"*Her Last Affair* is filled with wry humor and compassion even as the novel sweeps the reader from charm and romance to the depths of dark suspense. I was captivated from the first page and watched with awe as Searles wove the three storylines into a single, heart-pounding climax. Devastating, and yet at the same time, utterly romantic."

—Jean Kwok, *New York Times* bestselling author of *Girl in Translation*

"Love and revenge commingle until it's almost impossible to tell one from the other in the fascinating, character-driven *Her Last Affair*. As in his previous three novels, John Searles's low-boil plot hinges on slowly but forcefully building suspense, while subtly dropping clues to the characters' psychological makeup. . . . Insightful."   —Shelf Awareness

"How Searles weaves the stories of these fascinating, love-lorn characters together is nothing short of brilliant. . . . *Her Last Affair* is a book that builds the suspense with each turn of the page. The twist that Searles throws in will have you gasping. . . ."   —*Auburn Citizen* (New York)

"This story had so many twists and turns, it kept me guessing until the very last page."   —*First for Women*

"Eerie and captivating."   —*Woman's World*

"An intensely compelling book of suspense. . . . Treat yourself, read this novel! It has odd, fascinating characters, many surprises, and enough chills to keep one on edge. Searles is a master of suspense and delivers a bombshell with *Her Last Affair*. Mystery and psychological thriller readers and book discussion groups will find plenty to talk about."   —BookTrib

"All of these characters will meet in the final third of the novel, and it will be explosive. There is also a completely unexpected twist that is absolutely brilliant. The finale takes a sharp turn into a much darker place, and the ending is a satisfying one. I was not familiar with John Searles's work before, but he has won me over and found himself a faithful new reader."

—Bookreporter.com

HER LAST AFFAIR

ALSO BY JOHN SEARLES

Help for the Haunted

Strange but True

Boy Still Missing

HER LAST AFFAIR

A Novel

JOHN SEARLES

MARINER BOOKS

New York   Boston

HER LAST AFFAIR. Copyright © 2022 by John Searles. All rights reserved. Printed in the United States of America. No part of this book may be used or reproduced in any manner whatsoever without written permission except in the case of brief quotations embodied in critical articles and reviews. For information, address HarperCollins Publishers, 195 Broadway, New York, NY 10007.

HarperCollins books may be purchased for educational, business, or sales promotional use. For information, please email the Special Markets Department at SPsales@harpercollins.com.

A hardcover edition of this book was published in 2022 by Mariner Books.

FIRST MARINER PAPERBACK EDITION PUBLISHED 2023.

Designed by Michelle Crowe
Background art by Timothy S. Allen / Shutterstock, Inc.

Library of Congress Cataloging-in-Publication Data

Names: Searles, John, author.
Title: Her last affair : a novel / John Searles.
Description: First edition. | New York, NY : Mariner Books, [2022]
Identifiers: LCCN 2021029176 (print) | LCCN 2021029177 (ebook) | ISBN 9780060779658 (hardcover) | ISBN 9780060779672 (trade paperback) | ISBN 9780063211018 | ISBN 9780062199447 (ebook)
Classification: LCC PS3569.E1788 H47 2022 (print) | LCC PS3569.E1788 (ebook) | DDC 813/.6—dc23
LC record available at https://lccn.loc.gov/2021029176
LC ebook record available at https://lccn.loc.gov/2021029177

ISBN 978-0-06-077967-2

23 24 25 26 27 LBC 5 4 3 2 1

For Birute, Mario, Paul, Beth, Lydia, and, of course,
the invincible Christian

HER LAST AFFAIR

ONE

"I think this is the beginning of a beautiful friendship."

—From *Casablanca*, shown at the Schodack Big-Star Drive-in,
June 1943

EVERY MARRIAGE HAS ITS SECRETS. I never used to believe that. Was it denial? Just plain stupidity? Who knows? But for nearly fifty years, I operated under the assumption that the life my husband and I shared was built on truth. On trust. He's been gone an entire cycle of seasons now, and so many nights I lie in our creaky bed with my cell beside me instead of him. "Hey, Siri," I say, since Little Miss Know-It-All is my only company and, well, why the hell not? "What are the ingredients to a successful marriage?"

It takes some back-and-forth, some specifying, but sooner or later, her no-nonsense voice rattles off: "Love. Commitment. Faithfulness. Humility. Patience. Forgiveness. Laughter. Mutual sexual satisfaction. Honesty."

"I thought we had those things," I say, though it comes out like a question: I thought we had those things?

Good ol' Siri must be as stumped as me by that one, because her only reply is a grim silence. Then again, maybe she's busy looking up other topics I've asked her about, like the half-life of fentanyl citrate and the proper dosage required to slow a person down without stopping the heart. Tricky work, even for a retired nurse like me, and I wouldn't want to make a mistake. Whatever Siri's up to in the quiet of the night, her initial lecture about the necessary ingredients for a healthy marriage presses down upon my chest. When so many swirling thoughts of regret and revenge make it difficult to breathe, I shove her beneath the pillow, smothering her there, while I stare wide-eyed into the darkness.

SECLUDED TWO-BEDROOM COTTAGE FOR RENT

I waited too long after Hollis's passing before placing that ad in search of a tenant to rent our—or rather, my second home. Those words, *second home*, might conjure the image of oceanfront property, of kicking back and watching the sun set over the waves while sipping a leafy mojito. But push that pretty picture out of your head right now. Located in a tiny town in upstate New York, the cottage offers a view of nothing but scraggly pines and the defunct drive-in movie theater beyond, where most days the tattered asbestos panels of the screen flap in the wind like a colossal flag of surrender. My second home isn't quite close enough to reach out and touch, though I often describe it that way, since it's only twenty-six steps from our—my front door. Yes, I've counted. Built from prefabricated kits, both homes are single story with cedar shingles and narrow front porches. Identical, right down to the crescent moons carved in the shutters, which weren't part of the plans, but a detail my beloved added with his jackknife. Those moons give the houses an air of side-by-side cottages in a fairy tale, the sort where Goldilocks would show up to test the beds, only to find herself in a heap of trouble when the bears came home.

My desire to rent had nothing to do with money, since Hollis was what you'd call a cheap bastard. (Said with love. Sort of.) Prior to his death, you could catch me regularly ribbing him about his Loch Ness Monster of a wallet, as in: "Sweet Jesus! Look what just surfaced from the abyss! Let me snap a picture before the thing vanishes again!" After his death, I regretted those jokes (sort of). Thanks to his miserly ways, I never have to worry about paying the bills—no small relief, since I found myself with far more troubling issues to keep me up at night.

And so, this tenant.

He was not the first to respond to the ad. Before him, a brooding young woman came to see the place. Wrists jangling with what I concluded were too many bracelets. Skin wafting with what anyone would conclude was too much patchouli. In the dragging voice so many kids speak with these days, she asked if I minded cats. I don't. In fact, I like most animals a great deal and have a compulsion for nurturing strays that wander out of the woods behind the cottages. What I minded was her. Perhaps unfairly, I took Miss Bangle Bracelets to be someone who wore too much eyeliner and vaped too many e-cigs while the candles she burned drooled all over the countertops. She might have turned out to be clean, courteous, and punctual with the rent check, but she was not what I needed in a tenant. And what I needed was such a nuanced thing, I could not exactly list it in my ad.

For that reason, also a great big . . .

. . . NO to the Manhattan attorney who wandered the

small rooms and banged on walls the way people kick tires on a car they might buy, while I stood in the doorway. His phone buzzed with the determined frequency of a mosquito on the make, and when he wasn't interrupting himself to check it, the man was enlightening me in oddly urgent tones about his scheme to "go off the grid." Which led to this Mensa-level inquiry: "Do the birds always chirp so loudly? Because the last thing I need in my life is more noise."

. . . NO to the couple who smelled like Starbucks and gave the toilet not one but three test flushes. All the while I stood by the door fielding questions, which included yet another high-IQ hit: "Does that depressing drive-in still show movies? Because that would be, like, majorly inconvenient."

There were others. But given my situation, looking for a tenant was not unlike what people often say about looking for love: it had to feel right.

At the start of my troubles, Dr. Leopold paraphrased a different quote for me. The words became taffy in my brain, which is to say I pulled at them every which way:

> *Security is mostly a superstition. It does not exist in nature, nor do children as a whole experience it. Avoiding danger is no safer in the long run than outright exposure. Life is either a daring adventure or nothing.*

Thank you, Miss Helen Keller.

Perhaps you've figured out by now that I can't tell you with any great certainty what those rejected tenants looked like. I can only report how they sounded (dragging . . . urgent . . .), the way they smelled (patchouli . . . coffee conglomerate . . .), the particulars of their movements (jangling . . .), not to mention certain touches manufactured courtesy of a hunch (eye shadow . . . drooling candles . . .). Which brings me to a point about that business on TV and in movies where a blind person runs her fingers over someone's face to form a vivid mental picture. For the record: we don't do that. I hope, by way of example, to have already laid out some marginally better sense of how it works for a person like me.

As for the adventures I'm recounting here—adventures of the heart, let's call them—they were set into motion by the diagnosis I received from that ophthalmologist not long after Hollis's passing, by the fleeting year that followed during which my time was devoted to battening down the hatches, so to speak, and by the newspaper ad I'd waited too long to place. In many ways, things began in earnest with a knock on the door of the matchy-match house where I'd lived alone— not counting that heartless, know-it-all Siri, and really, who would?—since my husband passed.

Despite the chill in the air that afternoon, I kept the windows cracked to breathe the loamy smells of November on the wind. Outside on the lawn, pinwheels, windmills, tiny flags, and fountains spun and whirled, snapped and splashed. Those sounds, along with the ruckus from the old movie screen, had long since become a background static to my days and nights. Soothing, if only to me. When I opened the door, cocking my head sideways, since my vision is firmly smudged at the center but does allow me the foggiest peripheral view, I managed to make out the blur of a presence before me on the porch, like some fuzzy figure in a Monet painting.

I knew he was coming.

No, not for any psychic reason. I knew because this blur had telephoned a few hours prior to inquire about the ad. Forgive me for using a word nobody does anymore, but there was a distinctly jaunty quality to the man's speech, and I felt a genuine sense of surprise at hearing such a lively accent on the other end of the line. South African? English? Irish? I've rarely left the state, never mind the country, so I couldn't have told you the specifics right away. But the cadence of this man's voice gave me an image of a dapper gentleman (rare these days, I know) who smiled with each word he spoke. He introduced himself simply as "Mr. Cornwell." In return, I introduced myself simply as "Mrs. Hull." After some polite chitchat, he asked if I minded him "popping by a bit later to have a look-see at the place" and . . . well . . . by then, I was smiling too.

Embarrassing to admit, but as the seconds ticked down to his arrival, I found myself carrying on like a teenager primping for a date. In my case, that meant feeling my way around the bedroom closet until grasping a fresh version of the outfit I wore most days. If my fashion choice sounds odd, that's because it was. But consider how easily a nursing dress slips over the head, how simply it zips up the front, how such deep pockets make it possible to carry a trove of items. And if I'm being honest, there was also this: after nearly three decades devoted to caring for a parade of head cases on the eighth floor of a hospital over in Albany, that uniform possessed a foolproof magic. It never failed to resurrect in me a sense of confidence and authority.

Once that dress was on, I indulged in a bit of makeup. Why not? The basics of application were among the many skills I'd rehearsed relentlessly during those steadily dimming months following my macular diagnosis. No more liquid eyeliner, that was certain. But blush I could manage. And the smile on my face since that call made it easy to locate the apples in my cheeks (crab apples, some might say, given my age, which was not yet at that daunting three-quarters of a century milestone, but stomping closer by the day). When it came to lipstick, I'd only ever worn the same pale shade that complemented my pale skin: Nocturnal Pink. Fitting, I thought, and not just because I used to work night shifts, but also due to a long-held, private impression of myself that, while I may be overlooked by the world in any sense of physical attractiveness, deep down, I believed I contained a secret, underappreciated beauty, the sort a person might only glimpse if paying attention at unexpected moments.

My Hollis. He saw that in me every single day of our nearly fifty-year marriage—or so he led me to believe. The bastard.

The knock came just as I was finishing a careful three-sixty around my mouth. Quickly, I blotted and licked my teeth to mitigate the risk of appearing like a woman who'd just eaten a Maybelline sandwich. My hair, still a snowy white far as I could tell, was clipped low at each side of my head in modified pigtails, which I'm aware is not an appropriate look for anyone over the age of, say, eight, but is an easily managed style nonetheless. After adjusting my bulky necklace, then feeling the jumble of belongings in the pockets of my dress—creased retirement letter, wedding bands, monkey-faced finger puppet, a matchbook from a musty motel in Maine with only three matches remaining, among more harmful possessions—I opened the door to see, or rather, not quite see him standing there.

While it will come as little surprise to report that some people in this world you just like right away, it is perhaps more remarkable to discover that the same holds true even when you can scarcely make out the person. How I felt in that moment meeting him on the porch was akin to another thing people say about love: I just knew.

"What a magnificent slice of heaven tucked away back here . . . I couldn't help but notice the drive-in . . . Such a brilliant stitch of Americana . . . Makes one curious about the final film to have flickered on that screen . . . Perhaps some menacing Hitchcock number, like *Psycho* . . . Or a daft old romance, like *Roman Holiday* . . . And look at these doodads on your lawn . . . Why, it's a miniature carnival come to life on a windy day . . . Do those paint splotches on the trees behind the houses mark a path to somewhere? . . . Ah, yes, the rail bridge spanning the river . . . Bet there's good fishing there . . . I quite enjoy fishing and would make bloody good use of that path . . . Apologies for getting ahead of myself . . . Would you care to show me around, madam?"

As we stood on the porch—a stray mewing at his ankles, him gabbing away, me trying to keep up—much of what he said raced through my mind in the way of those speeding trains over that bridge deep in the woods. Even so, the man's enthusiasm for this place where I'd spent the lion's share of my life felt undeniably meaningful. So, with that dopey smile on my face still, I told him, "I'd be happy to give you a tour."

Without aid of a cane or Seeing Eye dog, I led the way across those twenty-six memorized steps. At the door, I reached for my necklace—really just a beaded chain purchased at the hardware store months back. Dangling from it was every key to every place on the property I considered off-limits to the world: the toolshed and the bedroom safe; the strongbox in my closet with a museum of meds I'd curated from the hospital before retiring; Hollis's pickup and my hatchback, neither of which anybody drove anymore; the gun cabinet and bullet box; and the squat cinderblock building that housed the old projection room and concession stand at the drive-in, which we—or rather, I now owned. Thanks to a self-designed, tactile system involving duct tape, Band-Aids, and rubber bands marking each key, I managed to find the one I needed by moving my fingers over the mishmash. Unlocking the door, pushing it open, I announced, "Welcome to your new home!"

I know, I know . . . A bit much. But the man gave no indication of being put off by my enthusiasm. In a peripheral blur of blues and flesh tones, he stepped by me into the house. It was then I noticed the smell, however faint, of marijuana on him. I let it slide. After all, parents used to puff away on a daily basis at the camp in the next town where I grew up. And while the man's feet padded from room to room, I braced myself for things to go south the way they had with the other would-be tenants.

Instead: "Lovely." That's what he offered upon his return to the living room.

It so surprised me that I responded, "Pardon?"

"The place. It's quite lovely. No frills. No fuss. What more does a man need? I do, however, have one small concern."

Here it comes, I thought. "Oh? And what's that?"

"Should it worry me that the landlord herself seems reluctant to step foot inside?"

This was a first. No one before had removed their head from their ass long enough to notice little old me lingering by the door. If only to appease him, I took a step into the front room. Then another. On my third step my shin banged into who knew what, which revealed my primary motive for avoiding that place: other than my old paperback romances packing the shelves and piled on the floor, plus the minefield of boxes of Hollis's fishing and camping equipment, I hadn't committed the arrangement to memory the way I had my overstuffed palace next door. Pushing aside a pinch of pain and humiliation, I said, "Happy now?"

"Indeed," he told me, and I had the sense he was smiling once more. "Who built these homes anyway?"

"My husband. He's gone, though. Little over a year now. We were just days away from celebrating our fiftieth when he passed. Unexpectedly. It was a freak accident."

"Oh, dear. I'm terribly sorry. One doesn't hear of many marriages lasting that long. Certainly not mine. I divorced after ten. And before you say you're sorry too, don't. Smartest bloody decision I ever made. We weren't in love the way you and your husband must've been."

Those words—*in love*—stirred shadows in my mind. As the man prattled on, I imagined his voice in the way of a flashlight's beam sweeping over the room—over my memories as well. I thought of a woman named Maureen Mooreover, dressed all in black and gaping at me from across the ER after Hollis's first accident. I thought of our wedding night years ago, back when Hollis's folks were alive and owned the drive-in. How brilliant we thought it was to skip any churchy formalities and get hitched in front of the movie screen, lit up with a spliced reel of scenes from black-and-white romances. (*Casablanca*, an apt choice; *Brief Encounter*, not so much.) Our wedding landed a half-page in the Albany *Times Union* and even made a small splash with an itsy-bitsy write-up in the *New York Times.*

"But why a matching house?" the man wanted to know when the bright beam of his voice swung my way again. "Why side by side?"

"It's a funny story actually. I'll tell you sometime. I mean, if you . . . if we . . . if . . ."

It felt difficult to focus, my mind still on that long-ago memory of Hollis lifting my veil, of my looking at his narrow lips, his steely blue eyes, his hair, thinning even then, as we sealed our union with a kiss and a sea of cars began madly honking in celebration—blame all that, but what came out next was, "Have you ever been in love?"

The question made him laugh. "Isn't a typical landlord meant to ask about my employment history, my bank account, my references?"

Embarrassed, I was the one who laughed now. Sinking my hands in the pockets of my dress, I felt the familiar comfort of that creased letter, the wedding bands, the monkey-faced finger puppet, the matchbook with only three matches remaining. Also, pills. So very many. Thanks to my endless fussing, they had come free of their amber containers and mingled in the way of loose Tic Tacs collecting lint. Finally, there was the sealed 21-gauge Ultra-Fine syringe, not to mention the outdated but surely still potent 5-milliliter vial of fentanyl. "Haven't you noticed? I'm not your typical landlord."

"I did notice, actually. But coming from one eccentric to another, I quite fancy it. Anyway, the answer is yes. I was in love. Once. A long time ago. Back when I was a teen. In Florida, of all places."

If only I'd pulled the plug on that impromptu Barbara Walters interview of mine, it might've been the end of our discussion—the end of so many things before they'd ever had a chance to begin. But I nudged. "What was her name?"

"Her name? Well . . . her name was Linelle. Feels funny to say it aloud now. I mean, it's only been a lifetime. We were kids. Both of us terribly young and unsorted. You know how the story goes."

At one time, I suppose I must have. But the notion of youthful foolishness felt so far in the rearview, I suffered amnesia on the topic. "Have you ever tried to contact her?"

Considering the way things turned out, you might say I'm to blame. My words acted in the way of those keys, unlocking emotions in the man, which he revealed to me, a stranger he'd only just met. While speaking of this woman from his past, this Linelle, the bright beam of his voice grew dim with regret. He told me how beautiful she was. How he kept pictures of her in a shoebox still and looked at them some nights. How more than anyone in his life, more than his ex-wife even, the mother of his child, it was Linelle he had most loved to hold close. "All these years have passed, and I've never truly gotten over her," he said after a long while of speaking, which I didn't mind, since I'm a sucker for a love story, even if it starts out sweet and hopeful and a tiny bit funny, only to turn dark and strange and—I may as well warn you now—more than a little twisted, as the ones in these pages do.

"So find her," I told him. "After all, none of us lives forever. Ticktock."

"Fairly certain Linelle is married now. Has been for years. Can't imagine she'd be too keen on a sorry bloke like me resurfacing out of the blue. Besides, even if I did get around to looking her up, I'm not sure I'd have the nerve to actually reach out. I mean, look at me. Would you—" He stopped. "My apologies."

"No need. It's no secret that I can't see."

"I just meant, if you could see me—then and now—you'd know I'm not remotely the man I was back in the day."

This was the moment when any well-mannered person would parade out assurances: "You look great!" "You haven't aged a day!" "Those jeans don't make you look—" You know the routine. But given my condition, how could I? Instead, I let the topic go. "The place is yours if you want it."

His employment history. His references. His finances. Even his name. I had not asked a single one of those landlord-y questions. Silly me.

"I would like it very much. I should warn you, though, I'm late all the time. Not with rent. I'll pay promptly. In cash. I just mean in life. My mum used to say I have two speeds: slow and stop."

"I'm not your mother. And that's fine by me."

"Also, I like my privacy. Don't get me wrong, I love a good chat and would very much enjoy getting to know you. However, I don't want a landlord marching through my private space, criticizing my lack of housekeeping skills."

"I don't want anyone marching through my private space either."

"And sorry to say, but I'm not handy in the least. If a pipe bursts, afraid I won't be of much use."

"I know how to call a plumber. Also, my nephew, John, comes up from the city to help now and then. Though if I didn't know better, I'd say it sounds like you're trying to talk me out of the offer."

"Not at all. I just prefer to be up front. That way there's no disappointments later."

"Understood. So let's try this again: Do you want the place?"

"I do."

As we stood in that extra house, November wind gusting outside, an unlikely image skittered through my mind. I pictured us holding hands before that screen at the drive-in, only it wasn't tattered and vacant, but lit up again with scenes from black-and-white romances. *Casablanca. An Affair to Remember. It Happened One Night.* In this vision, I wore a different white dress. In case you're getting the wrong idea, I didn't place the ad in the hopes of finding a new groom. Hardly. What I wanted, what I needed, what I hoped for in a tenant was another set of eyes. I craved a person nearby—not some malcontent on the payroll or that self-satisfied fembot, Siri, but a bona fide, caring human being who might allow me to see the world as he saw it, even for a few minutes a day. And though I've now made a skyscraper of a point insisting I didn't have my mind set on romance, I hope I don't have to explain that we form all sorts of unexpected attachments in this world. I formed a special one with this man.

How I miss that attachment.

How I miss him.

But on that first day in the matching house with moon shutters carved by my husband's sharp knife, what I recall this new tenant of mine saying next was, "Very well, then. Since we're going to be living in such proximity, I suppose the obvious next step is to ask your first name."

"Ah, yes. My name is Skyla. Skyla Hull."

"Nice to meet you, Miss Hull. I'm Teddy Cornwell."

Why, in his brief time in my life, did the apparition of this man give me such solace? Perhaps if I explain it this way: Imagine some humorless ophthalmologist dropping stinging liquid into your cloudy eyes, and then, even as the excess streams down your cheeks, instructing you to read a thicket of random letters at the bottom of a chart, letters that to you look like:

Now imagine struggling and squinting and willing yourself to see what's there, though for the life of you, it's not possible. Until a person comes along who says, "Hold on a sec . . . allow me to see those things for you." That person then takes it a step further, saying, "Not only will I see for you, but I'll be your friend. I'll listen to you. I'll laugh with you. I'll even dance with you. Most of all, I'll distract you from the ugliness of this world in this, the final phase of your life."

Before the unusual series of events I'm about to describe took place, events that involve that woman Linelle for one, a peculiar man named Jeremy for another—that is what Teddy Cornwell did. He helped me glimpse those letters floating at the bottom of the chart, letters that, as it turned out, weren't so random after all, but added up to the one thing each of us wants most in this world. He made me see, clear as those black-and-white romances, or even the final film that flickered briefly on the drive-in screen and was gone, before Teddy himself was gone too—killed, resurrected, killed again—for one last time in my life, the man showed me how special a thing it is to feel:

L O V E D

TWO

"Wouldn't it be lovely if we were old? We'd have survived
all this. And everything would be easy and uncomplicated,
the way it was when we were young."

—From *The Way We Were*, shown at the Schodack Big-Star Drive-in,
September 1974

ON THE NIGHT HER MARRIAGE FALLS APART, Linelle Dufort
spends nearly half an hour attempting to take a flattering picture of, to put it bluntly, her crotch. Two hours, if you consider
the time devoted to simply contemplating the idea while lying
in bed beside her husband, watching one of those shamelessly
manipulative news series that poses as hard-hitting investiga-
tive journalism, though really, it's just an excuse to string view-
ers along, teasing the reveal of the killer's identity between
Cialis and Boniva commercials.

"It's obvious the wife did it," her husband, Marcus, keeps
saying. "Look at her squinting. Look at her constant blinking.
She's clearly a total psycho. Case closed. Boom!"

Just that fall, he'd acquired the habit of punctuating sen-
tences with the same final burst of a word. At first, it made certain declarative things he said more declarative. But it's since

devolved into him "booming" even after the most innocuous comments. "Gonna nuke that leftover pizza in the microwave. Boom!" . . . "This dude who came into the bank asked if I'm still in my thirties. Boom!" . . . "Got a request to show the 67 at the Tallahassee Car Show this weekend. Boom!" On and on these explosions go. If Linelle were some poor, defenseless country, she imagines he'd have reduced her to rubble by now. And anyway, try as she might, Linelle cannot focus on that show, since her gaze keeps gravitating to the alarm clock on the nightstand:

10:53 P.M. . . . Speeding steadily closer to midnight.

That's the magic hour when she promised to send a picture of her privates to a man from her past. This man, Teddy Cornwell, turned up Thanksgiving morning with a simple Facebook message: I've been thinking about you for years, Linelle. And with her full participation, things escalated online deep into December, culminating in a flurry of heated messages and a deal struck in a moment of unbridled lust the evening before:

Tomorrow at midnight, I'll show you mine if you show me yours.

When Marcus fails to fall asleep, even after credits flash on the screen and a relic of a sitcom comes on, Linelle's insides roil with a mix of despair and relief that she might not be able to keep her end of the bargain. Years ago, she used to strap their daughter, Georgia, in a car seat and drive around the neighborhood until the girl passed out. Now Linelle fantasizes about using the same trick on Marcus. Since strapping all five feet nine inches and 193 pounds of him in a car seat is unlikely, however, she keeps right on watching his belly rise and fall beneath the sheets while stealing glances at those glowing numbers:

11:11! . . . 11:18! . . . 11:21! . . .

Between that initial sweet message from Teddy and the more recent raunchier one, there'd been plenty of respectable communication. In the beginning, they leapt with abandon into memories of the summer they met working at a certain Orlando theme park. All the back-and-forth made that time in their lives feel so palpable, it seemed they could walk right back into it, punch their time cards, and there they'd be, making out behind Space Mountain.

What followed was a sobering phase of catching each other up on life since, their marriages and Teddy's divorce, their children, their successes and failures, and all the many ways things did not turn out how they once envisioned.

When that line of conversation risked becoming melancholy, they retreated into a second round of nostalgia, firing off old photos. Finally, since Linelle's Facebook profile was a picture of Lollipop, her recently deceased cat, and Teddy had only a distant shot of him surfing years before, the notion of sending each other more current pictures was raised. That's when Linelle nervously tapped out a message warning him she did not look the same as way back when. And that's when Teddy messaged back saying he most definitely did not look the same either. Then, he suggested they take it slow and, in something of a joke, sent a photo of his thumb. Slow was just fine by Linelle, who sent a photo of her thumb in return. This game—like a hostage trade-off, only fun and flirty, which hostage trade-offs presumably never are—kept them busy for weeks.

His knees for her knees.

Her ears for his ears.

His belly button for her belly button.

On it went until they'd exposed every inch of their bodies except their faces and R-rated nether regions. And that's how Linelle came to be lying beside her husband on this night close to Christmas, watching his belly go up and down, watching the clock too:

11:24! . . . 11:27! . . . 11:35! . . .

At last, Marcus flops onto one side and goes night-night. Ever so quietly, Linelle picks up her cell, then eases out of bed and slips away down the hall. Boom!

After walking by Georgia's room—empty—she heads into the bathroom at the top of the stairs. Door locked, heart thrumming, she hikes up her recently resurrected T-shirt with crackled tangerine letters spelling UNIVERSITY OF FLORIDA. Those letters do not look as cheerful as they did when she enrolled back in the nineties. Then again, Linelle does not look as cheerful either. What's that saying about needing to choose between saving your ass or your face as you age? At forty-nine, Linelle had come down firmly on the side of her ass, subjecting herself to grueling boot camp classes and humiliating Zumba marathons, even strapping on her wrist one of those devices that tracks every step like a demented parole bracelet. All that effort has kept her body fit over the years, though her face, or so she believes in her most self-critical moments, is another story.

Linelle inches her tee higher. Positions the cell between her legs. Finds the shutter icon and begins tapping away. Back in her UF days, she studied art history before abruptly leaving school her junior year. Fumes of that abandoned major help her envision an O'Keeffe orchid, sensual and lush. But when she checks her phone, the images on screen look less evocative and more like something out of a medical textbook.

11:43!

She switches off the flash. Dims the vanity lights. Hunts around for a pair of scissors, finding only nose-hair trimmers but using them anyway to attempt a bit of grooming below.

11:48!

Linelle embarks on a reshoot, experimenting with angles and positions: leaning against the sink, propping a leg on the toilet, lying on the floor in a birthing position.

11:57!

Is it safe to say most people have no idea how exhausting it can be to take a decent photo of their genitals? On this December evening, Linelle contemplates exactly that. Giving up at last, she heads downstairs to where her laptop waits on the counter, where pictures of Teddy's penis have already arrived in a chat box.

Before getting to the specifics of those pictures (and yes, there's more than one), it seems important to set the scene on the first floor of the Dufort home, particularly given the great big boom to come later that night. Among details worth mentioning: a floor-to-ceiling mirror reflecting the entire living room and dining area. Recognition for that dubious décor choice goes to a teller at the branch of SunTrust Bank that Marcus manages. Referred to by Marcus as BFTB—as in "Barb From The Bank"—the woman considers herself an expert at interior design. Having honed her skills rigorously watching reality decorating shows, BFTB specializes in stripping away every personal detail and making things look like someone got a little too excited in the home department of TJ

Maxx. But in the midst of an argument about Linelle's clutter habit, Marcus suggested they hire BFTB to "you know, make the place look more presentable for dinner parties and crap like that."

A concession Linelle regrets.

While she's gotten used to the jute throw rugs everywhere and the endless candles in an array of nauseating scents, from "Cedar Tobacco Sunrise" to "Vanilla Dandelion Puff Daydream," what she cannot stand are the decorative signs that offer instructions. Giant letters and slabs of wood hanging in the kitchen spell COOK. Plates and mugs say EAT and DRINK. On a wall over the wine rack: UNCORK THE VINO. And on the new sofa, the color of a highway safety cone, pillows order people to CHILLAX and GET COMFY and FIND YOUR HAPPY.

Another thing Linelle detests: that mirrored wall, which serves up an endless, real-time playback of her every move.

She sees herself lighting a candle.

Sees herself blowing out the match.

Sees herself, yet again, tossing the match in the sink, since a slip of the kitchen can be viewed in that mirror too.

Linelle feels downright hunted by her reflection. Her face, mapped with faint wrinkles and weary-looking pouches beneath both eyes. Her hair, brown losing a war to gray, not long enough to suggest any particular style, though there's enough of it that she has to fish Cousin It out of the shower drain each morning.

Forcing her gaze away, she goes to the counter. Pushes aside the mess of Tallahassee real estate magazines and flash cards she's been studying in preparation for a real estate entrance exam. ABSENTEE OWNER . . . ABANDONMENT CLAUSE . . .

ACCELERATED DEPRECIATION . . . In truth, all that terminology bores her, same goes for the overhyped lingo in those listings: "Dazzling light and closets galore in this sexy split-level will have your friends drooling!" But since being pushed out of her job as a high school art teacher months ago, Linelle has been doing her best to put her mind on something new.

When she opens her computer, there they are: let's call them three "intimate self-portraits" of Teddy's junk. A sight she's not seen since the summer they broke up and, far as she can tell, things have held up over the years. What she finds odd, however: he's posed his penis alongside props. In the first photo: a tube of Colgate. In the second: a remote control. Third: a can of Diet Coke. Was she meant to do the same, Linelle wonders, and pose her privates beside various household items? If so, what would those be? Oven mitt? Pottery Barn catalog? Bag of lima beans? Then it dawns on her: in a typically male move, Teddy is attempting to convey a size comparison.

> **Teddy:** U there?

The sudden ping of his message causes Linelle to flinch. She'd been sitting at the counter, perusing the pictures, noting that the comparisons work, since his penis looks more impressive in length and girth than she recalls. Certainly more than the only penis she's known these last twenty years: the temperamental one belonging to her husband.

> **Linelle:** I'm here. Your . . . um . . . friend and I were just taking a moment to get reacquainted. You know, "Hey there . . . You again . . . Long time no see . . ."

Teddy: Funny. Meanwhile I've been feeling like a bloody fool since I sent mine at midnight as promised but u didn't send yours or even reply

A few things worth mentioning about Teddy: His full name is Ronald Theodore Cornwell III. Regal as it sounds, Teddy, which he's been called since birth, comes from a long line of alcoholic prison guards in East Kent, England. He and Linelle might never have met except when he was a teen his mother passed from lung cancer and his pub-dwelling father shipped him overseas to live with an auntie in Cocoa Beach. In turn, she sent him to work, with the help of a borrowed Social Security number, at that Orlando park. Rather than lose his accent as he stayed on in the States, Teddy allowed his to thicken, all the more so these days from what Linelle can gauge in these online chats. Another thing that hasn't changed: his inability to comprehend basic constructs of time.

Linelle: It's only midnight now. So u actually sent the pictures early

Teddy: Bloody hell. Better than late per usual I suppose. So don't I get a reaction? I mean most women *gasp* at the sight

Linelle: I gasped all right. U didn't hear it all the way in . . . wherever u said u live these days?

Teddy: Told you . . . a cottage I rent from a daft old nurse near Albany. And I don't seem to be in receipt of your photo as per our agreement

Linelle: Yeah . . . well . . . about my photo . . .

Linelle glances at the colossal mirror. Sure enough, there she is in the flickering candlelight, fingers poised over the keyboard. She put on softly playing Fado music earlier and the forlorn arrangement of instruments fills her with a pang of guilt about whatever this is between her and Teddy. Though she reminds herself that, whatever this is, it is not an affair. A few times, Teddy sent his number and suggested calling to hear each other's voices again, yet she resisted for fear of moving even a step closer toward the realm of real life. One thing Linelle likes best about whatever this is, is that the volley of flirtatious messages remains safely bridled in glowing boxes on the screen. It allows her to scroll back later, swiping in a way that feels akin to pulling the lever of a slot machine, landing on any number of silly or serious or sexual exchanges between them, which never fails to brighten her day.

In comparison, the most exciting messages between her and her husband go something like:

Marcus: Craving a burger. We got beef in the freezer?

Linelle: We have it. You want it?

Marcus: I want it. Thaw it for me babe. Home soon

Not one bit of that, rest assured, is an attempt at double entendre.

Now, Linelle is faced with the awkward business of putting Teddy off again. Rather than delay the inevitable, she resumes typing with the intention of laying out the truth. But just as in actual conversation, when a person means to say one thing and something else pops out, so it goes with online chatter.

Linelle: I've not had sex with my husband in almost a year

Teddy: Suppose I shud say I'm sorry to hear that tho selfishly it's not true. May I ask why?

Linelle: Hard to explain

Teddy: These things always r. But u brought it up luv . . . so try

Linelle: For so long the sex wasn't great. We said we were going to work on it but who wants to "work on" sex?

Linelle: My point: I'm rusty at this sort of thing

Linelle: Also I shud have mentioned this when we first came up with the idea but DD (remember her?!) found an old Polaroid months back and . . . looong story . . . but it made me think twice about going thru with this kind of photo. Sorry.

Teddy: Don't be luv. And please . . . no pressure from me. Guess we did get a bit carried away. Ha . . . We don't have to go any further

Certainly, part of Linelle feels relieved. But now the two have arrived at a first in the course of whatever this is between them: an uncomfortable cyber-silence. Linelle thinks of Teddy as he was years back: youthful green eyes, spiky blond hair, big feet slapping around in worn flip-flops, a rotation of dingy tanks showcasing a new tattoo on his arm spelling his mother's name, Bridget, above a broken heart. Illogically, it is that Teddy she envisions waiting for her reply. But what is there to say if they've decided not to take whatever this is any further?

The longer the silence, the more Linelle feels a sense of something coming to an end, of film credits rolling, of lights

being turned on, of people shuffling out of a theater and returning to their humdrum lives after only a brief burst of excitement. And a voice in her head shouts: *No! No! No! Sit back
down, everyone! Dim the lights! Unroll the credits!*

Linelle does not want to go back to her humdrum life.
That life where her classroom has some other teacher in it
and silence blares from her daughter's empty bedroom. That
life where her mother lives so impossibly close that her endless needs are a constant weight. That life with no sex, no easy
tenderness, and no escape. This, then, is the very heart of her
dilemma: she does not want to be the sort to engage in an
affair, but does not desire a run-of-the-mill friendship either.

But what to do about Teddy?

How to keep things alive without keeping them too alive?

As the cursor pulsates, as the candle flickers, as the Fado
music plays, the mirror gives Linelle back to herself in a ripple-
like fashion, and those questions ripple in her mind too. At
last, she fires off a message:

Linelle: What if we Skyped for a minute and I showed you?

Plenty of people are seasoned experts when it comes to
getting naked in front of a laptop. Linelle is not one of them.
The prospect makes her so self-conscious that she clarifies:
no faces, not yet anyway. Just sixty quick seconds, that's all, so
she won't have time to chicken out. When Teddy messages
back a thumbs-up, her pulse quickens. She logs onto Skype.
Types in a contact request. Tilts the camera away until she's
ready. Once the green light flashes on, the first thing she sees
is a packed bookshelf in his rented cottage. It reminds her of
how he used to keep an alternating array of small translation

dictionaries in a pocket of his cutoffs, practicing phrases on her all the time.

Veux tu danser avec moi? . . . Would you like to dance with me?

Uma só língua nunca basta . . . One language is never enough . . .

Ya lyublyu tebya . . . I love you . . .

As for his initial glimpse, Linelle figures he must be taking in the worst of BFTB's handiwork. She decides to get on with it, lifts her tee and steps in front of the camera. "Do you, um, see it?" She hears a timid hitch in her speech.

"I see it, luv," he says. Teddy's voice. Deeper with age, a bit gravelly too, probably on account of the cigarettes he used to smoke and, for all she knows, still does. But the accent, the lilt of words, the bravado—traits altered by time, though familiar just the same—envelop her in feelings of comfort and desire. "You again . . . Long time no see . . . How've you been?"

"Guess that serves me right."

Teddy pauses just briefly before he continues addressing her vagina directly, albeit more sincerely. "You're a sight for sore eyes, you know that? I've missed you. It may sound soppy, but you're as beautiful as I recall, *l̦ibetok.*"

L̦ibetok. Plucked from an old translation dictionary, that ungainly-sounding word was the pet name he used for that part of her anatomy back in the day. It means something sensual, though what exactly Linelle cannot remember. And anyway, it's been ages since a person used that other word, *beautiful,* to describe some part of Linelle. Not her bright, open face. Not her delicate hands with nail-bitten fingers. Not her lean, often stubbly legs. Not her gently curved ears. Not her feet with streams of blue veins and crooked pinkie toes. Not her lips. Not her eyes. Not the hollow of her neck. Not one single part of her, despite the fact that, like all of us, there are many beautiful parts of Linelle Dufort.

Given all that, how can she help but allow things to go on longer than sixty seconds? She takes a breath, conjuring her usual confidence in situations unlike this one. For the camera, for the man who'd been her first love, she begins moving her hips. Just a little. Side to side. Back and forth. All her life, the thought of dirty talk seemed like nothing but a bunch of idiotic clichés. Yet Linelle feels a need to say something slightly dirty. In an effort to avoid things coming off as canned, she searches for a different edge to it all, glancing at her flash cards and real estate magazines, latching unexpectedly onto the lingo used in the sample listings she'd been digesting for months.

"This cozy—" She stops as a swell of nervousness moves through her.

"This cozy what?" Teddy's voice—sexy, gravelly as ever—prompts.

"This cozy suburban vagina," Linelle manages, surprised as you may be too by her choice of words, "is in need of some TLC but was once a real stunner."

Teddy doesn't miss a beat. "Looks to me like more of a turnkey situation. In fact, I'd like to move right in."

"Well, just so happens I'm having an open house. Care to look around?"

"Would I ever! A nice slooooow look around . . ."

When it comes to this sort of heated flirtation, there reaches a point when the parties involved either return to their senses or lose all reserve. The latter is what happens with Linelle and Teddy. Linelle finds herself trailing a hand from her breasts to her stomach, fingertips stopping at the smooth expanse of skin inches below her belly button. Breathless now, she says, "First thing you should know: there's ample storage space if you decide to move in."

"Good. Because I've got lots I need to put away." Teddy shifts his camera and there it is: not his face, but his penis, before her once more.

Unlikely as it seems, the sight causes Linelle's mind to fill with the sudden, asynchronistic thought of her daughter: her long, grasshopper legs, so often bug-bitten, her lean, graceful shoulders, so often sunburned, despite Linelle's obsessive nagging that Georgia spray and slather and cover up. Why should she think of those things now? Maybe it's the broken-heart tattoo on Teddy's arm along with his mother's name, Bridget, glimpsed during the fumbling of the camera, that makes her consider how fraught motherhood is with the risk of loss. Maybe it's because the only reason she downloaded Skype in the first place was in hopes of keeping up with her child, though in the four months since she's been gone that's seldom happened. Whatever the reason, Linelle glances away from the screen. Looks around the room, seeing things not as they are, but as they'd been for years: cluttered and mismatched, but comforting nonetheless. Especially on Sundays when Marcus was off at the car shows with his Camaro, leaving Linelle to stretch out on the old plaid sofa as Georgia practiced her violin, squinting at sheet music behind thick glasses, and Lollipop purred between them.

"I know it's unusual for the buyer to meet the seller," Teddy says, prompting Linelle to return to that image on the screen. "But here we are."

"Sometimes it's good to break the rules," she tells him, because why stop when this is the most sexually exciting event to happen to her in ages?

Things might have felt all the more exciting if not for that sound, like a mosquito buzzing in the air: "Linelle."

She feels overcome by an urge to raise a hand and shoo it away.

"Linelle."

There it is again. This time, the sound has a way of tugging her more forcefully into the present. Slowly, she lifts her head. Looks into the mirror. Sees herself, shirt hiked, skin looking oddly bloodless and blue in the glow of the computer screen, the most private part of her body on display. Behind her, across the room, at the bottom of the stairs, stands her husband.

Linelle lets go of her shirt, turns to face him.

"What are you doing?" Marcus asks.

It's a question that lingers in the air a long while, until finally, in the darkest hours of that December night, she tells him the truth.

THREE

"The boys around here call it 'The Black Lagoon.' Only
they say nobody has ever come back alive to prove it."

—From *The Creature from the Black Lagoon*, shown at the
Schodack Big-Star Drive-in, October 1954

LINELLE ONCE READ that a couple can add some oomph to
their "how we met" story by simply tacking on the words *in
Paris*. "We met on a senior citizen dating website . . . in Paris."
"We met in line at the pharmacy buying wart remover and de-
pilatory cream . . . in Paris." "We met puking in the filthy toilet
of a crowded bar . . . in Paris."

Easy, right? As the French say, *Voilà*.

When it comes to the story of how she met Marcus, Linelle
always feels tempted to add that same jolt, since "An ATM ate
my card and I went into SunTrust Bank to complain" is hardly
the stuff of Hollywood rom-coms. For obvious reasons, no
one ever asks about her relationship with Teddy, so Linelle
never gets to say, "We met working at Disney . . . the one in Orlando, not Paris." She also never gets to say, "It started with my
wisdom teeth." When all four became impacted the summer
Linelle graduated from high school, she had all four extracted

at once. In the days that followed, she lay in the small second bedroom of the wood-paneled apartment she and her mother shared above a Goodwill in Lady Lake, Florida. Mind woozy. Mouth stuffed with gauze.

"We need to talk, pickle," her mother said early one morning when Linelle woke to find her sitting on the edge of the bed, clutching some sort of booklet. Before each night's shift at Lost Logs Casino Barge, the woman appeared done up: fresh eyeliner and lipstick, choppy hair sprayed into place, maroon vest and matching uniform pants ironed, "Hiya! I'm Trudy!" name tag pinned on straight. After the shift, all that faded, wrinkled, and went crooked. "You know the business of my bum arm?" the wilted version of her asked.

Linelle nodded, aware of the basics: Growing up in Tennessee, Trudy had been bumping along in the back of a pickup when the wind blew her brother's Vols hat off his head. She leapt up to catch it and tumbled out of the truck, breaking her arm. Rather than rush her to a doctor, her father reset the arm on his own. No surprise but the bones didn't heal properly. She was forever left unable to fully extend her arm, which made dealing at a blackjack table challenging, working the roulette wheel less so.

"Old Beverly who deals the baccarat said there's a way I can make easy cash on the side, renting myself out as a kind of tour guide at Disney."

"Disney?" Linelle said. "But you hate amusement parks."

"Not if I'm being paid beaucoup bucks to get people the VIP treatment." That's when she held up what turned out to be a Florida DMV handbook. "Says here your ol' ma qualifies for a disabled permit due to my limited mobility. According to Bev, Disney allows up to six people to accompany one handicapped guest. A staff member hauls the group around in a golf cart, making sure they don't wait in lines with all the riffraff."

"And by riffraff, you mean honest people who aren't so immoral as to hire a person with a minor disability just to float around on It's a Small World faster?"

"Try two hours faster, pickle. That's how long the lines can be."

"The waiting time wasn't really the point."

Trudy waved her hand in the air, as though swatting away a pesky detail. "Whether you approve or not, I already gave my name to this private concierge guy who arranges the whole deal, top-secret-like."

"Well, congratulations on your new career," Linelle said in a thoroughly unenthused voice, meant to send a clear message that she had zero interest in the scheme.

"Congratulations on yours too." Her mother pulled a scrap of newspaper from inside the booklet and held it in the air.

LOCAL AUDITIONS ANNOUNCED:

DISNEY PRINCESSES WANTED!

"You're kidding, Ma. Right? Me?"

"Not kidding, my little Aurora. Or should I call you Ariel? Or maybe you'll be an old-school Cinderella or Snow—"

"Stop it! There's no way I'm being some theme-park princess. The whole thing is degrading. It encourages passivity in young girls. Also, it—"

"How about you get off your high horse and consider the thousands of sick children who make a pilgrimage to Disney? Think of sick little Jessica from Cincinnati, or sick little

Cooper from San Diego, whose parents scrimped and saved so their precious little one could meet a favorite princess in what might be the last days of their lives."

"You mean because your golf cart full of rich people might run them over?"

With that, her mother stood, planting the newspaper clipping on Linelle's chest. "I don't know if you're expecting the tooth fairy to leave a wad of cash under your pillow, but guess what? The tooth fairy doesn't exist. And the jury's still out on God. So if my bum arm can put some ka-ching in our pockets, so be it. If that pretty face of yours can make us some money, so be it too. Now, you're getting your ass to that audition!"

As her mother stomped out of the room, Linelle shouted, "Never!"

In this instance, "never" amounted to one week later, when she found herself at the audition. Two weeks after that, she found herself in a subterranean "Co-Co Room" beneath Disney, surrounded by bins of makeup, shelves of wigs, and racks of bright, big-eyed costumes. An army of stern middle-aged women, nearly all of them sporting a chopped, utilitarian gray hairstyle, oversaw "actors" like Linelle. Known as the "WWWDs," on account of the buttons they wore that asked, "What Would Walt Do?," the women ruled the labyrinth of tunnels under the park with an iron fist—or, as they might have phrased it, an iron mouse paw. It was that sort of lingo that Linelle had to hurry up and learn. The Co-Co Room, for example, was what they called the Cosmetics & Costumes area. "On set" was their way of referring to any of the aboveground locations where Mickey, Minnie, Donald, Daisy, Goofy, and the gang appeared to mingle with throngs of guests who shoved their way around the park.

After she was cast as Belle from *Beauty and the Beast*, Linelle's training involved watching the film eight times, which was seven and a half more than she ever cared to. After each viewing, she filled out a worksheet testing her knowledge of the character, which included the question: What is the greatest irony in *Beauty and the Beast?* Linelle was always tempted to answer: "I'M TRAPPED IN A BUNKER PREPARING TO PLAY A PRINCESS FOR $9.54 AN HOUR WHILE MY MOTHER IS ZIPPING AROUND THE PARK IN A GOLF CART PIMPING OUT A MINOR DISABILTY FOR $50 AN HOUR!!!" But since she needed money to buy textbooks and art supplies for college in the fall, not to mention to put a dent in her dental bills, she refrained.

Once released on set, Linelle did her best to "disappear inside the role" and "smile at all times" as the WWWDs drilled into her head. That meant smiling as hundreds of sweaty kids hugged Belle and tugged at Belle's dress and whispered comments in Belle's ear like, "My brother sucks balls, and I want to drown his sorry ass on the Jungle Cruise." That also meant smiling when, during photos, she felt the hand of yet another pervy dad slip down her back. Finally, that also meant maintaining composure when an astounding number of slack-jawed guests approached on Main Street to ask, "What time is the three o'clock parade?"

"Why, I believe that would be at three o'clock," she informed them, leaving out the "you fucking idiots" part.

Luckily, Linelle made a friend right away: a rail-thin girl named Dana, who drove an hour from Daytona to play Snow White. In those early days at the park Linelle found it impossible to keep names straight; however, "Dana from Daytona" stuck. Linelle felt an odd comfort in never fumbling over it the way she did names of guests at the park or the endless parade of cute (but unfortunately for her purposes) gay male dancers, who all seemed to come from Ohio. It just felt easy to call out, "Hey, Dana from Daytona, is my wig on straight?" or "Hey, Dana from Daytona, is my makeup smudged?"

Dana picked up on this playfulness too, calling Linelle "Land O' Lakes," since Linelle drove an hour from Lady Lake to play Belle. As their mutual affection grew, the nicknames were shortened to simply "DD" and, years prior to its present-day definition, "LOL."

DD loved to smoke—high on the list of no-no's while in costume. The girl's need for cigarettes led to her curiosity about a covert, though legendary, sub-chamber beneath the park known as the Black Lung. One day, when they found themselves on break and free from the watchful eyes of the WWWDs, Dana guided Linelle through the maze of sloping corridors to a dwarf-size door at the end of a stray hall.

"Are you sure we should be doing this?" Linelle asked when she laid eyes on the sign: DO NOT ENTER—PARK ENGINEERING STAFF ONLY.

DD didn't answer. She shoved the door open and waved the glowing "bejeweled scepter" that was part of her costume. Linelle stepped inside and peered around. In the dim light, she could see a bench made from two buckets and a gray slab beside a laundry basket filled with the random left-behinds you might find at a stoner camp in the woods: drained vodka bottles, crushed beer cans, old lighters.

DD dug a Camel Light from her bodice. Not only didn't Linelle smoke, but she worried about the smell getting on her dress. She stepped away, over to the bench, squinting to read the words etched in the slab:

DEAR DEPARTED
BROTHER DAVE
HE CHASED A
BEAR INTO

"A cave," DD said, filling in the missing part while puffing like a locomotive. "Obviously, a broken tombstone from the Haunted Mansion. Don't ask me how it got here. But makes for a decent seat. Go on, LOL. Don't be afraid to pop a squat."

Reluctantly, Linelle gathered her Belle dress at the hem and sat down. "Keep away from me," she ordered DD. "I mean, aren't you worried about the smell of smoke getting on your costume too?"

DD waved her scepter again, revealing a large box of dryer sheets and a spray can of Lysol among the shadows. "Nope. Because here's what members of this exclusive club do after a smoke: we give our costumes a good rubdown with a dryer sheet, then spray a cloud of Lysol and step through it, the way some rich bitch would put on Chanel Number Five."

"And that does the trick?"

"Guessing the combo is part 'fresh off the clothesline' and part 'bathroom after someone has gone a little crazy with the air freshener after a dump.' But hoping it works. Anyways, I want to ask you something, LOL."

Linelle sighed. "If you're going to ask me again which dwarf I think Snow White sleeps with, can we skip it? I told you yesterday, there's an eighth dwarf no one ever talks about: Humpy. For obvious reasons, he's her favorite."

DD laughed, exhaling a stream of smoke into the shadows. "No, LOL. It's not that. Though you crack me up. I swear to God you better be my friend for as long as we work here.

Longer even. Like when we're ancient, in our forties, and tired of screwing our husbands. We'll get drunk and go to the mall and spend their money on random shit when we're not getting our nails done."

"Can't wait," Linelle said, even though that future held little appeal. Beyond buying books and art supplies and getting to college in the fall, Linelle's plans got fuzzy. But she knew enough to realize what she didn't want. "So what's the question?"

"It's about that gay dancer from Ohio."

"Evan from Cincinnati?"

"Not him."

"Sebastian from Cleveland?"

"Not him either."

"Jasper from Dayton? Or, wait. You mean Kyle from Akron?"

"Chill for a sec, LOL. I'm talking about Blake."

"Blake? But he's from San Diego."

"He is? Oh. I just assumed he was from Ohio like the rest of them. Well, that kind of gets to my point, which is that Blake doesn't seem as gay as the other dancers. So I was just wondering, like how gay do you think he is?"

"Call me crazy, DD, but when a guy spends his days doing fan kicks and cartwheels on a parade float down Main Street Disney, it's pretty much a lock." Linelle had meant to make DD laugh—sort of—but no luck.

DD frowned. "You're stereotyping, LOL. Not nice."

"Sorry. But why are you even asking? Do you, like, like him or something?"

The girl had a way of sucking cigarettes down to the last possible puff, something she swore Walt Disney used to do as well. Linelle watched her work at what remained of the butt until finally DD answered, "It's just that Blake flirts with me all the damn time. So I get a not-one-hundred-percent-gay vibe off him. Besides, don't truly evolved people believe sexuality is a sliding scale? I'm so man-starved around this place, I figure it can't hurt to see where things go if Blake and me hang out over a six-pack."

"Of raspberry wine coolers?"

"Of beer, LOL! Anyway, just forget it."

"I will. And I think you should too. It's not going any-where with that guy."

Alas, having offered what Linelle believed to be sound ad-vice, though clearly not the advice DD wanted to hear, she sensed irritation radiating off the girl.

Linelle had her own reasons to feel irritated later that eve-ning, when her shift finally ended and she waited in the staff parking lot for her mother. (Staff, on account of Linelle's of-ficial employment status, unlike a certain someone's.) When Trudy came limping up to the car, Linelle said, "It's your arm that gives you special status. Not your leg. So what's with the limp?"

Her mother shrugged. "I figure it adds to the mystique."

Trudy had proven highly skilled at ingratiating herself into the hearts of all those line cutters. Sometimes, Linelle found her loading gifts into the trunk of their paint-peeled Pinto: T-shirts. Sweatshirts. Wine. Champagne. Once, she was even given a new Polaroid camera. On this particular night, she brandished a bright yellow Walkman.

Linelle acknowledged it as little as possible and climbed into the passenger seat, where she opened her book, *Bizarre*

Romance: True Tales of Couples Who Committed Unthinkable Acts in the Name of Love, even though reading in the car made her queasy.

"You've got to meet Linda and Rick and their daughter Michaela!" Trudy gushed as she merged onto the highway. "She's the sweetest little angel and wears the most adorable dresses in all sorts of pretty prints! Yesterday, she called me Auntie Trudy. It just about melted my— Are you even listening, pickle?"

Pickle, or rather, Linelle looked up. "Not really."

Her mother groaned. "What's going on in that horrid book of yours anyway?"

Linelle had found the book abandoned on a random shelf in the Co-Co Room and figured she'd read it in hopes of better understanding the psychology of a princess who'd fall for a beast. So far, the stories inside were nothing short of demented. "Let's see, right now, I'm deep into a chapter about a man named Carl Tanzler. Back in the thirties, he worked as a radiologist in a Key West hospital, where he fell for a tuberculosis patient. Despite his desperate treatments, the woman died. Tanzler was so heartbroken he stole his love's decomposing corpse from the cemetery and attempted to bring her back to life. The guy used wax and wigs and plaster to replace her skin and bones and even an eye. At night, he used to find comfort in talking to her, in lying by her side, in—"

"Jesus! Enough! Why the hell would you read such a thing?"

Linelle stared out the window, where traffic thinned the farther away from the park they got. "Guess it's interesting to see how love can make some people lose their minds. The book says Freud believed falling in love always verges on the abnormal, by a compulsiveness, by a blindness to reality. It's not rational."

"Yeah, well, I loved your father, but didn't go digging him up when he was gone. After all the nonsense, Linelle, love comes down to paying the bills, watching TV together, and taking a nice vacation once a year."

"How romantic."

"It is romantic. You'll see someday."

And so, over the course of that sweltering summer, the collision of so many absurdities became an almost banal routine. There were the stealthy trips to the Black Lung, where DD contemplated the sex lives of Snow White and the dwarfs when she wasn't dissecting the details of her dogged attempts to convert Blake, either permanently or for a few minutes so she could make out with him. There were the car rides with her mother, listening to her gush about whatever family she was escorting, then watching her fake a limp. There were those gifts, more generous by the week, astounding Linelle, until one day she opened their apartment door to find two delivery men asking her to sign for a large-screen TV sent "With love and utmost gratitude" from Peggy & William Beaumont & Willy Jr. of Westport, Connecticut. In an unexpected way, the juxtaposition of the macabre love stories in Linelle's book, which she read and reread all summer, and the Technicolor cheer at the park made her job easier. In contrast to the oddities of that book, the people who clamored for a piece of Belle did not seem so exasperating after all.

Then came a July day when Linelle had a meet-and-greet with a sick child, something she'd encountered plenty of times before in her role as Belle and had actually been part of her training. But this particular girl, with her hairless scalp and frail mouth that looked drawn onto her pale face, had caught Linelle off guard by offering her a lollipop and insisting Belle keep it. Such a small gesture. But thinking of that girl and the grim circumstances of her life brought tears after all.

Without realizing it, Linelle had stopped smiling. Almost immediately, she felt a tap on her shoulder and turned to see a WWWD. "I think you're forgetting something, Belle. Do you know what that is?"

Linelle told her only that she did not feel well.

Since it was required that actors greet 172 guests per hour, the WWWD looked at the clicker in her hand. With seven minutes to go, Linelle had already cleared 201—that's how good she'd become at her job.

"We better get Belle back to the castle," the WWWD said loudly. "The Beast will be wondering where she's gone off to." The announcement drew groans from the crowd, though people quickly dispersed.

Once in the Co-Co Room, Linelle wiped off Belle's makeup and changed out of Belle's gown, all the while forcing back tears. At last, she headed out to the parking lot, expecting to find her mother loading God knows what into the trunk. But there was only a slip of paper beneath the windshield wiper.

Hey Pickle! Gatsby and Suzette are taking yours truly to the 8-course tasting menu dinner at the Magic Castle! We've had such a special time, how could I say no? Enjoy the park off-duty for a change while your old mom is wined and dined. Meet you back here around 11. Plan on driving home since I plan on getting ~~a little tipsy~~ seriously sloshed. Smooches—M

The last thing Linelle wanted was to be seen melting down in the prickling heat of the parking lot, so she ventured inside to the Black Lung. After a day spent baking in the sun amid the commotion of the park, the whir of ventilation fans and darkness offered solace. Linelle ignored the smell of pot in the air and sat on the broken tombstone, burying her head in her hands. Once begun, the buildup of so many oddities that summer, from her mother's antics, to the weird pressures of that job, to the disturbing details of that book, all of it made her cry harder.

"You alright there, luv?" a voice asked in the darkness.

Linelle jerked her head up, stared into the shadows. Back behind the laundry basket and dryer sheets and what was now a battalion of dead Lysol cans, a face came into focus. At first, just the slant of a jawline and an eye glistening in the dark. Then she noticed a patch over the other eye, a full-lipped mouth and square chin. *Handsome* was the word Linelle would think later, though in the moment, she was too surprised by his presence to arrive at any such conclusion. "You scared the crap out of me."

"Sorry, luv. I worried you might be one of those vile battle-axes who crack the whip around here. Since I didn't want to get tossed in the clink for smoking, I kept quiet."

"So that pot smell is you?"

"Guilty as charged, madam."

Linelle's eyes adjusted still more. He sat on a stray bucket, boots propped on another, back against the cinderblock wall. He wore a bandana over his head and a striped shirt. Where his left hand should have been, a hook protruded from the sleeve. "*Pirates of the Caribbean*," he explained, waving the hook.

"I figured. I'm a Belle."

"Figured that too. You're pretty in that way, if you don't mind me saying."

It had been a while since anyone over the age of twelve had paid Linelle a compliment, so she didn't mind in the least. "Thanks. And you can ditch the accent. We aren't on set."

He used his hook, impressively, to reach up and flip the patch in the direction of his forehead, revealing his other eye. After that, he removed the hook altogether and set it on his lap beside a small unlit flashlight and a book she hadn't noticed before. "News for you. I may not be a real pirate. But my accent—that's authentic."

"Oh."

"Now that sounded like a skeptical *oh* to me."

"You can read that into a single syllable?"

"Yes," he said, speaking the word in such a way that it sounded definitive, then again so it sounded doubtful, "Yes." And finally, giving it a hopeful spin, "Yes."

"Impressive. Did you learn that from the acting coaches here?"

"Afraid those hacks just taught me pirate-speak. Which I'll spare you. So why the skepticism?"

"Don't know. Guess I just assumed you were from Ohio like the rest of— Never mind."

"Not never mind," he said, playful but determined. "Like the rest of the what?"

"I was going to say, like the rest of the ridiculously good-looking gay guys around here," Linelle admitted, figuring it was, in its way, a compliment. "It's something my friend and I noticed. So many of you seem to come from Ohio. It's like they bus you all in."

That made him laugh. Linelle glimpsed a flash of gold teeth. For his sake, she hoped they were part of the getup and not unfortunate dental work. "While I fully own up to the ridiculously good-looking part, I've got news for you, princess: I'm not gay."

"Oh."

"Oh?"

"Yeah, just oh."

He smiled, and there were those gold teeth again, front and center. "You're funny, you know that? I'm Teddy."

"Linelle."

"If it's not too intrusive, may I ask why the crying, Linelle?"

"It was nothing," she said, not wanting to talk about that poor girl.

"I see. My dad used to say that whenever my mum uttered the words, 'It was nothing,' it was always something."

"Well, in this case it really was nothing—nothing I want to get into anyway."

"Okay, then." Teddy leaned back on his bucket, clicked on the flashlight. "I'll let you carry on with your crying about nothing, while I carry on with what I was doing."

"Getting stoned?"

"That . . . and this." He held up the book: *Everyday Russian: 673 Easy-to-Learn Expressions.* "Lest you think I'm a complete cretin, I'm doing a bit of studying too."

"Russian?"

"*Da.* That means yes. See, you just got your first lesson. Bet you weren't planning on that when you strolled through the wee door over there."

Linelle hadn't been planning on any of this. "Why Russian?"

He shrugged. "I'm good at languages. French, Italian, Spanish—most of the Romances I've got a handle on. Now I'm on a quest to crack the basics of a Slavic language. Proving a bit tougher, thanks to the bloody Cyrillic alphabet."

"What can you say so far? Besides *da*, I mean?"

He held one hand visor style over his forehead, as though to block a light that wasn't there in an effort to better see her. "At the risk of sounding like a show-off, I recently mastered this gem: *Kak seledka v boshke*."

"Which means?"

"'I feel like a herring in a barrel.'"

"Handy. Particularly around here."

"There's also the ever-popular *Delat iz muhi slona*, which translates to 'Don't make an elephant out of a flea.'"

"Also handy. Sounds like you're off to a good start."

"*Spasibo*. That's 'thank you.' And since I'm on a roll, there's a phrase perfect for a moment like this."

"Russian for, 'It reeks of pot in here'?"

"Afraid not. But give me a moment. I want to be certain I say the words right."

Teddy opened his book, flipping pages. "Here we go. It's a question actually. And the question is this: '*Ya khochu potselvat tebya?*'"

"Please don't talk about my *khochu* or my *tebya*. It's bad manners."

"Be serious, luv. You want to know what it means?"

"*Da.*"

"*Da?* I see you're a fast learner. Okay, then. It means . . . 'Can I kiss you?'"

"Oh." This time, when that single syllable slipped from Linelle's mouth, the sound indicated every bit of her surprise.

"Oh?" Teddy said.

"Oh, as in, are you really asking me?"

"I'm really asking you."

"Well, I don't make a habit of kissing guys I just met. Never mind in some barely lit drug den at work. And never mind when the guy is dressed as a pirate and flashing his gold teeth at me like somebody's creepy uncle."

"Ahh. These. Bit more difficult to pop off than my hook. If you don't mind, I'm keeping them where they are. But I promise they'll make the kiss more memorable."

Teddy glanced at his book and Linelle attempted a furtive study of his face. His nose, vaguely Roman in shape, looked slightly askew, and she wondered if it had been broken at some point. Even so, it did not mess with the pleasant arrangement of features, set off by a sturdy jawline and strong cheekbones. Linelle understood why he'd been cast as a pirate instead of a prince. There was something scrappy about his looks.

Teddy closed his book suddenly and stood. Ducking, so as not to hit any pipes, he carried the bucket closer, placed it across from her, and took a seat.

Handsome—that word rooted more firmly in Linelle's mind now that he was so near.

"I can tell you are considering it," Teddy said.

"You can?" Linelle said.

"I can. Am I right?"

The truth was that Linelle lacked solid experience in the kissing department, a fact she felt embarrassed about, given her age. Back in high school, any attempts boys made to kiss her happened at some tailgate party and had all the romantic timing of a mugging. Bold as Teddy's question was, in contrast to that history, it felt old-fashioned, more so given the pluck of his accent.

"I am considering it," Linelle admitted, "if you want to know the truth."

That was enough of an answer for Teddy. He leaned forward

and pressed his lips—softer than she might have imagined—to hers. Despite the taste of pot, that softness and the gentle feel of his hand reaching up to touch her cheek and her hair, well . . . it placed their moment of contact in the realm of something sweeter, more tender than other kisses Linelle had known. When they parted, Teddy smiled and said, "Tell me, princess, would a gay pirate from Ohio kiss you like that?"

"Probably not," she said, doing her best to maintain a casual tone, though things felt less casual now. "But one from Pennsylvania might. Or maybe Nevada."

"There you go again. Being funny when I'm hoping for a real answer."

"If you're wondering if you've proven your status as a heterosexual male, the answer is yes. The jury is still out on the British thing until I see your customs papers."

"Will be sure to bring my passport along to work tomorrow." Teddy stood and stretched. "Now I've got to get back to set. One hour left of acting pissed out of my mind and shouting, 'Blow me down!' and 'Skuttle me skippers!' Are you done for the day?"

"I am. But I'm stuck waiting for my mother. She's not finished until eleven. And before you ask, I don't want to get into the fact that my mother works here too."

"Sounds like another 'it's nothing' that's indeed something. But I'll respect your wishes. If you like, we could meet back here when I'm done and hang out until then."

Linelle did like, though not the idea of waiting around the Black Lung. Instead, they came up with a plan to meet in the park and make their way to Epcot. "Who knows?" she said as they gave themselves a crop-plane-style dousing of Lysol. "Maybe there's a mini-Moscow where you can impress people with your fancy talk of herrings in barrels and elephants made from fleas."

However, when they met later that night (twenty-five minutes later than agreed, which was Linelle's first experience with what she came to call "Teddy Time"), the two discovered there was no Russia at Epcot. Instead, they wandered to France, where cobblestone streets wound past dimly lit cafés with names like L'Esprit de la Provence and Galerie des Halles, which Linelle made Teddy pronounce in a French accent, and which she promptly mimicked, imitating the nasal sounds. In some weird way, this was fun for them both, and they kept at it until coming upon a fountain in a square surrounded by flickering lampposts. They reached into their pockets for pennies, turning up only nickels. Better, they decided, because that meant five wishes apiece. Linelle closed her fist around the coin, closed her eyes too, and came up with a list of four things she hoped for. She couldn't settle firmly on a fifth, but figured it wouldn't hurt to save a spare for when she really needed it. At last, she blew on her hand, shaking it the way she imagined gamblers did at Lost Logs Casino Barge, and tossed her nickel in the fountain.

"Must I really do all that, luv? Seems a bit labor intensive."

"Make your wishes whatever lazy way you want. Just don't blame me if they don't come true."

"I'll take my chances." Teddy hurled his coin in the air, and it fell in the water. As they walked away, he put his arm around her. "May I ask what you wished for?"

"If I tell you it won't come true. So let's just say, nothing."

"Ahh. I'm beginning to notice a pattern. Perhaps I should start keeping a list. My little list of Linelle mysteries."

The idea of this list gave way to him peppering her with

questions, like what she ate for breakfast and what she wanted to do with her life. He kept up until they reached a footbridge across a river inspired by the Pont des Arts. In the midst of crossing, while weaving through the mob of parents with kids on their shoulders, grandparents snapping photos, and all the rest of the tourist hullabaloo, an explosion sounded in the distance and the night sky lit up with fireworks.

Linelle and Teddy lingered there, watching the bursts of color behind the Eiffel Tower. They kissed again, which Linelle admitted to herself might have been that fifth wish on her list.

And so, ever since that night, if anyone had asked, this was the story Linelle could have told: "We met working at an amusement park . . . it started with my wisdom teeth. . . ." Or, what she might have said was, "We met in a place called the Black Lung. He was a pirate. I was a princess. He found me crying but helped me stop. We kissed right away, and I considered it to be the first real kiss of my life. Later that night, we found ourselves watching fireworks from the Pont des Arts over the River Seine with a view of the Eiffel Tower . . ."

Of course, it was not the real bridge or real river or real tower. But what did it matter? Theirs was a "how we met" story that felt romantic and auspicious to them both, a story that required no amount of exaggeration. It was perfect, exactly the way it happened, thousands of miles from Paris, right there beneath the Orlando sky.

FOUR

"When your head says one thing and your whole life says
another, your head always loses."

—From *Key Largo*, shown at the Schodack Big-Star Drive-in,
September 1948

AFTER LINELLE CONFESSES TO MARCUS—her husband of
nearly twenty years, a man who goes off to work each morning and returns home each night, who shares equally in the
myriad duties of raising a daughter, whose worst traits amount
to his juvenile eating habits, his juvenile sense of humor, and
his juvenile love affair with the 1967 candy-apple-red convertible Camaro in their garage—that he's caught her carrying on
with someone from her past, he surprises her with a question:
"Do you want a divorce?"

"A divorce? God no, Marcus. I haven't even seen him in
person yet."

"Yet? So you're planning on seeing him?"

"No. Or, I don't know. I mean, of course not. That's not
what this is."

"Then what is it?"

Linelle feels ridiculous. And humiliated. To make up for

her lack of underwear, she tugs at the hem of her T-shirt while looking at Marcus. He stands at the bottom of the stairs. What little hair he has left is mussed from sleep. The Florida Gators tee he wore to bed hugs his drooping pecs and belly. The man may never have been an Adonis, but in their early days, he put in some effort when it came to nutrition and the gym. Back then, his furry chest and bulky arms conjured for Linelle a kind of sexy gorilla. And though such things are not supposed to matter, he's since let himself go to such a degree that his body now conjures for her . . . well . . . a not-sexy gorilla.

"Please," Linelle says. "Do we have to talk about it? Can't we just—"

"I want to know his name," he says in a tone that makes it clear he will not let the topic go until she tells him.

"Okay, then. It's Teddy."

"And are you planning to fuck this blast from your past named Freddy?"

"Teddy! And no, Marcus! I told you, it's not like that. He lives nowhere near here. Even if he did, it's just . . . an online distraction. He wrote me. We were catching up. Then things got weirdly out of hand tonight. It was stupid. But there's nothing more to it, I swear."

There will be more questions, she assumes, like for starters, where and how exactly had Teddy written her. But a trait of Marcus's Linelle has long admired is his superhuman ability to avoid any lure of social media. While the rest of the world fell prey long ago, losing countless hours scrolling and swiping and liking and tweeting, he maintains a pure lack of interest in any of it. And now that the truth, or some scrap of it, is in the air, Linelle watches him cast a gaze at her laptop, at the mess of real estate magazines and flash cards, at their reflection in the mirrored wall. At last, he looks back at her. "You know, after all the trouble that old Polaroid caused, you should be more careful with this sort of thing."

The comment sends another wave of humiliation washing over Linelle. *That stupid photo!* she wants to scream. Instead, she takes a breath, tells him, "You're right."

"Okay, then. You promise that's all it was?"

"Promise. I won't ever talk to him again. You have nothing to worry about."

And just like that, there goes the escape and joy and comfort Linelle found in those late-night chats with Teddy Cornwell. The knowledge that he will be gone from her life once again and, most likely, once and for all, brings some unnameable force gathering in her chest, gaining strength, before fleeing her body in a sudden, tremulous rush. A feeling Marcus cuts short by saying, "Okey-doke. Let's go to bed."

"To bed?"

"Yeah, Linelle. Unless you have some other idea?"

"I don't. But . . . it's just . . ." The most sensible course of action obviously involves not challenging her husband's easy acceptance. Yet Linelle can't help herself. "That's it? I mean, just like that, you believe me?"

"Of course I do. You're my wife. I've known you forever. And I know you're not the type who would ever do anything so selfish as to have an affair."

"I'm not?"

"You're not. And you and I both know it. Think about it, Linelle. You're always just . . . there. For me. For old Trudy downstairs. For Georgia a million miles away. So let's put this BS behind us and go to bed."

Linelle tells him she'll be up in a minute, then heads to the counter. She blows out the candle. Tidies up the magazines and flash cards. After a moment, Marcus joins her. For a while, they say nothing, quietly gathering the cards. COBROKER . . . COLLATERAL . . . CREDIT REPOSITORY . . . Each one feels like an invitation to the next phase of Linelle's life, an invitation she wants to decline.

Finally, Marcus breaks the silence. "How are you, Linelle?"

After so many years of marriage that simple question is not one they often ask each other; it catches Linelle off guard. "How am I?"

"Yeah. I mean, are you okay?"

Linelle thinks of all the reasons she should feel okay, all the reasons she does not. It seems too much to speak of, the risk too great he won't understand. "I'm fine."

"You don't seem fine. And I was thinking, maybe it would be good if we started working on things . . . you know, in the bedroom again. I'm feeling pretty ready."

"If you want," she says, though after so many awkward attempts, no part of her wants to try.

"Also, maybe you should get out. See friends. I mean, DD has been your friend forever. I know what she did was messed up, but—"

"Messed up? Marcus, she cost me my job. My reputation. Not to mention our daughter's last year of living at home before college."

"We've talked about this. You know it wasn't intentional."

If she says much more on the topic, Linelle won't be able to sleep tonight, so she remains quiet, putting her mind on the flash cards.

"Okay, then. If you don't want to give it a go with an old

friend, at least try making a new one. BFTB tells me she texts you all the time asking to grab lunch and you blow her off."

The magazines and flash cards are now arranged in neat stacks. So Linelle gives Marcus what he wants. She taps out a late-night text to BFTB, tacking on an obscene number of smiley faces and hearts, slipping a lone sad face into the mix, since even in the world of emojis, she believes there should be some hint at a person's true feelings. Linelle presses Send, holds up her cell, and says, "Done."

But she's not done. BTFB texts back immediately:

Hey u! I c u r a night owl too! Let's grab lunch after Christmas. I'm planning a costume party for ur hubby's 25th anniv at SunTrust and I need ur help. The theme is superheroes so #getreadytoslaygrrrl! But shhhh . . . it's a surprise!

Seconds later, another text appears:

PS I've got dibs on Wonder Woman. Pick someone else.

Not long after, Linelle follows Marcus upstairs to their bedroom, where the evening began. After he drifts off to sleep again, Linelle stares at the ceiling and thinks of the lunch she now has to look forward to, of the superhero surprise party, of endless nights marooned in bed watching TV. She thinks, too, of the obligatory sex she and Marcus might start having again, since he mentioned resuming their efforts to "work on it." What all this thinking leads to is Linelle crying for the first time in a long while. Tears slide down her cheeks until her pillow feels damp.

You alright there, luv?

How many years has it been? And still, she longs to hear that voice in the dark, for it to offer the same comfort and happy distraction it did forever ago.

Finally, when she can't take lying there any longer, Linelle gets up once more. Outside in the hall, she rubs her face dry, pausing at her daughter's door before going to the basement, snapping on lights, squinting against the brightness.

Along a far wall, there's the closed door to her mother's tiny in-law apartment.

Along another, the tattered couch that served as the centerpiece of their home for years. Piled all around it are boxes filled with art supplies from her old classroom, plus relics and clothes from Linelle's past, purged from drawers and closets thanks to strict orders from BFTB. Linelle promised her that she'd host a tag sale, or take the boxes to Goodwill, though for now she has put off both. Spying a stray bit of Lollipop's calico fur beneath a strip of duct tape on one box, she looks away. Goes to a smaller box instead, one that's been mined many times since Teddy first made contact on Thanksgiving Day. Reaching in, she pulls out that old book, *Bizarre Romance*, and skims the back cover:

> For some, love is ordinary business. For others, the heart leads to a darker place. . . . Consider Emperor Nero, who in 67 AD employed barbaric methods to turn his young male lover, Sporus, into a woman resembling his dead wife. . . . Consider Queen Victoria, who in 1861 suffered such bottomless grief after King Albert's death, she held nightly séances to keep their love alive. . . .

Linelle puts the book aside. Goes back to digging in that box. Not searching for any specific thing, but rather the cumulative effect of a feeling those relics deliver. There is her laminated Disney ID with her younger self smiling. There is the Polaroid camera, the bright yellow Walkman, those long-ago gifts to her mother from one wealthy couple or another. There is a crumpled Denny's napkin filled with cramped handwriting:

> <u>My Little List of Linelle Mysteries:</u>
> *Why was she crying when we met?*
> *What wishes did she make in the fountain?*
> ~~*What does her mother do at the park?*~~ *(SOLVED)*
> *Will she always be so bloody obsessed with me?! (Hoping so)*

The list keeps going, filling up that napkin, filling up Linelle's head too, in a way that feels both painful and oddly pleasant. At last, she pulls out an envelope she'd found tucked away in the glove compartment of his auntie's VW Bug. For a long time after their breakup, Linelle carried that envelope inside her purse. Even now, she does not need to look at the letter inside to recall what's written in prim cursive on the page: *Mon cher cœur, Je ne m'attendais pas à développer des sentiments aussi profonds pour for vous . . .*

If not for those words, how would things have turned out for her and Teddy?

They'd been so young. Surely, it never would have lasted. At least that's what Linelle tells herself when she leaves that past, so freshly conjured, there on the floor and moves to the sofa. It's late—2:14 AM! Rather than sleep, she finds herself scrolling through contacts on her phone. She pauses on DD, who lives in Jacksonville now with her new husband, and allows her thumb to hover over the Delete option, though moves on before doing the deed. Then she comes to Teddy, to the number he sent when they flirted with the idea of calling to hear each other's voices again. Her thumb taps a message:

> Sorry about before. The Wi-Fi cut out. . . . I just wish I could see you Teddy. In person. Face to face. Wish I could hold you. Wish I could kiss you too

A moment later, her phone buzzes.

> **Teddy:** I want the same things. Believe me. I spend a great deal of time wondering what it would be like if we could erase the years and restraints of adulthood so we could have ourselves a proper date. But I'm aware of your situation. So tell myself it is never going to happen

What can Linelle say to that? She simply texts him goodnight and, after he wishes her a goodnight too, allows the cell to rest on her chest. Although her eyes fall shut, Linelle does not sleep. Not fully. Or, at least not right away. Her mind is too busy working something out in a fuzzy, dreamlike manner, until finally, the first stray beams of morning light seep through the high basement windows.

That's when she stands and stretches, having made a decision at last.

Quietly, Linelle opens the door to her mother's in-law setup, where a small artificial Christmas tree blinks away, the lone sign of the holidays in that house, since Linelle and Marcus decided to skip it this year. Spared from BFTB's clutches, her mother's space looks not all that different from the apart-

ment she and Linelle once shared in Lady Lake. Wood pan-
eling. Giant TV forever turned on. Reclining chair forever
reclined. Long ago, her mother developed a weird aversion
to sleeping in bed and spends her nights dozing in that chair.
On account of so much contact with Teddy, so much excavating the past, Linelle almost expects to see her mother from
the past too: choppy red hair, Lost Logs uniform, name tag
pinned to her chest. But there on the recliner, fast asleep, is
the current version of the woman: cloud of gray hair, mouth
dropped open, eyebrows knitted together, culminating in the
same befuddled expression she's worn since the stroke she
suffered Linelle's junior year of college.

"That you, pickle?" she asks, stirring suddenly.

"It's me, Ma. You doing okay?"

"Never better. Georgia home yet?"

"Not yet. It'll be a while."

"I still don't get why she isn't coming home at Christmas."

"We talked about this, Ma, like a million times. Her studies. She's too busy."

"Too busy for Christmas? Please."

Her mother's eyes close again, and Linelle thinks she's
fallen back to sleep. But then she speaks up, saying, "I'm sorry,
pickle. You know that, right?"

This apologizing is something her mother does so compul-
sively that Linelle has ceased asking what she's sorry for, since
there's never any specific answer. Instead she says, "Hey, Ma.
You remember that boyfriend I had a long time ago? Teddy
Cornwell?"

"Nope."

"Yeah, you do. The one I met at the park the first summer
there. British guy."

"Ohhh. Him. What a looker that one was. Handsome as all get-out. Nice ass too."

Linelle smiles, despite herself. "Not just that. Sweet. Funny. Charming. The two of us, we always just fit. Right from the start, everything felt so easy. On our days off, we'd borrow his aunt's car. Scrape together gas money and just drive. We ended up in Key Largo one time, Cape Canaveral another. Once, I remember, we had a picnic in some orange grove with junk food bought at a 7–Eleven. It was all, I don't know, simple."

"Until it wasn't. That boy broke your heart. Remember?"

Mon cher cœur, Je ne m'attendais pas à développer des sentiments aussi profonds pour for vous . . .

Of course she remembers, though she does not say so. And while the reminder should serve as warning enough about the decision Linelle has made, has she ever listened to her mother when it comes to matters of the heart or pretty much anything? Trudy drifts off to sleep again, this time for real, and Linelle adjusts the blanket over her thin body and kisses her forehead. The home health aide will arrive soon. Marcus will be getting up to start his day soon too, showering and shaving, heading off to the bank right on schedule.

Rather than go upstairs to their bedroom, she grabs her purse from the kitchen, then returns to those boxes and bags in the basement. After pulling out old jeans, tees, a sweater, curating whatever looks presentable and still fits, she makes her way to the garage, where her hulking SUV is parked next to the 67. Linelle reaches for the rack of keys on the wall, then pauses. Studies the candy-apple-red convertible, parked facing outward in a way that suggests a rocket ready for takeoff. Only once has she driven that car, back when Marcus first bought it. But she's surprised how easy it is to climb inside and adjust the seat and mirrors. To press the garage door opener and watch sunlight flood in, warming her skin already. To start the engine, to step on the gas too.

5:52 AM!

That's the time on the dashboard clock this December morning, just two days before Christmas, when Linelle rolls the Camaro out onto the driveway. She hangs a left on Orange Blossom Lane. A right onto the main road beyond. Yes, she's aware of the long drive ahead, of the many miles between where she is now and the cottage Teddy rents from the retired nurse.

As Linelle reaches I-95 and picks up speed, moving faster, faster still, her mind is elsewhere, replaying her husband's words from last night, about how she's always just . . . there. And when she no longer wants to think about that, her focus shifts to Teddy. Of course, she has no idea that during these last weeks, things between him and the old nurse have become darker and far more complicated. For now, she simply imagines that handsome face of his, made all the more handsome by age, as she opens her mouth and tells him, "After all these years apart, you and me, we've got ourselves a date."

FIVE

"One final thing I have to do . . . and then
I'll be free of the past."

—From *Vertigo*, shown at the Schodack Big-Star Drive-in,
June 1958

I FORGET THINGS. PHONE NUMBERS. Dates. Exactly which
pills are round, which are oval, and which are shaped like
submarines or teardrops. But I remember where the good tablecloth is kept. The fancy napkins. The silverware and bulk
box of tapered candles. My Hollis, he never liked to go out to
dinner. Or, allow me to correct that: he never liked to go out
to dinner with me. Still, that didn't stop me from doing what
I could to make things special. On our anniversary, I used
to transform our dining nook into something resembling a
private booth at a restaurant, minus the waitstaff and chef.
I've never been much of a cook, but how hard is it to follow a
recipe? Dump Campbell's mushroom slop—I mean soup, or
do I?—over thawed-out chops, throw that concoction in the
oven along with my carefully assembled Towering Tater Tot
Casserole. Crank up Patsy Cline on the ancient record player,
and those evenings felt pretty damn romantic.

No secrets between this hubby and wifey.

Just love and trust.

What a crock of shit.

But that's all in the past now. And the past, as they say, is a different country. Here in the present, it takes a great deal of fumbling to make things nice for this December date night with Teddy. He's been living next door in the matching house for five weeks now, and our Tuesday ritual is something I look forward to more than anything else.

"Tell me," Teddy says tonight, toward the end of the same special meal I served to celebrate my apparently not-so-special marriage. "What's the dishonorable hag's name?"

I wave my hand in the air. Heat from a candle tickles my palm, so I make a fist and slip it into the pocket of my dress, where those sources of comfort are waiting: retirement letter, wedding bands, monkey-faced finger puppet, matchbook with only three matches remaining, 21-gauge Ultra-Fine syr— Well, surely by now, you know the drill. "Don't make me say it out loud. It's like conjuring a ghost."

"But she's not a ghost. She's alive and well. Living twenty minutes from here."

"Says who?"

"Says you, Skyla! After we polished off last Tuesday's Chianti."

"Oh. Right. Well, speaking of wine . . ." I tap my glass.

Teddy pours for us both. The sound is heavenly, made all the more so by his company and Patsy's lush voice crooning about how she's got her lover's picture, but some other girl's got him. Tonight marks one week til Christmas, and though we've gathered pine branches on our walks in the woods and arranged them around my cottage as a kind of olfactory decoration, I resist playing carols in favor of more genuine sentiments.

"You know," he says, after some sipping and silverware clanking, "you're always banging on about how I should reach out to Linelle. Perhaps you should reach out to this woman who you talk about incessantly but whose name you refuse to say."

For a moment, I feel too bothered to speak. I close my eyes, allowing the thought to settle, before opening them and asking, "Why on earth would I do that?"

"Hmmm . . . Let's see . . . Maybe a little something called . . . closure?"

This time, when I wave my hand in the air, I'm careful to avoid any near miss with a flame. "Spare me that closure crap. There's no such thing."

"How do you mean, there's no such thing?"

"I mean, it's just poop people shovel as an excuse for prolonging a painful situation when they'd be better off simply swallowing whatever crap and moving on."

"Well, if you don't mind my saying, it's hardly moving on if you mention her all the time. And you can't even bring yourself to say her name."

"Maureen," I whisper.

"Pardon?"

"You asked her name. There you go."

"I see. And what a ghastly name at that. I don't want to risk sounding like a psychic, but I'm having visions of a cow. You know, time to milk old Moooo-reen."

"Even worse: her last name is Mooreover."

"Oh, how positively beastly! Mooo-reeen Mooo-reover!"

That makes us bust up laughing. Before his arrival in my

life, laughter had become an unfamiliar sound in this house. Now, it makes me think of a bird that's gotten inside, only instead of flinging its feathered body about in search of an escape, the creature is perched among those branches, or perhaps on a stack of my old paperback romances that clutter this cottage too, filling the air with joyful noise. We throw back more wine as Patsy finishes her bruised-hearted wailing about how it sucks to be the jilted party, then starts in about how damn crazy she is. In both cases, I know the feeling. The music gets in my bones, inspiring me to slide right out of that tarted-up dining nook in hopes of asking Teddy for a dance. Unfortunately, my necklace of keys catches on the tablecloth. I feel a sudden tug, followed by the clatter of objects crashing to the floor.

Glasses! Plates! Pyrex dish!

A hell of a lot of Tater Tots must go rolling across the braided rug, plus a slew of uneaten chops, which I picture, illogically, flopping on the floor in the way of fish yanked from the sea.

"Speaking of closure," I say in an effort to turn the moment into a joke, rather than admit how pathetic it all makes me feel, "our meal, which you so kindly carted over from the freezer at the concession stand, has hereby come to a close."

Teddy claps and whistles, shouting in his bright voice, "Bravo, madam! Well done! An impressive finale!"

I smile, do an awkward half-bow half-curtsy.

That's when he excuses himself and retreats to the kitchen, returning with a damp towel. "I hereby request permission to press this around your lips, madam."

"Permission granted," I tell him, puckering up as though I'm about to be kissed. And while I'm aware he's only wiping away crumbs or wine stains or smudged lipstick, my mind can't help but imagine he's erasing more lasting imperfections: my sunspots, my slivery wrinkles, even the doggish yellow from my teeth. In this vision, he keeps at it until I'm young and beautiful, prettier than I ever was in the first place, prettier than he ever found that Linelle woman to be too. "Thank you, Teddy," I say, once he's done dabbing, not in my fantasy, but here in the real world, "for making me feel special. For making me feel beautiful too."

When he speaks again, his accent has a quality that puts me in mind of air gone out of a tire—punctured, flattened. "Funny, isn't it? How certain people can make you feel downright exquisite and others can make you feel . . ."

"Feel what?"

"Ugly. Know what I mean?"

"I do." I'm thinking of Hollis and that final film that played on the screen at the drive-in, cut short halfway through.

It doesn't occur to me to ask who Teddy is thinking about. Though my understanding shifts something in him, because the cheerful pluck of his voice returns. "More importantly, luv, where were you rushing off to anyway?"

Suddenly, the notion of us moving together to the music seems absurd. I'm the man's landlord, after all. I have some twenty-five-plus years on him. But Patsy is wailing away still so, bad idea or not, I spit it out. "I thought maybe we could dance." And since he doesn't answer right away, I start in on a joke to conceal my nervousness. "Don't make me ask Siri, because I hear she's—"

"Yes, Skyla?" that icy voice pipes up from my cell.

"Oh, shut up!" I yell at her. "I was talking about you! Not to you!"

"I'm searching for coffee shops near you," she says. "One possibility is the Schodack Diner at 1842 Columbia Turnpike—"

"I don't want coffee shops near me, so for God's sake, butt out!" Siri thankfully goes silent, and after a hesitation I say to Teddy, "Sorry. I was saying please don't make me ask you-know-who, because I hear she's all left feet. Or all no feet. Get it?"

He laughs, but not hardily enough to make me think of that joyful bird. A lukewarm response that sends a message: the man is going to turn me down. The prospect brings the kind of gloom that leads a person to stare into a mirror while slapping her face and screaming, "You pathetic piece of shit!" What's that? You've never done anything of the sort? If so, lucky you. I used to catch my patients having a vindictive go at themselves too often to count. Hell, I've hurled a solid number of insults and whacks at my face over the years as well, at least back when I could witness such self-flagellation.

But good news: Teddy steps closer. His presence, an inviting mass of warmth, beckons me with a brand of comfort so different from those usual sources in the pockets of my dress. In his most dapper voice, he asks, "May I?"

"You may."

We are an unusual puzzle, this man and me, so our coming together requires a bit of arranging. I'm grateful that Teddy takes charge, moving my body in the way of a doll's, draping one of my arms around his shoulder, the other around his waist. Considering the frequency with which he mentions letting himself go, I'm not surprised to feel the slight pudge of his midsection between us. Yet, what does that matter, since I'm living proof of that old "love is blind" business?

Not that I'm in love. I know better. Of course I do.

"Your necklace," Teddy says. "Care to take it off?"

A question he's asked before, each time for a different reason.

On our walks in the woods: "All that jangling scares the birds . . ."

Over dinner: "You're dipping them in your supper . . ."

Whenever I pull off the keys to the concession stand, so he can bring food back from the freezer: "Why not just hand me the entire necklace?"

And now that we're about to dance: "They're poking me."

Usually, my answer is the same: "Wherever I go, the keys go." This time, however, I say in a playful voice, "Who knows? Maybe one will unlock your heart."

"Given our height difference, at the moment they seem better positioned to unlock my stomach."

I laugh, but the keys stay right where they are. As we begin moving together, I ask, "Did your ex-wife like to dance?"

"At weddings. She was very much an Electric Slide creature."

"As in 'boogie woogie, woogie'?"

"Afraid so. When that song came on, Lord help us all." He spins us around the room faster than the music. "What about your late husband?"

"The man worked for the power company and had all the grace of the telephone poles he climbed. So, no. At least not with me."

"Speaking of Hollis, you never did tell me the story behind the matching houses. Why two? Why side by side?"

Too much talk of Hollis and I worry we'll tiptoe back to the topic of Mooo-reen. Or worse: that second accident out in the woods, which did him in. I wave my hand. "Did you ever reach out to Linelle?"

"Looked her up? Yes. Reached out? No."

"I bet you'll be tempted come Christmas next week."

"Christmas? Why then?"

"You know how the holiday has a way of making people nostalgic."

"Yeah, well, not this person. Not this Christmas anyway. But now that you mention it, I did recently reconnect with someone else from my past."

"Oh? What's her name?"

"It's a him. A guy I used to tutor in French. Pretended to anyway. Long story. I said he should come visit sometime. He's an odd bloke, but you know how certain people from your past get grandfathered in? That's the case with Jeremy. He mentioned looking for a place to live. Wants to get out of the city. If ever I move on, I thought, maybe Jeremy could take my place."

I cannot speak for a moment, then say in a voice filled with dismay, "Move on?"

"Not right away. But eventually, I mean."

"Well, that day better never come. I'm hoping you'll stay here with me forever."

Teddy laughs and whirls us around, faster now, until I feel something squishy beneath my feet. "Oopsy. I'm fairly certain I'm stepping on something."

"We both are, luv. It's the pork chops."

"Oh. Well, I've heard of dinner dancing, but never dancing on your dinner."

"You're a funny one, Miss Skyla Hull."

And just when I'm feeling dizzy from it all, we slow down, begin swaying to the music. That's also when I dare to do something I've imagined since we first stood inside the house next door and I asked if he wanted the place and he said I do, since I envisioned us before the drive-in movie screen with me in a different white dress, since just about every second of our talks on the porch, every one of our walks in the woods, every one of our candlelit dinners. Yes! Yes! Yes! I'm aware I've denied any such extracurricular desires—to you, and even to myself—but am I the first to shove down such feelings? Am I the first to let wine get the better of me? Am I the first to look up at someone and make an unexpected and intimate request, in this case, asking, "Can I have a . . . hold?"

"Pardon?" Teddy says.

Hug—that's the word I intended to say, though *hold* seems more fitting to describe what it is I crave from him. After all, Hollis may have kissed me and had sex with me, but he seldom held me tight in his arms. So, I stick with it. "Can you please . . . hold me? I mean, for just a little bit. If you don't mind."

Thanks to all our maneuvering around the room, his body is sweaty. Mine too. But what's more unexpected: he has a beard, or at least a fair amount of scruff run wild, which brushes against me as he wraps his arms around my waist and pulls me to him. He feels good, this man, the only man aside from Hollis with whom I've ever been this close. (Always clean shaven, that one. Mornings, I'd return from a night shift, feet aching, and there he'd be at the kitchen table: cornflakes, newspaper, blood-spotted bits of tissue pressed around his face, courtesy of his frugal no-shaving-cream, disposable-razor method. He'd look up with those steely blue eyes and give me a warm, welcome-home kiss before clearing out to go climb telephone poles. Supposedly. The bastard.)

It's just my luck that the record comes to a sudden end,

making that *thump-thump* party's-over sound nobody likes. Teddy takes that as a cue to guide us toward the sofa and helps me sink slowly into the cushions.

"That was nice," I tell him.

"Quite nice indeed. Now stay put, Skyla, while I clean up the mess."

I pat the couch. "Leave the mess."

But he doesn't hear. And so, I lean back. Listen to him picking up tots and chops, sweeping broken bits into the trash. I stick my hands into my pockets, eventually pulling out the letter and holding it before me, as though I can still see the glowing praise on the page: SUCH STELLAR SERVICE! SUCH IMPECCABLE CARE! SUCH EMPATHY AND PROFESSIONALISM!

"What's that?" Teddy asks, and I'm overcome by the oddest sensation: time, or so it seems, has lurched forward somehow.

On these Tuesday evenings together, Teddy is forever warning me not to light candles because of the obvious dangers. Now, I sense he's snuffed them out. The air carries the faint, smoky smell of an evening that's all but over and ready for the history books. Looking up, in the direction of his voice, I wish desperately to see that face of his even once, but I'm met only with the usual shadowy abstractions.

What does he look like, this man?

What other women has he held?

Linelle, comes one answer. And more questions: Does she still think of him? If he does someday reach out to her, will he invite her here? How will I feel when his attentions are showered upon another?

All too much to think about, so I vow never again to bring up Linelle. Never to ask Siri to look her up either. Not that those searches produced more than the most trivial details of the woman's life: She lives in Tallahassee with her bank manager husband, a man whose prized possessions include a vintage Camaro and a collection of superhero action figures on a shelf above his desk. (Thank you, "Get to Know Our Staff" section of suntrustbank.com.) Their daughter is spending her final year of high school in Berlin, courtesy of some fancy music scholarship. (Thank you maclay.org, the girl's school website.) This past year, Linelle abruptly lost her job as a high school art teacher after what was described only as "an objectionable photo" of her surfaced on social media. (Thank you, tallahassee.com.) The point is: bye-bye, Linelle.

Nice not knowing you.

As for the letter, without my realizing, it has come to rest on my chest, atop my necklace of keys. "This? Well, it's a letter the head honchos at the hospital gave me when I retired. Since no one wanted me to leave, they went out of their way to commend me for my outstanding service. I carry it because . . . because it makes me feel good."

"Well done, luv. Let's have a look-see, shall we?"

I hesitate, nervous to share this part of me, before finally handing it over. Teddy reads: "Dear Ms. Skyla Hull, This letter is to notify you of your immediate term—"

He stops.

"Go on."

Silence.

"I said, go on! I was a real superstar up on that eighth floor. Yes, there was that unfortunate blip on my record, no thanks to that mix-up with Amanda Quigley. She was what we called a 'frequent flyer,' had been in and out dozens of times.

But other than that nonsense—one patient, out of hundreds, thousands, I cared for in a decades-long career—the administrators loved me!"

Still, nothing. Not a peep. Rather than nudge again, I reach wildly for the letter, like a child playing that dreadful pool game, Marco Polo, arms flailing, splashing about. "Either keep reading or give it back!" My yelling brings the realization that we are having our first fight.

My fellow nurses on the ward were always grumbling about their relationships. Lazy . . . limp-dicked . . . drinker . . . gambler . . . pervert . . . porn addict . . . drug addict . . . deserter . . . Name whatever horror show of a husband you can, and one of them would be attached to him. I'd stand there in my crisp white uniform, staring at them in their wrinkled scrubs in all sorts of pukey colors, not to mention clogs—or worse, those godforsaken Crocs!—and after a perfunctory expression of sympathy I'd say: "Guess I'm one of the lucky ones. My Hollis and me, we rarely ever argue. Matter of fact, I can count on one hand the number of times . . ." Here, I'd pause and hold up four fingers. The audacity! Sometimes I'd even go so far as to bend my pinky, joking that our last fight—"over his obsession with washing our bed linens and towels"—was so minor, it barely counted.

What an idiot I was to believe that our lack of conflict was evidence of marital purity.

"I'm sorry. It's just . . . Something caught in my throat," Teddy says at last. He makes a fuss of clearing it, then continues, "Dear Ms. Skyla Hull, This letter is to commend you on your years of impeccable service. What a stellar nurse you were. The bloody best. It is with utmost gratitude that we wish you well in retirement." He presses the paper into my palm.

"Told you," I say.

"You certainly did. Now, I want to talk to you about old Moo-Moo."

"Old who-who?"

"You know, Mooooo-reen Mooooo-reover."

"Oh. Her."

"Yes, her. While I was cleaning and you were napping—"

"I napped?"

"You don't remember?"

In truth, I do not. But admitting my forgetfulness, never mind my need for a nap in the midst of our dinner date, is not something I wish to do. "I closed my eyes for a few. I'd hardly call it a nap."

"Righty-ho. Well, while you were closing your eyes, I took the liberty of looking her up."

"In the phone book?"

"My dear, the phone book may as well be the Dead Sea Scrolls at this point. I looked her up on Facebook. And before I get into particulars, let me say, you are far more attractive. That should make you feel better."

"Oh, Teddy." Briefly, I bury my face in my palms, making a show of my embarrassment. The gesture, the compliment itself, are such unfamiliar territory that I can't help but feel that I'm playacting at being someone else. That is, a woman who dances with handsome men, a woman who has to swat away so many compliments about her beauty. "You're only being nice. I saw her, remember? In the waiting room at the ER when Hollis had his first accident. Dressed all in black. A good twenty years younger. A good twenty times prettier too. Gaping at me with—"

"An unmistakable expression of guilt. You've only told me

a hundred times, dear. Which is why I believe you need to face this piece of your past head-on. So you can get your answers, then put this bollocks behind you. So why not allow me to message her from my account, explain how I know you, and ask if she'd be willing to meet you in person?"

I begin to protest, to say absolutely not. But then I close my mouth.

"What?"

"I just realized that, well, you're looking out for my well-being. And other than my nephew, John, who comes up on occasion to help me, I can't remember the last time anyone did that. Thank you."

"You're most welcome, Skyla. So you'll think about it then?"

"I don't want to. But, fine. I'll consider it."

"Good. On that note, I best be going."

Normally, on these Tuesday nights, I make a point of walking Teddy to the door. But this Tuesday is different. Maybe because we've had our first hold, our first fight too. Whatever the reason, I stay put on the sofa and ask, "How about a hold goodnight?"

Again, that pause, during which I fear that I've asked too much. And again, I think of those self-inflicted slaps across my face, of my shouting, "You pathetic piece of—"

"Why not?" Teddy says after a breath.

I hear his footsteps coming closer. Sense him leaning over me. He slips his arms down around my body and I reach up and slip mine around his shoulders. We stay that way for a moment that's longer and far more intimate than a simple hug. We both feel the tenderness of it, I'm sure. When Teddy pulls away, I'm unable to keep from smiling. "Goodnight, darling," I tell him. Then a thought occurs to me. "Don't forget to inform your friend Jeremy that he's welcome to visit, but you aren't going anywhere."

"Will let him know. Night, luv."

I listen as he walks to the door. Listen as he ambles across those twenty-six steps to the second cottage. Listen as his door opens, then closes. And when I'm done with all that listening, I stay put on the sofa, soaking in the silence as my mind churns with thoughts of our holding each other, of our dancing, of our conversation and laughter. That's when I hear myself say, "Hey, Siri."

"Yes, Skyla."

In this manner, she's akin to the most loyal of dogs. No matter how ferocious a scolding you give the creature, the moment you need her again, there she is. Ready and willing to serve.

"If you're going on a date with the enemy, what should you bring?"

My cell is quiet. Siri must be thinking, if that's what you call whatever mysterious thing she does. At last comes her reply: "I'm not sure I understand."

Haven't there been enough disagreements for one evening? For that reason, I keep from hurling insults in her direction. She's just a stupid machine, after all. If she possessed even a shred of human intelligence, she'd know the answer. I know it. Something tells me you know it too.

My hands are already moving in my pockets, already feeling that outdated but surely still potent 5-milliliter vial of fentanyl, already feeling that sealed 21-gauge Ultra-Fine syringe as well. All the while, my mind recalls the way such needles look once unsealed.

So very pointed.

So very silver.

So much glinting in the light.

I may forget things. Phone numbers. Dates. Exactly which pills are round, which are oval, and which are shaped like submarines or teardrops. But certain details, I'll never forget. Like the first time my husband injured himself climbing one of those telephone poles, and I arrived in a breathless rush at the ER to find another woman by his side, dressed all in black, gaping at me with an expression of unmistakable guilt before rushing away through the exit doors. I'll never forget looking at his admissions paperwork afterward, seeing her signature scrawled at the bottom. I'll never forget sheepishly calling the wives of his friends, one by one, to say, "I'm sorry to put you in this position, but do you happen to know a woman named . . ." How hopeless it all felt, that is, until one of those wives said, "I do know of her, Skyla. And let me fill you in on what I know . . ."

So, this is what I tell that idiotic machine: "If you're going on a date with the enemy, you bring something to protect yourself. To harm her. If it comes to that. After all, this enemy thought nothing of sleeping with your husband. Not once. Not twice. But for years. While you were going off to work, grocery shopping, making dinner, making the bed, making plans for what you believed was a simple and happy life, a life full of love and trust—while you were doing all that, this enemy thought nothing whatsoever of harming you too."

SIX

"Inga! You don't shove the food down Shitake's throat. You place it on her tongue. Don't they have dogs in Sweden?"

—From *Overboard*, shown at the Schodack Big-Star Drive-in, April 1988

1. Pretty needs 5 walks per day. <u>No exceptions</u>. When you bring her inside, wipe her paws. They are sensitive to grime on the sidewalks.

2. Pretty needs to be brushed thoroughly at least once daily, but preferably twice. The full process should only take 30 to 40 minutes. Begin with brush #1 to loosen her fur, then finish with comb #5.

3. Pretty <u>must</u> practice her "Stand for show!" command. Blocks and measurements are in her bag along with her kibble and a separate list of instructions for feeding, plus an aromatherapy candle for her anxiety.

4. Pretty is competing next week (at the Boardwalk Kennel Club All Breed Dog Show in Atlantic City!!!) and I intend for her to win. So please don't fuck it up, Jer. That means <u>no giving her pepperoni pizza</u> like you did when we were dating and again when

you came by to try and change my mind after we broke up.

5. Btw, I saw those <u>disgusting</u> magazines on your nightstand. Can't you whack off to porn online like the rest of the depraved male population? See you when I get back from the funeral Sunday night.

Tiff

THERE ARE A NUMBER OF reasons why Jeremy Lichanel should not be packing for a last-minute weekend trip to Providence, Rhode Island. Pretty—his ex-girlfriend's overcoifed, angel-white standard poodle—is just one. Here's another: at the age of forty-four, Jeremy is still single. If you look at his relationship history, you might blame his "let's go Dutch, or better yet, you pay" approach to dating. Or his habit of saying whatever pops into his mind, like the first time Tiff invited him to dinner at her apartment in Astoria and he blurted, when she served him a mesclun salad with raspberry vinaigrette, "God, how I despise raspberry vinaigrette. Makes me want to vomit almost as much as mesclun. Give me a wedge of iceberg and ranch dressing any day." (This was also the last time Tiff invited him to dinner, since she dumped him that night.) Or you might even blame other more basic turnoffs, like his seventh-floor walk-up studio apartment in a sketchy section of Queens, New York, and his ancient Lincoln Town Car with a trunk full of old books and jumper cables used far too often on account of the car's faulty battery, not to mention a passenger window that doesn't roll up and an engine that is forever breaking down.

But Jeremy Lichanel does not blame his chronic single status on any of those things. Instead, he has come to believe that the problem lies in his appearance: specifically his face, with its undefined chin that melds into his neck in such a way that it's not quite clear where one begins and the other ends, his jowly cheeks not unlike Alfred Hitchcock's, his drooping eyes, meaty ears, too large teeth, too thin lips, and, worst of all, his skin riddled with acne scars. And so, that morning, before a trip to Providence was even in the cards, Jeremy finally did something about one of those problems, withdrawing a hefty sum from his surprisingly robust bank account and blowing it on the first in a series of fancy laser treatments from a fancy dermatologist on the fancy Upper East Side of Manhattan. The treatment was akin to taking a blowtorch to Jeremy's face, something Jeremy felt he had not been adequately prepared for by the doctor, a Barbie-beautiful woman minus the exaggerated breasts. That doctor had poked and prodded at his face as though feeling a questionable beefsteak tomato at a farm stand. In the most matter-of-fact voice, she gave labels to Jeremy's scars: "These 'icepick' scars down here on your chin—those I can help. But these 'rolling' and 'atrophic' scars on your cheeks are going to be trickier and will require me to go deeper with the laser."

All of this brings us back to the reason Jeremy should not be packing his suitcase and corralling Pretty and hunting down the dog's harness and two types of leashes and her bag with kibble and a lawn-scented aromatherapy candle and "Stand for show!" blocks, in preparation for a trip to Providence. The doctor had warned him that the skin on his face would turn increasingly red in the coming days—so red he would look like he'd been sailing. In forty-mile-per-hour winds. In the scorching sun. Without sunscreen. And perhaps slathered in baby oil. When all that was over, the outer dermis of his face would begin to crust, then flake, then peel away, snake-like, and the great hope was that it would reveal the beginnings of a smoother, clearer, slightly more beautiful face—the face Jeremy Lichanel was meant to have.

"Until then, you're going to be pretty scary to look at," she told him before exiting the treatment room, "so I suggest you just lay low."

Laying low had been Jeremy's only plan for this brisk, early November weekend as he rode the crowded E train back to Queens and hiked the seven flights to his apartment. Jeremy is something of an eighties movies buff, and it just so happens that there's an eighties movie marathon on TBS. He could hardly wait to sprawl out on his futon and pump his fist at the words "I'll be back . . ." (*Terminator*) and "Sometimes you gotta say 'What the fuck'" (*Risky Business*) and "Wax on, wax off" (*Karate Kid*). He's got a freezer full of Stouffer's French Bread pepperoni pizzas and that stack of old *Playboys* on his nightstand to keep him busy as he awaits the arrival of his new and improved face. And now there's also Pretty: a dog with the proportions of a midsize farm animal, only nowhere as useful, since she does nothing more than lift her head and put it back down when he opens his apartment door. Quite unexpectedly, Tiffany called that morning to inform him of her favorite uncle's equally unexpected passing due to a brain aneurism. She needed to fly home to Buffalo but was too broke to board Pretty. Sensing where the conversation was headed and, frankly, sensing a slim chance at romantic reconciliation after the raspberry vinaigrette debacle months before, Jeremy cut to the chase and told her where the keys were hidden.

But no sooner does he arrive home to read her preposterous list of instructions, while pressing a bag of frozen peas to each side of his tingling face, when his cell buzzes. Turns out to be a guy Jeremy has privately nicknamed "The Kid" (his actual name, Jeremy cannot recall). The Kid is an editor at a travel website Jeremy's been lucklessly pitching stories to for months. "How'd you like to go to Providence this weekend?" The Kid asks.

"You mean, Provence? Sure, let me get my passport."

The Kid does not so much as titter at the joke, but Jeremy fills the void by letting out a sharp burst of laughter all his own. That's when he feels the pain—so raw and pure it is akin to a jellyfish glomming onto his face. No laughing at jokes until further notice, he tells himself, pressing the peas more firmly to his skin, not yours and not anybody else's. No moving your face at all.

"You and that Provence trip," The Kid says. Jeremy desperately tries to dredge up his name: Destry? Dale? Dillon? Even though they've never met in person, his mind fabricates a picture based on nothing more than the youthful lag of his voice: he pictures The Kid as a twenty-something in skinny jeans, thick glasses, and the woolly beard of a Civil War soldier. "I told you last time, the South of France has been done. Like a million times. I mean, how much can people read about lavender and sunflowers and bouillabaisse?"

"Quite a bit actually," Jeremy tells him. "I don't believe there's a limit."

"Yeah, well, we cover more unexpected places. There's a

restaurant opening in Providence. The dude who was supposed to cover it is blowing me off. It's your gig if you want it. I can only pay you a hundred bucks but I've lined up a hotel that'll give you a free room tonight and tomorrow in exchange for a mention. Besides, didn't you used to, like, live there?"

"How do you know that?" Jeremy asks.

The Kid pauses. "Don't know. Maybe you put it in one of your pitch emails?"

"Nope."

"Oh. Well, maybe it's on LinkedIn?"

"I'm not on LinkedIn."

"Facebook?"

"Not on Facebook either. I deplore social media and avoid it at all costs."

While not entirely true, it is among Jeremy's favorite things to say, mainly because of the grave concern it never fails to rouse in people. You'd think he'd announced that he dislikes eating or breathing or fucking the way they carry on.

The Kid does not disappoint. What comes next is a hackneyed lecture about the myriad ways social media can raise Jeremy's profile and help him network and increase awareness of his brand. Network is the raspberry vinaigrette of words and brand the mesclun, far as Jeremy is concerned. Still, he listens, while flipping open a worn composition notebook in which he carefully tallies every penny he spends. In this case, minus $5.50 for the subway to and from Manhattan, and minus the $1,672.00 for the first laser treatment, bringing the grand total of his bank account to $1,372,321.93.

Yes, that sum raises questions about his dilapidated car, his crappy walkup studio, and his even bothering to pitch travel stories in hopes of scoring free trips, not to mention his habit of hanging up on the army of financial experts from Citibank who call to suggest he invest, rather than keep all that money in a run-of-the-mill savings account. At the moment, however, while performing this basic act of accounting, Jeremy does his best to feign interest in what The Kid is saying. "Well, dude, however I came to know it, you did grow up in Providence. Am I right?"

"Much of my growing up was done in a U-Haul, since my father's university jobs kept us moving every few years. I spent my senior year of high school in that armpit of a city. Another four at Brown. A few years later, I came to my senses and skedaddled."

"Skedaddled? Not a word I hear often."

"Well, I am a writer, after all. You and I, we're in the business of words. Isn't it our job to bravely trot out the very utterances others are terrified to use, rather than saddle up the same tired warhorses, day after day after day? You should see the way I boldly canter such rare breeds as *callipygian* or *absquatulate* or that exotic beauty, rarest among rare, *floccinaucinihilipilification* . . ." By the time Jeremy has beaten the dead horse of his equestrian metaphor, the line has gone silent. "Hello?" he says. "Hello?"

"I'm here. Anyway, um, where were we? Oh, this assignment. You could bring your experience to the piece. Throw in details about returning to the city and how it's changed. There's been a renaissance since you must have lived there back in the—"

"Late aughts," Jeremy says before The Kid can say the nineties, which is true. But Jeremy has come to understand that people The Kid's age dismiss anyone over forty as "old." So he does his best to keep his senior citizen status a secret.

"Whatever, man, you in or out? I have to get this assigned, then catch a train. I'm heading upstate to a writers' colony for the next two weeks."

Once upon a time, quite desperately in fact, Jeremy wanted to be the kind of writer who went away to writers' colonies. Instead of having affairs at those places the way most writers do, he actually hoped to use the time and space to write. He longed to write a grand, sweeping, thinky book of the sort his mother used to read back in the days when she hauled him around to endless appointments with doctors and theater auditions—the book Guy de Maupassant (a favorite of hers) would've written in his final years if only he'd put down the absinthe and picked up a pen. But Jeremy no longer thinks about that forgotten dream, except when he hears of someone else fulfilling it, as is the case now. "I'll go," he tells The Kid.

And so, after a quick back-and-forth about logistics and a deadline, Jeremy hits End Call. The moment he tosses his cell on the counter, there comes a rustling from the corner of the room. He looks to see Pretty, awake now and scrutinizing him from her position on his futon. The dog's fur is pure topiary—a carnival combo of mountainous white puffs and shaved-to-the-skin patches that would make Edward Scissorhands proud. Her eyes, however, are something else altogether: black and beady and downright sanctimonious in their gaze. The only time those eyes soften is when Jeremy slips Pretty a slice of pepperoni pizza, which is why Jeremy did just that on more than one occasion, even if it led, quite literally, to a shitstorm. But unlike his opinions on raspberry vinaigrette and mesclun and the words *network* and *brand*, Jeremy's observation about Pretty's eyes is something he has never once articulated to anyone, least of all Tiffany. That dog is her greatest possession. That dog is her biggest hope of winning what he assumes to be a substantial cash prize at the absurdly long-named kennel show in Atlantic City. Other than her favorite uncle in Buffalo, who passed away so horribly and unpredictably, that dog is the one thing that matters most to Tiffany. More than anything else in the world, the woman cherishes her precious Pretty. And though he knows she'd never want him to take the pooch on a road trip, he's about to do it anyway.

SEVEN

"That's easy for you to say. You're a mannequin, you'll
always have work. Me, I'm gonna wind up in the nuthouse
after this. . . ."

—From *Mannequin*, shown at the Schodack Big-Star Drive-in,
August 1988

OCCASIONAL WHIMPERING FROM THE DOG, the steady rush
of wind snapping the plastic duct-taped over the passenger
window of the Lincoln, the sporadic jostling of books knocking about in the trunk along with the jumper cables kept
back there since the prehistoric battery in that car needs a
boost on a regular basis—those things punctuate an otherwise uneventful ride to Providence. The thoughts that fill Jeremy's mind, however, are substantially more eventful. While
hurtling north on I-95, past signs for bucolic-sounding Connecticut towns—Milford, Madison, Mystic—the *zoom-zoom*
pace of the highway leads him to think of his parents on an
equally hurried car ride along an autoroute between Paris
and Provence years before. Even though the chatter of French
radio had likely transfixed his mother, while his father had

likely remained focused on the road ahead, Jeremy imagines her softly singing as his father hummed along:

"*Tout le monde est sage, dans le voisinage, Il est l'heure d'aller dormer, le sommeil va bientôt venir.* . . ."

When he glimpses the big blue sign that proclaims WEL-COME TO RHODE ISLAND, THE OCEAN STATE, Jeremy realizes that he has begun singing the old lullaby too, and that realization leads him to fall into a somber silence. He squelches all thoughts of that trip—a trip he refused to join them on despite their insistence. Instead, his mind wanders to yet another off-limits place.

The memories that unfurl in his mind have their beginnings in the spring of 1999 in a squat, single-story warehouse in downtown Providence, and come to an abrupt end on a summer evening of that same year in a shadowy playground behind a nearby elementary school. How easy it is to picture that younger version of himself, standing in the buggy woods behind that school, face and hands bathed in moonlight, crickets and cicadas making night sounds all around. How easy it is to recall watching a woman he'd known briefly, though perhaps more intensely than any woman since. Unlike his other exes, whose marriages and divorces and babies and careers Jeremy monitors with the help of the various social media accounts of "Courtney Goodale," he knows not a single detail of Maryanne's present life—or even if she is alive, since she's the lone female from his past he does not permit himself to look up.

Divine City Retail Rental—that was the name of the company on Rucks Street where, at the hopeful age of twenty-four, Jeremy had been employed. Dan Nicastro, the red-faced, black-bearded, muscle-pumped man who owned the business, made a killing charging stores in the Warwick Mall bundles of money to rent shelving, counters, cash registers, hangers, and a slew of other supplies. Why those businesses did not simply purchase their own equipment escaped Jeremy. And if it sounds like a deadly dull place to work, that's because it was. The single most intriguing aspect: mannequin rentals.

Whenever a supply of mannequins was returned to the warehouse at the end of a shopping season, a surprising number looked as though they'd been caught in a freak stampede. Fingers snapped off. Limbs wrenched from bodies. Faces marred by what looked to be footprints. What happened that they came back so brutalized when their only job was to look pretty in a window display? Jeremy once asked that question of Dan Nicastro only to get his booming, scratchy-voiced answer: "Who fucking cares how it happened? All I know is, when it does, I keep the security deposit, which means more money for me!" No matter how ruined the mannequins, none were ever thrown away; rather, they were deposited in a pile just outside a closed red door at the far corner of the warehouse. On a schedule so random Jeremy could not make sense of it, a person arrived to "pretty the dummies up" as Dan put it, and that person was Maryanne.

Voluptuous, curvy, busty—Maryanne had a body that could be described using all the words people do for a woman who carries a bit of extra weight in a way that looks undeniably sexy. Her clothes were a rotating uniform of black leggings and oversize pastel sweaters that stopped mid-thigh. If there was something standardized about her wardrobe, her hair was quite the opposite. Maryanne was forever chopping, coloring, curling, and straightening it, and Jeremy quietly studied each new coiffure from his desk while filing leasing forms and flinching whenever Dan Nicastro barked out a new order.

In his early months at DCRR, Jeremy's greatest fascination was Maryanne and the mysterious brand of magic she practiced behind that red door. He watched her lug those mannequins, so damaged by their time in the outside world, to the room on the other side. Days later, he watched her lug them back out, each one made whole again, beautiful in its own vacant, soulless way. Dan reacted critically to just about everything Jeremy had to say, so Jeremy remained as unobtrusive as possible. That meant, unfortunately, never saying more to Maryanne than "hello" and "goodbye" and, on one occasion when she asked after Dan's whereabouts, "He's on the can."

The palpable hush between them became an unspoken decree of sorts, one Jeremy wished desperately to un-decree. At last came a day when, unlike so many wishes in his life, this wish came true. Dan began leaving early with suspicious frequency that spring, slapping Jeremy's shoulder and telling him he was "Captain of the Ship" until Dan got back. Not long after Jeremy heard the sound of his truck speed away, there came the familiar thump of bass from Maryanne's Plymouth Turismo drawing closer outside. When the bass fell silent, the Turismo door slammed and the warehouse door opened. Maryanne stepped inside, wearing her black leggings that hugged the length of her calves and thighs, a muted pink sweater that hugged her ample breasts too. The collar of that sweater, Jeremy noticed, was cut loose and ragged. A style that put him in mind of *Flashdance*, a movie he often thought of while working that job, because of the warehouse setting and because Jeremy had a fair number of fantasies about Jennifer Beals.

"Hello," Maryanne said.

"Hello," Jeremy said.

Per usual, that was the only conversation between them before the familiar hush pressed down on the warehouse, the only sound the mannequins' fiberglass feet being dragged across the cement floor as Maryanne hauled one injured party after another through the red door. And then there was the *scratch-scratch* of Jeremy's pencil against the pad of paper he pulled from his desk. Whenever Dan appointed him "Captain of the Ship," Jeremy used the time to make notes for the novel he planned to write.

The dragging of fake feet, the scratching of the pencil— those sounds went on for some time until Jeremy heard a sudden crash and whipped up his head to see Maryanne looking startled, having let slip a decapitated, alabaster-white mannequin from her grasp. Thanks to the ragged neckline of her sweater, he managed to catch a glimpse of her breasts cupped in a silky bra as she bent down to pick it up. *Look away,* he told himself. But it was too late: her wide brown eyes flicked upward and met his gaze. Her expression, to Jeremy's way of thinking, conveyed one message and one message only: *I see you looking at my tits.*

"Can I help you carry those?" Jeremy asked in an effort to conceal his ogling.

"It's about time you did something gentlemanly and offered. I've only been waiting for you for, like, ever."

Maryanne's voice, he realized now that he heard her speak more than a few words, had a pleasingly mush-mouthed quality that put Jeremy in mind of yet another favorite eighties movie. It was not the plot of *Working Girl* he loved so much, but the way Melanie Griffith delivered a single line, her mouth moving sloppily over consonants, even more sloppily over vowels. And then there were the words themselves, which never failed to give him an instant erection: "I have a head for business and a bod for sin."

"Oh. Forgive me. I didn't realize you wanted me to—"

"I'm just teasing," Maryanne said. "But yeah, I could really use a hand."

Together, they picked up the mannequin, perfect except for that missing head and newly dented shoulder, and carried it, gurney-style, through the red door. This was Jeremy's first time on the other side, and he looked around to see that things weren't much different than the rest of the warehouse, if you didn't count the arms and legs and torsos piled haphazardly on shelves against the walls. When they placed the stiff body on the floor, he noticed a weight-lifting bench by the window. Not far away, a claw-foot tub, painted red but peeling in hundreds of slivers, was slowly filling with water.

"That's how I clean them," Maryanne said when she saw him looking. "They take baths. Same as you and me. I mean, unless you're more of a shower guy. Are you a shower guy, Jeremy?"

"I am," he managed. "But what about the weight bench?"

"Well, that's how I get them back in shape. What did you think?"

Jeremy wasn't sure how to respond to that, so he just studied her a moment. Maryanne's hair, sun-kissed blond weeks before, had returned to a bookish shade of brown that put him in mind of a librarian, or more specifically, a naughty librarian. Maybe it was the way she wore it, using simple bobby pins to hold things up, though her chronic chopping and restyling meant much of her hair fell free around her face. Jeremy

marveled at that face, made pretty by the simple genetic bless-
ings of symmetry and full lips and a delicately shaped nose at
the center. The imperfections—a blemish on her chin, a small
mole by her right eye, an overlapping tooth—only added to
the perfection. Maryanne made herself up with eyeliner and
pale pink lipstick and whatever else women use, the specifics
of which remained a mystery to Jeremy.

He would have gone right on staring, right on smelling
her perfume too, a heady mix of musk layered over the faintest trace of sweat brought on by so much mannequin lugging,
but Maryanne broke the spell by throwing her head back and
laughing. "I'm just teasing you again. That stupid gym stuff
belongs to Dan." She let out a series of exaggerated, animal-
istic grunts, pushing her arms up and down in unison. "He
pumps iron in here when I'm not around."

"Oh," Jeremy said. "I see."

Maryanne went to the tub, full now, and turned off the
water. "So what do you say? You want to help a girl wash some
mannequins tonight?"

Dan did not return that evening, and so the two stayed
at the warehouse far later than usual. As they ran washcloths
and soap over so many limbs and blank faces, they fell into
easy conversation about each other's lives. Jeremy gave Maryanne the basics about his father's work as a physics profes-
sor, and the places they'd lived, from Seattle to Orlando to
Wichita and so many others. He made the briefest of mention
of his time spent auditioning, at his mother's insistence, for
child roles in musicals like *The Music Man, Oliver!,* and *The
Sound of Music* at community theaters along the way. Since
he'd been one hell of a cute kid, a skilled actor, and a decent
singer to boot, Jeremy always landed a part. There was much

he left unsaid, however, including all the doctors he'd seen along the way, and the fact that his acting career had been cut short when adolescence struck. It seemed those features that had once made him such an adorable kid—what doleful eyes! what pinchable cheeks! what floppy ears!—did not work their equivalent magic on a more mature face. Not to mention the tsunami of acne that swept in like a FEMA-level disaster, sealing the fate of Jeremy's acting career.

Instead Jeremy told Maryanne that his family arrived in Providence during his final year of high school. Since his classmates were firmly entrenched in their social circles, he didn't bother to make friends. And when he stayed on in the city to study literature at Brown, he lived in his parents' home on Arnold Street instead of a dorm, and lost out on the college friendships struck up over Pong and puking up last night's beer. And then, as graduation approached, his father landed a teaching position in Paris.

Jeremy did not think he had ever seen his mother so ecstatic, or more aptly, so *en extase.* She had been born in the City of Lights and lived there until the age of eleven, when her parents brought her and her sisters to America for good. Quite stubbornly, the woman managed to hold on to her accent even as her siblings lost theirs. She also clung to other French-isms—air-kissing, walking whenever possible (which led to some very unpleasant moments and even near-death experiences on major roads the year they'd lived in Orlando), scoffing at anyone she deemed undignified. And just because Jeremy was her son did not mean he was immune. When she happened upon him pigging out on frozen food and watching, for example, a DVD of *Caddyshack* in their living room, she shouted: "When I was a girl growing up in France, my parents took us to the Camargue, where I saw all sorts of beautiful animals. Flamingos! Wild stallions! Rhinos! But there was one creature I found grotesque. The armadillo. And why? Because it did nothing but sit on its ass all day. Is that what you are, Jeremy? A Do-Nothing, Ass-Sitting Armadillo? Because that is what you make me think of, sitting here and watching this idiotic film! *Tu es un armadillo!*"

If his mother was *en extase* about the news of the transfer abroad, Jeremy was *misérable.* He was tired of relocating, never mind to a whole new country. And so, after much discussion, it was agreed that his parents would allow him to remain in the house another few years. He was supposed to use the time to do the opposite of a do-nothing, ass-sitting armadillo—look for a real job or apply to grad school—but instead, he ended up working at the warehouse.

As for Maryanne, she was an only child, adopted by perfectly pleasant parents who had lived all their lives in Lincoln, Rhode Island. Without their knowledge, she was trying to get her birth records unsealed by the courts—not out of any dramatic need, but simply to satisfy her curiosity about the circumstances from which she came. "And to find out if my biological parents are as boring as the ones who raised me," she said, laughing. In the meantime, Maryanne had found an apartment in Federal Hill and worked at the warehouse for quick cash, which Dan paid her under the table.

Once they'd both unloaded their stories, Maryanne walked to the shelf full of torsos, where she fished out a bottle of Johnnie Walker Red. "For emergencies," she told Jeremy.

"But there's no emergency."

"Maybe not for us." She unscrewed the cap and gestured at the spray of body parts all around. "But for certain others, it's fucking triage around here."

There was only a single glass, so they took turns sipping. The more they sipped, the more absurd the prospect of the job they were doing became. Soon, they began making up names to match the mannequins: Miss One-Eye and Mrs. Four-Fingers. Mr. Dented-Crotch, who was a long-lost relative of the We-Have-No-Genitalia family. As the names grew more outrageous, and as more scotch was consumed, Maryanne and Jeremy began posing the dummies in sexual positions. Doggy-style. Missionary. Sixty-nine. A discombobulated heap of bodies meant to be a circle-jerk but ended up just a plain old homosexual orgy. Their antics produced such uproarious fits of laughter that it bounced off the high ceilings of the warehouse and echoed all around. The sound grew so loud that a person eavesdropping might have thought the mannequins had come to life and were laughing along with Jeremy and Maryanne at the ludicrous things people do with their bodies for pleasure.

Maryanne brought the fun to a halt when she said, "You know, Jer, I'm not going to be Little Miss Magic-Mannequin-Fixer forever. I've got other plans."

"Me too," Jeremy blurted, thinking suddenly and quite soberly of that pad on his desk.

"Oh. What are yours?"

"I'm going to write a novel." This was a piece of personal information that he felt shy revealing, since he did not often admit it to people. The way Jeremy saw it, writing was a method of channeling his performance skills onto the page, using words instead of his physical form, which had so utterly betrayed him. That all sounded good, at least in his head, but when he told his studious, midwestern father (who was, by the way, an odd choice in a mate for his mother) about his hope of becoming a novelist, the most his dad had to say was, "Don't be ridiculous, son. You need a viable career." And when he told his mother, the most she had to say was, "*C'est une mauvaise idée.* While you exhibit the complete instability, utter irrationality, and pure *frappadingue* of a writer, in my opinion, you are simply not bright enough." In his early days on the job, before he understood the severe intellectual and social limitations of his boss, Jeremy had told Dan Nicastro that he dreamed of one day writing a book, only to hear the man say, "Really, buddy? I think I read one once."

"Wow," Maryanne said, that flirty little voice of hers full of wonder. "I bet you're going to write the best story ever. I can just feel it. Sometimes, I'm a little bit psychic."

"What about you?" he asked. "What are your plans?"

"Well, they're not going to make me as rich and famous as yours. But I'm going to become a hairdresser. Actually, I've already signed up for classes at Empire Beauty School right here in Providence. I start next week."

Jeremy felt a lump in his throat. "Does that mean you're quitting? Because you're the best thing about—" About working here—he was going to say, but she interrupted.

"Don't be silly. I need this job. How else am I going to pay for my tortellini habit?"

"Tortellini habit?"

"Sounds funny, huh? Well, one night next week, if you're free after work, I'll show you. Would you like that, Jeremy?"

"I'd like that a lot," he told her, that lump still lodged in his throat as he found himself looking around at the mannequins frozen in any number of lewd positions.

"Okay then. But for now, let's call it a night. Don't know about you, but I'm beat. Let's leave these dummies to their gang bang and get out of here. Can I give you a ride?"

The new four-door Lincoln Town Car that Jeremy had talked his parents out of selling before they left was parked in the alley behind the warehouse. But he liked the idea of getting a ride from Maryanne, to extend their time together, and because he hoped to work up the courage to kiss her goodnight.

And so, he soon found himself settling into her gold Plymouth Turismo, a car she referred to as "the Tiramisu" because "it's one damn sweet ride." Before starting the Tiramisu, Maryanne lit up a Benson & Hedges mentholated cigarette and offered him one. Jeremy had vowed never to smoke, because a dermatologist his mother once dragged him to, among the more troublesome head doctors, had told him it risked further irritating his skin. But vows were broken every day.

Once they'd both had a few puffs, Maryanne turned the key and the car roared to life with the thump of bass. As they drove through the dark streets of Providence, windows cracked to let in the warm spring air that mingled with the smoke inside the car, the Gap Band sang, "You dropped a bomb on me, baby . . . You dropped a bomb on me . . ." Now and then, the Tiramisu swerved to the wrong side of the yellow line, and though it might seem Jeremy would feel alarmed, in fact, he felt quite safe and happy. However, he soon began to hear a knocking sound from somewhere in the back.

"I think maybe we've got a flat," he told Maryanne.

"Huh?" Maryanne said over the loud music. One of her hands steered, one of her hands drummed the wheel, and the lit cigarette dangled dangerously from her lips.

Jeremy decided that he must have imagined the sound. But a moment later, there it was again: the knocking, the banging about. He repeated himself, louder this time.

"Ohhhh." Maryanne pulled the cigarette from her mouth, aiming for the ashtray but missing the first few times and singeing the dashboard. Judging from the multitude of burn marks on the vinyl, this happened frequently. "That's just Olivia in the trunk."

"Olivia?"

"Yeah, when I signed up for beauty school, they gave me a fake head to practice perming and coloring and cutting. All the other girls were so excited, but me, well, I've seen my fair share of fake heads. Anyway, the instructor told us we should name ours. So I did. She's Olivia, and she rolls around the trunk whenever I take a turn."

As if to prove it, when Jeremy pointed to his street up ahead, Maryanne took the turn extra hard. Sure enough, the knocking sounded and Jeremy pictured a head tumbling around the trunk.

When the Tiramisu came to a standstill, Olivia bumped to a standstill too. That's when Maryanne leaned toward Jeremy. He breathed in her musky perfume mixed with the scent of soap. For a moment, he thought she was going to initiate a kiss goodnight, but then he realized she was simply trying to get a look at his family's old house looming over the sleepy street. All the windows were dark; since his parents had recently announced that he was responsible for paying the electric bill, he left the lights off when he wasn't home and sometimes when he was to save money. The most anyone could make out in the moonlight was the slant of the roofline, the boxy windows on all three floors, and the faint glimpse of a tin rooster over the mailbox by the front door. "Doesn't it get lonely in that big place without your folks around?" she asked.

Jeremy thought briefly of the days when he used to return home from a stretch of classes at Brown to find his father at the dining room table hunched over a stack of student papers while his mother banged around the kitchen, making so much noise for what always resulted in so little a dinner. "Not so much," he answered. "But when it does get lonely, I nuke something good in the microwave and pop a movie into the DVD player to keep me company."

The Gap Band tape had come to an end. He watched Maryanne's hands with their long painted nails fuss with the stereo buttons, eventually pressing Rewind. Except for the faint electric whir of the stereo, the only sound in the car was the two of them breathing. If this were a scene in an eighties film, it would undoubtedly be the moment when the male character leaned over and kissed the female character. *Do it*, Jeremy commanded himself. But his heart beat hard in his chest and some unnameable force kept him motionless in his seat.

Then Maryanne reached over and put her hand on his forearm. He could hardly stand to feel so aroused in the seconds before she asked: "What do you think of Dan?"

"Dan? You mean, Nicastro? Our boss?"

"You know another Dan?"

"Well, actually I do. A guy I went to Brown with who lived in the dorms and once took a dare to eat a vomit omelet the morning after a kegger and—"

"Well, I don't know your Dan. So of course I mean our Dan."

"What about him?"

"I don't know. He's kind of sexy, don't you think?"

All that scotch and cigarette smoke, which had filled Jeremy with such warmth, turned into something sludgy and unpleasant. He felt as though he had just eaten a vomit omelet. Maryanne must have sensed the change, because she pulled her hand away. "Well, I don't look at guys that way," he told her, before adding, "But I'm sure Dan's wife finds him attractive."

"Oh, yeah: her. I've never seen his old ball and chain before. Have you?"

"One time when she came by the warehouse to get money from him."

"And what'd she look like? A total dog?"

"Actually, she's very pretty." In reality, the woman had been average, skinny in the most unappealing of ways: Olive Oyl to Dan's Brutus. But Jeremy wanted to move Maryanne away from thinking about Dan's sex appeal. That's why he tossed out this tidbit too: "She brought their kid in a stroller. God, that kid was cute. It's obvious the three of them are a happy family. It's nice to see people so completely and totally in love."

Maryanne let out a sigh. "Yeah, well, I still think there's something, I don't know, animal about the man. Not sure what it is. But he's beautiful to look at in his own way."

Jeremy reached for the door handle and stepped out into the warm spring air. This was back in the days when he did not blurt the first thing that came to mind, so he said only, "Goodnight, Maryanne. And thanks for the ride."

"It was fun. And don't forget, I'm going to show you my tortellini habit next week."

"I won't," he said, and then turned and walked up the stone steps to his parents' dark and vacant house. After opening the front door, he flicked the outside light on and off, letting her know it was okay to leave. Maryanne waved and Jeremy paused just inside the house, listening to the toot of her horn and the thump of bass start up again as the Tiramisu rolled away down the street. All the while the words he wanted to say burned inside him, though his mouth seemed incapable of getting them out, just as those mannequins back at the warehouse would have been incapable of articulating whatever it was they might want to know. In Jeremy's case, it was the answer to a question he longed for, and the question was this: "What about me, Maryanne? Don't you think I'm beautiful too?"

EIGHT

"That's two priests driving a Ferrari. When's the last time
you saw two priests drive a Ferrari?"

—From *The Cannonball Run*, shown at the Schodack Big-Star Drive-in,
May 1982

THERE'S A PRIEST CONVENTION AT the Omni Hotel in Providence, which would have intrigued Jeremy plenty if not for a far more pressing development discovered upon his arrival. No sooner does he walk through the lobby—Pretty prancing at the end of her retractable leash while a gaggle of men in white collars *oooh* and *ahhh* over her as though she's a beatific sighting—than the plain-faced girl behind the counter says, "Sir, we don't allow dogs."

"Really?" Jeremy's first instinct tells him he might reverse the situation with an attempt at humor and charm. "What about all those creatures over there wearing collars?"

"Those creatures are priests," she tells him in a voice as plain as the rest of her, "and they're wearing clerical collars, not dog collars."

"Right. Okay. What if I told you she's one of those ubiquitous therapy animals?"

"I'd say show me her ubiquitous therapy animal paper-work."

At last, when Jeremy shifts tactics and mentions the travel website and the story he's writing, a manager appears to offer this solution: "We've got a first-floor room in need of professional cleaning, since a guest was smoking inside when he shouldn't have. We can tidy it up, and you and your dog can stay there, if you don't mind a little stale air."

As it turns out, the "little stale air" rivals that of a cigar bar in Havana, but Jeremy and Pretty settle in anyway. While the dog sniffs around, Jeremy examines himself in the bathroom mirror. His skin still tingles, though, to his surprise, barely looks red at all. Even better, the swelling has a way of filling in the depressed areas, giving him a hopeful glimpse of things to come. The acne began plaguing him when he was thirteen and living in Orlando with his parents. At the first sighting of pimples, his mother dragged him to a dermatologist, who prescribed Accutane. But after Jeremy read the list of possible side effects—joint pain! seizures! dark urine! clay-colored stools!—he flushed those pills, pretending he was taking the poison as directed. Considering how many years he's spent living with the aftermath, it's no surprise he developed a compulsive habit of checking his face in every reflective surface to gauge how noticeable the scars are at any given moment.

She can really see them now, he used to think when sitting across from so many dates in so many restaurants and catching sight of his pocked face in a silver tray or a wineglass or, worst of all, a mirrored wall. *She can really see them and she thinks they make me look ugly because, well, they do . . .*

And so, there in the privacy of his bathroom, Jeremy slides the dimmer switch slowly up and down, pausing along the way to determine exactly how the varying levels of light play on the planes of his changing face.

All that keeps him busy until he hears a strange sound coming from the other room. Jeremy leaves the mirror to find Pretty walking in circles the way she does whenever she feels agitated. The dog keeps releasing a wheezy exhale and stopping to sneeze. The stifling air is undoubtedly wreaking havoc on her respiratory system, and Jeremy regrets agreeing to the trip, never mind his idiotic decision to bring her along. He worries for the dog, but also worries for himself, because if Pretty becomes sick and unable to compete, Tiffany will never speak to him again. And though their brief relationship—which began unremarkably on OkCupid and led to a half dozen dates over a couple of months—had hardly been the stuff of romance novels, she'd been the first woman in years to overlook his shortcomings and give him a chance.

Thankfully, Jeremy does not need to take that line of thought any further because he notices drab paisley drapes on the far side of the room. He walks over and tugs them back to reveal a sliding door that leads onto a small, walled-in patio. With great relief, he pulls open the door, then thrusts out his hand in a ta-da! motion, presenting Pretty with his grand discovery.

The dog makes a beeline for the fresh air. While she trots around the patio, sniffing and peeing and pooping, Jeremy sets out to improve the conditions in the room for both their sakes—cranking the ceiling fan and riffling through Pretty's bag for the anti-anxiety candle. Soon, the air is at least partially masked by what's described on the label as "the scent of a freshly mowed lawn at an elegant Hamptons estate when the sun is shining and the ocean breezes are blowing and the hydrangeas are in bloom." Or, Jeremy thinks, gunk scraped off the blades of a lawnmower. Either way, he decides things are improved enough that he can call the dog in and tackle the more absurd duties involved in her care.

First up: he places the "Stand for show!" blocks on the carpet, measuring the distance between each the way he's seen Tiff do. There's a block for each paw and, when he gives the command, Pretty is supposed to stand on them, thereby training her to maintain a "stacking pose"—hind legs further back than natural, her chest puffed out and head lifted.

"Okay, Pretty," Jeremy announces, clapping his hands. "Stand for show!"

The dog looks at him with an expression that communicates the unmistakable message: *You've got to be fucking kidding me.*

"Stand for show!" he says, louder, clapping again. Then again, "Stand for show!" And again and again: "Stand for show! Stand for show!"

At least a dozen more times, Jeremy keeps at it, even kneeling and arranging his hands and feet on the blocks to demonstrate what Pretty is meant to do. When that fails to inspire her, he gently tugs her paws toward the blocks, an effort met with a growl so fierce it seems to come from a wildebeest rather than a domesticated show poodle. After that, Jeremy gives up on the blocks and digs out Pretty's array of combs and brushes, numbered by Tiffany and varying in size and style. Brush #3 has a cluster of pinprick wire bristles so minuscule they look positively dangerous. Still, he's determined to keep his end of the bargain, so he lines them up on the dresser. When he turns around, however, the dog is gone.

Jeremy searches the patio and the bathroom, but it isn't

until he gets down on the floor and lifts the bed skirt that he sees her shiny black eyes staring back.

"First, no blocks," he says, because he has reached the point people do when reasoning with an animal seems the best hope. "And now, no brushes. We're batting a thousand tonight, aren't we, girl?"

As Jeremy keeps trying to coax Pretty out, he thinks of the one thing that never fails to make her obey: the sight of her slip leash. Not the everyday retractable leash Jeremy has used so far, but rather, a leather cord with what can only be described as a noose at the end. "Slip leashes," Tiff once explained to him, "are what professional trainers use to make sure their dogs obey at shows."

To which Jeremy replied, "Sort of like the leash a dominatrix uses to make sure her slave behaves. Except, in this case, the dog lacks the benefit of a safety word."

Tiffany was not amused.

Even though Jeremy knows damn well Tiffany would've produced the slip leash then and there, and even though he knows the dog would obey at the sight of it, he does not do it. He hates the thought of that thing around her neck so much that he left it in the trunk of the Lincoln with those piles of used books and tangled jumper cables that knocked about the way Olivia used to in the Tiramisu.

"Tell you what," he says in a softer voice, "I'll put the TV on some animal show. You come out when you want, Pretty."

And that's how Jeremy finds himself lying alone on the king-size mattress, picking at the remains of the overpriced junk food raided from the minibar and drinking his third puny but potent bottle of scotch raided right along with it. At some point, while watching whales crest and dive and slap their enormous tails against the surface of the ocean, he reaches for his cell and begins poking around online, doing what thousands of others do in down moments like this: checking out the social media posts of his exes. While it's true that he does not have his own account, Jeremy long since created one on Facebook under the name "Courtney Goodale" to keep tabs on various women who broke his heart. And though the pain has long subsided, he checks in occasionally, not unlike the way a person tunes into a once beloved soap opera to see if the characters are up to anything new.

As it turns out, none of their recent posts are remotely interesting, so Jeremy taps over to Tiffany's profile. There, he sees a new post featuring a picture of a sweet-faced bald man. Tiff has engaged in that headscratcher of a habit, treating social media like it's a portal to the afterlife, and has addressed her uncle directly in the caption: "I'm going to miss your weekly calls and funny cards and the snow globes you brought me from every trip you've taken since I was a girl."

That's the thing about Tiffany, Jeremy thinks: despite her harsh exterior, she sometimes reveals a sentimental side. That softer version had been on full display the evening she invited him to her apartment in Long Island City. Before they sat at the table, before she served the now infamous salad, before he ruined things with his blurted opinions, which led to a screaming match, which led to him slamming his fist on the table, which led to still more regrettable things, before any of that, Tiffany had shown him a bookshelf in her living room full of those snow globes. As they took turns shaking them and showing each other the cherry blossoms at the foot of Mount Fuji or the flurries over the Acropolis, Tiff spoke about her love for her uncle and her love for Pretty and her love for the little pleasures in life, such as sitting at the counter at Ben's Best on Queens Boulevard and ordering a Reuben after she got off work from Bubbles & Biscuits where she'd been a dog groomer for years. Or, another small pleasure: the scrapbook on her coffee table, which she showed him when they were done making it snow around the world. Inside, Tiffany had written quotes that made her think, like this one Jeremy remembers:

> *I learned there are troubles of more than one kind. Some come from ahead, some come from behind. But I've bought a big bat. I'm all ready, you see. Now my troubles are going to have troubles with me!*
>
> —Dr. Seuss

When Jeremy is done thinking about that quote and done thinking about the softer side of Tiffany, the side he likes best but no longer gets to see, he finds himself staring at the tiny Facebook search bar on his screen. A blank bit of cyberspace that brings temptation for so many when it comes to investigating some part of the past better off forgotten. And as the whales cry out onscreen in their strange sonar mating language, Jeremy wrestles with an urge brought on by the fact that he's back in Providence and by those memories he allowed himself to revisit of those days and nights at the warehouse on Rucks Street. He fights it, putting down his cell. But soon he picks it up again. He stares at that search bar. He stares at the whales. And this is the way of it for some time: search bar . . . whales . . . search bar . . . whales . . . search bar . . .

Fuck it, he finally tells himself as his thumb begins moving against the screen, typing the name: "Maryanne Popadowski."

What comes next: a surprisingly long list of Maryanne Popadowskis all over the country. Jeremy scrolls until he sees his Maryanne, still living right there in Providence. The manner in which she looks directly out from his cell, and directly out from the distant past they briefly shared, causes his heart to bump in his chest. He feels the same mix of emotions stir inside him as the first night he sat so close to her in the Tiramisu. Should he take those conflicting feelings as a sign and put away his phone for the night? Probably. Instead, his thumb presses the screen, conjuring more of her.

While he waits for Maryanne's full profile to emerge, Jeremy remembers his first visit to her apartment in Federal Hill, not long after the night they bathed the mannequins. He remembers her boiling fresh, beef-filled tortellini from the nearby Italian market and shaking a blizzard of Parmesan over the top before they took their seats on a blanket she laid out, picnic-style, on her living room floor. He recalls Olivia too, that practice head of Maryanne's, situated on the blanket like a centerpiece, because Maryanne wanted to marvel at the perm and color she had tried on her that afternoon. And then, as the tiny pinwheel keeps spinning on his cell, Jeremy's mind lurches from that memory to the last time he saw Maryanne. Even after so long, it all comes back: his standing in those buggy, moonlit woods behind that elementary school, her stumbling up a ladder, sliding down a slide, swinging on the swings. Her shouting in slurred words, "Jeremy Lichanel! Jeremy Fucking Lichanel! Think about it: if you say it the way it's spelled it sounds like Lick Anal!" Jeremy winces, not so much at that moment, but because of the one that came next, which sent him running from the woods, running from Providence soon after, never to return, that is, until now.

Before he can relive any more of that night, the pinwheel quits pinwheeling and there she is: nearly twenty years later, Maryanne Popadowski is brought back to life in the form of a Facebook profile. Jeremy studies the photo closely, noting how time has chipped away at the pleasant roundness of her face, sharpening the angles of her cheekbones and chin. She still looks pretty—no doubt about that—though in a mature, less accessible way. For some time, he continues navigating around her page, stopping on one particular photo of her in a low-cut cocktail dress. He makes another discovery as well: Maryanne has two sons. Tall and beefy and dark-haired, those boys look nearly the same age Jeremy and Maryanne had been while working at DCRR. And even more curious: those boys look like Jeremy and Maryanne's old boss. The resemblance leads Jeremy to tap over to her marital status, where he prepares himself to see the words: "Married to Dan Nicastro." Instead, he sees only: "Divorced."

"Can you imagine?" she calls out from those swings, howling in his memory. "Can you fucking imagine?"

The memory, the profile—every last bit of it—is enough to make him shove his phone beneath a pillow. On TV, the whales have been replaced by giraffes. Jeremy watches them chomp the leaves of a tall tree. Since the animal channel has done nothing to lure out Pretty, he turns it off. Down the hall, he hears the gaggle of priests carrying on a rowdy conversation in the bar just off the lobby. Earlier, when Jeremy saw so many of them with cocktails in hand, he had not been able to keep himself from inquiring about their excessive drinking.

"People don't call us whiskeypalians for nothing," a few answered in unison, laughing and raising their glasses.

Good for them, Jeremy thinks, considering crashing their shindig as a distraction from those glimpses of Maryanne lurking in his mind. Before he can decide, though, his phone buzzes. He slides a hand beneath the pillow and pulls it out to see a text:

> **Tiff:** arrived in buffalo:-(. if u hate mesclin sald u shud try my cuzin's ambrosia sald. how can something w/ marshmallows even be called a sald? so ttly nasty:-/ anyways how is pretty? she better not be eating pepp pzza, jer or i will kick ur ass when i get home >:-O!!!

Jeremy has never been much for texting, and whenever he receives a text from Tiffany, he can't help but feel like he's communicating with an adolescent girl. Something about all those abbreviated words and exclamation points, never mind when she gets on a roll with those old-school emoticons she favors over actual emojis. The tone at the end of that particular text would normally irk him, but the booze and memories of them shaking snow globes and flipping through her book of quotes have him feeling sweet toward her, which leads Jeremy to type a sweet reply, which leads to this exchange:

> **Jer:** Pretty is fine. No need to worry. Also, I want to tell you that I'm sorry about what I said about the dinner you made me. And I'm sorry for what happened after. It was wrong of me.

> **Tiff:** np. u said srry alredy. just let it go. good abt pretty. thx.

> **Jer:** what is np?

Tiff: no problem. i swear u need a textionary. and don't ask 'what's a textionary?'

Jer: i won't. well, i know this may seem out of the blue, tiff, but i was hoping maybe we could try again.

The moment Jeremy hits Send, he wonders if that was a mistake. Probably smarter to play it cool, to take care of Pretty and get her back safely, then ask if he can treat Tiff to a Reuben at Ben's Best to show he's making an effort to be more thoughtful. Too late. He watches anxiously as dots fill the bubble at the bottom of his screen until his cell buzzes with this reply:

Tiff: u always blame the sald comment. but it wasn't just that. it was so many things. we are 2 different pple, jer. those dumb arguments always happened and i got tired of it. Not to mention your temper.

Jer: but can't we try?

Tiff: i'm sorry. but i am done trying. i appreciate u watching pretty. but i just can't with u anymore. not in that way. besides, i'm at a funeral this weekend so have enuf on my mind. don't do this to me. c u sunday.

Plenty of replies race around Jeremy's mind, but he refrains from sending any, knowing they will come off as either pleading or pissed. Instead, he lies there, phone in hand, doing nothing, until at long last his thumb, seemingly on its own, presses 4–1–1. Moments later, he's scratching down a number on an Omni Hotel pad. He just wants to hear her voice saying hello—that is his only plan, if she even answers. He'll listen to that lone word before hanging up and shoving the past back into the dark corner of his mind where it's been festering for years.

One ring. Two rings. Three rings. Four . . .

Jeremy is about to give up when he hears, "Hello."

Tired—impossibly so—that's how Maryanne's voice sounds. And even though she spoke only two syllables, Jeremy can hear in them that the mush-mouthed quality he once found so alluring is gone from her. The woman is worn out, beaten down by a lifetime of disappointments. Jeremy is supposed to hang up—that was the plan—but instead he finds himself saying, "Hello, Maryanne."

"Who is this?"

"I bet you can't guess."

"I bet I can. Give me a hint." A dog barks. Not Pretty, still on hiatus beneath the bed. The sound comes from Maryanne's end of the call. "Hold on," she tells him. "Would you shut it already, Bingo? Okay, I'm back. Sorry, the pup hates the ringing of the phone. And no one ever calls this landline except for telemarketers and crap. I thought you were going to be the Policemen's Union asking for money again. Anyway, where were we? Oh, yeah, you were going to give me a hint."

Jeremy speaks just three words: "Mr. Dented-Crotch."

"Pardon me?"

"I said, 'Mr. Dented-Crotch.' Or how about the 'We-Have-No-Genitalia family'?"

"Listen, I don't know what kind of sick perv you are but—" She stops suddenly. The line falls silent. And then, "Oh my God. Jeremy?"

"It's me."

"I can't believe—" Again, she stops. "I mean . . . I . . . I tried to contact you over the years, but you never . . . you never—" Her voice sputters as she struggles to find the right words to connect the now to the way back then. He could still hang up, Jeremy tells himself, because surely any moment now he will feel the acute agony of that memory: Maryanne, swinging on the swings, heels kicked off, bare feet thrust out, toes pointing upward toward the moon as she swings up, pointing downward toward the earth as she swings down. *The moon, the earth, the moon, the earth, up and down, up and down, on it went until—*

"I heard you moved away," she says, finding her words at last. "But you never, well, you never said goodbye, Jer."

"Yeah, well. It was a long time ago. I had my reasons."

"I see. Tell me, did you end up writing that Great American Novel of yours?"

Jeremy does not recall ever describing the book he wanted to write quite that way. In fact, he hates when people use that idiotic phrase. His mother would have been quite proud of this opinion, but he finds it annoyingly American for a country to obsess over its own great novel. Does anyone ever talk about the Great Belgian Novel? Or how about the Great Albanian Novel? No, as far as he's aware. And why? Because those countries aren't so utterly fixated on their own greatness. But he doesn't bother telling any of that to Maryanne. Instead, he says only, "I wrote a novel."

"But I looked in Books on the Square. On Amazon too. I didn't see it."

Jeremy thinks of the rejection letters he received when he finished all 972 pages about a young man whose parents die in a wreck on an autoroute between Paris and Provence. He thinks of the truths slipped in between the polite language from all those literary agents: "Your prose does not take enough risks . . ." "Your plot did not grab me . . ." "Your writing is not sensitive enough . . ." All of it added up to the same message his mother and father had intimated: "You, Jeremy Lichanel, are simply not good enough." Never mind that other, more hurtful prognosis his mother summed up with that out-of-fashion French word she liked to hurl at him: *frappadingue*.

More to the point, though, after all that rejection, Jeremy let go of his literary aspirations and found a job writing restaurant reviews for a neighborhood paper in Queens. From there, he began pitching stories to a women's magazine; not the mainstream glossies, this was a cheap imitator that supposedly had millions of readers, though he never actually saw anyone reading it. The editor there found Jeremy's writing lacking in sensitivity too, but it just so happened that was exactly what she was looking for.

"The saying is not 'the pretty truth,' the saying is 'the ugly truth,'" she told him during their first meeting at her crummy office, tarted up with a purple sofa and zebra print pillows. "And that's what our readers need to hear from a man, whether they like it or not."

The Ugly Truth turned out to be the name she gave his column. And The Ugly Truth, as she encouraged Jeremy to tell it, was that no matter how much chardonnay women made men drink, they would never be like them. The Ugly Truth was that most men think about sex—dirty, filthy sex—so often it would alarm most women. The Ugly Truth was that sometimes men did not want to talk or cuddle or be romantic; they simply wanted to fuck, and not the same woman either, but lots of different women. There was no end to the horrors Jeremy could serve up, and soon The Ugly Truth rippled out to the more emotionally raw truths, like: sometimes you could love a man, you could give him the very best of yourself, you could listen to his problems day in and day out, you could boost his confidence and help him make a better life for himself and yet, despite all that goodness you gave, this man simply could not love you back—or at least "not in that way." Or: that same man could string you along, taking all the goodness you offered, until he had what he needed, before moving on to someone else, leaving you adrift on a raft of heartbreak and sorrow. The more ugly the truth, the more angry the letters, the more giddy it made Jeremy's editor, who, it seems worth mentioning, was bitterly divorced, not once, but twice. "It's a beautiful thing, because it means people are talking!" she'd tell him excitedly over the phone. But then she was fired and so was he.

After The Ugly Truth, Jeremy decided to reshape himself as a travel writer, beginning with this trip to Providence, but longing for a trip to Provence for more personal reasons. Instead of explaining all of this to Maryanne, though, he keeps it simple, telling her only, "Just because you write a book doesn't mean someone will publish it."

"Oh," is all she says in reply.

Pretty comes crawling out from under the bed then, so unexpectedly it startles Jeremy. Her flattened hair is dotted with so many dust bunnies it looks as though she's been swept up in a cyclone and dropped back down to earth. He'd set out her collapsible bowl of kibble earlier and she goes to it, sniffing but not eating. "Hold on," he says, then tells Pretty, "I suggest you have at it, girl, since I'm not giving you pizza again if that's what you're hoping for. Last time, you had indigestion for days . . ."

"Are you talking to your wife?" Maryanne says when he comes back on the line.

"My wife?" He wonders what sort of spouse Maryanne envisions for him given the things he's been saying. "No. That's my dog. Well, not my dog. I'm just taking care of her. It's a long story. Anyway, I'm not married."

"Me neither. At least not anymore. Thank God. So can I ask, where are you?"

"Providence."

"You moved back?" The lift in her voice is unmistakable.

"Sorry to disappoint, but I'm just here for a travel story I'm writing."

"A travel story? In Providence?"

"Normally I only cover major international destinations. I've got an assignment coming up in Provence, for example, but this was last-minute." He hadn't planned to lie, but the words had come so easily it gave Jeremy a thrill. "My editor is paying me a bundle because he likes my narrative style. I'm here to cover the opening of a restaurant on Chalkstone."

"You mean that new place, Voilà?"

"Yes, actually. That's the name of it."

"I live over by there now. No more Federal Hill for this girl. Anyway, I hear it's supposed to be amazing. I'm dying to try it."

"You should come," Jeremy blurts.

"Really?" Maryanne says. "Wow. This is a total mind bender. But okay. When?"

Ever so briefly, the thought of the laser treatment that morning flutters through Jeremy's mind. But last he looked, his face was not nearly as red as the doctor had warned. At most, things have ended up a little swollen, making his scars less apparent, creating the illusion of smoother skin already. "Tomorrow night," he tells her.

"Okay, then," she says without so much as a pause to consider what a reunion might mean for them. And then she adds in that old *Working Girl* voice of hers, "It's a date, Jer."

The moon, the earth, the moon, the earth, up and down, on it went until—

Jeremy closes his eyes, telling himself to stop thinking of that evening. Instead, he summons the happier moments they once shared, like the dozens of nights when he and Maryanne got off work and cruised around Providence in the Tiramisu, the Gap Band playing that song she loved—"You dropped a bomb on me, baby! You dropped a bomb on me!" They puffed away on cigarettes, laughing and telling each other secrets and swerving to the wrong side of the yellow line and taking turns too sharply at too high a speed, making Olivia roll around in the trunk. Jeremy thinks of the smell of Maryanne's musky perfume mixed with the mentholated cigarette smoke. He thinks of all the tortellini dinners they consumed, all the scotch they consumed as well. The two of them used to eat and drink and talk for hours until falling asleep, side by side and mid-sentence, on the blanket she always laid out on her living room floor.

With those warmer memories fresh in his mind, Jeremy blinks open his eyes to see Pretty eating her kibble at last. He feels a lump—both painful and oddly pleasant—forming in his throat when he takes a breath and says, "Okay then. I'm glad I called, Maryanne. Because after all these years apart, you and me—we've got ourselves a date."

NINE

"You go around like an open nerve saying, 'Oh, yes, I'm cheating . . . but look how guilty I feel! So, I must really be a nice guy.'"

—From *Same Time, Next Year*, shown at the Schodack Big-Star Drive-in, May 1979

I HAVE A DATE, OF SORTS. Today at noon. At the Schodack Diner on Columbia Turnpike, where I'm scheduled to meet you-know-who. As though it's a romantic date, rather than a fact-finding and quite possibly vengeful one, Teddy and I argue about what I should wear. This leads to him pulling outfits from my closet and, in the way of an overly solicitous salesman, describing the possibilities.

Him: "I'm holding up a lovely red cardigan. With Christmas days away, it's the perfect color. What do you think?"

Me: "We aren't meeting to bake cookies. So, no."

Him: "Very well. How about this woolly fisherman's sweater? Warm and comf—"

Me: "That ratty old thing? No again."

Him: (*sighing*) "Righty-ho. Ahhh . . . I've found just the

one! A rather dignified-looking blouse with delicate flowers on the—"

Me: "Puffy sleeves?"

Him: "Bit puffy, yes."

Me: "No. No. No. I told you already, this is a waste of time. You could unearth the ballgown worn by your precious Belle back in your Disney days, and I wouldn't touch the damn thing. I'm wearing my nurse's dress and that's final. My hairstyle. My necklace of keys. Those things are staying put too. So don't start on them again either."

It's not only when Teddy speaks a sad truth—like the other night when he mentioned the way certain people can make you feel exquisite and others can make you feel downright ugly—but also when he's exasperated, like now, that his voice goes flat. "Skyla, I don't know how to say this other than to just say it, but you should not be wearing that dress. Especially in public."

"And why the hell not?"

"Let's see . . . Well, do off-duty cops go around in their uniforms?"

"Some might."

"Most don't. Because it sends the wrong message."

"And what message is that?"

"That they're on duty! See what I'm getting at here?"

"Not really."

"Okay, then. More to the point, I don't think the people who wrote that letter in your pocket would want you wearing your uniform. Frankly, in the spirit of just saying things that need to be said, I bet they'd—"

Teddy stops abruptly. I reach in my pocket, careful not to touch that unsealed syringe, locked and loaded by yours truly first thing this morning. My fingers find the letter, caressing its corners and bringing all the praise to life in my mind: SUCH STELLAR SERVICE! SUCH IMPECCABLE CARE! SUCH EMPATHY AND PROFESSIONALISM!

"They'd what?" I nudge.

"Nothing. Never mind."

"Good idea," I say, before asking Siri for the time.

When she informs us that it's 11:34 A.M., Teddy surrenders on the issue of my attire. "Suit yourself, luv. Now enough folderol. Let's get a move on."

Ever since that first moment of tenderness we shared a few days before, I find myself looking for excuses to make physical contact with Teddy again. Sometimes it's just a playful swat on his shoulder. Other times, I feign anxiety about tripping so that he'll reach out to take my hand. When I think about the feel of his arms wrapping around my body, pulling me close, my heart falls into a girlish pitter-patter, though I've yet to work up the nerve to suggest another hold. As we head outside to the driveway, however, I make a show of worry that I might fall and, like that, his hand is in mine once more.

Six weeks together, and I've never ridden in Teddy's car. Not sure what I imagined, but it wasn't this. The air inside is stale. Empty bottles, or at least that's what I assume them to be, collect at my feet when I settle in. As I nudge the mess away with my nursing shoes, Teddy starts the engine. I reach in the direction of the radio, but he informs me it's broken. Rather than force Siri to DJ, I give her the address of the diner. After bumping down the long dirt drive to the main road, she instructs us to hang a right.

Snow-covered fields.

Barren, branchy woods dotted with crows.

The occasional lawn with inflatable Christmas decorations, deflated in the daytime, giving the appearance of a bizarre holiday massacre.

Out there in the blur, those are the things I imagine us passing. Normally, Teddy and I do nothing but chatter, but an unusual hush falls between us as we drive. Anyone's guess, the reasons for his silence. As for me, my nerves are to blame. The closer we get to this strange date of mine, the more I feel, deep in my bones, that it's a disaster in the making. What will I say to Maureen? How will I find the words to ask what I want to know? And what hideous truths will her answers reveal?

In my pocket, that syringe waits. Just in case.

The pills wait too. If only I could recall which was which, I might slip one between my lips for the promise of instant calm. The risk of ingesting the wrong medication worries me, though, so I strangle the temptation.

Instead, I take a stab at conversation. "My Hollis . . ."

"Yes, Skyla?" Teddy prompts after I utter those two words with no follow-through.

Unthinkable as it may seem, I've already forgotten what it was I intended to convey about the man who was my husband for just shy of half a century. Certainly not the fact that so long a marriage meant listening to your spouse tell the same stories, over and over and over, never mind sitting across the dinner table from him, night after night after night, listening to him chew while thinking I simply cannot bear the sound another moment. And certainly not the contrary fact that a marriage so long brought unexpected moments of sheer, overwhelming gratitude and love for this person who chose to share life together, day in and day out, which was not always as exciting a prospect as the words "happily ever after" promised.

"Skyla?" Teddy says.

"I'm nervous," I admit.

"Then why don't we take your mind off your jitters? How about unveiling the reason for the two matching houses? I've only been waiting on that mystery for ages."

"That's a funny story, and I'm not feeling the least bit funny at the moment."

"Understood. Well, speaking of Hollis, you never did tell me how you met."

I need to do something—anything—to beat back my anxiety, so I give the man what he wants: "Once upon a time, there was a girl with deadbeat do-nothings for parents. They lived with a bunch of people just like them in a bunch of rusted trailers and an old school bus over in the town next to Schodack. This girl did not want to end up like them, wasting her life making anti-establishment picket signs, strumming guitars, getting stoned. No offense about the stoned part. At the ripe old age of fourteen, this girl got herself a job as a paper girl. Mind you, this was back when there were only paper boys. So it made her something of a small-town Joan of Arc, though she didn't care about that. She just wanted money."

"Hold up, luv. To be clear, is this girl you?"

"Of course, it's me, dummy!" I swat Teddy's leg. Since that makes him laugh, I feel emboldened to leave my hand there, my palm and fingers atop his thigh. "On my route each afternoon, I used to pedal down the same road where I . . . or rather, we . . . you and me, I mean . . . now live. Looming out in the field was that movie screen. I'd look up at the sign by the entrance, showing the titles of the films playing: *The Killing* . . . *The Man Who Knew Too Much* . . . Back then, I liked the scary pictures. And let me tell you, it would've been a dream to roll up some Saturday night in this couch on wheels we're driving now. And I don't mean for a game of Backseat Bingo like so many horndogs who frequented the place."

"So why didn't you?"

"No driver's license, for one. Never mind a car. Plus, I was not so stupid as to blow my hard-earned cash. I was saving for nursing school, even then. My parents rarely bothered to bring me to a doctor, so when I was unwell I'd visit the school nurse. I always liked the idea of being someone like her, a person who helped others. I liked the orderliness and dignity of the occupation too. Anyway, my lack of discretionary funds didn't stop yours truly from pedaling to the edge of the field on weekends and watching the movie. Of course, I couldn't hear without the speakers paying customers hooked to their cars. But that was okay. I used to look up at the actors—falling in and out of love, telling lies, confessing truths, pointing guns, shedding tears—and in some ways, not having the sound made more of an impact. Because I had to pay careful attention to get an exact sense of what was happening in that world. When that failed, I simply imagined whatever story I wanted, which is a skill we can all use in this world, let me tell you."

Siri intrudes on our conversation then with a bunch of "turn rights" and "turn lefts" and one thousand feet this and five hundred feet that. Once she finally shuts her trap, Teddy says, "This might sound like an odd question, Skyla, but do you feel you have an exact sense of what's happening around you now?"

Something about those words causes his leg to tense beneath my touch. I tell myself it's just his foot shifting to the brake as we turn. But then his hand picks up mine, returns it to my lap. In a cool, clipped voice, I say, "If my hand bothered you that much, you could've said."

"No bother, luv. It's just, well, I'm driving is all."

I stay silent. Furious at myself as much as him.

"You know what?" Teddy picks up my hand again, places it back on his leg. "There. All better. We're getting close. So forget that question. There's still time to finish your story. You left out a crucial detail. Meeting Hollis, remember?"

Speaking more quickly now, I tell him how Hollis's parents owned the Big-Star, how one night his father caught me free-loading at the edge of the field, how scared I was he'd call the cops. "But that man was every bit as cheap and conniving as his son turned out to be. He'd been watching me for weeks. Tally-ing every film I saw. Biding his time before busting me. Then offering a deal whereby I worked off the cost of the movies, helping at the snack bar, selling tickets at the entrance. Hollis was the blue-eyed boy manning the projector."

"Ahhh . . . So it was love at first film?"

Easier, certainly, to simply agree with that assumption. Yet, I'm tempted to divulge a truth about those early days, one I've been turning over in my mind since this business of Maureen Mooreover began. I swallow the lump in my throat. "When we first met, I fell for his family as much as him . . . since mine . . . well . . . we weren't much of a fam—"

"Arriving at your destination."

For once, Little Miss Metalhead's timing is spot-on. Quickly I say, "Anyway, we all thought exactly that: love at first film. So innocent . . . so tender . . ."

While I lay on an extra-thick layer of Hallmark hogwash, not mentioning the last film to play up there, cut short in the middle and still on the projector too, Teddy turns into the lot.

Finds a spot. Cuts the engine. After carrying on about what an "absolutely brilliant beginning" Hollis and I had to our love story, that odd silence takes over again. My nervousness takes over again too. I must've eaten at the Schodack a dozen times with my nephew, John, when he comes up for a visit from the city, but now I can't bear to go inside. "What's the place look like?" I ask, stalling for time.

"Let's see . . . it looks, well, dinery. In that American way. Fake-stone facade. Stack of steps up to the glass doors. One of those maddening claw games in the vestibule with a pile of stuffed animals impossible to pluck out."

"You see Moo in any of the windows?"

"Hmmm . . . Only know the beast from Facebook photos, but looks to be mostly burly trucker types at present."

"She must've chickened out. Loser. We should go."

"Nice try, luv. We're a bit early is all. Better this way. We'll get you situated so old Moo can approach you at the throne. Kiss your ring and all that."

"Kiss my ass is more like it."

That makes us laugh. Makes my nervousness subside too. Unfortunately, the feeling is akin to a wave at high tide, washing out a moment, then crashing back with more force. My hands begin to shake. I slip them into my pockets, comforting myself with the treasures there, careful to avoid that unsealed though capped needle. When my chauffeur gets out of the car, I retrieve a pill at random. A submarine. *We all live in a yellow one,* I think, recalling that dreadful song people like my parents used to strum on guitar with such allegiance you would've thought it was the national friggin' anthem. Taking a chance, I push this non-yellow sub between my lips, swallowing it dry.

Old habits. They really do die hard, because I flip down

the visor for a glimpse of my reflection. No luck. Obviously. Blame my nerves, but I wonder if Teddy was right about my appearance. Not the dress. But my pigtails, my necklace of keys. Perhaps I should have reconsidered those things before venturing out into the world.

Teddy must sense my second-guessing. He opens the passenger door and says, "Sure you don't want to shed that chain?"

Though part of me does, I tell him, "No can do. My entire life is on this thing."

"Your call, Skyla. Now remember, all kidding aside, the point is to get your questions answered. To gather the full facts of their affair at last. To speak your truth to this woman. Take it from me, it's not worth getting caught up in anger and doing anything rash. Better to strive for acceptance and move on . . ."

This cloying pep talk fills my head as he takes my arm and escorts me across the lot, up the stairs, past the coin-sucking claw game, and into the diner. I interrupt only to insist on the most private table possible, which is how we end up in no-man's-land way in the back and, judging from the smell, not far from the restrooms. Lovely. Right away, a waitress swings by, inquiring in a surprisingly chipper voice what she can get us. After she's gone, Teddy says, "You'll be okay, won't you?"

In the grand scheme of things, probably not, I think with a sinking feeling. But for now, knowing he'll be right across the diner, I'm sure I'll survive. "Will Moo be okay? That's the question."

He laughs, but without his usual cheer. "I worry," he tells me.

"Worry? This whole thing was your idea."

"I know, I know. It's just that you and I have spent loads of time talking about our pasts. I know that mostly I've told you about Linelle. But—" He pauses for a weighted breath, and when he speaks again, his voice has that flattened effect. "I'm ashamed to admit, Skyla, that I've made some unfortunate choices in my life. I know firsthand what deep pain one human can inflict upon another. How impossible it can be to shake the sadness about the regrettable things we've done. About the regrettable things that have been done to us too. This business of your husband's affair? It keeps you from feeling true happiness. So if meeting with Moo . . . with Maureen allows you to shed even a little of the hurt in your heart, it'll be worth it."

Maybe. But I just want revenge. I consider cracking that joke, but the man sounds so plaintive, I say only, "Thanks for looking out for me."

"Of course, dear. And remember, I'll be back in exactly one hour to fetch you."

"Back in an hour?!" The words cause an unpleasant flutter in my chest. "When you first suggested this nightmare, you said you'd wait right here at the counter. Or did you forget?"

"Oh. I did say that, didn't I? Well, I just figure I can use the time to run a quick errand. Get some manuscripts I finished translating off in the post."

No big deal, I tell myself. I don't need a babysitter. And yet, it's one thing to be alone in my house, where every inch is memorized; entirely another to be by myself out in the world. So, no sooner does he say goodbye than the sound of his receding footsteps sends panic flooding through me.

"Wait!"

Does every last person in that diner stop to stare at the old nurse in the back? The one with toddlerish pigtails and a cumbersome necklace of keys? The one who is crying out and making such a scene? I imagine so.

"What is it, luv?" Teddy calls back.

Don't go. That's what I want to say, though the words won't come. But Teddy must sense my fear. He walks to the table again, leans down, and whispers in my ear, "Promise I'll be back. Don't be cross with me. You know I love you, Skyla Hull."

It hardly takes a medical professional, like yours truly, to know how unlikely it is any pill could work its magic with such expediency—never mind whatever outdated mystery medicine I plunged into my system. Which can only mean the sentiment uttered by Teddy is no delusion. I look up at that beautiful face whose features I imagine so well. The blue eyes. The square jaw. The sweeping head of blond hair. "I love you too, Teddy Cornwell. I really do."

I reach up. Tug free the brightly bobbled elastics holding my pigtails. Hand those elastics over to him. When I set about finger-combing my hair, he says, "Bit last-minute for a make-over, luv. Don't you think?"

"You know what they say: never too late to make a change."

He laughs. "What about the necklace? Why not give it to me for safekeeping? Hope you don't mind my saying, but it looks like something a custodian might wear."

Is it that logic which convinces me? Is that pill finally work-ing its magic? Is it everything to do with his proclamation of love? Whatever the precise alchemy of motivations, I grip that key-filled chain, thinking for a moment of all the locks it opens: the deadbolts on both cellars . . . the toolshed and bedroom safe . . . the strongbox in my closet with a museum of meds curated from the hospital . . . Hollis's pickup and my hatchback . . . the gun cabinet and bullet box inside . . . plus, the buildings that once housed the projection equip-ment and popcorn machine at the drive-in . . . I lift it over my head, fingers brushing clumped duct tape and Band-Aids and twisted rubber bands, and I place the necklace in Teddy's hands. "Remember what I said about my entire life being on this thing? I wasn't kidding."

"You have my word, darling: I'll guard your life with my life. Don't you feel happier without that hundred-pound albatross hanging from your neck?"

"You're exaggerating. It can't be more than fifty. Though, yes. I feel happier. Not so much because of the necklace coming off, but because of your loving me."

Teddy laughs. "I do love you, Miss Skyla. You're a dear friend. More than a friend, in fact, you are like the mum I never had . . ."

My mind goes so muzzy with disappointment that I find it difficult to focus on what he's saying.

". . . My mum, she was distant and downright cruel. You, on the other hand, are an angel who's been incredibly caring and loving to me when others haven't . . ."

The keys jingle in his hands. Tis the season, as they say, so shouldn't the sound make me think of Christmas, of "ho ho ho" and all that? But no. I think of so many collars with so many tiny bells, bought for so many strays over the years who wandered out of the woods behind the matching houses. My Hollis always warned me to avoid getting attached, though I never listened . . .

". . . Actually, it was Jeremy's mum who was truly unkind. Mine passed from cancer when I was young. Too many Mayfair cigarettes. But there's a certain cruelty, too, in not caring for yourself when you've got a child who depends on you. Know what I mean?"

Tins of tuna. Bowls of water. Claw trees on the back

deck. Always, I got myself in deep. So whenever those scraggly, mood-disordered felines quit coming around, or worse, scratched or bit me the moment I attempted to pet them, how utterly betrayed I felt. That's the way I feel now too. I reach in my pocket for another pill. A teardrop this time. How appropriate . . .

"Know what I mean?" he says again.

I swallow the teardrop. Do my best to force my mind into the moment. "I've got my own losses to sort out, Teddy. So I don't want to hear about your dead mother just now. Go on. Get out of here already."

It's every bit my intention that those words sting. Judging from the punctured quality of his voice as he fumbles a goodbye, mission accomplished. As he turns to leave, I have the last-second thought to snatch back my keys, but it's too late, his footsteps are already receding on his way out of the diner.

Once he's gone, I crave a time-out to calm my mind. Unfortunately, things have more of a revolving-door effect. "Skyla?"

I look up into yet another face I cannot see, though presumably one I've glimpsed before, at the ER after Hollis's first accident. "That you, Moo?"

"Moo?"

"Oopsy. Inside joke. I mean, Maureen?"

"It's me. Sorry I'm late. Guess that's the first of many apologies I owe you."

"You're right about that."

"Mind if I sit?"

"Free country. Do what you damn well please. Apparently, you always do."

I hear the scrape of a chair. Hear her place something heavy on the table. Her purse, I'm guessing, which is a habit

I've never cared for. Tables are for eating, not for parking your filthy pocketbook.

"I wasn't really late," she says after a moment. "I sat out in the lot for a long time. I even watched from my car as you walked in with that guy. But I was afraid to face you after all this time. Plus, my sitter didn't show. Janine is almost eleven now, but I still don't trust her at home alone. So when the sitter canceled, I felt relieved to have a reason to cancel on you too, but your friend didn't leave his number."

I don't reply right away, so busy am I trying to picture the details of this woman before me: the straight part of her dark hair, perhaps, revealing the pale moon of her scalp, or maybe small gold hoops dangling from her fleshy lobes. But my lazy mind conjures only the image of her that day I glimpsed her in the ER, a look of guilt on her face.

Then a different waitress rolls up to the table. This one, far less chipper, gets down to business ASAP, asking Moo what she wants. Seeing as it might be her last meal, I can't help but chime in, "Get whatever you want, Maureen. I insist. It's on me."

"Gosh. Wow. That's nice of you, Skyla. I mean, considering the circumstances. Hollis always did say you were a kind woman."

I just smile. Feel around my pockets. Touch that letter. Touch the wedding bands. Touch the matchbook too. I find that monkey-faced finger puppet. Slip my thumb inside the worn fabric, wiggling it for comfort. Question: If someone offered to treat you to anything on a menu, wouldn't you order more than a measly cup of tea? That's all this loser wants. Or so it seems until the waitress is about to beat it and Maureen stops her, saying, "If you don't mind, could you break this five into quarters and bring them to my daughter? She's in the front vestibule. Playing the Crazy Claw."

"Your daughter is here?" I say once the waitress is gone.

"That's apology number two, of the hundreds I owe you. What choice did I have without a sitter? Awkward, I know. But don't worry. Obviously, I didn't tell Janine who you are. And you certainly don't have to meet her."

My thumb wiggles inside that monkey as I think back to Hollis giving it to me. In fact, he hadn't—given it—until after I found that goofy-looking thing in a pocket of his denim jacket one afternoon while hanging it in the closet. A finger puppet is not the equivalent of lipstick on a collar, yet odd nonetheless. When I questioned him, Hollis spit out some story about stopping at a gas station where there'd been a box of them by the register. Ponies. Puppy dogs. Bears. To hear him tell it, the selection was worthy of Noah's ark. And to use his words as he slipped it on his finger and wagged it in my face, he'd plucked out that particular puppet because: "You're my sweet little monkey, Skyla."

In this great big world, I'm sure plenty of people get called that cutesy nickname. However, though my husband often told me I was beautiful, though he kissed me each morning at the kitchen table when I came in from my night shift, though he pulled me into bed to make love once a month—right on schedule, like paying the electric bill or some other every-thirty-days obligation—he did not call me by that name. Also, as we've established, the man did not like to part with a buck. So that story of his? A bunch of monkey shit. And I believed it for ten years, for the simple reason that I just plain wanted to. Not only that, but I began carrying the puppet in my pocket, the first of such items, for the comfort it gave.

Now, seated across from Maureen Mooreover on this un-likely date of ours, I open my mouth to ask the myriad ques-tions I came to get answered: Where did Maureen and Hollis meet? When did they meet? How often did they see each other? Did he tell her he loved her? Did he tell her he loved me? Did they call each other sappy nicknames? Did they have sex in all sorts of random places—countertops and rest stops and on the floor in front of a roaring fire—driven by passion, rather than obligation? Instead, what I ask is this: "Who am I?"

"I'm sorry, Skyla," she says, a bewildered but also circum-spect tone in her voice now. "I don't understand."

"A moment ago, you said you didn't tell Janine who I am. So . . . who am I?"

"You're Hollis's wife. His widow."

"Okay then. Who is Janine?"

"I told you. She's my daughter."

"Now tell me: Who's her father?"

Maureen is quiet, not answering.

"Well?" I say. "Well?"

For what feels like forever, I wait. Long enough that the waitress brings Maureen her measly cup of tea, saucer clank-ing on the table between us. Long enough that Maureen be-gins to cry, making all sorts of soft sniffling sounds, tugging tissues from what must surely be her purse parked on the table. Finally, through those tears, she tells me how terribly sorry she is. How she thought I was aware of the situation. That's the word she uses: *situation.* And speaking of what is and isn't said, only later do I realize she never actually comes out and utters my Hollis's name.

What does it matter?

The moment I asked that question, I already knew.

TEN

"Fasten your seatbelts, it's going to be a bumpy night."

—From *All About Eve*, shown at the Schodack Big-Star Drive-in,
July 1950

HE ARRIVES AT HER HOUSE on Angell Street, carrying a bou-
quet of pink tulips and wearing a turtleneck and brand-new
navy-blue blazer purchased that afternoon at the Warwick
Mall. Thanks to a display of sample lotions at L'Occitane, he
smells of lemon and lavender and all things Provence. Those
scents are meant to calm his anxiety, or at least that's what
the labels promise, though in reality, they only serve to make
Jeremy more nervous.

At the start of this momentous evening, there is something more to report: Pretty has come along on her retractable leash. That had not been the plan, but Maryanne left a
voicemail on the hotel phone earlier telling him she realized
their date—yes, she used that word again—meant he might
have to leave the dog alone. Since that didn't sound like much
fun for the pooch, she offered up a Plan B, whereby they leave
Pretty and Bingo to play together at her place while the two of
them go to dinner at Voilà.

In truth, Jeremy has difficulty imagining Pretty doing something as undignified as playing, never mind with a mutt named Bingo. Yet, given the day he and Pretty have had, which included his waking to find his face so incredibly red and swollen (beyond even the worst warning that doctor gave him), then the battery in the old Lincoln flatlining (beyond anything the jumper cables could resuscitate), followed by a rather distressing tow truck ride (speaking of things undignified) and an eternal wait for a new battery and alternator at Providence Auto Repairs (where a massive text war with Tiff ensued), he could not help but bring the dog. And so, there they stand in the November moonlight, gazing up at the surprisingly large, historic home where Maryanne now lives.

Her instructions were simple: walk through the gate at the side of the garage and follow the flagstone path to a set of stairs that lead to her kitchen door. Jeremy and Pretty do just that, but when they reach the stairs, the dog pulls back hard on her leash, planting her paws in the grass and refusing to go even an inch farther. What has her so suddenly spooked? There is the wind through the bare tree branches. There is the echo of voices from some nearby street. Other than that, Jeremy has no clue. He clicks his teeth against the side of his mouth, giving the giddyup signal Tiff so often uses. When Pretty still doesn't budge, the two engage in a brief tug-of-war, while he explains to her in a gentle voice how fun the night ahead will be, seeing as she'll have a playmate for a change, a puppy no less. Finally, for whatever reason, Pretty acquiesces and moves cautiously up the stairs beside him.

At the top, Jeremy stops to catch his breath. All day long, as the ticking clock brought closer the hour of this unexpected reunion, he found himself feeling oddly winded—hell, at times he felt practically asthmatic. Now he breathes deeply into his chest and blows the air slowly back out, glancing at his reflection in the glass of the kitchen door. He thinks again of his doctor and her many warnings about the time bomb she'd made of his face. How had he been so foolish to believe he'd somehow magically circumvented the redness and swelling and peeling she'd described in such detail? When he first woke and saw the ghastly way his face had transformed overnight, Jeremy had every intention of canceling on Maryanne. But then, on his walk to the hotel's complimentary breakfast buffet, he passed those priests crowded in the hall, on their way to a whale-watching expedition. At that very moment he found his excuse for Maryanne: I spent the day on a whale-watching expedition as part of the story I'm writing. Forgot my damned sunscreen and look how horribly burned I ended up. . . .

And so, since this unexpected date of theirs has a "now or never" feel to it, he did not cancel after all.

Still, much of the morning and afternoon had been occupied by staring at his face in the many reflective surfaces at the mall and in the windows of the Lincoln and the side-view mirror of that damn tow truck as the driver chewed tobacco and rambled on about the "shit-suckiness" of "Kraut-cars" and "Jap-mobiles." In fact, Jeremy has stared at his face so much today that he can no longer distinguish between the actual unpleasantness of his appearance and whatever horrid distortions might be at work in his mind. The most he knows is that there are moments, like in the dressing room at JCPenney, when he was trying on the blue blazer, when the image staring back at him looks nothing short of monstrous. Those lasers, it seems to him, drilled down into his scars and split them wide open, allowing the disappointment and anguish and sorrow Jeremy feels about his life to come seeping out, manifesting themselves right there on his face.

And yet—there is also the occasional shocking moment of optimism. At that very instant on Maryanne's back stairs, for example, Jeremy looks upon his image in the moonlit glass of her door and manages to see the promise of what those treatments might bring. If only for a few fleeting seconds, he imagines that wretched and unlovable face of his transformed into a new and improved version—a little bit closer to handsome even, dare he use that word.

But whatever the truth of his present and future situation, it is too late to turn away from this night. And so, Jeremy knocks.

From inside, there comes an explosion of barking, followed by Maryanne's girlish but tired voice yelling, "Hush up, Bingo! Hush up already! I said, hush the fuck up!"

A few moments later, the door opens and there she stands, dressed not in leggings and a long pastel sweater, but a black cocktail dress accented with sparkles. It looks to Jeremy like the sort of glitzy, two-steps-away-from-tacky outfit a magician's assistant might wear while being sawed in half. He notices two thin gold necklaces, one with a cross, the other with an Italian horn, dangling from her neck.

For a moment, neither says a word. The silence casts a spell all its own, allowing time to slow down, allowing each to think their separate thoughts about the sight of the other. Perhaps most important to Jeremy: the lights are dim enough on the stairs that he hopes for the best in terms of what Maryanne sees. He had intended to blurt that bogus explanation about the whale-watching trip right away, but somehow the moment doesn't seem to call for it, or at least not yet. Besides, as far as he's concerned, the woman in that dress is hardly the same woman he once knew. She looks too mature, too knowing, too . . . something. It occurs to him then that the pictures she posted on Facebook have been carefully curated and filtered to make her look better than she actually does, and he cannot help but compare them to the uncurated, the unfiltered, the real-life version of Maryanne Popadowski.

Among the most obvious of differences is her body, which has gone from curvy to curvier. One might even come right out and use the word *plump*. And there is the matter of her hair, colored brown and pinned up in that naughty librarian style he so readily recalls, but thinner and limper with age, not to mention so many years of overprocessing. The skin around Maryanne's eyes reveals the beginnings of slivery wrinkles and small pouches. Then there are the eyes themselves: Back when they'd known each other, those eyes had radiated a happy-go-lucky sense of adventure. Though Maryanne's eyes look happy still, they also look a lot less lucky, considering their world-weary and guarded quality.

All that and yet, to Jeremy, she is still every bit as beautiful. Just looking at her brings on the weightless flutter in his chest he used to feel in her presence. He finds himself blinking once, then twice, in the way people do when trying to fuse the past with the present. And in yet another kind of magic trick, it actually works. All at once, the Maryanne of his past melds with the Maryanne of his present. Suddenly, they are one and the same. That's when a conversation begins between them at last, exactly as it began so many years ago.

"Hello, Maryanne."

"Hello, Jeremy."

The moon, the earth, the moon, the earth, up and down, up and down— "Feels weird, huh?" Jeremy says, cutting short the memory of the way things ended last time.

"Sure does."

More silence, during which his cell vibrates in the pocket of his blazer and Pretty pulls on her leash. Ever since the explosion of barking, the dog has been attempting to move in those anxious circles of hers, but Jeremy keeps a tight grip. He makes a mental note to power down his phone the first chance he gets, since it could only be Tiff tossing yet another text grenade at him, and he knows damn well there's no way to diffuse her fury after what happened between them today.

"You know what?" Maryanne says, breaking the silence. "Let's not let it be weird. Let's just be together. How does that sound?"

More than the scent of lavender and lemons, her words blanket him with a sense of calm. "Sounds good to me. Oh, and here. I brought you these."

Maryanne takes the flowers and buries that delicate nose of hers in the petals. Jeremy watches, wondering if tulips have much of a fragrance. He doesn't think so but it's nice to see anyway. "So sweet of you, Jer," she says, without looking up from the flowers. "You were always so thoughtful, you know that? I was just too young and dumb to appreciate a guy like you back then. I learned that the hard way. Believe me. Anyway, why don't you come in while I find a vase? Oh, and this must be Pretty."

Maryanne leans down and pats the freshly fluffed Q-tip puff atop the dog's head. Pretty barely registers the greeting. Normally, Jeremy interprets her ambivalence as yet another indication of the dog's purebred snobbery, but he senses some-

thing else at work now. Pretty stares right past Maryanne into
the dimly lit kitchen, then sniffs the air, squints her eyes, perks
her ears, and stiffens her tail. All signs she's on high alert for a
glimpse of the dog she heard barking moments before.

When they step inside the small kitchen, with its white-
painted cabinets, oak floorboards, wooden beams, and clutter of cookbooks and pots dangling over the butcher-block
island, there is no sign of Bingo. Maryanne begins hunting beneath the sink and Jeremy lets Pretty off her leash so she can
roam the room, sniffing to her heart's content. After pulling
out a vase and grabbing a knife from a magnetic strip behind
the stove, Maryanne chops the stem bottoms before arranging the flowers. It seems obvious that she's made up her mind
to override any further awkwardness by talking right over it.
She asks about his parents. She asks about his life in New
York. She asks about the article he's writing. To all of those
questions, Jeremy gives the vaguest of answers before telling
her, "That's a longer story . . . one I should save for over dinner." And when he inquires about her life, she tells him more
or less the same thing.

So, with an evening of "longer stories" ahead, for the time
being, they wind up simply talking about Providence and how
much it's changed during Jeremy's years away. Most notably,
Maryanne informs him that the old warehouse on Rucks
Street has been transformed into condos. "Believe it or not,
they sell for a serious chunk of change."

The mention of the warehouse leads Jeremy dangerously
close to bringing up Dan Nicastro. He wants to know if the
guy left his wife and married Maryanne. But Jeremy holds
back, since he knows it will kill the mood. He feels proud of
himself for actually refraining.

"Anyway," Maryanne is saying. "Look at you. Mister Big-Time Writer back in town to cover a fancy new restaurant. You've done well for yourself, Jer."

Jeremy blushes, though given that Rudolph-red face of his, who could tell? Again, he thinks to mention the whale-watching trip, the lack of sunscreen, the strong winds, and all the rest. A couple of times throughout the day, he even tested that line of bull: at the mall, when he felt a salesgirl's gaze lingering too long, and in the tow truck, when that rambling, xenophobic driver made a crack about Jeremy getting a late start on Halloween. Both times, his explanation had been accepted with a bit of sympathy and no further inquiries. But Maryanne still does not seem to notice, since she keeps fussing with the flowers, testing out various locations around the kitchen to put them on display. "I was about to tell you the same thing," Jeremy says. "I mean, look at you in this big house."

"Thanks," she says, moving the vase from a window to the butcher-block island and leaving it there at last. "This is just the apartment in the back. I own the whole place, but now that I'm divorced and my boys have left home, I don't need so much space. I flip-flopped the situation and rent the main house to a family. They're away on vacation at Disney this week."

"Disney," Jeremy says and groans. "Just the mention gives me PTSD."

"That's right. I forgot you used to live near there."

"I do my best to forget it too."

"Yeah, well, I wish you could meet my renters. He's a schoolteacher, and she's a cop, of all things. Anyway, I live here, where my nanny used to live. Guess you could say it's a step up from my days in that crummy rattrap in Federal Hill."

The mention of her old apartment brings back a memory of the place where they once spent so much time. Jeremy can still see that kitchen with its beat-up cabinets, speckled Formica counters, and sticky linoleum in a dizzying geometric pattern. "Remember the silverware drawer?" he says. "The way it used to go off the track and crash to the floor whenever we reached for a fork or spoon?"

At last, Maryanne looks directly into his eyes, though without giving the least indication that she notices anything odd about his appearance. Quite the contrary, actually; she laughs and says, "Oh my god, yes! What a royal pain in the ass! Remember how eventually we just left all the cutlery piled in a shoebox on the counter because we were so damn sick of having to pick it up?"

Jeremy laughs too. And that's when a game of "Do you remember?" begins, as they bat memories back and forth in a high-speed volley:

Him: "Remember that crazy geometric pattern on the floor?"

Her: "Remember how it gave us migraines just to look at it?"

Him: "Remember the shower was in the kitchen instead of the bathroom?"

Her: "Remember how it was the size of a phone booth?"

Him: "Remember how you had to step up into it, like boarding some old train?"

Her: "Remember how we used to call my landlord Junkyard Joe, because he sifted through the trash and kept whatever weird stuff he wanted?"

Him: "Remember how whenever you'd complain to him about the lack of hot water he'd say in broken English—"

Him and Her: "You want hot water? I raise rent!"

Him: "Remember how you used to play that Gap Band tape all the time?"

Her: "Remember how I used to experiment on your hair?"

Him: "Remember that time you dyed it red by mistake?"

Her: "Remember how I tried to fix it but dyed it a weird swampy green instead?"

Him: "Remember how I finally just shaved it off?"

Her: "Remember those tortellini dinners? How I always laid out the blanket in the living room? And how we'd drink Johnnie Walker and cheap red wine and eat and talk and talk and talk until passing out mid-sentence?"

Him: "Remember—"

Jeremy stops. His mind clouds with the memory of them falling asleep, side by side, of all those times they woke in a confused and groggy embrace during the night. Her head on his chest. His hand on her stomach. Their faces so often inches apart, close enough that he could feel the warmth of her breath and smell the alcohol on her. One time, he opened his eyes to find her mouth impossibly near his, and even though her eyes were shut, he felt certain that over the course of so many nights like that, they had formed an unspoken agreement about the physical and emotional closeness they shared. He believed that closeness was a kind of secret between them, one that filled both their needs. And so, there in the dark, on that blanket in her living room, Jeremy did what felt most natural. He kissed her. But then her eyes opened, and he saw in them a look of surprise. Maryanne asked, "Jer, what are you doing?"

"Remember what?" Maryanne says now.

"Remember all the fun we had back then?" is the best Jeremy can manage.

"I do, Jer. Actually, I think about it all the time. It wasn't so long, really, that we were in each other's lives. But you and me, we had something special. Something I've never had since. I hope you don't mind me saying that."

Maryanne is smiling as she says those words, yet there is something unmistakably sad in her voice. He watches as she turns and goes to a cabinet and pulls down a bottle of Johnnie Walker, the same way she used to pull it from that shelf full of body parts at the warehouse. "What do you say? A shot for old times' sake?"

"Sounds good to me," he tells her, and as she pours, his mind returns to that long-ago night when he kissed her. He can still hear her girlish voice saying, "We shouldn't be doing this, Jer. I mean, I've got a date with someone else tomorrow."

"A date? With who?"

"I don't want to tell you, because I know you'll judge me. But I'm sure you can figure it out."

By then, it had been months since that evening in the Tiramisu when she first mentioned Dan, and not a single time since had she brought him up, other than to complain about how late he was when it came to forking over their pay. "First of all, Maryanne, Dan's married. I'm not," he told her. "Second of all, look at us: always together, having the most awesome times, being so close, falling asleep with each other, waking up with each other too. Doesn't that tell you something?"

"It does, Jer. And I know it feels good between us. But I just—"

"You just what?"

"I told you already that first night. So don't act like I didn't. I really like him. That's all. I can't help it. Believe me, it's stupid for me to even call it a date. We're meeting at some playground, where Dan says it's quiet and no one will see us. I told him to come here, but he's worried about Junkyard Joe seeing."

For a long while after that, they lay on the blanket, their bodies still touching. Outside the window, the night sky was slowly turning from black to blue. At last, Maryanne spoke up, asking, "You okay, Jer?"

"Yeah," he said, though he wasn't okay, not really. To cover up his feelings, in a perfect imitation of Junkyard Joe's broken English, he added, "You want me keep secret? I raise rent."

"To old times," Maryanne says now, handing Jeremy a shot glass. "To new times too."

After they clink and toss back their scotch, Jeremy looks down at Pretty, who is staring up at him like she wants a shot as well. Jeremy pets the tall puff on her head and asks Maryanne, "So where's this Bingo I've been hearing about?"

"Oh. I put him in the bedroom so Pretty could get used to the space before having to get acquainted with him. I read somewhere it's good to do that sort of thing when one dog is entering another's home turf. But she looks settled now so let me get Bingo and these two can make nice before we head to dinner."

She slips through a swinging door in the back of the kitchen. Jeremy listens to her heels click down a hall. A moment later, he hears her talking to the dog the way he did to Pretty. She tells him to be polite, then goes on about something else Jeremy cannot quite make out. He might have tried harder to listen, but his cell buzzes again. Rather than read the text, Jeremy pulls the phone from his pocket and powers it down. Doing so only makes him think of the disastrous way things unraveled with Tiffany earlier that day. After the tow truck hauled Pretty and Jeremy to a garage in some godfor-saken rundown neighborhood, there'd been an eternal wait for the new battery and alternator to be installed in the Lincoln, plus the mechanic offered to fix the window that refused to roll up while he was at it. To kill time, Jeremy decided to practice Pretty's "Stand for show!" command. Since her blocks were back at the hotel, he made do by piling old books from the trunk into four stacks, estimating the proper amount of space between each. The dog must have been as bored as he was, because she actually went along with the idea.

There in the dirt lot, surrounded by tow trucks and stripped cars, Jeremy clapped his hands and gave the command. Pretty put a tentative paw on a copy of *Dangerous Liaisons* by Pierre Choderlos de Laclos and another tentative paw on a copy of *Justine* by Marquis de Sade. (The books in the trunk were mostly leftovers from a short-lived phase in which Jeremy tried to understand his mother through the literature she read. Like all attempts to understand his mother, this failed, and Jeremy stashed the books in his trunk with the intention of donating or dumping them.) Once Pretty's front paws were planted squarely on those novels, her back paws moved to the two books Tiff had given Jeremy after their breakup: *Anger Management for Dummies* and *The Angry Brain: 10 Steps to Taming Your Temper.*

At last, just like that, the dog was exactly where she was supposed to be.

Despite all the bickering Jeremy and Tiff did about whether it was right to put an animal through such paces in order for her looks to be judged, he could not deny that there was something striking about seeing Pretty in such a proud and regal stance. As the sunlight glinted against her coifed fur, Pretty raised her head high and puffed out her chest. When she stepped off the books, Jeremy knelt to pet her. That's when his cell buzzed for the first time that day:

> **Tiff:** Sorry I was gruff last night. U know that's how I get when I'm stressed. The fam situation here has been trying:(makes me miss my uncle even more. My heart is broken. And speaking of hearts all of this has been making me think abt life & us & what happened & what u said . . . Anyways if u still want to, maybe we can try when i get back & see how things go. But let's take it slow. Sound ok Jeremy?

Once, twice, a third time—Jeremy read and reread the text. Despite his date with Maryanne, he could not help but feel a kind of lightness in his chest. Hope—that's what it was—an emotion that had not visited him in some time. He thought it best to speak Tiff's language for a change, and so sent back one of those smiley face emoticons she loved so much.

Tiff responded instantly:

> Thought that text might make you happy:-) Anyways how is Pretty?

Jeremy ignored the "*anyways*" (he'd told Tiff numerous times that it wasn't a word but she only seemed to say it more). Instead, he clapped his hands and gave Pretty her "Stand for show!" command. When the dog once again stepped up onto the piles of books in perfect formation, he snapped a picture with his phone and hit Send. A moment later, his cell buzzed:

> **Tiff:** WHERE R U?

By then, Jeremy was feeling so good about things he typed a chatty reply:

> **Jer:** Getting a new battery for the Lincoln since it finally died. Mechanic making other repairs too so taking a while. He says I can trade the old battery at some environmental agency for $20 so I strapped the thing in the trunk with the slip leash since he warned me not to let it tip over . . . The acid could easily spill out and apparently it's really harmful stuff in there. Anyway that's when I got the idea to use those books in the trunk to practice with Pretty

> **Tiff:** AND U R DOING THIS IN PROVIDENCE RHODE ISLAND?!?!

When those words appeared in the text bubble, Jeremy gasped and put a hand to his chest. How the hell had Tiff figured that out? Quickly, he began texting a reply claiming to be at a repair shop in Queens. Before he could finish, however, his cell rang. Back when they first broke up, Jeremy had been so desperate for Tiff to call that he set her ringtone to one resembling an alarm in a nuclear power plant, so that he would not miss it if she contacted him. Now, the phone erupted in his hand with the sound of an impending Fukushima-style disaster. Jeremy knew better than to answer it. Instead, he distracted himself by relocating himself and Pretty to a shadier spot in the lot, since it was best to get out of the sun, given the condition of his face.

That's when he heard another phone—this one releasing an old-fashioned jingle from somewhere nearby. It was coming from inside the garage, he realized. A moment later, the mechanic, who had tied back his scraggly hair with a bandana, stuck his head outside and spit a wad of tobacco, before shouting, "Yo, dude. Did you say your name is Jeffrey Lick Anal?"

"It's Jeremy. And it's pronounced Litch-In-Al. But yeah, that's me."

"Oh. Well, there's some chick on the phone for you and she doesn't sound happy. Says her name is Tiffany."

How had she figured things out? Jeremy wondered again, never mind tracking him down in a matter of seconds. He looked around at the rows of stripped cars in the lot, then over at a couple of bright red tow trucks that had surely been in the background of the picture he sent. And there was his answer: on the trucks' doors, bold black letters screamed a number with a 401 area code along with: PROVIDENCE AUTO BODY REPAIR. YOU WRECK IT, WE RESURRECT IT.

When Jeremy read those words, he had just one thought: *Ooohhhhhhh fuuuuuuuuuuuuuccccccckkkk.*

"Here comes Bingo!" Maryanne calls from down the hall over the sound of scampering paws on the wooden floor.

A moment later, the mutt bursts through the swinging door. The picture Jeremy had drawn in his mind of Maryanne's dog was of a midsize Lab mix, the sort with a slobbering tongue and a sweet but dopey disposition. How wrong he'd been. If Maryanne's sons resembled Dan Nicastro, then her dog might very well be the man in animal form. Bingo has a large muscley body, dark fur, and downright wrathful eyes. The beast gallops right past Jeremy and makes a beeline for Pretty, who freezes in her tracks a split second, startled, before turning and scampering away. Bingo begins barking, not the basic warning noises Jeremy heard earlier at the door, but ferocious howls, like those of some sort of uncaged wolverine.

"Give them a minute to get used to each other!" Maryanne

shrieks over the commotion. Then to the dogs: "Sniff it out, you two! Sniff it out! Sniff it out!"

But neither is doing much sniffing. Pretty keeps whirring round and round at such a fast speed it's like watching a greyhound at the track. Bingo remains, quite literally, hot on her tail. At last, Jeremy shouts to Maryanne, "I thought you said your dog was a puppy?!"

"He's only twelve months old!"

"And what kind is he?"

"Don't know exactly! They weren't sure at the shelter! Part Rottweiler, part Doberman, they think!"

Part Satan! Jeremy keeps from saying.

"But that's just a guess!" Maryanne goes on. "He's got some behavioral issues, but I've been working with him! I thought a little playdate would be good for him!"

"Apparently not, Maryanne! I don't think any of this was such a good idea!"

The moment those words are out, Jeremy looks to see a crumpled expression on her face. He does his best to soften things, over the barking and the cacophony of the dogs' paws and nails sliding across the oak floor: "I don't mean any of this was a bad idea! I just mean the dogs! You and me seeing each other again, well that was a great idea! Let's just leave Bingo in your room and Pretty in the kitchen. I don't want anything to happen to her."

Maryanne's face shifts to an expression of milder disappointment as she tries to grab Bingo. "Okay, Jer! Too bad they can't play nice!"

It's not they who are the problem, Jeremy thinks, *it's your demon dog.* But he refrains from saying as much, proud of himself for once again thinking through the ramifications before speaking. This time, when the beast whips by her, Maryanne manages to grab his collar. Against his will, she drags him back through the swinging door and down the hall, asking all the while why he couldn't just behave like a normal dog. Bingo's only answer is to keep barking.

Jeremy carries on a conversation of his own with Pretty, who is still making circles around the island. Seeing her so anxious makes him feel bad about bringing her in the first place, bad about letting Tiff down too. All he wants to do is get through this night with Maryanne and see where it leads, then deliver the dog safely home. After what happened today, he knows there will be no more trying between him and Tiff, but it is the least he can do. And so, as Pretty stares at him with increasingly expressive eyes, Jeremy says to her quietly, "I promise you, from here on out you have a mellow evening ahead." He reaches into the pockets of his blazer and retrieves two of the collapsible bowls he found among the things Tiff packed. He pops them open, fills one with kibble from a Ziploc bag, the other with water from the tap. Soon, Pretty calms down and begins drinking and eating, which leaves him feeling relieved.

"Guess my taste in dogs is as bad as my taste in men all these years," Maryanne says, when she finally returns. "Hope Pretty is okay."

Jeremy looks up and smiles. "She's fine. Not to worry."

After that, they both share a small laugh at the absurdity of the moment they'd just been through, each of them making some version of the same remark, that at least things are never dull when they're together. And then, at long last, they leave the dogs behind and walk down the back stairs and through the gate to the street. Along the way, they find themselves returning to that memory game. This time, however, they go about it more slowly, savoring many more little memories along the way.

"Remember how we used to watch cartoons on Saturday mornings?" Maryanne asks, which was a detail of their time together Jeremy had forgotten until then.

"I do. And they were good cartoons too. Bugs Bunny. Road Runner. Not the crap they churn out now. Remember how we'd finally get our asses up and drive over to Olga's Cup & Saucer for egg sandwiches?"

"I do," she tells him. "God, Jer, we used to laugh so much. I miss those times."

"Me too."

As they cross the street, Maryanne reaches for Jeremy's hand. She takes it in hers.

She does not let go.

ELEVEN

"It's no use going back to yesterday, because I was a
different person then."

—From *Alice in Wonderland*, shown at the Schodack Big-Star Drive-in,
May 1951

THE WINE FLOWS AND SO does the conversation at the candlelit table they share in a corner of that cozy Providence restaurant. It would be easy to assume they are a couple deeply in
love. When the two are not caught up in hushed and intimate
conversation, they are throwing their heads back and howling
with laughter, slapping the table and wiping tears from their
eyes, because whatever private joke they share is that funny.
And when, in a more serious and tender moment, Maryanne
tells Jeremy about finally tracking down her birth parents, who
turned out to be as boring as her adoptive ones, only clingy
to the point where she had to ask them to stop contacting her,
Jeremy watches as so many emotions flicker over her face.

"It was like they wanted to start over and try to be a family,"
she explains with a dimness in her voice. "Sorry, but it was a
little too late if you know what I mean. What about your parents, Jer? Did they come back to Providence?"

With a similar dimness in his voice, Jeremy tells her about that trip his mother and father took to Provence and how he regrets refusing to join them before moving on to a description of the novel he'd written, skipping over certain uglier truths about his mother and father that he cannot bring himself to articulate.

After all that is laid out between them, they each have the sense to move on to lighter topics, at least for a little while. Lighter topics are something of a strong suit for Maryanne: she launches into an animated story that begins simply enough with the ripped window screens in her old apartment. Before she can get to the punch line, however, one of the gentlemen waiters in crisp white shirts appears at the table with their salad course. The waiters have all fussed over Maryanne in such a way that confirms once more for Jeremy that she is still quite alluring, and this particular waiter has a difficult time taking his eyes off her breasts. Once their salads are on the table, he produces a rather large peppermill and goes so far as to joke with Maryanne, telling her, "Don't be alarmed by its size, because I know how to use it."

Maryanne laughs. "Well, you better get cracking, because I like lots of pepper!"

Jeremy pastes on a smile, waiting the whole thing out. After the waiter is gone, he finds himself looking down at the mountain of greens on his plate.

"Something wrong, Jer?" Maryanne asks.

"Oh, no. It's just the salad made me think of someone. Or something. Or, well, never mind."

"Not never mind," she says with a playful determination. "Tell me."

"No, no. We were talking about something important. I forget what it was, but I want to go back to that."

"I was telling you about the Mohawk and purple dye job I gave Olivia before I finally tossed her in the trash. And how months later I stopped at Junkyard Joe's apartment to complain about my ripped window screens, which were letting a million mosquitos into my place. I was standing there, bitching him out and showing him the dozens of bug bites on my arms and legs, when I looked over his shoulder and spotted Olivia on top of his TV."

"Did you ask her what she was doing there?" Jeremy says, grinning.

Maryanne lets out a cackle and swats him on the shoulder. "No!"

"Well, did you at least ask her how long she'd been screwing your landlord?"

She swats him again, laughing harder still. "No, Jer!"

"You should have. I'd be curious to know how that tramp Olivia had sex without a body. Then again, ol' JJ was missing a brain, so it probably equaled out."

Maryanne reaches over and slides his salad plate away. "Okay, buster. You can try to change the subject all you want, but my point is, what we were talking about wasn't important. Now tell me what you were thinking when you went into that little trance a minute ago. You're not getting this heap of greens back until you do."

Jeremy puts down his fork and releases a sigh. Luckily, there are no mirrored walls in the restaurant, and thus far he has staved off the compulsion to check his reflection in the silverware or wineglasses. Even though his bladder has been signaling the need for a trip to the men's room, Jeremy holds off for fear of facing the mirror inside. It occurs to him then that this might be as good a moment as any to unload the whale-watching story in order to explain the condition of his face, but things are going so well and Maryanne has still not given a single hint of noticing. And so, Jeremy sticks to the truth instead: "My last girlfriend broke up with me over an argument about a salad. She made one. I was quite vocal about not liking it. All hell broke loose."

"She broke up with you because of a salad?"

"Yes. Well, not just that. I mean there were other reasons, like she says I have a temper."

"You? You're a puppy dog, Jer!"

"Yeah, well. We started yelling, and I pounded my fist on the table. She told me to leave. The entire incident became a straw-that-broke-the-camel's-back situation. Anyway, Pretty belongs to her. I agreed to watch the dog because I thought it would be a way to get Tiff back. But then I was staring at this salad and thinking how it always felt wrong with her. You know, mesclun when what I wanted was arugula." Jeremy pauses and considers adding, "And you are my arugula, Maryanne." He aborts the comment at the last possible moment, because he is not certain Maryanne will find it flattering to be compared to a cruciferous vegetable, even an upscale one.

When he's done talking, she falls silent, playing with her thin gold necklaces—that small cross, that Italian horn.

This time, it's Jeremy who says, "Something wrong?"

"Nothing."

He reaches over and slides her salad away. "Same rules. Now tell me what you're thinking."

Maryanne lets out a sigh too. "Okay. Well, I guess I'll just come out and admit it. I have no right to feel this way, but I'm a tiny bit jealous thinking of you with some other woman."

Flattered as Jeremy feels, he cannot stifle the abrupt burst of laughter that escapes him. "After all these years you feel jealous?"

"I didn't say it made sense." She begins eating his salad, so he begins eating hers. "I just said it's how I feel. And feelings aren't always logical, Jer."

For a while after that, they eat each other's salads in silence. Jeremy tries to take advantage of the lull in conversation by making mental notes about the flavors of Parmesan and olive oil in order to reference them later in his review. He glances around the restaurant, taking a mental picture of the space, the rough brick walls and industrial-style windows. In truth, though, he is too distracted to focus on any of that. He grows even more distracted when Maryanne speaks up to say, "Do you mind if I ask about your ex?"

Sensing that the topic might pave the way for him to inquire about Dan Nicastro, he tells her he doesn't mind. "So long as you let me ask about yours."

"Okay then. Me first. I know it's shallow, but I can't help wanting to know: She's got this dog named Pretty, but is she pretty, Jer?"

Tiffany's picture from OkCupid rises up in Jeremy's mind. The first time he'd seen it had been late one night last summer. While suffering from a bout of loneliness, he'd begun trolling the site, looking at the photos but not bothering to read the profiles, as is custom among most people hunting for love online. Tiffany's photo wasn't so much a showstopper as it was a show-pauser. Frizzy black hair. Round Italian face. Sharp nose. Rather than smile, Tiffany smirked at the camera, giving the men on that site an "I dare you" sort of expression—a dare Jeremy accepted when he sent her a message with the romantic opening line, "Hey." To which she replied with the equally romantic, "Hey to you too." A week later, they met in a Queens coffee shop. In person, her face, which had looked the tiniest bit alluring on his computer screen, was, in fact, rather ordinary.

All of this is to say that the answer to Maryanne's question is no. Tiffany is not pretty, but she is not ugly either. Like a lot of people, she falls somewhere in the middle and does the best with what she has. Given his history with Maryanne, however, Jeremy offers a different response. "My ex is beautiful. Stunning, actually. Probably the most attractive woman I've ever been with."

"Really?"

"You sound surprised, Maryanne." Jeremy knows that if they go much further with this line of conversation, things could get, well, things could get ugly between them.

"No, no, no," she says, holding up her hands. "I'm not surprised at all. You're a great guy, Jer. I bet you can get any woman you want. It's just that, if she's the type to break up with you over a salad, then she doesn't sound very pretty on the inside. And that's where it counts, isn't it?"

Jeremy tosses back more wine, thinking that if being "pretty on the inside" really matters, that's what Maryanne would have asked about in the first place. But he doesn't point that out. Instead, he just says, "That's what people say."

Since Tiff is certain to extricate herself from his life once and for all after he returns her dog, there's little point in discussing her anymore. Jeremy puts down his glass and, at long last, raises a topic that has gone unspoken between them so far that evening. In his most serious voice yet, he says, "Seeing as we've found ourselves in the midst of a conversation about looks, there's something I want to say to you, Maryanne."

Maryanne lifts her gaze from the last of her salad—or rather his salad, which had become her salad. She stares intently into his eyes, waiting for whatever he might say next. For a moment, Jeremy sees the younger, drunker version of her. She is not sitting at a table at Voilà. She is swinging on a swing in a playground. She is not wearing high heels. Her feet are bare and pointing up at the moon as she swings, then down at the earth, then up at the moon, then down at the earth . . . "Can you imagine?" she howls into the dark. "Can you fucking imagine?"

"My face," Jeremy says to that woman in his memory, hearing the nervous hitch in his voice.

"Your face?" says the Maryanne before him now. "What about it?"

Difficult as it is, Jeremy does his best to shove that memory, to shove so many other unthinkable thoughts, back down again. More than anything, he wants to maintain the happy feelings this reunion has brought so far. He takes a breath and says, "No doubt you noticed that I have a severe wind and sunburn. It happened today when I went on a whale-watching trip as part of the story I'm writing."

Maryanne smiles. She leans closer, squinting the way you would if you were trying to detect something barely visible. Some part of him can't help but wonder if the gesture is all for show. How could she not notice? "Now that you mention it," Maryanne says, "it does look pretty red, Jer. It's peeling and flaking already too. My poor baby. Did you put some lotion on it?"

Jeremy has been putting lotion on it all frigging day, starting with the stuff he found in his hotel bathroom and moving on to the pricey tub of cream he bought at that gimmicky Provence store at the mall. Either way, Maryanne's mention of the flaking and peeling causes him to reach up and rub his palms vigorously against his cheeks. When he does, so many tiny flakes of dead skin drift down onto his salad plate, blending with the Parmesan. He should feel happy, since that means his old face is starting to peel away just as the doctor predicted. Soon, Jeremy's improved face will emerge. Somehow, though, he does not feel happy. In fact, suddenly, he feels quite sad.

"When we get back to my apartment, I'll give you an intensive hydrating lotion we use at my salon," Maryanne is saying. "Anyway, how were the whales?"

More than once, she has trotted out the words *my salon* in such a way that implies she owns her own place now. Jeremy has yet to inquire about it, because he's starting to see all the many ways that her life is appealing and, as is so often the case, his does not measure up. Instead, he finds himself launching into a line of bullshit about the fictional whales. Their breeching. Their diving. Their fin slaps and tail waves. He keeps going on, tossing out as much of the trivia as he can recall from that show the night before, crediting a made-up captain of the watch instead.

He tells her that fin whales pee the equivalent of three bathtubs of urine per day, to which Maryanne says she does too on days when she drinks too much coffee.

He tells her that blue whales have the largest penises in the world at eight feet long, to which Maryanne says that could put a lot of male porn stars out of business.

He tells her that blue whales also have the largest hearts in the world, the size of a bumper car and weighing some 438 pounds, to which Maryanne simply makes a sad face.

"Why a sad face?" Jeremy asks.

"I don't know. Guess I was thinking how much it might hurt if the creature ever had its heart broken."

Jeremy opens his mouth to respond, but the peppermill-as-penis waiter reappears to clear their salad plates, empty except for Jeremy's dead skin and uneaten Parmesan. Up until that moment, Voilà's owner and chef has not shown his face, though he sent over a steady stream of complimentary appetizers, not to mention an amuse-bouche. (If ever there's a French term Jeremy dislikes. It sounds like some sort of pre-meal mouth douche, and often tastes like one too.) Now Jeremy looks up to see the creator of this evening's pumpkin foam and pistachio mouth douche weaving between the tables, heading their way. A big-bellied man in a smeared white chef's shirt, he carries a bottle of wine in one of his meaty paws.

With the other, he shakes their hands upon arriving at the table. The man introduces himself as Liam, which Jeremy notes is a rather non-French name for the owner of a French restaurant. "Enjoying everything so far?" Chef Liam asks, keeping his eyes on Maryanne, even though the question is, presumably, aimed at them both.

"Oh, we are!" Maryanne says in her delighted, Melanie Griffith voice. "Aren't we, Jer?"

Jeremy thinks it best to save his review for, well, the review, so he says noncommittally, "So far, so good."

"Happy to hear it. I understand you're here from New York," Liam says, his gaze still trained on Maryanne. "Sent by Dennis at that travel site, right?"

"I'm from Providence," she tells him. "But Jeremy here, he's the big-city guy. And he's the big writer too."

At last, Liam has no choice but to fully turn his attention to Jeremy. In his eyes Jeremy sees the briefest flicker of surprise, perhaps even a tinge of disgust, when he sizes up the strangely rubicund face molting like a snake before him. At the same time, Jeremy's skin begins to itch. His cheeks. His chin. His forehead. It is all he can do not to lift his hands and scratch at it. To distract himself, and because he thinks more alcohol might numb the sensation, he looks at the wine the chef has carried over to the table and says, "So what's that beautiful bottle you've got in your hands, Liam?"

"Ah, this. It's one of our very best wines. I want you to try it." The chef pulls an opener from beneath his smeared smock and commences with the uncorking. At the same time, his gaze slides back over to Maryanne's more appealing face. "So what do you do here in Providence?" he asks her.

Before answering, Maryanne gives Jeremy a quick and uncomfortable glance. It makes him wonder if even she notices the way people prefer to put their attention on her rather than him. It was true way back with Dan and Junkyard Joe. It is still true with the waiters at Voilà and now Liam too. "I have a little salon," she says in a shy voice.

"Which one?" Liam asks, twisting the corkscrew.

"You probably don't know it. It's a tiny little place."

"Try me. We're both small-business owners in this city. I might have heard of it." Jeremy thinks this is unlikely, seeing as the man is completely bald.

"It's called the Sasha Stuart Salon over on Waterstone," Maryanne says, still speaking in a shyer voice than Jeremy is used to hearing from her.

"I know that place! But I guess I always assumed it belonged to someone named Sasha. Didn't you say your name was—"

"Maryanne," she tells him. "When I first bought it, I planned to change the name. But Sasha had such a following, I figured it was smart to wait a while in order to keep her customers. Except then I never got around to making the change. It's for the best. I mean, the Maryanne Popadowski Salon doesn't exactly scream, 'Oh my god, I want to get my highlights done there.'"

"I hear you," Liam says. "Why do you think I called this place Voilà? My last name is McDonald. Hardly French, for starters. And it's kind of already taken."

He laughs. She laughs. Jeremy pretends to laugh. Really, he's busy wondering if he should get up and go to the kitchen and finish cooking their dinners while Liam and Maryanne finish the date. He is close to at least doing the getting-up part when, at long last, Liam pulls the cork from the bottle. While blathering on about the "textural complexity" of the vintage, he splashes a taste into Jeremy's glass. Jeremy picks up his glass and gives it a good swirl, thinking of his mother, who taught him about wine. He used to resist her attempts at education, particularly the specifics of writing and speaking the French language, but what things she drilled into his head about wine stuck. Not surprisingly, his mother believed Americans made too big a deal about it with their ridiculous Robert Parker ratings and so much carrying-on about sulfite sensitivity. Her greatest wine lesson was what she called *la puissance de la pause* or "the power of the pause." In that precious moment after the first taste, the sommelier, the server, the other guests at the table, have no choice but to wait for the taster's approval or dismissal.

Normally, Jeremy doesn't carry on the way she used to, but in this instance, he keeps swirling the glass, examining the wine's legs, before taking a sip and embracing the power of the pause. He smacks his lips. He swishes his tongue. He makes a slight grimace while squinting at the label. All of this takes enough time that someone could have guzzled an entire glass. Still, Jeremy waits even longer, remembering the way his mother got a thrill out of making people believe she was about to send it back, and a subsequent thrill when they were that much more grateful when she did not.

"Well?" Maryanne says, unable to stand the suspense a second more.

"Everything okay?" Liam asks, obviously worried that he's poured a dud.

Jeremy senses that the dinner is back under his control. He does what his mother used to do: nods and says only, "You may pour."

Liam gives a weak smile. A new waiter approaches with their dinners. Steak au poivre for Maryanne. Bouillabaisse for Jeremy. With their glasses full and their dinners served, Chef Liam makes the sensible decision to tell them both to enjoy, before he and the waiter retreat to the kitchen.

After they are gone, Jeremy worries that the various intrusions have erased the happy mood from earlier. Neither he nor Maryanne says anything for a few moments. She slices into her steak, takes a bite, and chews, making a gratified *mmmm* sound. Jeremy smears rouille onto a crust of bread, which he sets afloat on the broth like a tiny boat, watching as it takes on liquid and goes lopsided.

"It's no tortellini," Maryanne says at last, smiling a little. "But I guess it'll do."

That might have been the perfect way to ease them back into their earlier mood, except that on the walk over, they'd already discussed those dinners. How fun to revisit a memory like that the first time, Jeremy thinks, how hollow it feels to revisit it again so soon. Maryanne returns to her steak while he begins fishing for that sunken crust of bread, certain their fun is dwindling fast. He wants to bring up the topic of Dan Nicastro, but decides to avoid that for the time being. Things feel tenuous enough already. And then, just when Jeremy determines that there really is not much left for them to say, Maryanne speaks up. "You must really know your wines, Jer. The way you tasted the stuff earlier, I could tell you're an expert."

"It's nothing. I just happened to remember some basic rules my mother taught me. You know how the French are about their wines. And she was a double threat: a French-born Francophile."

Maryanne stops cutting into her steak and says, "A Franco-what?"

Jeremy repeats the word.

"And what's that?"

He's about to explain but worries even that explanation might lead down some other dark road, one where he'll need to provide more information about his parents than the little tidbit she inferred when he explained the plot of his novel. Instead, he leans back from his steaming bowl of bouillabaisse and says, "Why don't you guess?"

"Okay, I will." Maryanne, who is always up for a challenge, wipes her mouth and leans back too. "Let's see. Well, I don't know. To me, it sort of sounds like a pedophile. But like, maybe one who touches your frank. Did she touch your frank, Jer?"

All of this was said with enough of a smile that, given the

warped sense of humor they share, the two start laughing. "Yeah," he tells her. "And she touched my beans too."

Certainly not the funniest of exchanges between them, but they each crave a return to that frivolous mood from earlier, and it is enough to get there. Soon, they are laughing again as Jeremy finds himself explaining the actual definition of a Francophile. Back and forth the discussion goes, growing more absurd and hilarious, at least to them. And then, in the midst of all their laughter, Maryanne leans closer, looks him in the eyes, and says, "I love you, Jer."

The words stop him. If such a thing is possible, they seem both years overdue and far too soon. Even so, Jeremy cannot help but take a breath. When he releases it, out come the words, "I love you too, Maryanne. I really do."

TWELVE

"To tell you the truth, I lied."

—From *Chinatown*, shown at the Schodack Big-Star Drive-in,
September 1974

PERHAPS IT BEARS REPEATING THAT there are a multitude
of reasons why Jeremy Lichanel should not have taken a last-
minute weekend trip to Providence. There is Pretty, of course,
and now there is the all but certain permanent loss of Tiffany
from his life too. There are the other previously established
matters of his face and that ever-failing Lincoln, its trunk
full of old books and now a dearly departed battery, gone
leaky with acid and strapped down by the slip leash. Finally,
of course, there is Maryanne and their hasty return to the past,
or, more aptly, their hasty rush to bring the past into the
present. Maybe all of those things would be fine; maybe the
reunion would be unremarkable, except for its sweetness and
the happy feelings it creates for them both, if not for that inconvenient and persistent memory of her on the swing.

Toes up. Toes down. Moon. Earth. Moon. Earth.

And so, while there are moments during the course of
the evening when Jeremy senses that the hand-holding and

her confession of petty jealousy and most certainly the I love you's are akin to constructing a house of cards (one, on top of another, on top of another . . .), at some point he ceases worrying. Jeremy allows himself to be caught up in the feel of her hand in his, the sound of her girlish voice in his ears, the joy of so much laughter bubbling between them after so many years of silence. That night in the playground was a very long time ago. . . . If Jeremy has any final, flickering thoughts of that memory as the two finish dinner and leave the restaurant, it might be that, and this too: We are grown-ups this time around, and it's clear how we feel about each other. . . .

Now, they stand in front of his parents' old house on Arnold Street. In the distance are the faintest sounds of a party—the thump of bass, the din of chattering voices, the occasional celebratory whoop in the night. While time has done much to alter Jeremy and Maryanne, it has done nothing to smudge the stoic New England beauty of that house. There is the same sharp slant of a roofline, the same barn-red shingles, the same paned windows giving off no hint of life from inside. Even the old tin rooster still stands guard at his post above the mailbox by the door. All those details make it easy for Jeremy to imagine his younger self slumped on the sofa in the living room, watching any number of eighties favorites (*Footloose? Tootsie?*) on the DVD player, every light in the house off on account of the electric bill.

"What are you thinking about, Jer?" Maryanne asks from where she stands impossibly close to him on the sidewalk, puffing on a mentholated cigarette.

Smoke wreaths in the air around them, reminding Jeremy of the way the Tiramisu used to smell. Even though he quit smoking after those long-ago days and nights with Maryanne, he'd gone along with her idea to buy cigarettes and puffs away beside her, bringing yet another element of their past into their present. It had also been her idea that they walk off dinner by taking the long route home to her place, stopping to see the old house along the way.

If Jeremy were to answer her question with honesty, it would require him explaining the way his brain works, and how thoughts of his younger self inside watching an eighties flick have put him in mind of a favorite quote from *Tootsie*: "I could lay a big line on you and we could do a lot of role-playing, but the simple truth is, is that I find you very interesting and I'd really like to make love to you. . . ."

He longs to say just that to her, which is yet another thing not so terribly different from the first time they found themselves outside that house on Arnold Street at the end of an evening. But rather than admit that every part of him is filling up with a longing to kiss her, a need to hold her in his arms, a desire to be as close as possible to the one woman he finds more alluring, more beautiful, than any he has ever known, Jeremy confesses only to a smaller truth, at least for the time being: "I was thinking of my mom and dad."

Maryanne sucks on her cigarette, stained a deep red at one end from her lipstick. The deli where they stopped did not sell Benson & Hedges, so she settled for Marlboro Lights, a tiny detail that bothers Jeremy more than it should. He keeps thinking of those gold cartons and how they so perfectly matched the gold Tiramisu. He wants everything the same, except for the things he does not want the same, like her love for Dan. "I bet you miss your folks," she says. "Do you ever wish you could talk to them still?"

Jeremy stares up at the house and imagines his mother

inside, shouting at him, "*Tu es un armadillo!*" Then he thinks of the very last time he saw her, not in that house, but in a small Paris apartment on the lone trip he ever took to that country. "You were not the son I hoped you would be," he can still hear her saying, her accent working full throttle the way it did whenever she divulged an ugly truth. In this instance, it happened to be her ugliest truth of all: "Not when you were young. Not now that you are grown. I'm sure you feel the same about me as a mother. I see little point in either of us pretending otherwise." And, of course, in the midst of it all, she threw out that outdated French term as her final diagnosis of him, "*Frappadingue!*"

"I trained my brain not to think about certain things from the past," Jeremy tells Maryanne, shoving his mother's words into the same dark sinkhole in his mind where the memory of the swing lives. He looks away from the house, having seen enough of that place for one lifetime, and returns his gaze to Maryanne's lovely face, watching as she blows more smoke from her lips.

"Like me?" she asks.

"If I'm being truthful, yes. Like you."

"I'm sorry, Jer. You know that, right?"

"Me too," he tells her, though it is unclear to him the specific things for which they are apologizing. At the very least, the moment presents a segue back to a puzzle that still needs solving. "I just realized that we never picked up our conversation before."

"You mean about Junkyard Joe and Olivia? Turns out they got married and have an entire brood of kids now. Of course, they had to adopt on account of her not having a uterus or fallopian tubes or—"

"I'm serious, Maryanne."

"Okay, okay. Which conversation do you mean?"

"Back at the restaurant, I was telling you about the whales and how the blue ones have such giant hearts. And you said how much it would hurt to have a heart that big broken. I was about to ask if you've ever had your heart broken when we got interrupted."

Maryanne holds up two fingers, the answer clearly a no-brainer. "Twice. My ex-husband and, well, you remember Dan."

"Our old boss?" Jeremy says in such a forced tone of surprise it sounds phony even to him.

"The one and only. Remember how stupid crazy I was over that idiot? It made no sense. But as I've gotten older, I've realized it's all about hormones. You just can't control who you feel that way about and who you don't. Dan and me, we carried on for far too long. Years, in fact. Years and years."

"I have to confess something, Maryanne," Jeremy says, without thinking it through.

She lowers her cigarette, flicking ashes onto the sidewalk so they skirt away in the breeze. "What's that, Jer?"

"I did a little snooping online last night when I called you. Nothing too intense, but I was nervous about seeing you, so I poked around a bit. I saw the pictures of your sons on Facebook, and I couldn't help but notice they look a little like Dan. I figured he left his wife and that you two . . ."

"You thought I married Dan?"

"I do," Jeremy says. "I mean, I did. You didn't?"

She lets out a huff. "God no, Jer! What a disaster that would have been. The truth is, I did marry a guy a lot like Dan. A gambler. A cheater. He pissed away money all the time. My boys are his, though. Not Dan's. And anyway, that's all in the past. Thankfully, I refuse to allow my hormones to control me that way anymore." Maryanne lets out a helpless little laugh, before asking, "What about you, Jer? Has anyone ever broken your heart?"

If not for that puffy red skin, she might have read the answer on his face: *You broke my heart, Maryanne. So did my mother.* Instead, Jeremy fumbles for an acceptable response. "Well, this last breakup with Tiffany threw me for a loop. Not exactly heartbreak, but it stings. Still, I'll tough it out. Guess that's what I've learned as I've gotten older: eventually, you bury your bad feelings and move on." And then, unexpectedly, he thinks of something more he wants to say. "I used to have this friend, back when we lived in Florida. Teddy Cornwell. We kept in touch long after I moved away."

"Oh, yeah," Maryanne says. "I remember you used to talk about that guy sometimes. Whatever happened to him?"

Thinking of what happened to Teddy leads Jeremy to take a deep breath. "Things didn't work out the way he might have hoped. Last time we spoke, well, it wasn't good."

Maryanne lets out a sympathetic sigh. "Sorry to hear that."

"Me too."

Back when Jeremy lived in the neighborhood, nights had been deathly quiet. Now, the sounds from that party on some distant street grow steadily louder, making the evening feel alive with possibility. "Anyway, speaking of Tiffany, should we head home and see how Pretty is doing? Bingo too?"

Maryanne's only answer is to snuff out her cigarette and take his hand. They walk in relative silence for some time, passing a gaggle of college students, all dressed in togas, likely freezing their asses off.

When they arrive at her gate on Angell Street, she swings

it open and together they head around back and up the stairs. At the door, Maryanne fusses with her keys in a trial-and-error method, working through several on her chain and cursing beneath her breath each time one fails to do the trick. Jeremy listens for some sound of the dogs inside. The silence has him worried that Bingo has gotten loose and terrorized Pretty. And he's also worried about kissing Maryanne—about screwing up his courage and taking her in his arms. Surely that's the endpoint of this evening.

At last, the proper key slides into the lock and the door opens. Maryanne steps inside. Jeremy follows. His eyes scan the small kitchen until he spots Pretty, fast asleep in a dim rectangle of moonlight on the oak floor. She does not so much as lift her head. Jeremy whispers a joke about what a good guard dog she is, which leads Maryanne to laugh and whisper back that they may as well leave the lights off so as not to disturb Sleeping Beauty. While their eyes adjust to what slivers of moonlight shine through the window, Maryanne asks in a hushed voice if Jeremy is in the mood for a nightcap.

Jeremy nods. Maryanne puts down her keys and goes to the same cabinet for booze as earlier. This time, however, Jeremy swallows back the lump that has formed in his throat. He rubs his palms quite vigorously against his cheeks and chin and forehead in hopes of sloughing off any bits of peeling skin. And then, when that frantic rubbing is done, he comes up behind Maryanne, threading his hands around her soft waist, nuzzling his face into the back of her warm neck, breathing in her scent of cigarette smoke and soap and perfume and the faintest trace of sweat.

For an instant, he feels Maryanne's body stiffen, and Jeremy braces for the same rejection that came years before. But

then the moment passes. He feels her body relax into his. After another moment, Maryanne turns to face him. His mouth
finds her mouth. His hands slide up her back. Her hands move
to his shoulders, then to his neck, holding him there, as their
kiss grows deeper. It might seem odd, it might seem downright
juvenile, in fact, to count the seconds of a kiss, but some part
of Jeremy's mind sets about doing just that:

One . . . Two . . . Three . . . Four . . . Five . . . Six . . .

His tongue slips into her mouth. It tastes of scotch. It tastes
of steak. It tastes of still more cigarette smoke.

Seven . . . Eight . . . Nine . . . Ten . . . Eleven . . .

His erection, more powerful than any he has experienced
in ages, presses against his zipper. His heart drums faster and
faster. The lump in his throat returns.

Twelve . . . Thirteen . . . Fourteen . . . Fifteen . . . Sixteen . . .

His fingers go to the sides of her face—that beautiful, exquisite face!—where he finds that her skin feels impossibly
soft.

Seventeen . . . Eighteen . . . Nineteen . . . Twenty . . .

Possessed now by an absolute hunger to touch all the
parts of her that have been kept from him for so long, Jeremy
moves his body greedily against hers. His legs press to her
legs. His crotch presses to her crotch. His hands drop from
her face to her breasts, which he anticipates will feel all the
more impossibly soft beneath her dress.

Twenty-one . . . Twenty-two . . . Twenty-three . . .

His hands travel from her breasts to her back. His fingers
scout out her zipper.

Twenty-four . . . Twenty-five . . . Twenty-six . . .

He has never been skilled at removing a woman's clothes,
but down the zipper comes! Jeremy imagines Maryanne's bare

back revealing itself in the moonlight, like some pale night-time flower opening to him at last.

Twenty-seven . . . Twenty-eight . . . Twenty-nine . . .

"Jeremy!" Maryanne says, pushing him away.

He stumbles back, losing his balance, reaching for the butcher block to keep from falling. A jingling sound comes from a corner of the kitchen, and he glances over to see Pretty lifting her head. The dog's shiny black eyes glisten in the dim light, watching him, watching both of them. Confused, he asks, "What's wrong?"

"Nothing. I mean . . . Sorry . . . It's just . . ."

"What?" Hadn't she been sending him unmistakable signals all night long? *We're adults now,* Jeremy thinks again.

Maryanne takes a breath. "Don't go so fast is all. There's no rush."

Oh, Jeremy thinks, a trickle of relief running through him. Rattled as he feels, he has the sense that she's right: he was going too fast. "I'm sorry," he says.

"It's okay," she says, standing up straighter and smiling. "Let's try again."

This time, Maryanne comes to him. As his hands resume their position at the sides of her face, his forearms graze those thin gold necklaces with the cross and the Italian horn. Her lips resume their position on his. Ever so gently, Jeremy pulls her body closer, moving his tongue into her mouth, resisting the urge to count this time.

As their kiss continues, Jeremy hears the sound of Pretty's collar jangling again. He does not allow it to distract him. When he senses that an appropriate amount of time has passed, he reaches around and trails his fingers up and down Maryanne's spine, then makes light circles on her skin with the pads of his fingers, before finally reaching for her zipper and tugging it lower, lower still, all the while pushing his tongue deeper into her mouth and—

"I can't do this!" Maryanne says, breaking the kiss again.

Unlike the last time, she does not push him away. Instead, she simply takes a few steps back, burying her face in her hands.

Pretty watches them both, black eyes blinking in the shadows. From somewhere down the hall, Bingo lets out a lone bark. Those are things Jeremy will recall later, but of all the many details that will return, the one he will remember again and again, the moment that will shake him awake in the night for the rest of his life, is this: he looks back across the small expanse of Maryanne's kitchen and sees her lift her face from the cradle of her hands and wipe their kiss away on her sleeve.

"What do you mean you can't do this?" Jeremy asks.

When she sees him watching, Maryanne brings the business of her mouth and her sleeve to an abrupt halt. "I'm sorry. I thought I could. But I can't."

"And why can't you?"

This answer requires some thinking on her part, Jeremy notes, because Maryanne does not say anything right away. "It's just . . ." she begins at last. "It's just . . . I don't know, Jer. I really did miss you all this time. I was telling the truth about that. And when you called last night, I started thinking about what a good guy you were and how stupid I was to turn you away back then. I wanted things to go a certain way between us tonight. I hope you saw how much I wanted that. But when it comes right down to it, even though I feel this intense emotional connection between us, and a closeness and comfort I've never felt with another guy, it just doesn't feel sexual to me. It never has. And I guess it never will."

They say animals can sense things, and Jeremy wonders if it's true, because down the hall, Bingo begins scratching at the door. Pretty stands and shakes herself, then pads over to one of the collapsible bowls Jeremy set out earlier and begins noisily lapping up water. For a moment, the only sounds in the kitchen are the scratching and the lapping, until, on the other side of the wall, there comes the muffled chiming of a clock.

Her tenants' clock, Jeremy thinks. And then, all at once, an unexpected clarity settles over his mind, a clarity that leads him to decide, *No, not her tenants at all.*

And in the light of that newfound clarity, Jeremy has the sense of something churning in the air around them, something taking shape, something gaining strength, whirling round and round.

"Say something," Maryanne pleads. "Please, Jer."

At last, he speaks. "I saw you that night."

"What night?"

"At the playground."

"Playground?"

Maryanne sounds genuinely confused, though who could tell any longer what's genuine between them? Jeremy says, "You know what I'm talking about."

The clock on the other side of the wall reaches its final chime, ushering in the arrival of midnight as Bingo scratches at the door and Pretty drinks her water. Jeremy studies Maryanne, waiting for some flicker of recognition. It goes on far longer than is natural, until all at once her mouth falls open and her expression turns to one of genuine alarm. "Oh my god, Jer. Your face . . . it's . . . it's bleeding!"

Jeremy's hands shoot up to his cheeks, then move to his forehead and the patchwork of pinprick scabs he first noticed in the mirror that morning. Sure enough, when he brings his hands down, blood glints on the tips of his fingers. Maryanne turns and goes to the sink, her pale back visible to him in that unzipped dress. He watches her tear a paper towel off the roll and hold it beneath the faucet. Jeremy reaches up again, only to discover there is more than just blood on his face: there are tears now too. He does his best to wipe both away, though what point is there in trying to hide the undesirable details from her and from the rest of the world? It never does any good.

Frappadingue! he hears his mother's voice hiss. *Armadillo! You disgust me!*

Maryanne comes to him and begins dabbing his face, before Jeremy snatches the paper towel and presses it to his own skin. A moment later, he removes it and examines the smeared dots of blood there.

"There was no whale-watching trip, was there?" Maryanne asks gently.

Jeremy shakes his head, mumbles, "How did you know?"

"How did I know? Please, Jer. I work in the beauty industry. I've seen my fair share of faces battered after laser treatments. The moment you walked in tonight, I pretty much knew what you'd had done."

"So why didn't you say something?"

"Because nobody ever wants to admit to that sort of thing. I learned a long time ago to let people have their secrets. Whenever I spot the signs on a client at the salon, I just go about my business, cutting hair and making chitchat."

Jeremy continues dabbing and blotting. "Speaking of the salon," he says, that sense of clarity still within his reach, "you don't own the place, do you?"

Her dress has begun to slip from her shoulders and, with some difficulty, she attempts to reach around and tug up the zipper. In that same sheepish voice she used when Liam prodded her about the salon, she says, "I guess that BS about why I own a place named after somebody else didn't exactly hold up, did it?"

Jeremy shakes his head.

"Well, you got me. It really does belong to Sasha Stuart. I just work there."

"And you also just rent this apartment from whoever lives on the other side of that wall, am I right?"

This time, Maryanne doesn't offer an explanation. She simply nods, then looks at Pretty, who has finished drinking and begins making those anxious circles of hers, round and round the butcher-block island. Down the hall, Bingo scratches at the door, incessantly now, releasing a loud bark on occasion too. Maryanne shouts at him to chill out, but the dog does not let up. Jeremy thinks to tell Pretty to calm down, though he knows she never listens once she gets going—not unless Tiff breaks out the slip leash, which is still in the trunk of the Lincoln wrapped around the old battery.

"Well," Maryanne says, "since we're unpacking the unpleasant truths about our lives, you don't write big travel stories about exotic places for fancy publications, do you? I did some snooping of my own online last night and couldn't find anything you'd written but some column for a women's magazine years back that sounded pretty angry."

The paper towel has grown warm. Jeremy removes it from his forehead. The bleeding appears to have subsided, the tears too. The mention of his anger leads Jeremy to think of Tiffany, of course, which in turn leads him to reach into the inside pocket of his blazer and turn on his cell. In no time, the frenzy of texts she's been sending since he powered things down earlier begins flooding his feed. He does not read them, but feels each one arrive with a frantic buzz, like small electric jolts to his waist. "Now you're the one who's got me, Maryanne. This is my first travel story. And it's for some rinky-dink website. So I guess that makes us even when it comes to the trumped-up versions of our lives we presented each other."

"Guess so," she says as Pretty whips by them in the shadows, and Bingo scratches and barks down the hall. And then, Maryanne tells him, "Well, not quite even. You said something earlier tonight. Something you were right about." She takes a deep breath, releases a sigh. "Okay, then. Here goes: Not both of my boys, but one of them. My oldest. I've always suspected he might belong to Dan. Nobody knows that but me, and now you. After I married another guy, Dan started coming around again. It was dumb of me to start up with him a second time. Even dumber not to be careful. Anyway, the way the math works out, not to mention the resemblance. I think you're probably right."

Maryanne pauses a moment. "While I'm at it, I may as well tell you: My biological mother was not so clingy that I had to ask her to stop contacting me. In reality, she wanted nothing to do with me. It took years to track her down. I wrote her dozens of letters. Dozens. Finally, after all my begging to meet, she wrote suggesting a date and time, and telling me I should pick whatever restaurant I wanted and she'd be there. Well, I chose a steakhouse in Boston, a place I'd been once with my ex-husband. I thought it would feel special. When the night came at last, it was absolutely freezing. I wore a fur coat my ex had given me after one of our many fights. I kept that coat on at the table, because I wanted my mother to see how well the daughter she'd given up had done for herself. But as it turned out, my mother waited for me to order prime rib before mentioning that she was a vegetarian. And not just a vegetarian but the hardcore kind—"

"A vegan?"

"Yes, a fucking vegan, Jer! She ordered a side of broccoli and a baked potato and sat there with a look of disgust on her face while I sliced into my meat. It was like a bad date. No, it was like the worst possible date, except it wasn't a date. It was my one and only meeting with the woman who brought me into this world." Maryanne's voice has gone wobbly. She sounds near tears.

"Why didn't you just tell me that?" Jeremy asks.

"Same reason you didn't tell me those things about you. Who wants the world to think they've failed? Who wants anyone to think their lives aren't perfect, that they're not happy and successful and fulfilled every second of every day? Who wants anyone to know the truth: that the things they wanted most from this life, they either messed up on their own or they just plain got screwed out of for no good reason?"

A silence falls over the kitchen. The dogs still carry on, though somehow, their commotion has slipped into a kind of background static.

"Are you mad at me?" Maryanne asks at last. "I don't want you to be mad at me. I don't want to lose you from my life again. I need you. Maybe that sounds corny, but I really do need you, Jer."

A laugh, one loaded with contempt, escapes him. She needs him? Whoever considered the things he might need? Rather than say that, however, he sticks with the truth. "The reason Tiffany thinks I have a temper isn't just because I pounded my fist on her table."

"It's not?"

Jeremy shakes his head.

"Why does she think you have a temper, Jer?"

"It's, well, sometimes, on sidewalks or on the subway, when people don't move out of the way because they're too busy yapping into their cell phones or just plain oblivious to the world around them or even just downright rude, I get what Tiff calls a little 'shovey.'"

"Shovey? As in, you shove them?"

"Not really. Actually, not at all. So that's a dumb name for it. What I do is tense up my shoulders and act as though I don't see them either, that way they bump into me. I figure it teaches them to pay more attention. You know, for their own good."

"I see," Maryanne says. And then, after a pause, "Well, the city is so damned crowded, I guess it's enough to make anyone a little crazy some days."

"Exactly. Plus, when I'm driving, if someone cuts me off, I cut them off right back. Tiff calls that my road rage. Well, I guess that's what everyone calls it."

"I see," Maryanne says again. "But that's not so abnormal, Jer. Believe me, I flip people the bird plenty when they steal my spot in a parking lot."

"Good," Jeremy tells her. "But there's more."

"More?"

"Yes. There's, well, Tokyo, Key West, St. Louis." Even the simple act of speaking the names causes Jeremy to look down at his feet. He pictures the bits of broken glass, the miniature artificial cherry blossoms, the toppled plastic Mount Fuji, the family of minuscule porpoises, and that white arch—the "Gateway to the West"—no bigger than his thumb, turned upside down like a horseshoe.

"Jer?" Maryanne says. "What are you talking about?"

He shakes his head against the memory, looks up at her. "Tiffany has a collection of snow globes that her uncle brought her from his travels around the world. The night we fought, it started about the salad. But things got heated and she told me to leave. On my way out, I—"

"You what?"

"I knocked a few off her shelf. Tokyo. Key West. St. Louis. Those places."

"That's awful, Jer." Maryanne steps away, to the other side of the butcher block. "You shouldn't have done that."

"You don't have to tell me, Maryanne. I know! But all I can say is, there are times when so much of the shit that gets piled on a person is too much to take." He stops, takes a breath, tries to modulate his speaking the way those asinine anger management books advise. "I just lost it. And believe me, I felt terrible and regretful and ugly as ever. I tried to make it up to Tiff by tracking down replacements on eBay. I even found the exact ones I'd broken and showed up at her doorstep with them in my hands. I stood there like an imbecile, shaking each one for her, so she could see the cherry blossoms falling over Tokyo, the porpoises swimming in the waters of Key West, the flakes collecting at the base of the arch in St. Louis."

"And what did she say?"

Jeremy shrugs. "That none of it was the same, since they weren't the snow globes her uncle had given her with so much love. She didn't want them. She didn't want me anymore either." He feels another of those small jolts to his waist. No doubt another text from Tiffany, and Jeremy cannot help but marvel at her timing.

Maryanne watches him, a kind of wariness on her face now. It is that nervous, expectant expression that leads him to unload one more paramount truth: "Both my parents aren't dead."

"What? You said they had an accident. You said—"

"No, Maryanne. I told you I wrote a novel about a guy whose parents died in an accident. You assumed that's what happened in real life. People always do that: assume the things a novelist puts down on the page are the truth of his or her life, when that goes against the very definition of fiction in the first place. In your case, that's the assumption you made, so I let you believe it. Really, though, it's only my father who's dead, and he passed in a rather ordinary manner. My mother is alive and well, far as I know. But after my father died, she said some pretty unforgivable things. I got my inheritance, a hefty sum thanks to my father's investments and family money. I carefully meted it out in order to avoid ever having to get a real job, and now she's dead to me in an entirely different way."

Maryanne is quiet, her mouth hanging open the slightest bit, her dress still sliding from her shoulders. "I don't understand. Why did you tell me you regretted not going on that trip to Provence with your parents?"

"Because I do regret it. Because it was my last chance to do something with them as a family. Because if I'd known how things would change after that, I would have gone. I should have gone."

Once more, they retreat to their individual silences. While the dogs go about their chaos, Jeremy finds himself thinking, oddly, of Teddy Cornwell again. Of a day in Orlando when

Jeremy's mother dragged him to a Disney audition that never happened. On the way out, she heard another voice speaking French. A voice that turned out to be Teddy's. Then Jeremy's mind shifts abruptly away from Teddy to "Courtney Goodale" and the nights he spends trolling Facebook. He thinks of all those perfectly curated photos on the profiles of his exes, so many of them filtered into some idealized reality. He thinks, too, of those little white Facebook fists with their thumbs up, signaling those godforsaken "Likes" everyone so desperately craves. "You'll never know," he says at last.

"Never know what?" Maryanne asks. That dress insists on slipping from her still, and she moves from side to side in order to keep it in place.

Jeremy reaches to his forehead to be sure the bleeding has not started again. He feels pieces of the paper towel stuck to his skin, and it brings back memories of watching his father shave at any number of bathroom sinks, at any number of the houses where they'd lived, the way he'd stick a piece of tissue to the dots of blood on his face afterward. Funny how that memory should return to him now, since he has not thought of that detail about his father in all the years since his death. "What I mean to say, Maryanne," Jeremy begins again, his voice foggy, disconnected, "is that you will never know what it's like to be ugly like me."

"Oh, Jer. Don't talk like that. You are not ugly. When you smile, your entire face lights up like nobody's I know," she says. "And when you're telling a funny story, well, your eyes, they absolutely sparkle."

Again that laugh, contemptuous as ever, escapes him. "A smile and occasionally sparkly eyes. How grand. But I'm afraid this isn't a case where the whole is greater than the sum of its parts. And anyway, Maryanne, you don't understand. People like to look at you. Tonight at the restaurant, it was Liam and that waiter waving his peppermill in your face. Hell, even those college boys in togas checked you out. I saw them—"

Maryanne slaps her palm on the butcher block. "I don't know where you're going with this, Jer. But—"

"Let me tell you exactly where I'm going with this, Maryanne. It must be nice to have the world open up to you, instead of shutting down the way it always does for me. And you know why it opens up? When it comes right down to it, it's because of your face. Because it is so lovely to look at. Unlike mine."

"Jer, you're acting like I'm some supermodel on the cover of a magazine, which is hardly the case. I've always been a bit heavy. God knows I'd do better if I stopped fucking with my hair. For years, I wore too much makeup until Sasha suggested I try a simpler look. I'm nothing like what you're making me out to be. Besides, everyone knows that it's not the way people look that make them ugly, it's the things they do."

That final platitude triggers Jeremy's laughter again. It bubbles up from his throat like bile. If ever there was a pile of horseshit, he thinks, it is that "pretty on the inside" business. It's no different than so many other lies about the world, like Christmas not being about gifts or gray hair looking dignified. But why waste his breath refuting any of that wrongheaded stupidity? Instead, Jeremy chooses that moment to bring things around to the one simple fact worth repeating: "I saw you that night at the playground."

"There you go again, Jer. I don't even under—" She stops. "Wait. You mean the playground where Dan and I used to meet?"

"That would be the one. Yes."

"What do you mean, you 'saw me'?"

How remarkable a thing: the past, Jeremy thinks. One moment, it is decades behind you; the next, it is there before your eyes, living and breathing and teeming with so many familiar and forgotten emotions. He felt it when recalling his father shaving so many mornings in so many different sinks. He felt it when thinking of his mother on her settee by the wall of windows in that Paris apartment, spewing those unforgivable things. And at that very instant, standing before Maryanne in her shadowy kitchen on Angell Street, he feels it as his mind wraps around the memory of those moonlit woods, of watching her on that swing, of hearing her howling laughter and listening to her shouted words, all of which he has never forgotten no matter how hard he has tried. The memory returns with such an absolute wallop that Jeremy wonders how he had ever allowed himself to look up Maryanne, never mind to call her, never mind to say hello, never mind to ask her to dinner, never mind to dream of kissing her again, then to actually kiss her again, only to end up back in those proverbial woods once more. His heart cannot bear it, Jeremy thinks, it simply cannot bear it. "I went there that night," he tells her, his voice shaky now too. "I watched you both."

"You what?"

"Do you remember that night?"

"I think you should go," is all she has to say, standing up straight, pointing toward the door.

"I'm not going, Maryanne. Not yet, anyway. Because I asked you a question, and the least you could do is answer. So tell me, do you remember that night?"

"Vaguely. I mean, there wasn't just one night at that playground. He and I used to meet there a lot. Did you come every time? Because that's downright creepy, Jer."

"Only the first. So I don't know what went on after that night. But let me remind you of what I saw. For starters, you might recall getting fucked on the hood of your car."

"Okay, that's it! We're done here!" Maryanne moves toward the door, holding up her dress as she goes, then holding open the door.

"You might recall sliding down the slide afterward, half-naked and drunk."

"I want you to leave. Now."

"You might recall getting on the swing. Dan pushing you higher and higher as the two of you began discussing—"

"I said, I want you to go! I don't want to talk about this. Take Pretty and leave."

"Oh, I'll leave, Maryanne." Jeremy watches as that dress slips a tiny bit farther down her shoulders. The thing seems to have a mind of its own, and it so clearly wants to be free of her. "And this time, I won't ever come back. But let me finish telling you what I remember about that night. From here on out, I promise to stick to the particulars as they pertain to me. Would that be okay?"

"Frankly, I don't see how my meeting another guy pertains to you in the least. But alright. If you insist. So long as you get the hell out of here the second you're done with this bullshit, tell me whatever you recall that's so damn imperative right now."

And so, at long last he begins telling her, each word breathing new life into that old memory, working a kind of spell in that kitchen. Soon, it is as though Jeremy no longer stands among the butcher block and white cabinets; rather, he finds himself in the woods on the perimeter of the elementary school playground. It is as though the dogs no longer make a ruckus; rather, crickets and cicadas fill the air with the sounds of a warm summer evening. And those wooden beams over Jeremy's head recede until only the large, lush leaves of so many oak trees are above, rustling against the moonlit sky.

He is about to relive it.

Like it or not, they both are.

THIRTEEN

"We all go a little mad sometimes."

—From *Psycho*, shown at the Schodack Big-Star Drive-in,

August 1960

"YOU SURE YOU WANT ALL the details, Skyla? It's the past now. Telling you such things will hurt, and I've caused you plenty of hurt already."

"You're right about that. But tell me, Maureen. Tell me everything."

"Okay then. If you insist. Here goes: We met during a storm, a nor'easter, many years ago. I was driving home in the heavy rain and whipping winds when a power line fell, like some giant snake crashing on the hood of my car. It scared the hell out of me. I couldn't go forward and worried backing up might pull down the whole damn pole. Forget getting out too, since I was terrified of being electrocuted. My cell had no service, so all I could do was sit there. Helpless. Radio playing. Blinkers blinking.

"Back then, I had this boyfriend. Norman. God, what a loser that guy was. Things between him and me were never smooth. We were always fighting. He was always gone when I needed him. I wanted to get married. All he wanted was to get laid. Sorry for saying it that way, Skyla, but you asked me to tell it like it is. Or like it was, anyway."

"It's okay, Maureen. Please. Go on."

"Of course Norman had no way of knowing I needed his help, but I felt pissed at him just the same. And then, after a while of sitting there, stewing in my fury, listening to the pounding rain and howling wind, some sad song came on the radio. The music got to me and I started bawling. Wishing things were different. Anyway, that's when I looked in the rearview to see a giant NYSEG utility truck rolling up behind me, lights flashing . . ."

"Sounds like fate."

Maureen is silent. I imagine her shrugging, looking down at the table, ashamed. "More coffee, Skyla?"

"No thanks. I've had plenty already. Believe me, I won't sleep tonight as it is."

"Sorry about that too."

"So many apologies. I hope they make you feel better at least."

"They do. A little. I've wanted to tell you how sorry I am for a long time."

"And look, now's your chance. So, let's get back to business. Go on with your sweet little love story."

"I'm not saying it's sweet. I'm just trying to take you through the facts as you—"

"Enough with the explanations. Just get on with it already. What happened next?"

"Well, um, okay. Let's see . . . He knocked on my window, and I looked up to see him. Rain pouring down his bald head, dripping from his eyelashes. He made some joke about being my knight in shining utility vehicle. Mine was hardly the only accident that night, so it would be hours before a tow truck would arrive. Hollis was on his way to deal with a mess of other fallen lines, impacting the grid for miles around. But he left all those people in the dark awhile longer to give me a ride back to my condo."

"Nice guy, that Hollis."

"I'm sorry, Skyla. This is too much."

"The only thing that's too much is you saying so every few minutes. Now cut the crap. Please. Keep going."

"Fine. But this feels masochistic of you, you know that?"

"That's my business."

"I suppose. Well . . . he showed up at my door, like, a week later. Said he wanted to check on me. I invited him in and that was the first time we were . . . intimate. Even though he wasn't wearing his wedding ring that day, I remembered seeing it the night he drove me home. So I knew he was married. I told myself it would be just that once. No way was I going to be somebody's mistress, never mind doing that to another woman. To you. But, embarrassing as it is to admit, I was lonely. Hollis was twenty years older than me, but handsome nonetheless. Attentive and sweet too. Especially compared to Norman. Still, the guilt ate away at me, and after a few more times, I told Hollis it was over. We didn't see each other for months. Until . . ."

"Until what?"

"Until I started missing him. Selfish, I know. My emotions got the better of me and I tracked him down. We started things up again. I used to make all sorts of stupid rationalizations, telling myself, 'It's just one hour a week . . . it's just sex . . . nothing more . . . what harm can it do?'"

"Let me guess," I say in an almost bored, condescending

tone that I hope makes her feel pitiful. "You got pregnant by mistake?"

"Actually, no. If you really want the truth, as you say you do, what happened by mistake was that I fell in love. We fell in love. Our daughter, I'm sorry to tell you this, Skyla, but we planned for her."

"Pardon me," I stammer, because I'm the one who feels pitiful now. "One second, please. I just . . ."

"Are you okay?"

It makes no sense. If not for my pride, that's what I would say, because I wanted a child, though Hollis always maintained that he did not. Instead, I summon my most nonchalant voice and tell her, "I'm fine. I just . . . realize it's time to take one of my pills is all. You know, some stupid medication doctors push on us decrepits to stave off death a little longer so they can keep charging our insurance companies buckets of money." From the pockets of my nurse's dress: another teardrop, another submarine while I'm at it. I feel that syringe waiting there too. The smooth plastic of the barrel. The wide wedge at the top of the plunger. The narrow metal of the needle, still capped, sharpening down to a finite point. I swallow the pills dry, then take a breath and tell her, "There. That should keep the grim reaper at bay. Now, the floor is all yours once more. I believe you left off with you and my husband planning your happy little family. Did anyone ever consider letting me in on the plan?" My voice, I realize, rises in pitch and volume with that last, so I do my best to dial things down. Flashing her a sweet smile, I say more calmly, "Sorry, dear. But I can't help but wonder is all."

"I understand," she says and I really do sense genuine remorse, not that I want her pity. "Believe me. But here's the thing: Hollis loved you, Skyla. I know that sounds strange given all I'm telling you, but it's the truth. He used to say all the time how special you were to him. How lucky he was to have met you at such a young age. And he made it clear from the start that, no matter what happened between him and me, he was never going to leave you. He said you were each other's family. That he couldn't break your heart in such a way. Even five years in, when I started telling him I wanted a kid, he insisted he'd never leave you. And by then, we'd fallen into a kind of rhythm. You went off to work each night at the hospital, and he came to stay at my place. Or, some nights, I . . ."

"You slept in my bed?" I say, struggling to keep my voice steady as I picture Hollis waiting with his cornflakes and newspaper and good morning kisses at the kitchen table when I arrived home from my shift. Sheets and towels tumbling in the dryer.

"Sometimes, yes. But never on your side."

"How courteous of you, Maureen."

"I'm sorry, Skyla. I really am. I know how wrong it all was. Horrible, in fact."

The needle. If ever there's a time to jab the thing into her chest, into her face, this might well be it. But my hands shake beneath the table, and before I can do any such thing, Maureen says, "You know the two matching houses?"

"Of course, I do. They belong to me, after all."

"Why are they there? Why two? Why side by side?"

I think of how Teddy asks those questions, how so many of the rejected, would-be tenants asked too. In some moronic, automated fashion, I give the same canned response: "Well, it's a funny story really."

"Tell me the story," Maureen says in what I take to be a

show of curiosity. "I've been telling you all these things. Now
you tell me."

"Fine. After we married, we lived in Hollis's family's house,
even after his folks passed. But the place was falling apart
around us. Hollis, always the penny-pincher, decided our best
bet was to order one of those prefab houses from a kit. So one
day, a flatbed truck rumbles up the drive and drops off all we
need to put together our new home. Which is what we did,
tearing down the old place too. Months later, another flatbed
pulls up the drive and delivers a second house kit. Hollis and I
couldn't believe the company would make such a goof! I mean,
it's one thing to order a bathrobe from L.L. Bean and get sent
two by mistake, which happened to me once. But we're talking two entire houses here! Me, I wanted to return the extra
kit, but Hollis wanted to wait and see if they came to reclaim
it. One month passed. Two months. Three. Four. Finally, he
decided it was safe to build the second house, which he—" I
stop, suddenly realizing why Moo wanted me to tell this story.
"That house wasn't a mistake, was it?"

"Afraid not, Skyla," she says in the sort of gentle voice a
person uses for breaking bad news.

We are both quiet after that. What an idiot I was to believe
that story all these years, never mind repeating it to people
like it was the funniest bit of luck on the planet.

Somewhere in the diner, someone is cleaning. The smell of
ammonia wafts in the air. Far as I can tell, those pills have had
little effect on my mind, though my stomach is another story.
Nausea rises steadily in me. I want to open my mouth and vomit
all over the table. Vomit all over Maureen and her purse too.

"Hollis had this idea . . ." she says, then stops, then starts again, ". . . this idea that we could all live together. Not under the same roof. But, well, almost."

"And how did he . . . how did the two of you . . . think this commune would work without my knowing?" My mouth has gone dry, and when I reach for water, I manage to knock a glass from the table. It crashes to the floor, and Maureen makes the expected fuss. In an instant, a cleaning person rushes to the table, bringing that ammonia smell closer, making my queasiness worse. Once the mess is taken care of, my mouth and lips feel impossibly dry, when I reiterate: "Tell me how that would have worked."

"It seems crazy now, Skyla."

"It most certainly does. But go on. Hit me."

"Okay, well, at first Hollis planned to finally tell you. He still wasn't going to leave, but he wanted you to know that he loved us both. And he really did think that once you were over the initial shock, you'd come to accept it. That you loved him enough to make it work. And that we could all live our lives together. Except he couldn't go through with it. So he came up with another plan whereby he'd put the cottage up for rent and I'd pretend to be a random tenant."

"Fucker," I say and feel a swell of rage and sadness inside that makes me think of standing beside him in the projection room, watching that final movie on the screen.

"I know. And while I'd like to tell you it was him who backed down from that too . . . it was me. Hollis ordered that second house. Told you that story. Built the thing. But when I saw you—"

"At the hospital, after his first accident?"

"No. That happened much later. This was a long time ago.

One morning in the grocery store, of all places. I'd just come from your house. Your bed, I'm ashamed to say. I was in line, waiting to pay for animal crackers, since my mom had taken Janine for the night and I was on my way to pick her up. That's when I heard the cashier call the woman in front of me, Mrs. Hull. It was you, Skyla. You must have stopped on your way home from the hospital, because you were still in your uniform, the way you are now. I watched you help bag your groceries. You smiled at me, and I smiled back. And the moment changed everything for me. I mean, everything. Suddenly, you were . . . real."

"I wasn't real when you were sleeping in my bed?"

"Sorry. But no. You were always just this, I don't know, abstraction. But after that day, I couldn't go through with it. I moved to a new condo with Janine. I saw Hollis less often, though he still came around to see our daughter. And for sex sometimes, if I'm truthful, though it wasn't the same. That extra house sat empty. Hollis used it to—"

"Mom," a voice interrupts.

"Janine. I told you to play the machine until I'm done."

"But I'm out of quarters."

"Ok, sweetie. Let me get you some more."

"Don't do that," I say, trying hard not to picture the girl and which features of Hollis's she might have inherited. His steely blue eyes. His thin lips. I don't want to see her, even if it's only in my mind. "I've heard enough for a lifetime. We're done here."

"Are you sure, Skyla?"

"Unless you're about to tell me he kept a harem in the second cottage, rather than my romance novels and his fishing and camping equipment, then I'm good. We can go."

Must be close to one, which means Teddy will be back to fetch me soon.

I ask Maureen to help me out to the parking lot. The least she could do. And though she never actually introduces Janine, when I stand—wobbly, nauseated, dizzy now too, thinking perhaps those pills have had more effect than I realized—the girl takes my hand. We move through the maze of tables, me bumping into backs of chairs, past the pie carousel and counter I recall from previous visits. At the register, I stop to pay the bill, scattering a bowl of breath mints by mistake, and the manager informs me that my "gentleman friend" left cash to cover whatever we ordered.

"See how lucky I am," I say to Moo. "That cheap son of a bitch I married is rotting six feet under. But my new boyfriend is alive and well and generous as hell."

Yes, I'm aware there's a child present. But isn't it her mother's fault for dragging her daughter along to this PG-13 showdown of ours? Anyway, it doesn't seem to bother the girl, who begins peppering me with questions as we walk through the front vestibule, past that coin game with the weak claw and piles of tightly packed stuffed animals: "Did you ever see an operation where a person's guts are hanging out of their body? . . . Did you ever hold a beating heart in your hand? . . . Why are the uniforms white anyway?"

I don't bother answering the first two, but pounce on the last. "In the past, nurses wore dignified white dresses, caps, and nursing shoes. Today they wear all sorts of colors. Pink. Blue. A pukey peach I particularly despise. Opting for individuality and comfort, wearing clogs, Crocs, crop tops, and baggy pants, which I find downright sacrileg—"

"Do you have to wipe butts all day?" she asks, cutting me

off and exhibiting the same poor manners as the woman who raised her.

By then, we've made our way outside and down the steps. I hear the steady *whoosh* of cars speeding by on the main road. Feel the sun on my face, the air so warm you'd never know Christmas is just days away. "I've wiped my fair share," I tell the girl. "But you know what? I've kicked my fair share too."

She breaks into a fit of giggles, before I hear her making what I gather are karate kicks around that lot, shouting "*Kiai!*" as she goes.

"You'll have to excuse her," Moo tells me. "You know how kids are."

"I don't actually. Seeing as I never had any of my own."

I mean this as a statement of fact. Also, I mean it to make her feel despicable, which let's face it, she is. To guarantee the job is done properly, I add, "Oh, believe me, I wanted kids. But my husband always said he didn't. He thought our life would be easier without them. Less responsibility. Less expense. Less burden. Apparently, what he meant was that he just didn't want kids with me."

"Oh, Skyla. I'm sorry. I don't know what else to say. But I really am."

It's now or never, right?

I reach in my pocket.

Wrap my hand around the syringe, spin the cap with my thumb.

The person before me has done me wrong—so many times, so many ways. *Merry Christmas to me,* I think, gripping that syringe tighter. *Ho! Ho! Ho!* Santa came early and look what a glorious gift he gave: the corpse of my husband's more-than-a-mistress, the mother of his child no less!

But before I can take the syringe out of my pocket, Moo shouts to Janine to quit karate-chopping the dogwood at the edge of the lot. And I loosen my hold. Blame the simple fact of her daughter—Hollis's daughter—but I simply cannot bring myself to allow the girl to witness what it is I want to do to her mother.

Someday, I tell myself.

"Someday," I tell Maureen.

"Someday what?" she asks.

I don't answer, giving myself the pleasure of a moment to consider all the many dangers out there in this world waiting for her, waiting for all of us: the host of horrifying diseases . . . the slim but possible chance of a plane crash . . . the risk of a grisly car crash too, each and every time we climb into one of those wheeled metal boxes . . . the chance of choking on a wedge of grapefruit or bite of steak or getting struck down by a stray bullet, which seems more likely all the time in this world. Who knows which nightmare it'll be when her number's up? In the meantime, I pull something different from my pocket. "Take these, Maureen."

"What are . . . Wait . . . Skyla, are these . . . ?"

"Wedding rings. Hollis's and mine."

Maureen tries to push them back into my hand. "I don't want them."

"What a coincidence. Neither do I. If you give them back, I'll just toss them on the ground. So keep 'em. Apparently, you were as much a part of my marriage as me." Before she can respond, I pull something else from my pocket. "Hey!" I call, unable to bring myself to say her name. "Come over here! I've got something for you!"

The kid karates her way back to me, and I hold out the

monkey-faced finger puppet, a gift from her father some ten years late. Although she thanks me, I get the feeling that puppet is less exciting to her than my joke about kicking asses earlier. Even so, she tells me to hold out my hands, then places a fuzzy object in my palms. "It's a whale," she informs me as I feel the plump body, the wide tail, the glassy eyes. "I won it in the Crazy Claw. You can have it."

"Why, thank you. I'll be sure to fill the sink soon as I get home and let the creature swim."

"She's just a baby now. Get ready. She'll grow a hundred times bigger."

"When that happens, I'll fill the bathtub for her."

"What about when she grows a thousand times more?"

"Well, then I'll just have to get a swimming pool."

"And when she grows a million times more?"

"I'll have no choice but to release her into the ocean."

"Won't that make you sad?"

Funny, how sad I feel then. In some unexpected way, I sense an attachment forming with this girl, not unlike how I feel when those strays wander out of the woods behind the houses. I should know better. "It will," I tell her.

"Skyla," Maureen says, interrupting. "Are you sure you don't want us to wait with you?"

Maybe it's the pills at work, but I forgot her standing there. "I'm fine. My tenant—I mean, my boyfriend, he'll be back any minute to fetch me."

"Okay, then. I don't know about you, but strange as it sounds, I think it's good we did this. It's a relief to have some sense of closure, know what I mean?"

"I've always believed closure is important in life," I say, piling on one last lie.

With that, we say goodbye. Moo and the girl climb in the car with the monkey puppet and wedding rings I carried for so long. Doors slam. An engine starts. I listen as they pull out of the lot.

Once they're gone, I feel alone. Incredibly so. Standing by the busy road, holding that whale, the midday sun beats down until I'm sweating, all the more wobbly, nauseated and dizzy too. Cars speed by, a few honking at random. What sounds like a bratty teenage boy shouts, "Yo, sexy nurse! Can you take my rectal temperature?!"

"Come back here and I'll shove more than a thermometer up your scrawny ass!" I shout back, waving my arms frantically. Even though the car must be well past me I add, "You're fucking hilarious! You know that, you little prick?!"

That's when another voice, this one older, kinder, says, "Ma'am, are you okay? Do you need help?"

"Help?!" I shout. "Why would I need help?!"

"It's just . . . you seem agitated."

"Because you're agitating me! So leave me alone!!"

I hear the person hurry away, then reach for my cell. "Hey, Siri," I say, but she's silent. "Hey, Siri!" Still nothing. "Siri, I need you to do your job for a change! Tell me what time it is! Text Teddy asking where the hell he is! I need him to come get me!"

All that screaming does nothing to make her answer. I feel the way a magician must when a magic trick fails. The obvious question: What now? If I've chosen not to use that syringe, chosen to give away my wedding rings and finger puppet, what is left to bring me comfort? The matchbook: useless at the moment. The pills: I've had plenty. I'd hoped for an Ativan or another benzo to make me less tense, but judging from my muddled state, I worry I took a Haldol or, worse, Zyprexa.

I think of the letter, which never fails to calm me. Except this time, when I reach in my pocket and touch that envelope, none of the usual praise comes to life in my mind. Rather, what I hear is Teddy's voice, exactly as he began reading the other night:

Dear Ms. Skyla Hull, This letter is to notify you of your immediate term—

"No!" I shout. I keep shouting over the parts he did not read, at least not to me, parts I've shoved down, pretending the opposite was true, ever since I first saw them.

—ination. This decision is not reversible . . .

"No! No! No!"

. . . in direct violation of hospital policy, as follows . . .

"No! No! No! No! No!"

More cars pass, honking at the spectacle I've become.

"Fuck you!" I scream, waving the letter, waving the whale too. Frantically, I begin to move from parked car to parked car, touching the warm metal hoods, leapfrogging in this weird way until I feel the fake-stone facade of the diner. I trail a hand along the bumpy surface, rounding a corner, finding a shadier, more private spot, where I slump down, back sweating against the building. Try as I might, I can't stop the words of that letter from whipping around my mind.

. . . ADMINISTRATION OF MEDICATION WITHOUT A PHYSICIAN/NP/LIP ORDER!

I pull the matchbook from my pocket. Strike one of the remaining three matches.

. . . FALSIFICATION OF DOCUMENTATION IN REGARDS TO MEDICATION ADMINISTRATION!

It does not light. Again, I strike.

. . . FAILURE TO RESPOND TO ACUTE PATIENT DIS-

*TRESS WITH APPROPRIATE ACTION AS OUTLINED IN HOS-
PITAL POLICY!*

Nothing. Again, I strike.

*. . . GROSS NEGLIGENCE AND DERELICTION OF DUTY
RESULTING IN—!*

"Ma'am," another new voice says.

"Not now!" I scream. "None of it is true, you know! They
lied! They ganged up on me!"

"Ma'am," the voice repeats, stopping me this time. It's a
deep voice. Almost familiar.

"Hollis?" I look up, though of course I can't see him. "That
you?"

"No, ma'am. I'm Officer Keegan. This is my partner, Officer Ludgood."

"Oh. Forgive me. I thought maybe . . . Well, never mind.
Nice to meet you fellas."

Fellas is a mistake, I realize, since the next thing I hear is a
woman's voice. "Hello, ma'am."

"Amanda?" I say, picturing her bulging eyes, her tempest
of salt-and-pepper hair, her jack-o'-lantern mouth with its
missing teeth, open wide as she shrieks and thrashes in her
hospital bed. "Amanda Quigley?"

"Nope. Officer Ludgood. Would you mind telling us what
you're doing here?"

"Oh. Waiting for my husband. Would you mind telling me
what you're doing here?"

"Certainly. We got a call about someone behaving strangely
outside the diner."

"Must be someone else. Because like I said, I'm just waiting."

"The person was described as wearing a nurse's uniform,

so . . . Care to explain what you're attempting to do with those matches?"

Their presence, their questions too, at last silence that letter in my mind. I crumple the paper and press it to the pavement before shoving the matchbook in my pocket, careful to avoid the syringe. "I was just killing time. These matches are ancient. They don't light. And so you're aware, I have difficulty seeing. In fact, I don't see much of anything at all anymore. Just a great big blur that used to be trees and people and a life I thought I knew but apparently did not . . ." It would be sensible to stop there, but they make no effort to interrupt, so I keep going. I talk about Hollis. I talk about Moo. I talk about the old drive-in and how, when business reached its slowest in the early nineties, we used to rent the land to a traveling carnival each summer, how those rickety rides made me dizzy and downright vomitous, which is how I feel now. While I'm speaking, I hear a radio squawking from what must be their squad car. The staticky voice on that radio drones about an accident on Route 78. And when I quit blathering at last, the female officer asks, with more kindness, if I'd like to wait in the back of the car until my husband arrives.

"My husband? He's dead. Don't you read the paper? Freak accident. Deep in the woods behind our houses. One night, over a year ago now, he decided to—"

"Can you tell us your name?" the male officer with the low voice interrupts. When I tell him Skyla Hull he follows up by requesting my address and other basics, like my emergency contact, which I tell him is my nephew, John, who lives in New York City, though I can't remember his number. "Okay then, ma'am. We're going to help you stand up. Then we're going to help you over to the car, and you can wait there until we straighten this out. Understood?"

I don't recall answering, but just like that, their hands are on my body. I feel them lifting me, the sensation similar to those carnival rides I never cared for. I'm floating. I'm spinning. I'm laughing, though I feel quite ill. Then I imagine it's Hollis beside me, his hands on me too. I tell him: "I love you, Hollis" and "How dare you, Hollis" and "I'll kill you, Hollis."

This whirly-go-round of sentiments keeps up as the police officers help me toward the car, where that voice still drones on about the accident. "Maybe it's Moo," I say. "Maybe karma has already done its job. Oh, but the girl. Poor thing. If she survives, she can come live with me, seeing as Teddy wants to leave soon. Or maybe he's already left. Maybe he took my necklace of keys and went back to my house and raided the safe and stole everything. There are men out there who would do something that dastardly to an old woman. There are men out there, the one I married, in fact, who would—"

"Ma'am, please duck your head when we help you into the car. We don't want you to hurt yourself."

I'm about to do as told when there comes a rush of footsteps from behind, and I hear a voice calling, "Officers! Officers! Hold a moment please. What's going on here?"

"Teddy?" I say, straightening up, shaking the police off, feeling my feet return to earth. Spinning still, though not nearly as much. "Is that you?"

"Yes. It's me, luv."

"You're late," I say in a voice full of so much resentment it conceals the overwhelming relief I feel to have him back. "I've been waiting here for hours."

"No, Skyla. I'm right on time. It's one on the dot. Now please, tell me what's going on."

Is he asking the officers or me? Either way, I feel all talked out, so I let them do the explaining. After they inform him about the complaint, about the matches, about "certain confusing statements Ms. Hull was making," they ask Teddy for his name. Reluctantly, he gives it to them. I can tell they'd like nothing more than to turn the problem I've become over to him, so they can head inside for lunch. They make quick work of confirming that Teddy is indeed the person I've been waiting for, and then he takes my arm and guides me to his car.

My keys are waiting for me on the passenger seat. Once we're in the car, once that beaded chain is around my neck, once we are on the road again, heading home, Teddy lets out an exasperated breath and asks what happened back there.

"With the police? Or with Moo?"

"Both. But the police first, because I don't fancy dealing with the law. Why didn't you just text me if you finished early?"

"Siri," I say and hold up my cell. "The bitch was giving me the silent treatment."

He takes the phone from me. "Skyla, your mobile is dead. I should've checked the battery before dropping you off. Anyway, I'll hook it to the charger. Now what happened with Moo?"

"I'm tired. Don't feel like talking about it."

I expect him to push on the topic, but he lets it go. As we drive in silence, I lean my face against the window. Imagine passing more of those blow-up Christmas decorations on people's lawns: deflated Santas and Frostys and Rudolphs, old-fashioned nativity scenes. Then I picture Hollis and Maureen with their child. Such a perfect little family. "How could you?" I mumble.

"How could I what?"

"How could you lie to me?"

Hollis? Teddy? Whoever it is behind the wheel sighs, then tells me in a flat, somber voice, "I'm sorry I lied to you, Skyla. I had a feeling you'd figured things out, or at least were starting to put two and two together. I wanted to tell you. Believe me. I've been trying to find a way. But it's been a confusing situation for me too."

"Confusing for you! What about me? All these years! I don't even know where to begin. The extra house! The company delivering it by mistake! I can't believe I bought that bullshit story for so long. Never mind Janine! It's cruel! It's humiliating, Hollis!"

"Hollis? Oh dear, Skyla. I think you're confused. Listen, you've had quite a day. Maybe we shouldn't talk anymore. Let's get you home and into bed. We can discuss all this tomorrow after you've had some rest and your head is clear."

By then, we're turning off the main road onto the long dirt driveway. My heart is beating so hard and fast it must be more than anger, but the work of those pills I never should have taken. The car rocks side to side as we navigate potholes and gullies. When we come to a stop, he cuts the engine. We sit a moment, nothing but the sound of our breath in that car, pinwheels and windmills and other doodads out on the lawn making their usual racket in the breeze, the tattered screen at the drive-in flapping away. Finally, my mind focuses enough to ask in a quiet voice, "What lie were you talking about?"

He sighs. "Remember how I told you that I've done things I'm not proud of? Well, it's a lot to explain. My past. Who I am. How I came to be here. But like I said, best to save it for tomorrow."

Not Hollis, I think, realizing how much those pills have scrambled my mind.

Whatever it is about him, this man who came to rent my house, who took my hand and walked the woods with me, who danced with me, who held me, I'm not sure I want to know. I've had enough truth-telling to last a lifetime. "Tired as I am, let's go inside and play some Patsy. Have a dance. Have another hold too."

My suggestion is met with the usual silence, the longest so far. This time, however, I refuse to allow my mind to scold and shame me. After all, what's so wrong about wanting some attention and affection in this world? I reach into my pocket, looking for some comfort. My fingers touch something soft and I pull out the whale.

"What's that?" he asks in that flat, somber voice.

"What's it look like?"

"Oh. Did you know that blue whales have the largest hearts in the world, almost the size of a small car and weighing hundreds of pounds?"

"I did not. How do you know that anyway?"

"I just do."

"I see. So . . . shall we go dance and hold each other?"

"Skyla, I'm not sure those things are such a good idea anymore."

"And why not?"

"It just . . . doesn't seem appropriate is all." He opens his door and gets out, walking around to my side. The sound of his footsteps makes me think of Hollis's boots. Hollis's low voice. Hollis's steely blue eyes and thin lips. The bastard. But then, I remind myself, *Not Hollis.*

Which is followed by an odd thought, *Not Teddy either.*

"Here we go," he says, opening my door and leaning in to help me out.

"Who are you?" I ask.

"Pardon?"

"You're not Hollis. You're not Teddy. Who are you?"

"I told you, Skyla," he says, that jaunty accent gone from his voice as I've noticed so often, though. I should've spent more time wondering why. "Let's save all that for—"

The syringe. Ever so quickly, there's no time for him to realize what I'm doing, no time for him to try and stop me. I grab it. Jab the needle in his thigh. Push down on the plunger with my thumb. Send that liquid shooting into his bloodstream.

"What the fuck?!" he screams, jerking away from me.

I pull the door closed and pound my fist down on the lock. Reach across the driver's seat and scrabble around until I've hit all the locks. "Who are you?" I ask again. "Who are you?"

I hear him out there, banging on the glass, yelling. But minutes pass and, eventually, the banging slows, finally so much so that I feel brave enough to open the door. That's when his body slumps forward, startling me as he falls like some sloppy drunk on my lap. Beneath the weight of him, I scream, "Tell me who you are! Tell me! Who are you?"

Before going silent and still, the last thing the man says is, "Jeremy. My name is Jeremy."

FOURTEEN

"I haven't lived a good life. I've been bad.
Worse than you know."

—From *The Maltese Falcon*, shown at the Schodack Big-Star Drive-in,
August 1941

HOW IMPOSSIBLY DARK THOSE WOODS had been when he parked the Lincoln on a nearby street and hurried toward the playground, without a flashlight, trespassing through a random backyard, past an aboveground swimming pool where a filter hummed and blow-up rafts drifted about, before slipping into the blackness between the trees.

Jeremy had bled that night too. Not his face, but his knees, when he tripped and fell while navigating his way toward the edge of the playground. After getting up, his eyes adjusted to the darkness, so that he could make out the rocks and gullies and unearthed roots and fallen branches underfoot. And when he reached a spot among the trees with a view to the seesaws and sandbox and the parking lot beyond, Jeremy found himself making a game of defining the shapes around him. Tractor tire. Safety cone. Soda bottles. A surprising amount of junk had been abandoned in the woods and, with nothing to do but wait, he cataloged it for no good reason, until head-lights splashed against the tree trunks and swept over the can-opy of leaves above.

Dan's truck, Jeremy saw, was rolling into the lot. He watched the vehicle swing around and come to a stop beneath the teth-erball pole. The headlights glared against the windows at the rear of the school building, all the windows empty except for one decorated with oversize construction-paper letters, fac-ing backward from this angle. As Dan waited for Maryanne, his radio broadcasting a Red Sox game, his cigarette burning red, Jeremy studied those backward letters.

SELIM. REPIP. YNAHTEB.

MILES. PIPER. BETHANY.

Names, he assumed, of the children who occupied that classroom. By the time he had worked out all but the few ob-scured by the glare, he could hear a stereo in the distance, thumping with the bass of the Gap Band—"You dropped a bomb on me, baby! You dropped a bomb on me!" Just the thought of Maryanne playing that song without him felt like a betrayal, even though Jeremy knew he had no right to that feeling. It was not their song. She was not his girlfriend. He should not even have come here in the first place. And yet, he could not keep himself away.

The song grew louder, and the Tiramisu's headlights swept over the tree trunks and leaves. Jeremy's heart picked up speed. The sensation grew so powerful that he placed a hand on his chest and felt it there, a fist knocking inside. He watched as Maryanne swung her car around and parked by Dan's truck. For a moment, both sets of headlights lit up that classroom window, shifting the glare in such a way that he glimpsed those few remaining names.

YDNIM. NAYR. EOZ.

MINDY. RYAN. ZOE.

They cut their engines. No more headlights. No more names. No more Red Sox. No more Gap Band. In the silence and darkness that followed, Jeremy worried he wouldn't be able to hear or see them. But then, in the moonlight, some thirty-odd feet away, he watched their silhouettes as they stepped outside and slammed their doors. They walked toward each other, pressed their bodies together, kissing and groping. Jeremy felt his heart knocking harder still. Every last part of him regretted having come, but he did not dare retreat for fear the branches breaking beneath his feet might lead to the humiliation of his being discovered. And so, he stood motionless among the trees, watching Dan maneuver Maryanne back toward the Tiramisu, where he pressed her down on the hood.

Soon he was tugging off her top.

Soon after that, he was unfastening her bra.

Soon he was peeling off the leggings she always wore, then slipping her underwear down her thighs and knees and calves and feet until, at last, she was naked.

For all Dan's effort to undress Maryanne, the most he did was yank his shirt over his head, exposing his muscular chest with a thatch of black fur at the center, before undoing his jeans and shoving them down, along with his underwear.

Jeremy felt overcome by a sickening sense of breathlessness, mingled in some strange and undeniable way with a kind of exhilaration. That mix of feelings, he worried, gave a clear indication that there was something wrong with him, the way his mother always said, the way those troublesome doctors from his youth once speculated too. But still, he did not retreat. And as Dan reached down to adjust himself in order to enter Maryanne, Jeremy found himself reaching down too. He found himself opening his jeans and taking himself out. His imagination grew feverish with the fantasy that he was the one giving Maryanne so much pleasure on the hood of that car, that he was the one making her moan the way she did, that he was the one grunting on top of her, pushing himself into her, burying his face in her breasts the way Dan did with such abandon.

When it was over, for all three of them, Jeremy wiped his hands on his jeans and zipped up again. Dan hiked up his jeans too, but kept his shirt off. Maryanne started to dress, clumsily pulling on her underwear and bra. But that's as far as she went. Jeremy had spent enough nights drinking with Maryanne to recognize when she was well on her way to being drunk, and the meandering, almost sluggish manner in which she moved to the open window of the Tiramisu made him realize that was the case now. He watched her lean inside the car and fish around, eventually pulling out a bottle of scotch. That feeling of betrayal swelled again, since it was what they drank during their nights together—likely the very same bottle they'd shared the evening before. After taking a swig, she handed it to Dan, who did the same. That's when Maryanne looked over at the moonlit slide and motionless swings dangling from their chains, sizing them up.

MILES. PIPER. BETHANY.

None of those children were inside the classroom at that moment—of course they weren't—but Jeremy could not stop imagining their small faces pressed to the window, their tiny hands perched visor-style above their foreheads, their puffs of breath fogging the glass as they watched and wondered about what things that man and woman were doing in their playground after dark.

"We should get dressed," Dan said. "If a cop swings through here, it won't be cool for either of us."

Jeremy had given Maryanne similar warnings on nights when she drove a little too fast or took a turn a little too sharply, so he knew it only translated into a kind of dare for her, compelling her to go faster, to turn sharper. Sure enough, she laughed. "Cool your jets," she told Dan. "I want to have a little more fun first." And then she began walking into the playground, past the monkey bars and on toward the slide.

MINDY. RYAN. ZOE.

While Maryanne climbed the ladder, Jeremy held the image of those children watching still, same as him, and same as Dan now too. When she reached the top, Maryanne looked back at Dan, stretching her arms skyward in the shape of a V and laughing again. "And now for my world-famous, half-naked, twisted-tuck, inward-reverse pike!"

Dan shook his head and laughed as Maryanne positioned her legs in front and gave herself a push down the slide. Like so many slides, this one was not nearly slippery enough, which led to her skidding and stalling, the situation made worse no doubt by her bare skin. She did not allow that to ruin her fun, however, and kept releasing howls of laughter, shoving her body back into motion until she reached the bottom. That's where Dan met her, offering a hand to help her stand. But Maryanne pulled him down to her instead. Soon, they were kissing and groping each other once more. Jeremy had seen enough—at least that's what he told himself—and yet, he kept right on watching until they moved to the grass, lying side by side, staring up at the moon and the stars, not unlike the way he and Maryanne did on the blanket in her living room.

After sipping from the bottle, then handing it to Dan, Maryanne said, "Nice. Isn't it?"

If Dan responded with more than a grunt, Jeremy did not hear. He couldn't help but think how different things would be if it had been him beside her. For starters, Jeremy would have at least agreed how nice it was to be lying there together under the nighttime sky. He might also have pointed out the handful of constellations he knew, thanks to his father, who used to love looking up at them from wherever they happened to be living around the country—the sky a more anchoring presence for him than the earth. Or, Jeremy thought, he might have gone so far as to softly sing to her that old lullaby his mother used to sing to him on starry nights:

Tout le monde est sage, dans le voisinage, Il est l'heure d'aller dormer, le sommeil va bientôt venir. . . .

All the world is wise, in the neighborhood, It is time to go to sleep, sleep will come soon . . .

"Something wrong?" Maryanne asked Dan.

"Nope," he told her.

After that, they passed the bottle back and forth between them, not saying much of anything. Eventually, Maryanne rolled onto her side and faced him. She put a hand on his chest, playing with the forest of hair there. "I just realized what's going on in your head, Dan."

"You did? Well, hell, if I'd known you were psychic, I'd have asked for your help when I went to Atlantic City last month. I lost a shit ton of money."

Maryanne gave his chest a slap. "You should've told me.

Because I'm a little psychic sometimes. But this is more of a guess."

"Okay, then. Let's hear it."

"Well, something tells me you're lying there thinking, 'I hope she remembers I have a wife, and that even though we just had some pretty hot sex, I hope she knows it can't be anything more than that.'"

Dan did not respond immediately, and Maryanne did not prod. Instead, she lay back and stared up at the sky again. The Big Dipper. The Gemini Twins. Orion. Jeremy imagined pointing them out, until Dan rolled onto his side, propped his head on one hand, and reached over to stroke her breasts with his other hand.

"So how'd I do?" Maryanne asked.

"Let's just say I'm glad I didn't ask for your help at the blackjack table."

"I was wrong? Well, it's not the first time. But now that we're on the subject, I don't want you to worry. I know what this is between us. I'm not stupid."

Dan dipped his head to kiss her breasts, saying something into them that Jeremy did not catch. When he came up again, he touched her chin with his fingers, touched her lips too. "Listen, this situation between you and me, it's pretty cool. So long as things stay casual, you know? Like you said, I've got my wife. And even though it makes me crazy, from what I can tell, you've got something going on with Jeremy."

"Jeremy?" Maryanne sat up, and Dan sat up too. He reached for the scotch, taking a final swig and then hurling the empty bottle into the woods with such force it was as though he knew Jeremy was there and had made a target out of him. The thing came rocketing through the leaves, spitting through the air not far from Jeremy's head, landing with a dull thud on the dirt over by the tractor tire.

When Jeremy turned his attention back to the playground, Maryanne was saying, "It's not like that between me and Jer."

Dan laughed. "Come on! You expect me to believe that?"

"Actually, I do."

"Okay, then. I get it. You're one of those girls."

"One of what girls?"

"One of those girls who knows a guy has a big ol' boner for her but conveniently pretends not to notice, because she knows damn well that if she shoots the dude down, she'll end up losing out on all the attention and whatever else he gives her. So tell me, now who's the psychic?"

"Fuck you!" Maryanne stood, brushing all the stray blades of grass from her pale legs.

"Would you look at that?"

"Look at what?"

"We're together no more than thirty minutes and already we're having our first fight. I think this might be a record."

"Very funny," she said.

"Apparently not. Anyway, forget I said anything. It's none of my business."

"Well, you're right about that much at least."

Jeremy watched as Maryanne looked over at the school, where he pictured those children huddled by the darkened window, looking right back at her. It might have been the moment when she chose to head to the Tiramisu, to gather her leggings and pastel top and go. But instead, Maryanne turned to Dan. "You're right about something else too. Jeremy kissed me last night. Tried to, anyway. But I made it clear I'm not interested."

Dan was quiet, mulling that over. "And why aren't you?"

"The question is, why do you care? You jealous or something?"

"Maybe," Dan said. "Actually, now that I know the little pecker put the moves on you it's more than a maybe. It's a yes. I should rip his dick off."

"Might I remind you that you're married? You don't have any right to be jealous, never mind ripping anyone's dick off."

"I have a right to fire his ass if I feel like it."

Maryanne let out a huff. "Just cut it out already. I told you, I'm not interested. Believe me, I let that be known last night."

"And that brings me back to my question: Why aren't you interested?"

Again, Maryanne huffed. "Do I really have to explain?"

Dan didn't give an answer, at least not right away. He simply waited, staring up at Maryanne, who occupied herself with peeling away more of those stray blades. "Wouldn't hurt," he said, finally. "I mean, if you want the dude to keep his job and all."

"You're being a total jerk right now, you know that?" Maryanne waved a hand at him, as though she'd had enough, and in that same meandering way, began walking toward the swings.

Maryanne did not so much sit on a swing as she did slump into it. The seat was made of rubber, and it hugged her ass while she wrapped her arms around the thick chains. At first, she just kicked out her legs and leaned back, staring up at the moon and stars. Futile as it was, Jeremy could not keep his mind from the final gasping thoughts of what this night might have been if only he was in the playground with her. In that alternate version of the evening, the two of them would be laughing and flirting. Jeremy would go beyond the constellations and that French lullaby; he would recite poetry from his lit classes at Brown:

> Art thou pale for weariness
> Of climbing heaven and gazing on the earth,
> Wandering companionless
> Among the stars that have a different birth . . .

But what woman wanted a man who recited poetry anymore, never mind one who knew constellations and could trot out French? What woman even wanted a man who was single and available and actually nice? None that he knew. Jeremy told himself to cool it with those outdated thoughts of chivalry. Not only did Maryanne not want poetry; she did not want him. If ever there was proof, he had just seen and heard it with his own eyes and ears. And yet, Jeremy wondered, how does a person turn off his heart? How does a person simply discontinue the feeling of wanting someone when that wanting is not returned? He knew with utmost certainty that the remedy had nothing to do with playing witness to her tryst with another man. Still, though, he did not move.

"Aren't you at least going to give a girl a push?" Maryanne called out.

Dan stood and went to her, gripping the chains with his big hands, pulling her farther and farther backward until it seemed the swing might break if he pulled any more. At last he let go. Maryanne sailed forward and upward with such momentum it looked as though she might come rocketing through the leaves toward Jeremy same as that bottle had. But then the swing reached its limit, and she swung down and backward toward Dan. When she reached him, he gave her a good hard push, sending her sailing in Jeremy's direction once more.

Up and down, back and forth, toes up, toes down, pointing to the moon, pointing to the earth—that's how it went. At first, the sounds Maryanne made were not so terribly different from the simple cries of pleasure any of those girls—PIPER, BETHANY, MINDY, ZOE—might have made on that swing. But the higher and faster things became, the more reckless and shrill her laughter became. "Okay!" she called to Dan finally. "Okay! Okay! You can stop now! Or at least quit pushing so hard!"

"Not until you tell me," Dan said as she swung closer.

"Tell you?" she shouted, zooming away from him, then zooming right back again. "Tell you what?"

"Why you're not interested in Jeremy!"

"You're still stuck on that?" she screamed, a boomerang effect happening with her voice, which grew louder as she came, then softer as she went. "You're really insane, you know that?"

Dan's only response was to shove her harder. The force and momentum led her to release a shriek of nervous laughter. But her laughter came to an abrupt stop when she must have realized, as Jeremy did too, that she really was going to have to tell him in order to make him slow down.

And so, she began with this: "Okay. For starters, on a most basic level, there's his name!"

"Crater Face?"

"No, you idiot!" Her voice boomeranged as she moved forward and back, up and down. "I mean, his actual name:

Jeremy Lichanel! Jeremy Fucking Lichanel! Think about it: if you say it the way it's spelled it sounds like Lick Anal!"

Dan laughed, but that response was not enough to satisfy him, because he kept pushing, sending Maryanne hurtling toward the woods again. Jeremy watched, his mouth dry, his heart pounding still harder, as he glimpsed the bottoms of her splayed feet each time she went skyward, the soles dirty from all her parading around the playground with her heels kicked off.

"Beyond that basic fact," she called, when Dan gave her yet another push and she shrieked into the night, "all anyone has to do is look at—"

"Stop it!" Maryanne says in her shadowy kitchen some twenty years later, her voice jerking Jeremy back to the here and now with as much force as that swing. In the present of Maryanne's kitchen, Pretty still circles, her nails making a *tap-tap-tap* on the oak floor. Bingo barks and scratches down the hall, the sound growing so loud it has taken on a downright ghoulish quality. "Just stop it, Jeremy!" Maryanne shouts. "Stop talking! I don't want to hear any more!"

"Why don't you want to hear any more?" Jeremy says in a voice far calmer than hers. "Is it because you remember what happened next, Maryanne?"

Her dress is still giving her problems, and she seems determined to get it back on. When she reaches her arms around again, struggling to do up the zipper, he thinks of the way she used to wrench the arms from the mannequins, temporarily amputating them before reattaching new limbs. "Of course I don't remember, Jeremy! It was ages ago. I was drunk, just as you described. Whatever it was I said next, I didn't mean it. Enough is enough. Let's call it a night."

But no part of Jeremy believes that she doesn't remember. And no part of him is ready to call it a night. Not yet. He begins speaking again, working that spell, filling the kitchen with the memory of all that he saw and heard while standing in those woods behind that playground so many years ago. And sure enough, in another instant, there she is, flickering back to life before them, drunkenly swinging in her bra and underwear as Dan pushes her harder and she tells him what he wants to know.

"Beyond that basic fact, all anyone has to do is look at Jeremy! I mean, how could someone like him even think someone like me would want to kiss him. I'm telling you, when he tried last night it was all I could do not to—"

"Please, Jeremy!" Maryanne shouts now, doing her best to break the spell.

But Jeremy does not stop. She will relive it all again, that much he is determined to make happen, just as he has relived it so many nights since.

"It was all I could do not to vomit! I'd rather—"

"I told you to stop, Jer! I'm begging you to stop!"

"I'd rather lick the scum off every last one of those filthy dummies when they get dumped at the warehouse at the end of the Christmas season! I mean, can you imagine? Can you fucking imagine? It's so disgusting. He's just so—"

"No more, Jer! Please, no more!"

"Ugly! He's just so unbelievably ugly! That skin. That face. I mean, his mother should have—"

"Stop it! I don't want you to say any more!"

"His mother should have given him away!"

"Please!"

"His mother should have put him in the middle of the

highway and run him over. In fact, maybe she did and that's why his face looks the way it does! What's that saying about a face only a mother can love? Well, I bet he's the one exception to the rule in the entire fucking world, because I doubt even his own mother loved looking at him!"

In that playground all those years ago, Maryanne was laughing. Dan was laughing too. Soon he quit pushing, and soon the swing came to a stop, and they began kissing again. As for Jeremy, he looked away from the sight, toward that school window where moments before he had imagined those sweet children. He did not imagine them there anymore. And then he turned and ran, sticks snapping beneath his feet, prickers catching on the cuffs of his jeans. He ran past that old tractor tire. Past the safety cone and soda bottles. Over the rocks and gullies and fallen branches. On through the woods and between the trees, large and small, out into that random backyard, past the aboveground swimming pool, where the filter hummed and blow-up rafts drifted about, and down the dark street of that sleepy neighborhood to where the Lincoln waited.

In that kitchen on Angell Street all those years later, Jeremy finishes telling that story. During the final moments, Maryanne pours herself over the butcher block and covers her ears. Her dress has slipped down her arms, nearly to her elbows now, her back exposed more than ever before. She's crying, making small whimpering sounds like the ones Pretty made in the backseat of the Lincoln on the drive to Rhode Island just the day before.

At last, Maryanne speaks up, though without lifting her head. In a muffled voice, weighted with sadness and regret, she says, "Oh my god, Jer. Oh my god. I was young. I was drunk.

I was cruel. I didn't mean it. I didn't mean any of it. Dan was jealous of you and me. I was just trying to prove to him I had no interest in you. I was trying to make it so he wouldn't fire you."

"I see," Jeremy says. "So you said those things to protect me, is that right?"

"Yes," she tells him. "That's right."

"How nice of you, Maryanne. But that also means you actually do remember saying it all, unlike the claim you made before that you did not? So tell me: Which is true?"

Slowly, Maryanne lifts her head and looks at Jeremy. Mascara runs in inky black streaks down her face. Despite that, despite everything, she looks beautiful to him. *She won't ever know what it's like to be ugly,* Jeremy thinks again.

"I remember," she says. "I wish I didn't, because who wants to remember doing something so hurtful to someone they love? Not me. But the sad truth is that I do, Jer. And I'm sorry. You will never know how much."

Just as he had done in the woods on that long-ago summer night, Jeremy reaches up and puts a hand to his chest, not because his heart is pounding so hard, but because he feels it—he really does feel it—break. Jeremy looks down at his feet and pictures his heart shattering like Tiffany's snow globes. And then he pictures the sad details of his life down there in miniature, spilled out like the scenes in those snow globes too: the futon where he sleeps, the stack of *Playboy*s on his nightstand, a freezer full of frozen pizzas, his crappy TV where he watches eighties movies no one cares about anymore, the seven flights of stairs he climbs day after day, and of course, the Lincoln—a car he has driven for nearly twenty years, despite the leaky battery and faulty engine and its other myriad problems. Thinking about what all his time on earth has amounted to leads Jeremy to move his feet, as though kicking it all away.

Maryanne remains stretched over the butcher block, face down again, her back rising and falling as she weeps. When Pretty dashes by, Jeremy thrusts out an arm for her so they can be on their way. But the dog dodges out of reach. The next time she passes, he flings out an arm again. And the same thing happens: she dodges out of reach. For the time being, Jeremy gives up on Pretty.

"So," he says to Maryanne's shapeless form. If not for the motion of her back, she might have been one of those broken mannequins. "Now that we've unpacked every last unpleasant truth between us, I want you to do something for me."

Maryanne lifts her head again and stares at him with that inky face and those watery red eyes. "Anything, Jer. Anything so long as you don't leave here hating me."

"I want you to look at me and tell me to my face that the reason you don't want to kiss me, that you can't love me in some romantic and physical way, is because of the way I look."

"No. I won't say that, Jeremy. It isn't true."

"It is, Maryanne."

She shakes her head.

"Say it. Say it's because of my face."

She is quiet.

"Say it!" he screams. "Say that the reason you cannot love me is because I'm ugly. You said it that night on the swing. Say it now."

For a long while, she is silent, staring at the butcher block. Bingo scratches and barks. Pretty circles, dashing out of reach when he tries once more to grab her. And then, Maryanne wipes her cheeks, mascara streaking in all directions. She looks at him with those big brown eyes. "Okay, then. The reason I can't kiss you, that I can't love you in that way, is because of your face."

"Because I'm ugly?" Jeremy says.

"Because you're ugly," she tells him.

"Thank you. That's the last bit of truth I wanted tonight."

Again, Pretty zips past. Again, Jeremy thrusts out an arm to grab her. Again, the dog dodges his reach. To say he's had enough would be an understatement, and so Jeremy scoops up her collapsible bowls and heads toward the door. If Maryanne calls to him as he clomps down the stairs and around the side of the house, he does not hear. He is too lost in his thoughts, and his thoughts are this: that, as with all the medications people take, there should come a list of possible side effects from simply trying to make your way in this world. Jeremy is thinking specifically about the risks that befall anybody trying to find love and value in one's self, while trying to create art, or even just trying to pay your bills and feed yourself and walk down the sidewalk without some clueless stranger ruining your day.

Jeremy pushes open the gate and steps onto Angell Street, considering, Possible side effects of life: Broken heart! Or worse, a hardened heart! Unfulfilled dreams! Unshakeable memories of cruel things people said and did that haunt you at night! Moments of insufferable loneliness! Fear of death! Longing for youth! A desire to hurt the person who hurt you and to make that person feel as horribly as you felt!!

Oh, how that list goes on, Jeremy thinks. *It really does go on and on.*

These are the thoughts that race around as Jeremy arrives

at the Lincoln. When he pops open the trunk and reaches in for the slip leash, he is careful not to touch that ancient, leaky battery, remembering the mechanic's warnings. He unwraps the slip leash. But then his hands freeze. Standing there, staring down at the leash and battery, Jeremy thinks that some people in this world will find love, they will find value, they will make a legacy for themselves, make beautiful art and leave the world a better place, or they will simply make a paycheck or make themselves a sandwich and get by without inflicting too much damage on themselves or anybody else. But it is too late for any such hopeful outcome for him, Jeremy Lichanel.

Frappadingue! his mother hisses in his mind. *There is something wrong with you! You disgust me!*

Jeremy's mind and Jeremy's hands move back and forth between what he now sees as the two choices that remain for him. This goes on for some time until, at last, he considers Pretty's collapsible bowls in his trembling hand. He takes what he needs from the trunk, and slams it shut.

Jeremy turns and walks back down the sidewalk, then through the gate, then around back, then up the stairs. Inside, he finds only Pretty in the kitchen. But the sound of him entering leads Maryanne to appear through the swinging door. Bingo tries to follow her, but she shoves the dog back, pressing her body to the door to keep him from breaking through. Quite unexpectedly, she's changed into a simple white nightgown that falls to her knees. Jeremy looks at her legs a moment. They appear as pale and lovely in the moonlight as they did that evening on the playground when he watched her peeling away so many blades of wet grass.

Behind her, Jeremy sees the dog's ghoulish shadow moving frantically back and forth at the bottom of the door, its tongue licking at the floor, its teeth bared now too. All of that leads Pretty to circle the island still faster, round and round, again and again.

"I'm glad you came back," Maryanne tells him. "I really am. Let's start over. Let's calm down and try things one more time. I treated you badly. I see that now. But there must be some way we can work things out."

Jeremy steps from the shadows. He thinks of beautiful things. Those priests out on the Atlantic, watching whales crest and dive and slap their tails. The wondrous sights his parents must have seen on that trip to Provence, sights he has dreamed of seeing for himself ever since. Fields of sunflowers and fragrant lavender. Children talking in little French voices, saying such sweet words like *beau* and *jolie* and *charmant*. He thinks of his face and the way it will look when the last of the dead skin peels away in another few days, on his way to something even a tiny bit closer to beautiful, though he knows he'll never truly get there. And in his hand, he grips the choice he carried with him from the trunk. He steps closer to Pretty. He steps closer to Maryanne.

At last, the dog stops circling. She lets out a loud and alarming yelp. Eyes wide, Maryanne asks in her girlish voice, "What's that, Jeremy? What's that in your hand?"

Now you'll know, Jeremy thinks.

"Now you'll know," Jeremy says.

And in this way, she knows.

FIFTEEN

"A man lost in the mazes of his own mind may imagine
that he's anything."

—From *The Wolf Man*, shown at the Schodack Big-Star Drive-in,
August 1941

IT'S BEEN YEARS SINCE I had to lift a body, years since I had
to move one from place to place. In my early days as a nurse,
before I switched to the psych ward, I did time in the ER and
PACU. There, I was forever lifting people off gurneys and
onto examining tables, off examining tables and onto beds,
off beds and onto chairs or toilets. Manageable, if the patient
was a featherweight, a hell of a lot tougher when the person
packed some pounds. That's the case with Teddy. Or Jeremy.
Or whoever this man is, slumped on top of me in the passenger seat of his car.

I take a moment to calibrate. His breath is slow and shallow. I have some time, though maybe not much, before he re-
gains consciousness. The first thing I need to do is reposition
his body. I give him a good hard shove. He falls backward,
landing on the dirt driveway. I stand. Step over him. Straighten
my dress. Take a deep breath and then bend down and rifle

around his pockets, producing a wallet and phone, a couple of necklaces. I feel a small cross on one, a narrow pendant I can't identify on the other. Tossing all that on the seat in the car, I do my best to get my bearings. He probably parked in the same spot as before, which means I can't be far from my front door.

"Hey, Siri," I call out, overwhelmed by it all.

"Yes, Skyla," she answers from inside the car, freshly charged and raring to go.

"What should I do now?"

"I'm afraid I don't know what you should do."

"Thanks," I say. "You're a big help. As always."

Every part of me wants to make my way inside, twist the deadbolt, and climb into bed, skip the rest of this day and night, skip Christmas and New Year's and the rest of my life as well. But leaving the man out here in the driveway seems unwise. So I do what I would have on the ward when a patient rolled in unconscious from an opioid OD. One hand beneath his nose, another on his chest, I count his breaths, slower and shallower than I first realized: a troubling ten breaths per minute. I press my index and middle fingers to his inner wrist, below the base of his thumb, feeling the sluggish *thump-thump*, confirming his radial pulse is problematic too. Making a fist, I press my knuckles to his sternum and rub with great force, shouting, "Hey! Hey you!" These disruptive stimuli might cause his eyes to flutter open and shut—a good sign—but I can't gauge that. Instead, I listen for even a remote verbal response. Not so much as a grunt.

If this was happening in the hospital, I could do any number of things to help him. But this is not the hospital. Far from it. And so, for the time being, I leave him and Siri behind.

Make my way through that minefield of pinwheels and wind-mills and all the rest, stepping on, over, and around, tripping more than once, though I manage not to fall. At last I arrive at my door. Inside, I run the faucet. Shove my lips beneath the stream of water, gulping, my mouth dry as a box of cotton swabs thanks to those pills. After, I sit on the sofa, rocking back and forth, my mind spinning in all directions.

Past, present, future—they all seem equally dangerous to contemplate. I suppose that's why I get up again. Why I begin pacing my little house. Familiar as it is to me, I bump into chairs and tables anyway, knocking objects from shelves, pictures from walls. Hands deep in my pockets, touching whatever's left there, I mumble what must sound like a sin-gle, mashed-up, runaway train of a question: "Who is he why did he come here where is the Teddy I knew was he ever the Teddy I knew the one who loves me the one who I love too the one I danced with and walked in the woods with and shared so many dinners with why did he come here and why did he want me to see Maureen and what about that woman Linelle from his past and who is Jeremy anyway and why and why and why . . . ?"

Finally, I come to a stop in the bathroom. I stare at the mirror above the sink, imagining my withered face in the re-flection. I suck a good number of deep breaths into my lungs, before saying to the murky image in the mirror, "You've got to calm down, Skyla. You've got to get a grip and take control of this situation."

Somehow, this self-imposed pep talk makes me feel more stable. I make my way back to the living room and yank a wool blanket from the back of the couch. Hunt down my stetho-scope, my sphygmomanometer, a fresh syringe, and a vial of fentanyl too, just in case. Outside, I zigzag back to the car and that near-motionless body sprawled on the ground. Laying my hands on him once more, I determine there's been no change in breathing, no change in pulse. I wrap the blood pressure cuff around his upper arm, place the stethoscope over the brachial artery, listen to the *woosh-woosh-woosh* of blood pumping, concluding that both his systolic and diastolic pressure are low. Best to get him inside, where I can monitor his vitals while making preparations to protect myself should he come to.

I lay the blanket beside his body and roll him onto it. Gripping the corners, I muster every bit of strength and pull. At first, he barely budges. I tighten my hold, shift my feet, try again. Ever so slowly, I begin to drag him across the driveway, my hands quivering with the weight. Every minute or less, I need to stop. To catch my breath. To wipe sweat from my neck. To wonder what the hell I'm doing.

The porch step of the matching house surprises me; I bump against it and fall backward. My head whacks against the porch railing as I go down. For a long while, I lie on the step in a daze, feeling a lump rise on the back of my skull, feeling a trickle of blood move along my scalp and down around my left ear. Finally, I wipe the blood with my hand, grab the man's wrists and heave him up onto the porch, leaving the blanket behind. I feel for the key around my neck and unlock the front door.

I don't want a landlord marching through my private space . . .

It's been six weeks, give or take, since that November morning when he showed up here and spoke those words to me. Out of respect for his wishes, I always made a point of inviting him to my place instead of coming here. What's been going on under this roof and between these walls?

"Hello!" I call out. "Hello!"

Some part of me can't help hoping to hear Teddy's voice in reply, hoping the last hour was nothing but some strange, dark delusion brought on by those pills. After all, I've seen it countless times on the ward: patients, under the influence of any number of drugs, calling out to people who weren't there, reliving or just plain hallucinating the most harrowing events in their minds.

"Hello?" I call again, this time saying the word like a question.

Alas, no answer comes. The silence that greets me drains any remaining reserves of my energy. I'm exhausted, plain and simple. I leave the man there on the floor just inside the door and begin searching for Hollis's hunting and fishing equipment, banging my elbows and shins as I do. Eventually, I manage to dredge up a few feet of rope from those boxes. I never was a Girl Scout, but that doesn't stop me from doing my damnedest to tie the man, by the ankles for now, to the nearest thing I can find, which happens to be an old wooden rocking chair.

No, it won't stop him from moving.

Yes, it will slow him down a bit.

All I want is some advantage should I need one when and if he comes to.

What time is it when I finish with my lumpy mess of knots? Outside, the air is quiet, no trace of chirping birds, so I figure it's nearing dusk. A guess that cannot be confirmed by Siri, since my cell is still in the car. *Go get it*, I tell myself, even as I sit in the rocker. *The car door is wide open, so go get it. Go get it.*

"Hello! . . . Mrs. Hull? . . . Hello!"

I open my eyes. The voice is the slightest bit familiar. I also hear persistent knocking. Close at first, then farther away. I fell asleep, I realize, though for how long I could not say.

"Hello! Mrs. Hull?"

My hand goes to the back of my head. That lump, larger and more tender than before. The blood in my hair, sticky now. That's when I remember: the syringe, the host of worrisome vitals, the body at my feet. I thrust a hand down, fearing two opposing outcomes: I'll find him dead or I'll find him gone. To my relief, my fingers touch his ankles. I do a check of his tibialis posterior pulse, which, upon palpating, I gauge is far better than—

"I'm alive, if that's what you're attempting to determine."

The sound of him speaking so suddenly startles me. I gasp, flinch in my chair. Quickly as I can, I scramble to my feet and move across the room.

"Don't worry, Skyla," he says in the voice I recognize as that deflated, somber one Teddy used when discussing something sad, like how certain people can make you feel exquisite and others can make you feel ugly, or the regrettable things he'd done in his life, things he never specified to me, things I should have wondered more about. "I'm not going to try to hurt you. I'm not going to try to escape either."

Why not? That's what I intend to say, but what comes out is the same question I asked before he blacked out: "Who are you?"

That irksome knocking interrupts. The vaguely familiar voice calls, "Hello! Mrs. Hull?"

"Looks like we've got a visitor," he says. "You might want to find out who it is."

I hear the static chirp of a radio outside just then. A police radio. All at once, I understand: the female officer from the diner. That's who's out there. Calling to me. Knocking on the door to the other cottage.

"She's been at it awhile now, Skyla. Something tells me she's not skedaddling anytime soon. It started on this door, then moved over to your—"

"Oh, shut up! She can wait!" The man is so many things to me at the moment—my tenant, my victim, my patient, my prisoner, my passion, my mystery—that I can't help but keep my focus on him. "Now what I want to know is, are you Teddy?"

"I'm afraid not."

Those words are what I expect to hear. And yet, they do something wretched to my heart anyway, because I don't want to lose Teddy. I don't want to lose the tenderness and closeness we shared. I don't want to lose the hope and joy and excitement he brought into my life. Most of all, I don't want to go back to feeling unloved. Of course, I say none of this out loud. Instead, I tell him, "Then zip your fucking lips, asshole. Understood?"

His silence sends the message that he does. I step over his lump of a body, open the door just enough to slip onto the porch, and shut it tight behind me. The birds are chirping once again. A gentle sunshine warms my skin. It must be morning. Apparently, I slept in that rocker all night.

The temperature is cooler than yesterday, and I cross my arms against the chill, pasting a big smile on my face and calling in a breezy voice toward my house, "Good morning."

"Oh, there you are, Mrs. Hull. It's me, Officer Ludgood. We met yesterday at the diner when you—"

"I remember, dear. It's all so embarrassing. Please don't make me relive it. My meds. Sometimes, I have an adverse reaction to them. Anyway, you and your partner were very kind to look after me."

"Just doing our jobs," she says from across those twenty-six steps. Her rich voice, her professional demeanor, conjure the image of a formidable woman with unwavering confidence in the power of her badge.

"Well, thank you," I say. "So what can I do for you now? I was in the midst of some much-needed beauty sleep when I heard the racket you were making out here."

"Sorry to be so persistent. It's just, well, when I started my shift this morning, I thought I'd come check on you. Make sure you got home okay. Then when I got here I saw the open car door, the blanket tangled on the ground, the lawn decorations toppled. Things just felt . . . off. Are you okay, Mrs. Hull?"

"Do I look okay?" I ask, stepping off the porch.

Wrong move, wrong question too: her footsteps come closer. It occurs to me I should have loaded that fresh syringe I took from my cottage the day before, because it was empty in my pocket now. "Actually, Mrs. Hull, you don't look okay."

"Suppose I could use some lipstick and my hair's a mess. But like I told you, I just woke—"

"I'm not talking about your makeup. Or your hair. Mrs. Hull, are you aware there's blood on the side of your face? Bruises on your arms too."

"Oh. It's nothing. I mean, I understand how it must look. But remember, I'm a thousand years old and blind as a bat. Last night, I slipped and fell."

"I see. But . . . ouch. Must've been a bad one."

"Nothing I won't recover from."

"Hoping so." I hear her moving papers around, possibly

pulling something from her pocket. "Still, since I'm here, mind if I ask a few questions?"

"Not at all." I keep the smile pasted on my face, thinking of the man on the other side of the door, wishing I'd shoved a sock or dish towel or that stuffed whale in his mouth before stepping outside.

"The man who picked you up yesterday. You said he's your tenant?"

"Yes."

"Where's this tenant now?"

"I'm his landlord, not his prison guard. I don't make a habit of tracking his every move."

"His name is Teddy Cornwell, correct?"

"I never said that," I tell her, because I don't recall giving the police his name, and why is it her business anyway?

"He did. When he showed up and we asked him."

"Oh. Then you already have your answer."

"Mrs. Hull, if this gentleman, Mr. Cornwell, is engaging in any sort of elder abuse toward you, it's not right. You know that, don't you?"

Her skewed perception of the situation so stuns me that it takes a moment to answer. "Oh, my. That's—"

"And you don't need to hide it or deny it, ma'am. It's very common and nothing to be ashamed of. If that blood and those bruises are the result of his mistreatment, you can report it. Matter of fact, you can tell me right now."

"Officer Nogood," I say, mangling her name on purpose, since it's a surefire way to stop a person in their tracks and the change in meaning is convenient besides. "I'd appreciate it if you allowed me to get a word in."

"Ludgood," she corrects, and I can sense she's perturbed. "Go ahead."

All I want is to tell her how wonderful Teddy is to me, how much happiness the man has brought into my life. I don't want to think about the other man in the cottage, the one who could call out for help at any moment. And yet, he doesn't call. Why not?

"You were saying, Mrs. Hull?"

I don't fancy dealing with the law . . .

As those words he spoke on our ride home yesterday stir in my memory, I have the flickering thought of informing her about the man's presence in the cottage and letting her know I'm not certain of his identity after all. But given what I've done to him, given my own troubled history too, I decide against it. Better to get rid of her, then force an explanation from him before coming up with my next move. And so, I tell her, "I'm sure you must get bored as hell writing traffic tickets and ruining people's days. After all, what else is there for a small-town cop to do? Not much, and we all know it. While it must be fun to play detective, you've got the wrong idea here. Teddy and I were bringing in groceries last night and left the car door open. That blanket was hanging on the porch to dry when the wind blew it off the railing. And my lawn decorations are forever tipping over. Much like myself nowadays. You will too when you're my age. Sorry to ruin the excitement, Sherlock, but case closed. Got it?"

The second I'm done laying into her, I can't help but feel a tiny bit bad. After all, the officer is looking out for my well-being, and shouldn't I be grateful for such kindness?

"Apologies, Mrs. Hull," she says in a far cooler tone. "Didn't mean to bother you. I'll leave you alone now." I hear her walk to her car, where the police radio squawks. Her door squeaks open. "By the way, Mrs. Hull. You told us yesterday to look up what happened to your husband. So I Googled him last night."

"It was a freak accident," I say automatically. "We were just days away from celebrating our fiftieth when he passed."

Normally, that bit of news elicits a wave of sympathy. Not from this officer. She's quiet. I imagine her staring into the woods behind me, at the paint splotches on the trees. Picturing Hollis packing up his tent and fishing pole and heading off for the night, never to return alive. "You know," she says at last, "I'm surprised he wasn't more cautious. Working for the power company and all, you'd think he'd have known better."

"Yes . . . well . . . I worked in a hospital for years. And if there's one thing I learned about life it's that accidents happen all the time."

"Funny you should mention that. While I was searching, some articles came up about your work at the hospital too. About what happened. It was before my time in Schodack, so I wasn't aware of any of it."

I strain to keep smiling and say, "Yes, well, I crossed the picket line during a strike. Put my patients ahead of a paycheck, unlike those do-littles I worked with. Didn't exactly make me popular with my fellow staff, but I've never cared about being popu—"

"That's not what came up. It was about a patient of yours."

Her bulging eyes. Her tempest of salt-and-pepper hair. Her jack-o'-lantern mouth with its missing teeth, shrieking from the hospital bed, begging me to make it stop. To make it all stop. I shake my head, wishing the memory away. "What happened there was an accident too. It was the early days of my condition, and I didn't realize just how bad it had become.

Could've happened to anyone in my situation. Never once in all my years had I made that sort of mistake. And given such a stellar record of perfect service, you'd think those fuckers would've taken my word for it." Instinctively, I plunge my hands into my pockets, searching for the letter. Last I recall having it was in the parking lot of the diner, but where's that paper now?

"If that's all true, then I'm sorry, Mrs. Hull, for all you've been through."

"Of course it's true! And if there's nothing more you want to chap my ass about then I'd like to get back to my day."

"Understood. Well then, goodbye, Mrs. Hull. You be careful not to have any more accidents."

What is there to do but listen as she gets in her car and shuts the door? As her tires roll down the driveway, leaving me breathing in a cloud of kicked-up dust, I stand there. Smiling. Waving. Like we just traded knitting patterns.

When she's gone, I listen to the birds, feel the sun on my face. A stray wanders up, mewing at my ankles, so I kneel to gently stroke the kitty's rough fur, all the while beating away thoughts of how terribly I've botched things.

"She'll be back," I say aloud, because I feel it all through my bones.

After the feline scampers off, I stand and slip my hands into my pockets. Pull out the fresh syringe and vial. Unseal. Uncap. Push the needle into the rubber top. Draw back the necessary amount. Flick my index finger against the barrel, popping any bubbles, before recapping and returning it all to my pocket. Then I turn toward that second cottage. Sighing. Wishing things were different, wishing for, well . . . "Teddy?"

I call. "You're in there, aren't you? Please tell me you're in there . . ."

No answer.

No Teddy.

In case that other man has designs on a jailbreak, I make my way to the car. Scoop my phone and his off the seat, along with those necklaces. Then I feel for the switch to the head-lights and turn them on, thinking of the way certain morons used to drain their batteries at the drive-in back in the day. I'm aware I should head inside that second cottage and deal with the situation there. Get him some water. Get some an-swers too. But I need to take care of myself first.

"I've got your wallet!" I shout. "Which I'm guessing means I've got your driver's license too! You even touch those knots and I'll have that officer on your ass pronto! Understood?"

Again, no reply.

I should be worried, though with his personal belongings in my possession I sense I've bought some time. I head to my cottage, locking the door behind me. Inside, I allow myself to rest on the sofa awhile before managing a shower and putting on a fresh white dress. I transfer the contents of my pockets, consider redoing my pigtails, but in the end simply brush my hair, not bothering with makeup. Feeling a bit more myself again, I go to the kitchen. Pull out the lone remaining fro-zen dinner, making a mental note to grab a fresh supply from the freezer over at the drive-in. After zapping it in the micro-wave, I carry the tray along with a bottle of water across those twenty-six steps. To avoid any number of risks, when I open the door, I set the food on the floor and slide it in his direc-tion, send the bottle rolling his way too.

"Lunch is served," I announce.

"Let me guess. Chateaubriand?" he replies in a weary voice, though his efforts at sarcasm tell me he's alert enough to answer some questions.

"More like Lean Cuisine."

"I see. Well, I'm not hungry. Just thirsty."

"It's the medication. I brought you water. Drink up."

"Speaking of . . . might I ask what you were so kind to inject into my thigh?"

"Never mind that." I move into the house, cautiously checking the knots around his ankles. I expect him to flinch at my touch, or to try and fight me off, the way patients sometimes did on the ward, but he remains perfectly still. "Care to fill me in on why you didn't alert that cop to your presence here? My guess is you're hiding something. What?"

"Oh, Skyla." He sounds every bit defeated when he tells me, "It's all so shameful, so painful to relive."

"I see. Then allow me to rephrase my request. I've got another needle here in my pocket. Unless you want it jammed into your deltoid, you better start talking."

The man lets out a heavy breath. I hear him sit up, which makes me nervous, because I don't want any funny business, though the only thing I hear next is him fussing with the water bottle. After steadily gulping, he says, "Where do I start? Orlando when I was thirteen? Providence when I was twenty-two? Six weeks ago in New York City when I set out to improve this unlovable face of mine, not to mention agreeing to watch my ex's show dog—" Here, he pauses to laugh. Not a little laugh either, but a fit of breathless guffaws that goes on so long I consider interrupting. "—I mean, the absurdity of . . ." he chokes out at last. "Stand for show! . . . Sir, those are clerical collars, not . . . Begin with brush number one to loosen her fur! Well, anyway, then came the travel assignment I never should have accepted. And I really never should have looked up Marya—"

"Stop! Stop! Stop! What I want to know about is Teddy. Did I ever know the real him?"

He is quiet, drinking, breathing, saying nothing.

"Well?"

"Sorry," he tells me at last. "But, no. You never knew him. It was always me."

Embarrassing to admit, but tears prick at my eyes then. Being on my feet feels unbearable. So I go to the sofa, closer to him. As I settle into the cushions, I feel the weight of grief pressing down upon me, squeezing my heart, but I do my best to fight it off, to stay focused and figure out a plan.

"Are you okay, Skyla?"

Of course I'm not okay, but I don't bother saying as much.

"Would you like me to keep going?" he asks.

There were nights on the ward when my patients started speaking, unexpectedly opening themselves up to me, the calamitous details of their lives pouring out. I was always good at listening, which made me a good nurse too. I sense I'm about to hear the same sort of confession now, and though I worry that whatever I learn will lead me to regret sending that cop away, I say to the man on the floor, "Go ahead. Tell me how all this came to be."

And so, he begins talking. "The first thing you should know about my mother is that she loved being French. The second is that she was of the opinion that I exhibited questionable behaviors as a child. Tantrums. Long spells of not speaking. When I got angry, I tore up my bedsheets. I loathed most other children. We moved all the time, and at one miserable school in Tulsa, I spent every recess walking the perimeter of the playground, obsessively. All that and worse led to her belief that I was . . . well . . . *frappadingue*."

In my time at the hospital, I encountered plenty of patients who exhibited all sorts of questionable behaviors, though that word is unfamiliar to me. "Sounds like plain old oppositional defiant disorder."

"Let's not get into my various diagnoses now. As for that other word, it's an old Frenchism no one uses anymore. Means crazy. Most often, intended in a playful way, though that's not how she meant it. And my mother had no clue what to do with her crazy child and his odd behaviors, so she hauled me around to auditions. I was a cute kid and good at pretending, so I got a lot of roles: Kurt in *The Sound of Music* . . . The Artful Dodger in *Oliver* . . . Winthrop in *The Music Man*. My mother would sit in the front row, happy, because on a most basic level, she liked me better when I was someone else."

Despite all I'm being told, my mind clings to the notion of Teddy. I think of the diner yesterday, the voice I knew to be his saying, "My mum was distant and downright cruel . . . Actually it was Jeremy's mum who was truly unkind. . . ."

One clue among many, I think, *if only I'd been paying better attention.*

"At the age of thirteen, we moved to Orlando. By then my face had exploded with acne, so I wasn't getting cast and my mother's interest in me waned, to say the least. I wanted to please her so I came up with an idea that I could play one of the dwarfs at Disney. My mother hated that park, but off we went to an audition. Turned out their employment rules meant I was too young to even be considered. A waste of time. Except, as we were leaving the audition room, she overheard someone speaking French. This thrilled her, because it normally provided the chance for her to correct mangled pronunciation and make people feel less than her, which was something of a hobby for the woman. However, the French flowing from this person's mouth was near perfect. Which is what she told the young man, who happened to be handsome and charming, and whose name turned out to be Teddy Cornwell."

"Teddy?" I say, realizing I must sound like some dopey schoolgirl.

"He was older than me. Eighteen. From a seaside town in England, he told us, living in the States for the summer. Early in life, he developed a knack for languages, having spent so much time in his mother's collectibles shop, chatting with tourists who came in looking for souvenirs, for directions, for the toilet. He'd taught himself French. When we met him, he was attempting Russian. My mother was impressed. She offered Teddy a deal on the spot whereby she'd pay him to come by a few times a week and tutor me. It used to annoy her to no end when I garbled the most basic words: *merci* was mercy . . . *beaucoup* was bucup. The first day he showed up, I said to him, '*Je parle parfaitement le français, connard. Mais feignez de ne pas le faire parce que cela agace ma mère, ce que j'aime faire. Donc, voici le marché que je propose: vous prenez son argent et nous l'utilisons pour nous amuser.*'"

"I don't understand."

"Neither did he. At first. It means, 'I can speak French perfectly, you asshole. But I pretend not to because it annoys my mother, which is something I love doing. So here's the deal: you take her money and we'll use it to have some fun.'"

"Oh," I say, getting it now.

"Genius, right? Teddy's response was an instant yes. Or, *oui,* to be exact. My mother was so smitten with him that he had no trouble convincing her that it would be best for me to learn a language while out experiencing the world. So off we went. To arcades. To burger joints. To the beach where we smoked pot with a bunch of Deadhead surfers. All on her dime. I don't think I ever had so much fun. And you know what? My French did improve. So did his, since we spoke it to each other all the time."

I never knew the real Teddy—that much he's made achingly clear. And yet, the confused attachment I'd formed with him, with the idea of him, leaves me wanting to know more about the man. I can't help but ask, "What did you talk about?"

"All sorts of things. His mother, whom he'd lost. My mother, whom, frankly, I wouldn't have minded if she met a similar end. Sounds harsh, I'm aware, but at the time I believed it to be true. Also, I told him what I knew of the stars from things my father taught me. Quasars. Black holes. The randomness of the universe. But what I remember most is that we talked about love."

"Love?"

"Yes. That summer he'd fallen for a girl who he said was everything to him."

"Linelle?" I say, feeling the way I used to those nights on the ward, when pieces of my patients' stories began dropping into place.

"I'd only glimpsed her around that summer. She was beautiful, but a stranger to me. Looking back, thanks to my mother and so many doctors she took me to see, I believed I'd never find love. I was too crazy. Too ugly, inside and out. So I used to ask Teddy what it felt like to care for someone so deeply, to have that person feel the same desire in return. Also, as an adolescent boy, I was curious to know what sex was like. Whatever I asked, he told me. Not in a prurient way, but like a big brother, which is what he became to me, if that makes sense."

"I suppose. Though I don't think Linelle would have appreciated it."

"Clearly not. But it was a long time ago. I meant no harm. At the start anyway. And Teddy, I think he was so dazed by his feelings that it made him happy to talk about it. After all, aren't we told in endless songs and movies and stories that there's no greater joy on the planet than finding love?"

"We are," I tell him, thinking of the love I felt in my marriage, which was more of a pragmatic steadiness than any feral passion. Then I think of the flutter of feelings I developed for Teddy. "But where is Teddy now?"

"That bit is quite sad. Teddy's life didn't turn out the way one might've thought. But six weeks ago, when my circumstances went tits up—to use a phrase he would have—I found myself fleeing Providence and heading to Buffalo to return my ex's dog. When I stopped at an Albany area mini-mart, I was waiting for the key to the restroom and flipped through a local newspaper in a desperate effort to distract myself from . . . from . . . well, never mind. That's when I saw your ad. It was an elegant solution to my little problem, and when I called you, while the phone was ringing, while I waited for you to pick up, I realized what I wanted, what I needed, was to be someone else. Anybody else! Please, God! For once, not me with my Everest of troubles! With my self-loathing and dead-end decisions! And then you said hello, and I—"

"You became him," I say and feel a strange kind of—not relief exactly, but a reluctant understanding of the facts.

"Yes. Imagine: To be handsome! To be so easily adored! To be loved! I opened my mouth and, without quite deciding to do it, out came that accent. From the very first sentence I spoke to you, it felt good. . . . It felt . . . free. And I've loved being him, these past six weeks, loved doing and saying all the things he would. At times I almost believed it myself. But it wasn't true. I want to apologize to you, Skyla, for bringing him to life for you, for allowing you to feel a love that wasn't there."

Tears press at my eyes again, spill down my cheeks. I feel foolish, ashamed, all the more so when I tell him, "I don't want to lose Teddy. I've had enough loss already."

"I'm sorry," he says. "For what it's worth, I'm grateful for the love you showed him. It's not something I've had a lot of in my life. So it was exquisite to feel, even in such an unusual way."

And that's when it comes to me. "You know, you don't have to do it," I say. "You could just keep on . . . being him."

"Skyla," he says, and I hear the instant dismissal in his voice. "I can't—"

"From what you've told me, you don't want to be Jeremy either. You want to be Teddy. I want you to be Teddy. You and me, we've both experienced so much sadness in our lives. Why suffer now when we have the means to do otherwise?"

"I hear what you're suggesting, but it won't work. That cop seemed suspicious and might even be running the plate on the old Lincoln right now. The reason I had to leave Providence is . . . well, I did something I regret."

In an effort to persuade him, I speak in a quiet voice, admitting what I never do, not even to myself. "I've done things I regret as well, so that makes two of us."

He pauses, and I sense he's considering what I've said. "In my case, the police won't stop until they find me."

"Until they find him. So enough. Bury that past. Do whatever you can to forget."

The cottage grows quiet. I hear the sound of our breath, rising and falling. The ticking clock, the breeze outside, the old movie screen making its usual commotion. I think of Fright Nights at the drive-in years ago. *Carnival of Souls. Eyes Without a Face. Night of the Living Dead.* Also, *Frankenstein.* I think of that monstrous creation stitched together from parts dug up in a graveyard, of the mad doctor screaming, "It's alive! It's alive! Now I know what it feels like to be God!"

And then, into the silence of that room and the clamor of my mind, a familiar voice says, "Hello, luv."

"Teddy?" I whisper.

"Yes, my dear."

I go to him. Kneeling, I can't help but touch his arms, touch his hands, touch his fingers. And, for the first time, I touch his face—that beautiful, lovable face of his, with his square jaw and sharp cheekbones and perfectly smooth skin and full lips and full eyebrows and full lashes too. "I missed you, Teddy. You have no idea how much."

"I missed you too, luv. I really did."

I wrap my arms around him for a long, deep, and tender hold. And then we begin working on those knots. Despite my lack of scout experience, I'd managed to tie them tight, so they require time and effort to undo. We begin making plans to celebrate his return with one of our dinner parties, with food and wine and Patsy spinning on the record player, with us spinning around the room too. I'm about to tell him that we need to walk over to the concession stand for tots and chops when Teddy shushes me abruptly.

"Shhh . . . Listen, luv. Hear that?"

"Hear what?" I say.

Then comes my answer: the sound of a car moving up the long driveway, bumping over potholes and gullies. I pay attention to Teddy's movements, the creaks in the floor as he stands, slowly, and goes to the window. After a moment, he says, "Oh, dear. Oh, no."

"Is it that officer? Because if so, I'll march out there right now and give her a piece of my mind."

"It's not that officer. Skyla, it's that old girlfriend of mine. The one I never got over."

"Linelle? But you said you didn't reach out to her."

"I know. That's because I could sense you were jealous. But the truth is, I did reach out to her. And after all these years apart, she's come to see me again. She's come for one final date with the past."

SIXTEEN

"Redrum! Redrum!"

—From *The Shining*, shown at the Schodack Big-Star Drive-in,
June 1980

NINETEEN HOURS BEHIND THE WHEEL. Five uncomfortable
hours sleeping (or trying to) in the lumpy bed of a roadside
motel somewhere in Delaware. Twelve cups of bad coffee. Dozens of texts, calls, and voicemails from Marcus. Not a single
text, call, or voicemail from her daughter, Georgia. And while
there'd been countless moments when Linelle thought, *What
the hell am I doing? Just turn the car around already and go home!*,
she kept heading north, possessed by the long-forgotten feelings of first love that stirred in her once more.

Now, here she is, bumping up the dirt drive and taking in
the sight of a ragged movie screen looming over twin cottages
with moon shutters, a scrawny cat grooming itself on a stump
at the edge of the woods. When Linelle cuts the engine, she
feels desperate for a shower. Desperate for a nap and a change
of clothes. Desperate to use a bathroom too. She settles for
messing with her hair in the rearview.

No sooner does Linelle get out of the car than a woman emerges from one of the cottages. Her face, pale and withered. Her hair, a spray of white. Her clothes, a nursing uniform, the sort you see more often in TV shows and films than real life these days. *All that's missing is the cap with a red cross on the front,* Linelle thinks. "Hi there," she calls. "I'm Linelle. An old friend of Teddy's. You must be his landlord?"

"The one and only," the woman answers, smiling big and wide as her hands swim in the pockets of her nursing dress. "I'm Skyla Hull. Nice to meet you, Linelle. Teddy's mentioned you. Quite a bit actually. Don't worry, all good things. Though I must say, this is a surprise. He never told me you were coming to see us."

Us. The word gives Linelle pause. "Yes . . . well . . . I wanted to surprise him. Silly as that sounds. He's mentioned the Big-Star. The distance from Albany. The cottages. It wasn't hard to find. You know how it goes with the Web these days. You can figure out pretty much anything."

"Apparently so," Skyla says. "Too bad it's not the same with people. Teddy left this morning."

"Left?" Linelle flinches at the news, disappointment rising in her. "For where? And when will he be back?"

"Seems I've said this already today, but here's an encore: I'm his landlord, not his prison guard. Beats me."

"Okay then . . . Let's see . . . I guess . . ." Linelle looks around the patchy lawn cluttered with flags and fountains, pinwheels and windmills, and wonders what to do next. "Sorry . . . it's just . . . when I imagined coming here, I envisioned a lot of scenarios. Somehow, Teddy not being home wasn't one of them."

"Well, that's what you get for dropping by with no notice. After all, none of us is a teenager anymore. People have lives, Linelle. Teddy has a life. Don't you?"

Linelle drops her polite smile. "Of course, I—" She stops, realizing it's ridiculous to reply to such a rude question. "We texted yesterday afternoon, when I was still in the Carolinas, and not that I told him what I was up to, but he didn't mention any plans to leave today."

"Disappointing, I'm sure. Now if you don't mind, I need to get back to my life. You get home safely, dear. Goodbye."

Skyla steps toward the door, opening it just enough to slip inside. Before she does, Linelle calls out, "Wait!"

Slowly, she turns around, studying Linelle in a birdlike manner, head tilted, watching from the periphery of her vision. "Yes?"

"I don't mean to be pushy, Mrs. Hull. But I came all the way from Florida. Not the most grown-up plan—you're right about that. I'm here now, though, so I'm sure you'll understand that I don't want to leave without seeing Teddy. Also, my bladder's about to burst. If you wouldn't mind, could I at least use a bathroom?"

Skyla sighs. Pulling the door closed, she mutters, "Fine. But after that, I really do suggest you go."

There's something so unnerving about the woman that it leads Linelle to reach into the Camaro for her phone. She swipes away a clump of new texts from Marcus, sending Teddy a message instead.

Um. . . . so here's a surprise. Guess who's on your doorstep?
Me. Right here in your "little town outside of Albany." Not

kidding. Only problem: u r not here and ur landlord is trying
to get rid of me. Help!

When she looks up, Skyla is stepping off the porch in
the direction of the other cottage, which confuses Linelle.
Uncomfortable as she feels, Teddy has yet to respond and
her bladder is about to burst, so she grabs her purse and
follows. It's then, while watching Skyla's careful, deliber-
ate movements, that Linelle realizes her vision is impaired,
a detail that makes even more sense the moment they step
into the living room and Linelle observes the state of things
there: Food mashed into the braided rug . . . Records strewn
about . . . Discarded nursing uniforms piled haphazardly on
an armchair . . .

"Bathroom's down the hall," Skyla says in the same inhos-
pitable tone. "Knock yourself out."

Linelle makes her way to the tiny bathroom and relieves
herself, while checking her phone. Still nothing from Teddy.
She finger-combs her hair. Pulls a travel toothbrush from her
purse that she'd picked up at a rest stop and takes care of that
as well. Finally, since none of this is turning out the way she
envisioned, Linelle does a quick search on her phone for a
nearby hotel.

Back in the living room, she finds Skyla waiting in the
chair on top of a tangle of nursing uniforms, looking anxious
and uncomfortable.

"Thanks, Mrs. Hull. Sorry to have bothered you. I'm going to head over to the Cedar Inn. When Teddy comes back,
you can let him know—" Linelle stops. She hadn't noticed it
before, but Skyla is holding a syringe. The sight brings an unsettled feeling creeping over her. "Never mind. I'll text him."

Linelle steps toward the door, but can't help asking, "Mrs. Hull, are you okay?"

"Just dandy. Why do you ask?"

"It's . . . well . . . the needle in your hand . . ." And the mess of this place, Linelle is tempted to add, but despite how brusque the woman's been, does not want to sound disrespectful.

"This?" Skyla holds up the syringe, giving a better view of the bright orange cap over the tip. "Just all part of my . . . aggressive regiment of self-care. While you were in the bathroom, I figured it would be smart to prep my next shot."

Diabetic, Linelle assumes. She thinks of her mother—the difficulties of aging, the care she requires too—and the unsettled feeling is replaced by a wave of sympathy. "I'm sorry you have to deal with that. It must be unpleasant."

"I was a nurse for over thirty years. Injections are as second nature as breathing, so it's nothing compared to my vision problems or losing my husband." Her voice grows quieter when she says, "Not to mention, the more recent disappointments of my life."

Gazing around, Linelle notices a framed wedding photo of a younger, happier-looking Skyla, hand in hand with her handsome groom. Behind them, the drive-in movie screen rises up, looking happier as well. "I'm sorry about your husband."

Linelle assumes that will be the end of the discussion. But Skyla seems lost in thought, as though responding to some inner dialogue as much as to Linelle when she says in a remote, more vulnerable voice, "Don't be. We were married nearly fifty years. For many of those he had Maureen."

"Maureen?"

"The other woman. One thing to want two lives. Suppose we all wonder about that on occasion. But entirely another to actually go through with it. That other cottage I rent was originally built for her, though I only just figured that out . . ."

The things she's saying bring more sympathy for Skyla, a twinge of embarrassment too, since what had compelled Linelle to come here was a similar desire to sample, however briefly, another life. The thoughts put her in mind of the book from her princess days about irrational things people have done for love: the brokenhearted radiologist who dug up his lover's corpse, the emperor who attempted to transform a boy into a woman resembling his deceased wife, never mind the endless tabloid headlines about deceit and betrayal and murder, all in the name of love too.

"But enough of that," Skyla says, giving her head a small shake. "I've got more pressing things to take care of. Time for you to go, Linelle. And if I might offer some advice, dear: Leave the past alone. Take it from me, it can be a painful place to visit. If I were you, I wouldn't wait for Teddy at that inn. Better you just go home."

Hardly an invitation to sit on the sofa across from Skyla, but curiosity compels Linelle to do just that. She intends to ask about Teddy, to stall a little longer in case he returns soon, though the vision of Skyla in that chair, surrounded by so many nursing uniforms, conjures one of the scant details he shared about her. Without quite meaning to, Linelle says, "I thought you were retired?"

"I am."

"But then . . . if you don't mind my asking, why the uniform?"

Skyla shrugs. "Comfort. Convenience. Also, some jobs you

leave, but they don't leave you. They're too much a part of who you are. Does that make sense?"

It might be the first thing the woman has said that makes sense to Linelle. She's not thinking of that real estate exam, but her job as an art teacher. Certainly, the position had its headaches, though working with students gave a sense of reward. That's what she intends to say, but what comes out: "Years ago, I left college to care for my mom when she had a stroke. Later, I finished a degree in art education. Taught for twenty years. I don't teach any longer, but as much as I miss it, there's another job I miss more: motherhood. My daughter's away for her last year of high school. I miss her every day."

"Oh, yes. Berlin, right?" Skyla says with a bit more warmth in her voice. "On some fancy music scholarship. Siri—. Teddy told me. Impressive."

"It is," she agrees. It's a glossy version of the truth she's been telling anyone who will listen: Georgia's fancy scholarship, how proud and happy she and Marcus are for her. Since Skyla seems more open to conversation now, Linelle takes a breath and says, "I wish my daughter didn't feel she had to go. But last spring, my husband and I cleaned out our house. Or my husband's colleague did." She laughs. "I came across an old Polaroid of my friend DD and me, back when we worked as Disney princesses. Dressed for a Halloween party. Short skirts. Teased hair. Hookers, that's what we were supposed to be. Funny to us at the time, especially the messages DD scrawled on our shirts that said, well . . . Sorry, I don't know you and shouldn't—"

"I worked the psych ward in a hospital. I've heard it all. So just say it, dear."

"'BJ's for a Buck. Backdoor Stuff for Free.' Stupid, I know.

But we found it hilarious way back when. Harmless too. I scanned the photo and sent it to DD. She thought it was funny and posted it on Facebook with the caption 'Princesses by Day, Prostitutes by Night. We've Come a Long Way, Babe.'

"After DD posted the picture, I started getting pointed comments from parents and teachers. I posted an explanation saying it was a joke and we were kids at the time. But that made things worse. Their consensus: 'Sex workers are an abused and disadvantaged population, and a person who treats them as a joke is not the sort we want at our school.' I was suspended indefinitely. And my daughter—absurd as it sounds, students made up all sorts of names, tormenting her too. So I helped her apply to that program. Before I knew it, we were signing papers, and she was gone. Ever since, there are moments when a picture of her as a little girl pops up on my phone and it stops me. Where did it all go? I think. Packing her lunch. Driving her to swim meets and soccer practice and birthday parties. Nagging her to get out of bed on school mornings. An entire life, just gone."

"I'm sorry," Skyla says, the warmth in her voice still present. "I know what it's like to have a person you love vanish from your life." She sighs, considering something. "The way it can make you do such foolish and desperate things. But in your case anyway, your daughter will come back. People will forget that photo. Give it time."

Having confessed such personal things to a stranger, especially one with outsize troubles of her own, makes Linelle feel silly and selfish. Yet, it solidifies a notion she's been turning over in her mind since leaving Florida: her sadness is not merely about missing her daughter or her job. Rather, it's what Georgia's absence has revealed about her marriage. Linelle fears she's shared too much already, however, so she looks around for a change of subject, noticing the towering stacks of romance novels: *Barely a Lady*; *Forever in Love*; *Take Me, I'm Yours*; and hundreds of similarly overblown titles. "You've read all these books?" she says.

"Back in the day. Or more accurately, back in the night, after my patients fell asleep. Those love stories used to bring me comfort. The good ones in particular."

"And what makes a good one?"

Skyla shifts in her seat, tilting her head toward the window where the sky is beginning to grow dark and the movie screen rattles in the wind. Linelle senses she's become impatient with her presence again, though Skyla continues the conversation. "I suppose the lovers need a unique 'how we met' story. Then there's the obstacles that make it seem as though they'll never be together. But, at the very last minute, by some bit of magic, in an unexpected twist, they end up face-to-face once more. Even if you don't get a happily ever after, you're left with hope for their relationship. That's my criteria anyway. Why do you ask?"

"Guess I was just thinking that real life usually doesn't measure up to what's in those pages. Like, I met my husband at a bank. Where did you meet yours?"

Again, Skyla glances toward the window. "About a hundred yards from here. At the drive-in. And I'm told you and Teddy met at Disney."

The mention of him leads Linelle to check her phone, where Marcus has bombarded her with texts the way he's been doing since discovering she took the 67: "Don't ride her clutch!" "Don't park her near other cars or her paint might get dinged!" "Let her engine idle for a solid ten minutes before

driving her again after any long stops!" Considering he's
shown more concern for "her" well-being than hers, Linelle
has sent just one text back saying only that she needed time
away. There's still no response from Teddy, which brings even
more of a sense that this surprise visit was a terrible idea. Now
that she's lulled Skyla into conversation, however, Linelle finds
herself going on about their romance. Her wisdom teeth. Her
mother's bum arm. The auditions. The WWWDs. DD. The
Black Lung. All of it, including that letter written in French,
which hadn't broken them up, but led to their first fight and
many others, until it was over. When she's done, Linelle says,
"I should leave you alone now, Mrs. Hull. Sorry to talk your
ear off."

"You seem like a nice woman, Linelle. Forgive my rude-
ness earlier. If this were some other time, I'd welcome your
company. But as I said, I've got things to take care of around
here . . . none of it pleasant."

"Anything I can help you with?" she asks, feeling sorry for
her and holding out hope for Teddy's return.

"Unfortunately, no. But I'll walk you out."

When they stand, a glint of motion on the couch catches
Linelle's eye. In the fading light of the cottage, she reaches
down and rescues two tangled necklaces about to slip between
the cushions. "I found some jewelry here."

"Jewelry?" Skyla says, sounding confused.

Linelle dangles the necklaces between them. "Two thin
gold chains. One with a cross. The other with an Italian horn.
Aren't they yours?"

"Oh, right." Skyla places the syringe in a pocket of her
dress, then reaches out. "Brought those in from the car earlier
and must've misplaced them."

Together, they head outside to the Camaro. Linelle digs the key from her purse, climbs in, and starts the engine. When she rolls down the window, Skyla calls over the roar of the motor, "You get home safely to Florida. Goodbye, dear."

"Well, maybe not goodbye just yet," she tells her. "It's almost dark, so I don't want to start the trip now. Think I'll stay at that inn after all. I'm sure I'll hear from Teddy by morning, so I'll probably come by then. If I do, I'll be sure to say hello."

The softer expression fades from Skyla's face as she glances at the dark windows of the second cottage. "You're determined, aren't you?"

Linelle laughs. "If you read the texts from my husband, you wouldn't blame me for not rushing home. I appreciate your advice, but I came this far, so I might as well see it through. Now, are you sure you don't need my help before I go?"

This time, Skyla takes longer to contemplate the offer, surprising Linelle with a different answer. "You know what? My kitchen is empty. I need to head over to the concession stand where I store food. Since you refuse to . . . skedaddle on home as I suggest, I could use your eyes, Linelle. Use your arms too."

"I'd be happy to help," Linelle tells her, getting out of the Camaro. "My husband says I'm supposed to let the engine idle for a bit anyway. So, let's go."

WELCOME TO THE BIG-STAR SNACK BAR

After they make their way through the row of trees and enter the low-slung, cinderblock building at the far end of the field, Linelle sees that sign above the service counter. The black magnetic board beneath is missing so many letters it makes a puzzle of the old menu, from "Big-St r Bur ers" to "Big-S ar Ba ana Boa s" and ice cream in all sorts of cryptic flavors. Behind the counter, there's a hulking fryolator and griddle. Skyla fusses with the keys on a chain around her neck before using one to unlock a freezer, nearly empty inside. Linelle begins pulling out the last of the frozen pork chops and tater tots, fish sticks and French fries, stacking packages on the counter to carry to the cottage. She becomes lost in the chore until a clacking sound causes her to look up.

"Mrs. Hull?" she calls, realizing the woman is no longer at her side.

The noise comes from another part of the building, where a flickering blue light spills through an open doorway. Slowly, Linelle steps toward it. She looks inside to see an enormous projector, switched on and bustling away. Film cannisters are scattered on the floor. The walls are plastered with movie posters: *Casablanca* . . . *The Way We Were* . . . *The Creature from the Black Lagoon* . . . *Key Largo* . . . *Vertigo* . . . *Overboard* . . . *Mannequin* . . . *The Cannonball Run* . . . *Same Time, Next Year* . . . *All About Eve* . . . *Alice in Wonderland* . . . *Chinatown* . . . *Psycho* . . . *The Maltese Falcon* . . . *The Wolf Man* . . . *The Shining* . . . *Roman Holiday* . . . *Mildred Pierce* . . . *Brief Encounter* . . .

In the midst of it all, Skyla stands with her hands in the pockets of her white dress, peering out a small viewing window, head tilted, tears shimmering on her cheeks.

"Mrs. Hull?" Linelle says, hesitantly, over the train-like commotion of the projector. "Everything okay?"

"I'm fine. I know I have things to take care of, and I'll do it, I really will . . ." She inhales deeply, shifting her hands inside her pockets, before letting out a weighted breath. "But all our talk of love, of missing happier times and a life that used to be, made me think of what's been on this projector for more than a year now. Don't know why I bothered, though, since I can't make out a damn thing."

Linelle goes to another viewing window and peers through to see a shapeshifting fog of images on the tattered screen across the field. "I don't understand."

"As a fiftieth-anniversary present for my husband, I found a service to transfer our home movies to thirty-five millimeter. I wanted to surprise him on the big night by showing them on the screen. But while fetching his waders for a fishing trip, he found the reel where I'd hidden it in a closet. Even though it was still a few nights before our anniversary, I loaded it on the projector. The two of us stood right here and watched."

"What a sweet thing to do."

"It was. Though I had an ulterior motive. I hoped seeing these moments from our life, being reminded of all we'd lived together, would make him quit what he was doing with Maureen."

"And did it?" Linelle asks.

Skyla looks out the window, tilting her head in an effort to see, not answering.

"You know, Mrs. Hull," Linelle says after a moment, "it's blurry, even for me. Which control helps focus?"

When Skyla points to the dial, Linelle adjusts it until the grainy images glimmering on the screen become clearer. Again, they look out the windows and Linelle follows her instinct to describe what she sees to Skyla. "There's a Christmas tree strung with colored lights, twinkling away . . . A family all around . . . Wait . . . The camera is panning the room and . . . there's you."

"A younger, happier me."

"Well, you're certainly smiling. And by your side, there's a boy. Brown hair. Bangs. He's opening a gift."

"That's my nephew. Hollis's sister's son, John. They used to visit at Christmas."

"He's shredding the wrapping paper the way my daughter did at that age. But . . . turns out he's been given a doll. He looks pouty. Disappointed."

"His mother and I used to wrap Santa's gifts for him and his sisters. Whenever there was a mix-up, we blamed the elves. Though, really, it was too much Chianti."

Linelle laughs. "The film just cut to some other time. Not Christmas anymore, but fall, I think. Leaves are swirling in the air. A man with a hard hat is standing in one of those cherry-picker things."

"Aerial lift. That's the technical name. And that's my Hollis."

"Right. I recognize him now. From the picture in your living room."

"He worked for the power company. A 'trouble man.' That's what they call emergency service technicians. Back when he finished his apprenticeship, I convinced him to let me film him in the bucket. I was so proud of him, though I used to worry about the dangers of that job."

"I don't blame you. And . . . wait, the film just jumped again. To the drive-in at night. It's pretty dark, so I can't see much, but a sea of cars fills the field."

"Our wedding," Skyla says with what sounds like pride.

On the screen, Linelle watches her in a simple wedding dress, hand in hand with Hollis in a tuxedo. But given what became of their marriage, rather than describe the joy and innocence on their faces, Linelle stays quiet.

"To answer your earlier question," Skyla says over the clacking of the projector, "I had no idea how involved things were between him and Maureen. So, no. It didn't work. On that night last year, my husband watched the movie for a few minutes. He made some comments about his sister and her kids, then planted a kiss on my forehead, saying I'd done a nice job, but he didn't have much use for the past. More like he didn't have use for me. Hollis said we'd finish some other time, because he wanted to pack up his fishing and camping equipment before heading off for the night."

On the screen, Skyla and Hollis, bride and groom, seal their union with a kiss. Linelle keeps from describing that moment too.

"Anyway, I've come to believe that every marriage has its secrets." After a pause, she asks, "What's your secret, Linelle?"

"Mine?" Despite her hesitation, the answer comes quickly and with such clarity it surprises even her. There's no one nearby to hear, but Linelle speaks in a hushed tone anyway. "I don't think I love my husband anymore."

Before Skyla can react, a snapping sound comes from the projector. Linelle looks to see the broken film whirling wildly on the reel.

"Probably grown so brittle this past year it was bound to break," Skyla says, feeling the various controls before switching off the machine.

The sudden quiet of the room serves to call attention to Linelle's confession. While she'd prefer to ignore the weight of it hanging in the air and simply get back to gathering food, Skyla says, "Thank you, Linelle, for helping me to see my old life. I can't help thinking that if we met under different circumstances, we might even become friends. So, I hope you don't mind me telling you: Don't let your love story end like mine. You're still young. You can change things. If that's the way you feel about your marriage, tell your husband. After all, it's only fair to him too. Nothing good comes from betrayal. Trust me. I guess that's why I keep urging you to go home. Understand?"

"I do," Linelle says, though all she wants at the moment is to finish up and get to the hotel, where she can run a bath and clear her mind before deciding anything.

As they step into the concession area again, Linelle informs her that the freezer is empty. Skyla begins pressing her fingers to the keys around her neck, undoing the lock on a chest freezer nearby. Linelle reaches in and begins pulling out more frozen food. When her hand touches a hand, at first Linelle does not understand, and simply attempts a firmer hold. Palm. Fingers. Thumb. Then she stops. Peers inside the freezer. What happens next feels grainy and dimly lit, swooping and herky-jerky, in the way of that film on the tattered screen. The sensation of what she's been touching is so cold, the realization of what it is so shocking, that her hand yanks back. Linelle wants to scream but feels on the verge of vomiting. Her mouth drops open. Her voice sputters. "There's a body in the freezer! Oh my god, there's a body in the freezer!"

"What are you talking about?" Skyla asks, fussing with the boxes in her arms, sounding more annoyed than alarmed.

"A woman's body! Right there! In the freezer! Look!"

And in her way, Skyla does look. She puts down the boxes. Leans over the freezer, as though leaning over a casket to pay her respects. Turning her head sideways, she peers down. All the while Linelle watches, confused, afraid, wondering what to do next. Every part of her is shaking as Skyla reaches inside, feeling the body for herself, placing a hand against the neck, then against the wrist, confirming its cold, dead presence, its obvious lack of a pulse. "Oh my," she says. "Oh, dear. Oh, no."

"I don't understand!" Linelle screams.

Still looking into that freezer, Skyla takes out those thin gold necklaces and drops them inside, saying, "I believe these belong to you."

Her voice is so oddly calm, it begs any number of questions, all of which begin tumbling from Linelle's mouth as she moves to the far side of the counter toward a row of exit doors. Already imagining herself running across the field, past the bent metal posts with their dangling wires and blown-out speakers. Already seeing herself slipping through the path between the pines, making her way to the safety of the idling Camaro. Already seeing herself climbing inside, locking the doors, grabbing her cell from where she'd left it on the seat, calling 9–1–1, and tearing the hell out of there. First, though, these questions spew from her lips: "Did you know about this? Did you know about her? Who is she? Why is she here? What is going on?"

"Of course, I didn't know!" Skyla shouts. "Would I have asked you here if I did? Would I have asked you to help me cart the food to my house? Would I have ever opened that goddamned freezer in the first place? I'm as horrified as you."

"We have to call the police. I'm going to my car to get my phone." Linelle steps closer to the doors, pushing one open.

"Wait," Skyla calls, stepping from behind the counter too. "Use my phone. It's right here in my pocket."

Linelle looks back. Skyla thrusts her hands into her pockets, fumbling for a few seconds before producing her phone. She holds it out to Linelle, who steps away from the door, so it clangs shut behind her. Taking the cell, she looks at the screen, doing her best to steady her quivering fingers as she presses 9, then 1, then—

"Ow!"

Linelle feels a sudden prick in her shoulder and looks up from the phone to see the old woman holding a needle, her thumb pressing on the plunger. Before she can push it more than halfway down, Linelle knocks her arm away. The sight of the syringe waggling from her body brings the swooping, herky-jerky sensation on full force. Linelle yanks out the syringe, tosses it to the floor. She feels as though the building is tipping. That the food is sliding off the counter, crashing onto the floor. That the hulking casket of a freezer is quaking. Overturning. That the body is toppling out, rolling across the floor, still wearing the white nightgown from that evening six weeks before when Jeremy paid a doomed visit to his past.

"What was in that syringe?!" she screams.

"I'm so sorry, Linelle," Skyla answers in a murky, underwater voice.

"Am I going to die?" That's the question she wants answered, though Skyla only stares at her in that odd, sideways manner. And since the phone is still in her hand, Linelle decides to finish that call to the police, her shaking thumb hitting 2 instead of that final 1, then pressing Delete and—

"Hey, Siri," Skyla says before Linelle can manage the correct digit.

"Yes, Skyla?" the familiar voice pipes up.

"Turn off phone! Now!"

"To power off your iPhone, first press and hold—"

"Just fucking do what I say for once!" Skyla shrieks, then lunges forward, knocking the phone from Linelle's hand so it sails in the direction of the freezer, landing on the floor, skidding beneath.

At last, Linelle does what she imagined moments before: she runs. Out the door. Across the field, where the ghostly movie screen looms and the earth rises up in rows of small hills so, once upon a time, cars could park on a slant to afford the best possible view. The farther she goes, the weaker her legs become. Her breath is shallow. Her mouth sticky. Her mind clouding over.

Where am I? she wonders, looking for the opening between the trees.

Why did I come here? she wonders, freefalling, against her will, into the muzzy world of that drug taking hold.

Finally, she spots the path. On the other side is a house. Two houses. Side by side. The idling car, not far away. The ache in her shoulder brings back the memory of Skyla's needle. Linelle orders herself to stay focused. To get to the Camaro. She begins moving again, but her knees buckle. The damp December ground welcomes her body, sucking it into the loamy earth, wanting to keep her there while the stars spin and the moon wobbles in the sky above.

How much time passes before Linelle stands again? She is too dizzy, too disoriented, to gauge. But those twin houses and the car beyond are still there. She manages to get on her feet. To walk, as best she can, through the path, reaching the nearest cottage first. *Teddy's cottage*, she thinks, noticing how the moon shutters give the place a feel of a fairy tale. In those stories, you never knew if the place was haunted or a safe haven until someone knocked and discovered what was waiting inside.

Behind her, Linelle hears footsteps and a woman's determined voice muttering something indecipherable until, all at once, she makes out what's being said: "I didn't want to hurt you, Linelle. I still don't. But just as you have secrets, I have secrets too."

The sound is coming closer now, and Linelle understands she won't make it to the Camaro in time, so she stumbles up the porch steps instead, falling again, though dragging her body across the splintery floorboards. In the final moment before the footsteps are upon her, Linelle reaches up, grips the knob and turns.

And the door opens.

SEVENTEEN

"I don't know how to say goodbye."

—From *Roman Holiday*, shown at the Schodack Big-Star Drive-in,
September 1953

YOU FEEL IT WHEN the end is coming. Summers, when nights begin to cool and leaves begin to turn. Holidays, when decorations in department store windows take on a weary look, and the same cloying Christmas carols have been played one too many times. You feel it in romance novels, movies too. Like those books I devoured nights at the hospital and the films that showed at the Big-Star, when the last of so many surprises has been revealed and the lovers meet again and declare their undying devotion—or don't. You can feel the end approach in real-life relationships too. When a person who used to say "I love you" and "You're beautiful to me" with such joy and ease scarcely offers those words anymore. Or, as was my case with Hollis, the sentiment is uttered in a rote fashion, checking a box, getting the job done.

Before Hollis passed, I felt the end coming.

Before Dr. Leopold delivered my diagnosis—"I've got

some news, Mrs. Hull. And I'm afraid it's not good . . ."—I felt it too.

I've told you how I memorized the twenty-six steps between the cottages, the location of light switches, cutlery, bug spray, and more. What I didn't tell you: sometimes I simply stood in my yard, amid that carnival of lawn clutter, watching leaves whirl about, watching snow falling, watching birds flit from branch to branch.

I suggest you do the same. After all, none of us gets to see this world forever. My advice: see it while you can.

At the pharmacy, where I stockpiled medications, Band-Aids, and bath oils, I watched faces with the wonder of a person stargazing. In my waning months of sight, so many features and expressions struck me as uniquely glorious. The hope shimmering in one woman's eyes, the sadness pooling in another's. The tight-lipped seriousness of a teenage girl examining a shampoo bottle. People can be so beautiful. So ugly too. If I needed any proof of the latter, while waiting in line with everyone gaping at their cell phones, I gaped at newspaper headlines. BLOODHOUNDS HELP FIND WOMAN CHAINED IN BASEMENT! . . . MAN SECRETLY LIVED IN FAMILY'S ATTIC, SNUCK INTO 14-YEAR-OLD GIRL'S ROOM AT NIGHT! . . . LOTTERY-WINNING COUPLE ARRESTED IN STRING OF BURGLARIES! Where did those stories begin? I wondered. What made those people step off the familiar path of everyday life, into such sinister, such bizarre, such ugly territory?

I've been thinking about you for years, Linelle . . .

Forgive me. Seems I've stepped off a path here too. No doubt what you want to know about right now is her. When Teddy, or the man I wanted so desperately to believe was him, looked out the window and told me she'd come for one final date with the past, I panicked. Used a needle on him a second time. Apologizing even as I jammed the syringe into his deltoid. Shushing my beloved while I urged him into the rocker from which he'd just been untied, hurriedly, haphazardly, knotting ropes. Around his ankles again, around his torso and upper arms, strapping him to the chair. Shoving a dishrag in his mouth this time. I needed to gain control of the situation in order to get rid of Linelle. But when it became clear she would not go home without seeing Teddy, I told myself to take more drastic action. But Linelle's kindness made it difficult to harm her, and maybe I never would have, if not for her discovery of the body, which left me no choice.

And so . . .

When I stomp up the porch steps, Linelle is slumped across the threshold of the second cottage. I trip over her, lose my balance, nearly whack my head again. Inside, I stand between them. Her on the floor behind me. Him in the chair before me. I pull the rag from his mouth, thump his chest, slap his cheeks, though there's no response but his slow, shallow breaths. Hers as well.

What is there to do but wait? The hours that pass make me feel as though I'm back on the ward, my patients asleep in their rooms, their usual commotion reduced to an occasional moaning or mumbling. Some part of me wishes I could lose myself in one of the paperback love stories piled around the cottage the way I once did. Instead, I'm left with my squall of dark thoughts until, at long last, that flat, punctured voice says, "What have you done to her?"

Startled, I sit up on the sofa and say, "I should be asking you the same question. Why did you contact her?"

He coughs, clearing his throat with a progression of

frustrated, guttural sounds, which makes me anticipate that he's about to ask for water. But then he says, "What do you mean, why? You're the one who suggested it. Remember that 'none of us lives forever . . . Ticktock' business the first day?"

"Yes. But that's when I believed . . ." I stop. Tilt my head. Attempt to see his face in the periphery, though I'm met with nothing but a useless blur.

"Who are you?"

A question I might have asked at that very moment, yet it comes from Linelle. The unexpected sound of her voice—woozy, distant, even while so close—surprises me. I go to her and, kneeling, press my thumb and index finger to her palm, checking her radial pulse as best I can. Forty beats per minute. Not good. "Can you hear me?" I ask, loud and clear, rolling her over, thumping her sternum, grasping her hand and instructing her to squeeze. Other than the faintest murmuring, she's unresponsive.

"We've got a problem," I say.

"Yes, I seem to be tied up. So, I need you to un—"

"I'm talking about the body parked in the freezer at the Big-Star. Linelle discovered your little secret over there!"

He's quiet for what feels like a long time. I hear him wriggling in the chair, straining against the ropes, and though he's able to move his hands and forearms, it's not enough mobility for him to get loose. Finally, he says in the voice I knew to be Teddy's, "I had nothing to do with that gruesome business, I assure you, luv."

I realize he's attempting to keep the reality we'd agreed upon alive, and though I'm no longer certain I can, I say, "Well, now you're involved. Linelle tried calling the police. When she comes to, no doubt she'll try again. If that happens, you and me, this life we've stitched together, it will become unstitched."

"It doesn't have to be that way, Skyla. I've read the letter from the hospital administrators and searched online. So I know what you did to Amanda. I'm aware how selfish, how cruel it would be, but . . . you could do the same to Linelle."

"What happened there was an accident!" I shout, insisting upon another more palatable reality too.

"Really? Because the letter's here in the pocket of my blazer. I picked it up in the parking lot of the diner yesterday. If you like, I can remind you what it actually says."

"Shut up! I didn't do it on purpose then! And I can't . . . I won't do it now! Besides, you said so yourself, it would only be a matter of time before the police, not to mention Linelle's husband, come sniffing around in search of the missing woman." I pause and say, "Women."

He offers no reply. Linelle moans, faintly, mumbling too. Taking her hand again, I lean in close and decipher what she's saying: "Help me."

The same plea Amanda Quigley made, and I remember her up on that eighth floor of the hospital. Her bulging eyes. Her tempest of salt-and-pepper hair. Her jack-o'-lantern mouth, open wide, showcasing her missing teeth. The hollow at the back of her throat, like some slick and shadowy sinkhole a person might slip into, vanishing forever. "Help me!" the woman shrieked from her bed, as I held a needle, hesitating. "Help me, please!"

"I can't," I repeat, then and now. "I won't."

In that woozy, remote voice, Linelle asks, "Who is he?"

I wait for him to answer, and when he doesn't, find myself making a final, futile attempt at keeping that world we agreed upon alive, telling her, "That's Teddy, dear. Your long-lost love. The man you came to see."

The words sound empty, even to me, and I feel a certain reality slipping away. I feel the end coming. My hand is still in hers, which is how I sense the subtle motions of her body. How I realize she's struggling to raise her head in order to see him. I help lift her neck as she turns in his direction.

"No," her faint voice says. "No, that's not him."

In that moment, I make up my mind about what I need to do, even if I don't know exactly how just yet. "The body in the freezer," I say. "Who is she, Jeremy?"

It takes time, but eventually he begins. "Maryanne. That was her name. She was beautiful . . ." He keeps talking, telling me about looking her up on the trip to Providence. About their date at the French restaurant. Each and every detail, including the events on the playground. The cruel things he heard Maryanne say. His attempt to kiss her years later. And when he arrives at the moment in her kitchen, the acid in the dog's bowl, the bowl ready to be launched in the air, Maryanne in her white nightgown, pleading, "What's that, Jeremy? What's that in your hand?" he stops abruptly.

"Did you?" I say.

"I'm afraid so, Skyla."

I stand, feeling the only thing left in my pockets other than some stray pills: the matchbook from my honeymoon. I'd come upon it in a box of keepsakes while excavating those home movies and began carrying it as a way to remember the earliest days of my marriage. I think of Officer Ludgood telling me not to have any more accidents. I think of Teddy, of who I believed him to be, warning me about the candles in my cottage. Then I go to the boxes belonging to my late husband, begin rooting around inside, touching and dismissing so many items.

Compass . . . Canteen . . . Countless fishhooks . . .

"What are you looking for?" he asks.

I don't answer. Don't ask him to keep going either, yet he does.

"The next morning, I came to on the kitchen floor, hearing the sound of Maryanne's tortured cries beside me as she covered her ruined face. Pretty at her side. The fear of someone hearing made me realize we needed to get out of there . . ."

Tent spikes . . . Mess kit . . . Tackle box . . .

". . . but I worried about taking my car or hers, both of which could be traced. That's when I remembered: the couple who owned the place was on vacation. I broke into their side of the house . . ."

Fishing wire . . . Bobbers . . . Gutting scissors . . .

". . . No luck finding car keys, but I found a joint in their nightstand. A gun on a closet shelf. A wad of cash. I took those things, got Maryanne and Pretty into my car, and drove away. But being in the car with Maryanne was unbearable. She kept moaning and wailing. I didn't know what to do. At last I pulled into a 7–Eleven. Warned her not to go anywhere while I went inside . . ."

Radio . . . Lantern . . . Kerosene . . .

". . . But when I came out and handed her everything I could find—Purell, Visine—Maryanne threw it in my face. She screamed, 'You think this is going to fix what you've done to me, you fucker!' She started hitting me. Pretty started barking. Maryanne opened the door and tried to get out. I panicked and grabbed her and . . . the gun from her landlord's closet had no bullets, but I used it anyway. As an object, I mean."

As his words give way to so many racked and anguished sobs, I quit searching, having found what I need at last. Tucking the small metal container beneath a blanket taken from a box, I go to Linelle. Lay the blanket over her feet, over her legs and torso, over her shoulders, right up to her chin, stopping at her face when she says, "Help me, please."

"Don't worry," I tell her, same as I did Amanda. "It will all be over soon."

I unscrew the cap. Tip the container. As liquid pools onto the pile of paperbacks between them, I wait for him to say something about the spill, about the combustible smell in the air, but he keeps talking, through tears, lost in his confession. "After it was over, I just drove. Smoking that joint. Muttering a lullaby my mother used to sing to me. *'Il est l'heure d'aller dormer, le sommeil va bientôt venir . . .'*" Those uncontrollable sobs overtake him again, before he catches his breath and translates, "'Time to go to sleep, sleep will come soon.' Eventually, I pulled down a deserted road and moved Maryanne's body to the trunk. Then, like I told you, I stopped for gas and saw your ad. After our call, I returned Pretty to Tiff in Buffalo, then came here. Early on, when you gave me the keys to the concession stand to get food, I moved her body to a freezer. I planned to move her again, to the woods when the ground thawed come spring, and copied the keys while you were at the diner to make it easier. And anyway, I liked being Teddy so much that I took your advice and contacted Linelle. To feel what that kind of love was like. It wasn't hard, since I had old photos of him. And to make sure she had zero doubt, I even got a tattoo of his mother's name on my arm. What did I care? One more step away from being me. Easier to be Teddy, since he didn't kill Maryanne."

Holding the matchbook in my hand, I say, "You did."

"Pardon?"

"You killed her, Jeremy. You dumped acid on her. You bludgeoned her with a pistol. And you deceived me. Deceived Linelle too." I break off the first of two matches that remain, so old and flimsy it feels almost powdery between my fingers.

"What are you doing, Skyla?" he asks, his voice sounding sharper now, more aware. He must realize what I poured over the books, because he says, "If you light that match, if you throw it on that pile, if you leave me here tied to this chair, you won't just murder me, you'll murder Teddy. You'll never be able to bring him back."

"Teddy's gone, Jeremy. You put an end to him when you told me what you did."

I strike the match, but it doesn't light.

"Help me," Linelle pleads from the floor. "Help me, please."

"If you untie me, this cottage can still go up in flames. Only with her in it. Not me. Please, Skyla. You did it to Amanda. You can do it again."

"I told you, I didn't kill her on purpose! I'm not a murderer! I'm not like you!"

"Oh, but you are. The paper here in my pocket says quite clearly: 'Dear Ms. Skyla Hull, This letter is to notify you of your immediate termination!'"

"I told you to shut up about that letter!"

"Then why don't you come get it, Skyla? Because it says that 'in direct violation of hospital policy,' you—"

"No!" My hands tremble when I try again to strike that first match.

"You administered improper medication!"

"No! No! No!" Nothing happens. Once more, I strike.

"You failed to respond to a patient's subsequent distress!"

"No! No! No! No!" Still, nothing. I keep trying.

"Your gross negligence and dereliction of duty resulted in—"

I toss that useless match to the floor. "Give me that letter!"

"A fatality, Skyla! That's what it says! You killed her! You killed her and tried to cover it up!"

Clutching the matchbook with the final match, I lunge at him in that rocker.

"It says your continued practice as a nurse presents a danger to the public!"

I thrust my hands in the pockets of his blazer but come up empty.

"That's why they suspended your license! That's why they got rid of you!"

I shove my hand beneath his blazer, search the inner pocket.

"So, you and me—we are the same! Now untie me!"

At last, I grasp that wretched paper. All those twisted truths I never again want to hear. As I yank it free, his hand grabs mine. I manage to shake him off, but before I can step away I feel a piercing sensation at the back of my right arm, grinding into my flesh. Like those strays I rescued who turned on me, like those more treacherous patients who turned on me too, the man is biting me.

Clenching his jaw.

Thrashing his head.

I release an agonized howl. Pull backward with such force it causes an even deeper pain to bloom inside. My flesh, my bones, my muscles—humerus, triceps, tendons—feel as though they're being ripped apart. Another cry escapes my mouth, and I swing my free arm around, my fist making contact with his skull.

"Let go of me! You bastard!"

But he does not let go. Again, I pull. He jerks his neck in the other direction. I find my footing and, despite the fresh burst of pain it brings, muster all my strength to yank in my direction. That's when I sense the rocker careening toward me. The chair with him in it tips forward, and the two of us crash onto the pile of books.

As we lie in a jumbled heap, stunned into silence, catching our breath, the wound on my arm begins to throb. Blood trickles along my skin, dripping onto the books doused with kerosene. I tell myself to light the match, but except for the crumpled letter, my hands are empty. I must've dropped the matchbook.

The chair pins my hip and shoulder, and I feel too weak to shove off the weight. Still, I move my fingers over the paperbacks in search of the matchbook. To distract him, I begin talking, telling the truth at last. "Amanda was a frequent flyer on the ward. She'd been in dozens of times. Dozens. To see her at the end. Missing teeth. Track marks up and down both arms. She was an addict. Her diagnoses too many to name. The woman's mind was a house of horrors, her body riddled with disease, her existence a misery. She begged me to make it stop. To make her life stop. Guess I don't have to tell you that being in this world is not easy for some people. Despite how the letter makes it sound, I felt compassion for my patients. In all my years, I'd never done such a thing, but one night, I came across her losing the battle with her mind and body. Convulsing. Shrieking. Pleading with me to put an end to her agony. I filled a syringe with risperidone, a drug she was prescribed. Insulin, too, which she was not. Any nurse will tell you never to mix insulin. It's a surefire way to bring on the end. Untraceable in case of an autopsy. And so, I hesitated, told myself I couldn't do it, but then . . . I did."

"It's true then. You and me, Skyla, we're the same."

"No," I say with an unexpected clarity, despite the circumstances of the moment. "Amanda was like the strays that wander out of the woods behind the cottages. Most of the time, I succeed in caring for them. I'm a good nurse, after all. But some strays are too far gone. The wounds so infected, they'll never heal. They're a danger to themselves and others. In those instances, the most humane thing to do is put them down. What I did for Amanda was a gift. It brought her peace after such torment. That's nothing like what you did."

Linelle moans again. My fingers continue creeping over the books in search of the matchbook.

Jeremy is quiet. After a long while, he says in a forlorn voice, "I fear I'm like one of your strays too. Too infected by life to ever truly heal. I knew it was over for me the moment I took the acid from the trunk. Even if I somehow evade the police, I'll never outrun what I did to Maryanne. Day after day, I'll see her beautiful face. I'll see the shock in her eyes when I took that collapsible bowl . . . when she realized I was . . ." He pauses for some time, then says at last, "Skyla, you can tell people what happened here was an accident. Though I can't help thinking it's a shame the world won't know the truth: that ours was a kind of love story, however peculiar. Also, Linelle won't ever know about that letter I wrote."

"Letter?"

"Never mind. They were kids. It never would have lasted,

even without my jealousy and interference. Just one in a long list of ugly things I did in my life. Unimportant now."

I hear a scratching sound nearby.

Jeremy says, "You can stop looking for the matchbook, Skyla."

All at once, I understand: when he grabbed my hand during our struggle, he grabbed the matchbook too. My fingers go still. I hear the scratching again, that final match striking, and then the sound of a flame being born, like a tiny gasp in the air between us. I picture the orange glow flickering before the man's face, a face I've never imagined before, since I always saw Teddy. Until now.

"Wait!" I shout. "Wait!"

EIGHTEEN

"Are you sure you want to know?"

—From *Mildred Pierce*, shown at the Schodack Big-Star Drive-in,
September 1945

TUESDAY AFTERNOONS AT THREE, I meet with Cheryl Foxx,
who boasts an alphabet soup of letters after her name: LSW,
PsyD. First time we met, nearly a year after my second cottage
burned to the ground, I told the woman those letters don't
impress me. After all, I've got two of my own: RN. Despite
everything that happened, I even tried a joke on her: "These
days, some might say a more appropriate set of letters following my name would be WTF?" But Cheryl Foxx didn't laugh.
Not even a bit.

Wednesday mornings at ten thirty, I attend a group therapy session with the drippy-dip label, "Facilitating Change
from Within." Sitting in a circle of chairs, cocking my head
sideways to take in the fog of faces around me, I listen to so
much verbal vomit in response to prompts like, "I feel angry
when ___" and "I feel calm when ___". A few times, I've trotted out a joke there too, saying, "I feel annoyed when group
therapy starts" but "I feel pretty damn relieved when it's finally

over." That gets some laughs at least, though not from the group facilitator.

Appointments like those, so many others too, keep me occupied, lessening the risk of my mind "venturing down a dark road" as good old LSW, PsyD, put it.

"Little late for that, wouldn't you say?" I replied.

Speaking of a little late, the intake doctor who listened to my heart when I first arrived told me I need to be careful with that too. Instead of a steady *lubdub-lubdub*, what he heard through the stethoscope, what I heard too when he let me have a listen, was a murky, discordant thudding. "I'd sound that way too if I was my heart," I told him, before his lecture about the risks of atrial fibrillation and the medicines I'd have to begin taking in hopes of correcting it. "After all, the thing's been broken. Not once. But twice now."

At the facility library, there's a slew of audiobooks. It's pretty much a "get what you get and don't get upset" selection. For obvious reasons, I'm not keen on romance at the moment, so I've begun dabbling in biographies. *Harry Houdini: The Legend of the World's Greatest Escape Artist.* There's a title that interested me. The man could make an elephant disappear! Meanwhile, I've failed to pull off the trick of making a host of unwanted memories vanish from my mind.

But never mind that.

The appointment I look forward to most: Hollis's sister's son, John, driving up from the city to see me. For some time now, he's been coming every Friday, staying at a nearby hotel and returning Saturday mornings to visit again. We've embarked on something of a joint project, and I don't just mean dealing with the legalities of my situation, though that's certainly been a force in our coming together. As my point of contact throughout the trial, John made every effort via the DA to lower my sentencing from attempted first-degree murder—on account of using that needle on Linelle—to aggravated assault and reckless endangerment. Speaking of magic tricks, it worked. These days, he's attempting another: filing all sorts of paperwork and appeals in hopes of having me transferred out of the mainstream penal system and placed in a straight-up psychiatric facility.

"It won't be home there either," he's told me, "but you'll be treated like a patient, rather than a prisoner."

Maybe so, though I prefer to be the one caring for patients.

While I can't tell you what the visitation room looks like, I can report that we're given a table and chairs. No need for thick glass between us; apparently, the guards aren't worried about my nephew baking me a cake with a file in it or slipping me a syringe. During these visits, we go back and forth about the myriad updates from lawyers and administrators and our plan to sell the property, where one of those moon-shuttered cottages still stands, not to mention the old movie screen out in the field.

After we've finished with business, John and I move onto plain old chitchat. About my life here, and the merry-go-round of meetings I attend. About his life in the city, and the dinner parties he and his partner host. We talk about those long-ago Christmases, before his side of the family moved away and fell out of touch.

It was during one of these discussions that I brought up an idea proposed by Cheryl Foxx purely as a therapeutic exercise. "I'd like to write a letter to Linelle." Then I raised a notion she did not suggest. "And once you help me do that, I'd like you to mail it for me."

"I don't think that's a good idea, Aunt Skyla," John said, sounding worried. "Better we leave her alone."

But I insisted, telling him, "She deserves my apology. Deserves an explanation too. Also, there's something Jeremy said that I think she should know."

"Speaking of all that," John said, dropping his voice to a conspiratorial tone, "forgive my asking. But I can't help wanting to know . . . What happened?"

I felt rankled by the question. But also, when you have secrets, there's always a small part of you itching to tell. At first, I resisted, saying, "You were at the trial, so you already know. Jeremy lit that match, I shoved him off, rolled Linelle onto the blanket, and got us both out of there."

"What I mean is, what really happened? Before all that?"

The whole truth, I realized, that's what he wants.

The story I painted for police and detectives and reporters was, as an elderly, grieving widow who had recently lost her sight, I decided to rent my extra cottage. How could I know my tenant was someone different than he claimed? Other than an occasional chat on the porch and a ride he once gave me to the diner, we hardly spoke. Linelle showing up unannounced, as well as her discovery of the body in the freezer, sent me into a disorienting state of shock. My instability and confusion were corroborated by Officers Ludgood and Keegan, based on our encounters preceding the fire. Such muddled perception, the attorneys argued, led to a misguided effort to protect myself, using the needle on Linelle. The jury might've bought it, if not for my history at the hospital. Still, in my version of events, when I confronted my tenant about the body, he became violent, which, according to records unearthed from various psychiatrists Jeremy had visited over the years, turned out to be his history. That's when he trapped us in the cottage and . . . well . . .

DRIFTER MURDERS EX-GIRLFRIEND,
SETS REMOTE CABIN ABLAZE!

FORMER CHILD ACTOR SLAYS BEAUTICIAN,
PUTS BODY ON ICE!

DERANGED TENANT TAKES LANDLADY HOSTAGE,
TORCHES HOME!

In that visitation room, with John seated across from me, I heard myself tell him, "Every marriage has its secrets."

"Pardon?"

"I said, every marriage has its secrets. I didn't use to believe that. Was it denial? Just plain stupidity? Who knows? But for nearly fifty years, I operated under the assumption that the life your uncle and I shared was built on truth. On trust."

There were rules in that room. Time limits, for one. No phones, for another. John couldn't simply tap a screen and record our conversation. (And I'm not allowed a phone in here at all, so if you happen to speak to Siri, please do give her my worst.) He simply listened as I recounted the details of Teddy answering my ad. On John's next visit, he arrived with a notebook, pencils, and a small sharpener. "I thought about it, and if you really want to write a letter to Linelle, I'll help you. Then, I thought we'd pick up where we left off, Aunt Skyla, with you telling me your story."

And so, after we finished the letter and he promised to send it, I took a breath and began talking. In order to reveal the whole of what happened, I had to tell not just my story, but pieces of Linelle's, pieces of Jeremy's too. My nephew started writing, stopping to ask questions, nudging me to fill in blanks, even if it meant speculating beyond the details Linelle shared in my living room and Jeremy shared within the walls of that rented cottage. For months, this was the way of things, until finally, one Friday afternoon in early spring, after we'd slaughtered an army of pencils and filled dozens of notebooks, he took a seat across from me and said, "I've got good news, Aunt Skyla."

"Linelle wrote me back?" I said, hope brimming in my voice.

"I'm sorry, but no. I even followed up over email, but no reply. I think we need to give up on hearing from her."

"Oh. Then what's your news? Have you finished editing and arranging our story?"

"Almost. But that's not it either. It's not official yet but looks like we're going to get you moved to the psychiatric hospital, where you can serve out the remaining years of your sentence."

In his voice, I sensed he expected excitement. At the very least a smile. What a disappointment it must've been when the most I did was close my eyes. Not that I didn't long to exit that place, believe me, but I'd gotten quite good at making my mind see what I wanted, no matter how much it differed from reality. When I imagined the facility where he and the lawyers had been working so diligently to send me, I envisioned nothing drab, nothing dysfunctional, though both were likely the case. Rather, I imagined white halls lit up with fluorescence, a bustling staff of nurses in those old-style dresses I favor, white shoes padding along the floors.

They were carrying clipboards.

They were lugging sorted bins of blood vials.

They were pushing IV carts from room to room.

Every last one professional, caring, focused on the task of helping the unwell get well.

I thanked John and told him it was wonderful news. What I didn't tell him: deep down, I still felt the end coming. I knew I'd never make it to that hospital.

Shuffling papers, he got back to the business of our joint project, which only lately had we begun referring to as an actual book. "Looking over the notes, I realize we need to make certain things clear. Like, what about the real Teddy? Where is he? And why did Jeremy say his life turned out so bad?"

"Can't help you there."

"Well, what should I do about it? In the pages, I mean."

"I leave all that to you. The piecing together. The coloring in and figuring out. I only ask that you change names and locations. You know, protect the innocent. Or in my case, the guilty. Other than that, do what you want with this story after I'm gone."

"Don't talk that way, Aunt Skyla."

"Too late, kiddo. I just did."

Before we could say anything more, a guard's voice boomed from the far side of the room, informing us that visiting hours were over.

"Guess that's it for today," I said, reaching for my walking stick, both new and necessary, since I couldn't be bothered to commit the place to memory. "See you next week."

But I didn't see him. The next week, before I did the *tap-tap-tap* trek to the visitation room, a guard informed me that no visitor was scheduled. Later that evening, I waited in an eternal line for the phone, and the moment my nephew accepted the reverse charges, I asked why he'd been a no-show.

"Oh, Aunt Skyla," he said over the sounds of what I gathered was a dinner party, soft music and the din of conversation, "I told you I couldn't make it this week, remember?"

"Must've slipped my mind. Sorry."

"Don't be. But I'm glad you called, because I have some news that'll make you smile: after all this time, Linelle finally wrote you back."

"She did?" I say, and it does make me smile. "Did she accept my apology?"

"Sounds like it. Also, she mentions opening a business. And there's something else unexpected. Do you want me to read it to you?"

"I do. But you get back to your party. We'll save it for when you're here next week."

"Okay. And wait, before you go, by the way, I looked up the dog."

"Maureen? Told you she's a beast, didn't I?"

That joke made me feel something I hadn't in ages: a pang of missing Teddy and our Tuesday nights together. Patsy playing on the stereo. Tots and chops warming in the oven. Candles glowing. Wine flowing. The chatter. The laughter. The dancing. The holding. How I missed that attachment. How I missed him. Even though I told myself there's no use in missing something that never really was.

"I'm talking about Pretty." John's voice crackled through the phone. "Turns out, the dog won first prize at the show with the absurdly long name in Atlantic City. Plus, she racked up two more wins in Vegas and Miami."

"Good for her!" I said, surprised by how happy that news made me too.

"Go, bitch! Go!" John said, which got us both laughing.

When our laughter died down, despite the pressure of the line behind me, I couldn't help but tell him, "It just goes to show, whether you're a snooty dog with a shady history, a person stuck in an unhappy marriage, or some other desperate character, the past doesn't have to hold you back. You can make a new life for yourself."

"It's true. And same goes for you, Aunt Skyla."

I think of all the secrets I told him about my past, and one I didn't. Finally, caving to the pressure of that line, I wish him goodbye.

Something I don't mind about this place: Fridays are movie nights. That means tapping my way to—if ever there was an inane marriage of words—the "cafetorium." A rare chance to choose a seat means most everyone vies, which is my polite way of saying shoves, to score a spot up front so as to better see the show. Not me. I seek my preferred location in the back. The films are the sort of pure eighties fluff Jeremy would've appreciated. Hardly my first choice, but that's okay. Once the lights go down, and I tilt my head to take in the shifting shadows, I'm no longer an old woman whose bad luck and bad decisions have landed her there in the last row.

I'm a teenage girl who's ridden my three-speed to the edge of a field on a summer evening in 1960. In an attempt at inconspicuousness, I forgo the kickstand and lay the bicycle down before sitting on the grass. In the distance, over the roofs of so many parked cars, I see a film flickering on the enormous movie screen, an old picture even then. And though I can't hear the voices of the actors up there—falling in and out of love, telling secrets, telling lies, making threats, making promises, breaking hearts—I don't mind, because those nights spent under the stars, conjuring the specifics of their stories for myself, are among the first real thrills of my life.

"What you're doing amounts to stealing. You know that, don't you?"

Startled by the low voice in the darkness behind me, I whip my head around. In confusion between two worlds—the past, the present—I expect to see a guard. But, no. I look up into the face of a man with pale skin and pale blue eyes, head bald but for the scattered gray wisps swept overtop. In his hand is a flashlight, switched off. Before I can say anything, he continues, "Do you know who I am, young lady?"

"The owner of the drive-in?"

"Exactly. And I'm running a business here. Which means no freebies."

Every dollar I earn from my paper route, beyond what my parents take for food and other basics, I stash away. Now, I reach in the pocket of my cutoffs, extract a crumpled bill, hold it out for him. "Here you go. For tonight's ticket."

"Hate to break it to you, but I've been keeping track. We both know you owe more than this. Last week, you hid back here watching *The Alamo* and *Butterfield 8*. Week before, it was *Anatomy of a Murder* and *Brides of Dracula*. Should I keep going?"

"I'll pay whatever I owe, sir. Just please don't call the police."

"Nobody's calling any police. But this ain't a charity. Bad enough all the trunks I have to pop open at the entrance to root out deadbeats smuggling their way into the show. Where are your folks anyway?"

"At the camp. Over in the next town. Please don't contact them either."

"Camp? You mean those rusted-out trailers and that old school bus? Don't tell me you're one of those do-nothings from that goddamned vagrant commune."

"My parents are. Not me. Not for long, anyway," I tell him.

"Good. I don't have any use for freeloaders. People should get a job."

"Couldn't agree more, sir. That's why I've already got one." Pointing to the baskets on my bike, I explain about the paper route, about my dream of nursing school, about my saving for it too. "Doesn't make it right, I know, but that's why I'm back here instead of parked in the field, taking in the show properly."

This news leads him to look upon me with more kindness in his eyes. Waving away my crumpled bills, he says, "Tell you what. You can settle your debt by working here a few nights. Prove yourself to be decent at it, and I'll even start paying you. Then you'll have two jobs to help get you where you're going. What do you say to that?"

"I say, when do I start?"

"This film's about to come down. Next one'll begin soon after. There's always a rush of activity between. So how's about you come get a sense of things now?"

As we make our way across that field, past all those cars with speakers hooked to their windows, I can't shake the odd sense that I'm leaving something behind. My bicycle back there in the grass, certainly. My parents too, since a job at the drive-in means one more move away from life with them. But there's something else—what is it?

When I step inside the cinderblock building, that question

is lost in the chaos of the moment, though the feeling does not fade. I'm introduced to his wife and daughter behind the concession stand, if you call pointing his flashlight at them an introduction. With their cat-eye glasses and bouffant hair, the women look more like sisters. Both give a warm smile and quick wave while excavating burger patties and fries from a freezer, tossing the former on the griddle, plunging the latter into a fryolator. I'm led past that commotion to an even noisier room in the back, where a film is threaded on an oversize projector, spinning off one reel into the machine, spooling onto a second when it emerges from the other side. Here, too, the man waves his flashlight, pointing at his son, who stares out a small viewing window at the credits rolling on the screen. "Tell him to show you the ropes," the man says. "I've got to deal with a moron who ran down his battery."

With that, he's gone. I find myself standing in that warm and cacophonous room, studying the boy's taut, lean body, his strong arms on display, thanks to a basic white tee. Already, I feel a kind of comfort in that place. The *clackity-clack* of the projector. The hullabaloo of the snack bar. And while I wait for him to discover me, I take a moment to finger-comb my hair, brush off my clothes. When he turns and sees me at last, I expect him to be startled, to ask who I am and what business I have lurking there. Instead, he says, "Let me guess. My old man caught you freeloading. Now you're his indentured servant and I'm meant to show you the ropes. Am I right?"

"You are." I take in his steely blue eyes and thin lips, his face, a younger version of his father's, dusted with freckles and set off by a full head of hair, clipped short.

"Okay, well, I've got to get this film off the projector and the new one loaded for the next show. If you want to bolt out the back door, now's your chance. I'll tell the old man you made a jailbreak when I wasn't looking."

His words bring on the feeling, more forcefully now, that I'm leaving something behind. As he returns to his work, I step to the door. I stare across the field in the direction of my three-speed abandoned out there in the grass. Somehow, strange as it may sound, I can see beyond to the caravan of trailers and old school bus across the town line, that not-quite-a-home where I live with my parents and a parade of people like them who come and go in no particular order. And somehow, I can see beyond even that, to a room where rows of chairs face a screen. A movie is finishing there too. Credits roll. Lights are flicked on. The women who'd been watching stand, no longer shoving, as they file into the hall. Soon, every chair is empty. Every chair but one. In the very back, an old woman sits, eyes closed, head to one side. A person in uniform approaches, snapping fingers, clapping hands in front of her face, before gently shaking her shoulders.

None of it matters, because she does not wake.

All at once, I understand what it is I'm leaving behind.

Turning away from that vision, I look at the boy across the room. He finishes loading the next movie onto the projector and carries the reel with the previous one to a workbench. I watch as he loads it onto some sort of apparatus, threading the film from the full reel onto an empty one, flicking a switch, causing both to spin.

"What are you doing?" I ask, moving closer to him again.

"Rewinding," he tells me. We gaze down at the march of frames in miniature, whirring backward, so many moments, so many faces, so many emotions and experiences to be remembered or forgotten—joy, sadness, fear, curiosity, jealousy, anger, forgiveness, laughter, suspicion, desire, shame, confusion, peace, and on it goes—speeding past in a breathless blur, the way life does too.

That room saw the beginning of my relationship with Hollis. Fifty years later, it also saw the end. I stood in that same space feeling angry, rejected, thinking about that woman I saw at the hospital after Hollis's first accident, about what his friend's wife told me of their relationship. Thinking about how Hollis couldn't even sit through the movie of our life together.

I walked back to the cottage. Pulled on his spare boots. Flashlight in hand, I wandered the paths, winding between trees. Those woods from which so many strays had emerged. Bare branches rustled wildly above. Leaves skittered just as wildly on the ground. Rain began to fall, the very reason he wanted to go fishing that night, since the surface of the water would be broken up by the drops, triggering the muskies and smallmouth bass to roam and feed. When I reached the bridge and walked out onto it, I saw him: a small and shadowy figure below in his waders. Thunder rumbled and lightning flashed so suddenly it felt as though my anger, my sadness, had summoned both from the heavens. The flickering light allowed me to see him more clearly, for an instant, as he stopped casting, reeled in his line, then began climbing back up the bridge.

Turn and leave, I commanded myself, though my legs refused to move.

When he reached the top, his hands gripped the railing. His face appeared before me and his eyes went wide. As more thunder rumbled, as lightning flashed, he said, "Skyla?"

There were so many things I could have said. Our marriage, our beautiful marriage. My devotion. My trust. My heart. My love. *How could you? Really, Hollis, how could you?* But I said nothing. I simply pushed. *A freak accident,* I told myself. Told everyone else ever since. Every marriage has its secrets. Mine had Maureen. But also, it had the secret of my husband's death, and how exactly his body came to rest, crooked and motionless, on the rocks below that bridge, which I never admitted until now.

"A MINUTE AGO, WE WERE at the end," says the young man beside me in the projection room on that long-ago summer night while the two of us stare down at the blur of images rewinding on the reel. "Any second, we'll be back at the beginning."

"Like magic," I tell him. "I think I'll stick around. For a little while anyway."

When the machine stops, he removes the full reel, caps it, then places it on a shelf with so many other movies, so many other stories. "I'm Hollis," he says, reaching out his hand to shake mine.

"Skyla," I tell him, reaching out as well.

"So, Skyla, you want to watch the next film with me?"

Since we're back at the beginning, since the show is about to start, and since I have no idea how it all will end, I smile and say, "I do."

NINETEEN

"And then I did see his face. It was rather a nice face."

—From *Brief Encounter*, shown at the Schodack Big-Star Drive-in,

June 1943

FOLLOWING THAT ILL-FATED TRIP, Linelle returned to Talla-hassee. There was the trial, the demands of which came in spurts, bringing bursts of unwanted attention and disruption, making the ordeal difficult to leave behind. Also disrupted: the relationship with her husband. Although Marcus initially expressed his sincere relief for Linelle's well-being, as months passed, he could not rein in his resentment about the trip, and in particular, that she'd helped herself to his car.

"I can't believe you took the 67 . . ."

"How could you have taken the 67? . . ."

"Don't you understand the 67 is not meant for long trips?"

Whenever he started on that topic, Linelle came close to erupting. Ultimately, though, she felt too lost to respond. Too muted by an exhaustive inner grappling with the events of that strange night in Schodack. Disbelief that it had happened at all. Humiliation that she'd been scammed—"catfished" on the internet, like so many people on those late-night news-magazine shows she and Marcus watched. Rage and fear when she thought of that nurse coming at her with that needle, despite the fact that, somewhere in the fog of memories, Linelle also recalled the woman dragging her from the fire to safety, saving her life.

Still, she did her best to reclaim some semblance of normalcy. She took the real estate license exam, passed it, and began working at an agency. What's that adage about how working at your passion leads to success? Maybe so, but Linelle discovered that working a job you're not the least bit passionate about can lead to success as well. In a spate of unexpected luck, she sold her first few residential listings with ease before being asked to represent a commercial space in a strip mall. As Linelle walked the bright and echoing 1,448 square feet, she began asking questions of the owner about various leasing restrictions, which led to haggling, in person and over email, until finally, *she* signed the lease. Her idea: to open an art supply store with the tiniest local gallery in the back, which brought the first bit of excitement to her life in some time.

> **BFTB:** Hey girl! We've put off your hubby's bash for over a year now. It would be a sin to let this Wonder Woman costume (not to mention all the Pilates I've been doing) go to waste so let's make it happen!!!

In the midst of preparing the shop and gallery to open, BFTB resurfaced the idea of a superhero theme party to celebrate Marcus's much belated anniversary at the bank. Someone else resurfaced too: Skyla, who sent a letter, which Linelle did not open. Also, Skyla's nephew emailed, politely introducing himself and explaining that he was hoping to speak with her in order to, as he phrased it, "share some information and begin a conversation in order to fill in some blanks." Beyond her necessary deposition, Linelle had no interest in reliving that nightmare, so she ignored the email. Though she did agree, however reluctantly, to the party. She put together a simple costume—flowery dress, flowers in her upswept hair, reminiscent of Frida Kahlo—and spent an evening in a hotel banquet hall, watching employees fawn over her husband while Barb paraded around in red knee-highs and a star-spangled mini, tossing a spray-painted gold jump rope over her coworkers and saying things like, "Admit it! You never fix the copy machine when there's a paper jam!"

But on the ride home in the 67 with Marcus, Linelle's cell buzzed. When she dug it out of her purse and tapped the screen, their daughter's face appeared. Linelle wondered if all parents saw a kind of reverse montage of their child the way she did with Georgia. There she was at the Miami airport with her luggage and violin case as they hugged goodbye. There she was jumping up and down while reading the acceptance letter from that music program in Berlin. There she was, years before, at gymnastics and soccer practice, and squealing when a monkey snatched a popsicle from her hand at the Gulf Breeze Zoo, and again, racing around their backyard in her nightgown catching fireflies, and so many moments in between, until finally, there she was, cradled in Linelle's arms, a warm, wrinkly infant with her eyes squeezed shut. At that moment, however, the girl they'd raised looked every bit a young woman, in a turtleneck and glasses, speaking to them from her dorm room at Northwestern, where she'd been accepted upon returning from Berlin. She told them about classes and music practice and new friends she'd made, then tried a little French on them, which she'd decided to study after giving up on German. "*Tu me manques, maman*," she said. "Guess what that means."

"I'm ready to come home?" Linelle said.

"Not yet. But I will on break. It means, 'I miss you, Mom.'"

After she hung up, Linelle felt a closeness and nostalgia toward Marcus. She even reached over to stroke his arm, significant since they rarely made physical contact anymore. But then he shifted gears and muttered that the clutch had been sticking ever since she took the car. Linelle removed her hand.

When they got home, instead of going upstairs with Marcus she headed downstairs to the in-law apartment. Linelle expected to find her mother dozing in the recliner, so it was a surprise to find her wide awake. Drinking tea. Picking at a slice of carrot cake. Watching the news. Linelle launched in about her marriage. About the tangle of emotions she had felt since the events in Schodack. About the unopened letter from Skyla Hull. About the woman's nephew who'd emailed yet again, asking if they could speak.

Surprisingly, her mother had become quite good at listening, and so each night after that, they came together to drink tea and eat carrot cake and continue talking.

"I'm sorry, Ma," Linelle sometimes said, halting in the middle of the late-night litany. "I know I've already unloaded all this."

"Don't be," her mother always told her in the more careful manner in which she spoke since the stroke. "You've got to make sense of it, pickle. Make peace with it too."

As still more time passed, this became a pattern: Days

spent readying the shop and gallery to open, juggling that real estate job, engaging in hot and cold discussions with her husband. Nights spent talking to her mother, usually falling asleep on the couch not far from her in the chair.

Then one evening, in the midst of their usual conversation, her mother said, "What's Teddy's real name again?"

"His real name?" Linelle assumed she was confused, which sometimes happened. "It's Teddy, Ma."

"No," Trudy said, more insistent. "It's some long, phony-baloney-sounding thing."

And that's when Linelle remembered. Rather than say it aloud, she picked up her mother's iPad and tapped: Ronald Theodore Cornwell III. In less than a minute, the two found themselves staring at a photo of the actual Teddy. Older now, though undeniably the same man she once loved. Linelle could not help but think back to all those years ago in the Black Lung when she first looked up to see his face come into focus: the slant of a jawline, an eye glistening in the dark, the other covered by that silly patch, his full-lipped mouth and square chin.

Handsome was the word Linelle thought then. It was the same word she thought now.

"Not too shabby," her mother said. "You should ding him."

"You mean ping, Ma. And no. Not after what happened. I still have too many questions about that man who pretended to be him. About the private things he knew."

But then, after finally opening the letter from Skyla and reading what she said Jeremy had told her, and after many weeks of returning to Facebook to stare at Teddy's picture, she pushed aside her misgivings and sent a message:

I've been thinking about you a lot lately. And you won't
believe the reason why . . .

She anticipated a flurry of messages in response and felt
disappointed when nothing came. But Linelle had the opening of the shop and gallery to distract her. She'd decided to
kick things off with an exhibition titled "Now & Then." After
purchasing a bunch of Polaroid cameras and film, Linelle sent
out invitations, encouraging guests to bring an old photo of
themselves, the less flattering the better. On one wall in the
gallery, they pinned the old photos. Bad perms. Bad fashion
choices. Awkward poses and smiles. On the other wall guests
pinned pictures of themselves taken right there at the party.
Linelle decided to invite DD too, who made the long drive
and arrived with a surprise of her own: she was pregnant, having frozen her eggs years before. "Getting one in under the
wire," she told Linelle, laughing, before they hung up that old
picture not far from a new photo of them looking nothing like
those teenage girls they used to be.

When Linelle made a toast, she expressed her gratitude
to everyone for coming, and cracked a joke about them being
required to spend a bundle on art supplies. Then, she took a
breath and said, "Also, here's to forgiving ourselves for who we
used to be, and whatever mistakes we may have made. Here's
to forgiving others too."

That night, when she returned from the party, Linelle
checked her messages to see one from Ronald, or rather
Teddy.

So sorry for the lag in my reply. I'm not on here all that
much. But wow . . . what a surprise to hear from you, Linelle!

Would be even better to see you in person. Joining my son and granddaughter on a trip to Disney—that's right, our old stomping grounds—this spring and would be fun to meet up if you'd like that. To be honest, life was hard for me for a long time. Sort of lost myself after my wife passed, though I'm doing much better now. Sober and drug free for a decade in fact. Will tell you all about that if you care to hear. Also, you can bring a calculator so we can do the math in person as to how the hell I can possibly have a grandkid. Until then, spare me the grandpa jokes . . . xo Teddy

Linelle skipped the grandpa jokes, though neither could resist the slew of Disney jokes and memories as they began writing back and forth. When spring came, they arranged a date to meet. Not at the park in the Black Lung, as they kidded about, but for breakfast at a diner in Orlando.

Before she left, Linelle did two things. First, she dug up that old letter, written in French to Teddy, which began: "My dear heart, I did not expect to develop such deep feelings for you . . ." All those years ago, it led her to suspect him of having an affair with the mother of the boy he tutored in French. An accusation Teddy denied, yet it did something to fracture their relationship anyway. Now, thinking of what Skyla informed her about the cryptic final thing Jeremy said, Linelle wondered if he really had written the letter, knowing what damage it would do when she found it. Whatever the truth, it was in the past now, so Linelle simply tore the letter up and tossed it in the trash.

The second thing she did was pull out the box of art supplies from her old classroom. Scissors. Sharpies. Glue. Then she began pulling all the signs and letters off the walls. COOK . . . UNCORK THE VINO . . . LOVE . . . BE

GRATEFUL . . . FIND YOUR HAPPY—they all came down. In their place, she might've spelled out any number of sentiments that swirled in her head whenever Marcus started in about that trip she'd taken with his precious 67: HOW DARE YOU or I COULD HAVE DIED or NOW THAT GEORGIA IS IN COLLEGE THERE DOESN'T SEEM TO BE A CONNECTION BETWEEN US ANYMORE or REMEMBER THAT NIGHT WHEN YOU ASKED IF I WANTED A DIVORCE? I'VE THOUGHT ABOUT IT A LOT AND I DO. Instead, for now, she cut a *V* from a canvas sign. She cut an *E* from another sign too. She broke off the entire *YOUR* from a wooden sign, then went in search of *S*'s, keeping at it until hanging them on a wall in an artistic masterpiece that read:

SHOVE YOUR CAR UP YOUR ASS

Boom, Linelle thought.

Dear Skyla,

I know it's taken me a long time to write you. For obvious reasons, I first needed to sort out what happened in my head and in my heart. Also, I've been busy making changes to my life—opening a new business, for starters, which has kept me occupied. There's a lot to say, and I'm afraid if I try to get it all down in this note, I'll put it off and won't write anything at all. So, for now, I'll start small and share one thing that I think might bring you comfort, like those books we talked about that day in your cottage.

I took your advice and told my husband how I feel. Also, I found Teddy. I wrote him and we agreed to meet for breakfast. When we sat down, he reached across the table and took my hand right away. We were quiet at first—each of us nervous, I guess—then, at the same time we said, "So, where should we begin?"

And Skyla, it was the strangest thing: after so many years of silence between us, by some bit of magic, the sort you'd find in the pages of a love story, in an unexpected twist, just like that, the two of us, we began again.

Yours in friendship,

Linelle

ACKNOWLEDGMENTS

DURING THE WRITING OF THIS BOOK, my apartment in New York City burned down, thanks to an arsonist who fled the country (a bizarre story I now try to tell in a funny way); the magazine industry in which I happily worked as an editor for twenty-plus years collapsed; and by far, saddest of all, on a beautiful, moonlit evening, my dad died in a motorcycle wreck. During a time of so much upheaval, my solace was waking in the early mornings to slowly craft this story. My other solace: the people who helped bring it to life. I owe each of them a huge and heartfelt thanks.

Most of all, my exceptional editor, Kate Nintzel, whose encouragement, vision, and devotion to these characters never wavered. Her hand touched every scene and sentence of this novel as she guided and pushed me to make it the very best it could be. I'm so lucky to have her. Also, the powerhouse team at Mariner Books/HarperCollins: my dear friend and publicist, Sharyn Rosenblum, plus the incredible Liate Stehlik, Jen Hart, Tavia Kowalchuk, Virginia Stanley, Danielle Kolodkin, Molly Gendell, Mumtaz Mustafa, Michelle Crowe, DJ DeSmyter, and Jessica Rozler all treat me with such kindness and make the publishing process fun.

My wise and enthusiastic agent, Deborah Schneider, takes excellent care of me and my work. I'm so lucky to have her too.

Also, Cathy Gleason, who handles every detail, big and small, with ease. And Matthew Snyder, my longtime film agent, has always championed my writing in that world.

Kate O'Connell, friend and nurse extraordinaire, answered my endless nursing questions and, on her days off from the hospital, took time to read and comment on this novel. She also showed up at my home with a purse full of syringes and demonstrated how to give an injection . . . on a lime . . . before we indulged in margaritas.

Patti Howard and Ed Caro of the Malta Drive-In in upstate New York welcomed me into their magical outdoor theater, shared so many fun stories and details, plus let me tour the projection room and take in a movie under the stars, complete with a giant tub of popcorn and every type of candy from their concession stand. (My teeth are still tingling!)

Joseph Lea, longtime library media specialist at York Correctional Institute for women in Connecticut, where I've visited, kindly answered my questions.

Bruce Gruner, a "trouble man" for the power company in Sag Harbor, obliged when I spotted him up on a telephone pole on a sweltering summer day and yelled up to ask if I could interview him.

Ron Krystofik, Lieutenant of the East Hartford, Connecticut Fire Department, kindly answered all my questions about the details of a fire.

My early readers offered invaluable support and insight at various stages of writing: Colleen Curtis, Carolyn Marino, Chris Bohjalian, Jessica Knoll, Stacy Sheehan, Elizabeth Barnes, and Susie Merrell.

For time and space to write, I'm indebted to the Hawthornden Castle Writers Retreat, the Studios of Key West, and Yaddo.

And, of course, Susan Segrest, Michele Promaulayko, Kate White, Amy Chiaro, Ann Hood, Scott Robinson, Amy Salit, Betty Kelly, Dean Shoukas, Donna Krystofik, Dave Vendette, Jay Torreso, Jeremy Coleman, Zoe Ruderman, Glenn Callahan, Liz Rend, Boo Whitnebert, Katrina Naomi, Lili and Rob Anolik, Vivian Shipley, Joanna Pulicini, Whitney Lee, Joyce Howe, Maia and Cristian Ventresca, Shannon Searles, and the many book clubs and librarians and hometown friends who cheer for my novels.

As always, I'm grateful for the love and support of my mom, Lynn Searles, and my husband, Thomas Caruso, who read and reread this story and gave endless inspiration and encouragement.

Finally, I'm thankful to the real-life Skyla Hull and hope all the "coloring in and piecing together" would have made her proud.